RAINB[O

RAINBOW BRIDGE

GWYNETH JONES

J'ai conjuré le terrible esprit nouveauté qui parcurait le monde

NAPOLEON BONAPARTE

The right of Gwyneth Jones to be identified as the
author of this work has been asserted by her in accordance
with the Copyright, Designs and Patents Act 1988.

First published in Great Britain in 2006 by
Gollancz
An imprint of the Orion Publishing Group
Orion House, 5 Upper St Martin's Lane,
London WC2H 9EA

This edition published in Great Britain in 2007 by Gollancz

1 3 5 7 9 10 8 6 4 2

A CIP catalogue record for this book
is available from the British Library

ISBN 13: 978 0 57507 976 2
ISBN 10: 0 57507 976 2

Printed and bound at Mackays of Chatham plc,
Chatham, Kent

The Orion Publishing Group's policy is to use papers that
are natural, renewable and recyclable products and made
from wood grown in sustainable forests. The logging and
manufacturing processes are expected to conform to the
environmental regulations of the country of origin.

www.orionbooks.co.uk

ACKNOWLEDGEMENTS:

Many thanks as always to my editor, Jo Fletcher, my agent, Anthony Goff; and to Peter Gwilliam and Gabriel Jones for their support, especially on the last burn. Thanks also to Richard Gwilliam, prince of geeks; to Li Li and Teng Hui (Jamie) for calligraphy, and for vetting my use of Chinese characters, history, literature and legends. Any daft mistakes that survived are entirely my responsibility. Thanks to the Sussex Wildlife Trust, the Fenland Lighter Project, the staff of Brantwood, Coniston, the Wasdale Web; and Sellafield Visitors Centre. Apologies: if a quotation from any source is deemed to exceed fair-dealing use this is entirely unintentional, and copyright holders should contact the author. This book is dedicated to all melodramatic fools, rockstars or not.

For full credits, booklists, out-takes, pictures, confessions, see the Rainbow Bridge feature at

http://www.boldaslove.co.uk

TABLE OF CONTENTS

Golden Abalone

All true fairytales are spun from the golden thread of a young girl's beauty, at that precious moment when she has just become a woman . . . It was a pity, thought General Wang, that the heroine of the tale he had entered was past that perfect moment. He would have liked to meet Frances Slater, known as Fiorinda, when she was the fiery teenager of legend, in all her angry pride. He had no complaints, however, about the grown-up woman with him tonight: white-skinned, divinely tall, with the most amazing emerald eyes. Her blatant use of cosmetic 'enhancements', one of the pernicious habits he was here to root out, didn't worry him. She was splendid.

An array of supper dishes covered the low table between himself and his guest. She had eaten hungrily, when she'd recovered from her awe at the spread – which he found promising. Wang liked a woman who could eat. He sat at his ease, his arm along the back of the sofa. He'd seen her eyes widen, when she took in the pictures of Fiorinda which lined this pretty little room, but she had made no comment.

'Do you like my place?'

'Oh yes,' she said. 'It's *very* cool.'

'I like to think it has the air of a haven given over to secret pleasure.'

He smiled, and she smiled obediently. 'But I interrupted. Please, go on.'

Dian Buckley had been England's top rock music journalist at the time of the invasion, she was the author of best-selling books on the phenomenon of the Rock and Roll Reich. She'd known Ax Preston personally, intimately. The General was well aware that Dian's part in the lives of the radical rockstars had been much smaller than she told it; but the facts he could get anywhere, fact was immaterial this evening. He was collecting impressions—

'What you need to understand—' said Dian, earnestly, alight with wine. 'I was a total insider, most favoured media-person, I saw it from the beginning— What you need to *get* is that it wasn't hype. They were our good luck mascots, ever since Massacre Night. You know? When the hippies took over, our violent green coup?'

'I know.'

'Whatever disasters happened, people felt that if the Few were okay, we'd all be okay. But it was more than celeb culture, it was totally *genuine*. When I had my own tv show, which I did, very young, and it was essential viewing, I wouldn't talk to anyone, no matter how big they were, if I knew they were bores. You'd dread spending five minutes with some of the megastars, trust me. *They* were incredible. All of them, not just the Triumvirate. Allie, Dilip, Rob and the Babes. Chip Desmond, Verlaine. And George Merrick, Bill Trevor, Cack Stannen – that's Sage's band.'

Wang's tame goddess counted on her fingers, listing her totems. 'Ax's band, the Preston family band, he left behind a long time ago. You don't have to worry about *them*. Fiorinda never had a band of her own, of course. Those names, those names I just told you, *they were the core*. If they talked to you, everything sparkled. The world had fallen apart, but the Few were still hot. You wanted to look like them, be near them, be in the gang—'

The General had a malicious impulse to inquire if Fiorinda Slater was included among the wonderful, light-the-room people. Dian wasn't disrespectful. The Chinese had made it clear that Ax and his partners were not war criminals and were not to be vilified. But he'd noted that she had reservations about the young woman whose harsh fairytale had been so strangely woven into Ax Preston's utopian dream.

The psychology of the *Dians* of this world is the same in any culture!

'Tell me about the Triumvirate.'

Her eyes darted to the photos – framed publicity stills – and to Wang's face, checking guidance. 'Ax was lovely: a total star. So unassuming. And S—' Dian laughed. 'Aoxomoxoa: we were once very close, more than good friends, you know?'

'I can believe it.' *Aoxomoxoa* was 'Sage Pender', also known as 'The Zen Self champion'. A violent bully, involved in highly suspect 'spiritual technology',˙ a notorious womaniser; and a hero tortured by the evil régime. An interesting character!

Dian blushed. 'In the end I had to tell him to cool off. Fio's so possessive.'

'Ah, I sense you were not entirely smitten with the rock and roll princess?'

4

Another wary saccade. 'Well, some of us saw through her a little. was an operator. Like, when she did that *unknown teen waif, coming off t..* *streets*, we all knew, everyone in the biz knew who she really was—'

The General raised his elegant brows. 'She traded on her father's name?'

Dian affected to be horrified. As well she might, considering the relationship between Fiorinda and her father, the wicked megastar Rufus O' Niall. 'Oh, God, no! But she definitely knew how to use the system.'

Wang felt kinship with the child of rotten privilege (untold generations of it, on the mother's side). It's a difficult burden. But his heart was touched by this other Englishwoman: thoroughly immoral, yet so gallantly determined to make the best of things. The press release folder that he'd provided lay in her lap, like a last scrap of decency. He saw her glance at the cover page, and shiver away.

In the cities, flower gardens; in the countryside, cultivated land.

The characters would mean nothing to her, she was no scholar. Nor the translation: she was no analyst. But not even a superstar journalist, about to become a courtesan, likes to face the fact that her country has been conquered.

He refilled Dian's glass with the Pouilly Fumé. She smiled, and nodded.

'The Reich was a *feeling*. They were never a government, they never tried to be, that's all wrong. It was who they were, it was the way they made us feel, I mean *us*, the media. The mediators. We passed that feeling on to the masses—'

'Allie Marlowe, she was Preston's chief administrator?'

'Allie was the only non-musician. But she had it, she had the glow—'

'What about Hugh Raven? Sometimes known as "Smelly Hugh"?'

Dian shook her head so the blunt-cut blonde wings of hair flew. 'I never, ever knew him. Smelly was marginal to the Few: he was a leftover from the Pigsty régime, the hippies. *None* of the people I knew were Counterculturals.'

'Of course not,' murmured the General. No one who insisted on professing that deluded faith had been spared during the invasion; nor would they be spared. 'What about Dilip Krishnachandran? What were his responsibilities?'

'Oh, DK was the DJ. He was *Mixmaster*. He *invented* the mass-market form of Sage's immix tracks, he brought immix to the dance floor—' Dian caught herself. 'Immix' or immersion code, the software for direct cortical stimulation, was one of the *serious* pernicious absurdities, the use of which was instant death. She stared at him, transfixed by terror. 'I *hated* immix myself. I wouldn't go near it. Such a horrible idea, building fake perceptions and zapping them into people's brains through their eyes. It was so invasive. How can something f-fake be good?'

Wang frowned, not letting her off the hook.

'By "Sage", you mean Aoxomoxoa?'

She giggled and covered her mouth; turning the laugh into a cough.

'I meant Aoxomoxoa. Sorry . . . Dilip's responsibilities? He didn't have responsibilities. That's not how it worked. The Few were called "Ax's rock and roll Cabinet", it's misleading, they had no c-conventional posts, except *hahaha*, Aoxomoxoa was called the Minister for Gigs, but that was more or less a joke—'

A pause, Wang giving no clues. Dian reached her chopsticks, with careful bravado, for a piece of lobster meat.

'Do you mind if I ask a question?'

'Please do.'

'What did you *really* come here for? Why England?'

Ah, he thought, she's quick. She has realised she already knows how to please and intrigue a powerful man. Be bold, Dian; but not too bold.

He laughed, so that Dian had to laugh too. 'We came for your gold,' he said. 'We have an insatiable lust for gold, in China.'

Dian licked fiery, sticky sauce from her chopsticks. 'But there isn't any. British gold's in Ireland, and Wales, and there's not much of it.'

The Celtic nations had not yet been touched.

'Ah, but we have our methods, and we are connoisseurs. Small amounts of a distinctive, native gold can be very precious.'

'Now you're teasing me.'

A cheeky, coquettish grin, a weapon from the armoury of a tv journalist, turning the interview into a flirtation. Suddenly her face changed. The English roses fled from her cheeks, leaving her chalk-pale, in panic.

'Excuse, sorry—'

In the space-capsule bathroom Dian threw up briskly, rinsed her mouth; applied breath spray and sat on the toilet seat looking at her watch. Two minutes for recovery time: it's always worth the investment. She had eaten as much of the show-off food as her stomach would bear. Unbelievable, the seafood especially. White flesh of squid and abalone, swimmy pools of oysters in the shell on crushed ice, all sprinkled with yellow glitter, Hong Kong millionaire chic. She'd been hoping for fragrant rice, or bread. Everybody longed for bread. Instead she'd been eating metal. And now she'd lost the lot, fuck, fuck. She *could not afford* to be thin in post-invasion London. It would brand her, it would make her look a failure.

Could he be serious about the gold? She imagined Snowdonia strip-mined, ground to dust, isn't there some gold in Cumbria? Ireland and Scotland were supposed to be safe, they'd capitulated to all the Chinese demands. Some of Dian's friends had fled there, but she hadn't seen herself as a destitute asylum seeker.

I was right to stay put. Nowhere is safe now.

I am going to survive.

The twentieth of September, the day the Chinese had hit Cornwall with their staggering sub-orbital ships, was six weeks in the past. The four 'Commanding Generals' had parcelled out England between them, but the military invasion had stopped dead after the eighteenth October executions. Sheng of the North East had taken a few major cities, hammered the Islamics in Bradford-Halifax, and retired to build a fortress in Newcastle. In the South West, where Wang himself was in charge, crops rotted in the fields. The South East General had established a cordon round East Sussex for some reason: but was doing *nothing* to restore the movement of vital food supplies. Londoners saw themselves facing starvation, as winter closed down. Hu Qinfu, Commanding General In Charge Of Subduing The Capital, responded to pleas for action with brute force and bewilderment.

They measure famine differently in China.

There was something people had started to say, at the height of the invasion. One of those mystery expressions that comes from nowhere, then suddenly it's everywhere, and everyone knows what it means. Is China going to take a card? The Chinese had leapt around the world, with the tech they'd been nurturing in secret through the years of chaos. Within a week they'd had Europe in a box, England and Roumania overrun. Almost at once the English had known that their only hope was if the rampage went on. If China attacked again, at once – say France or Ireland – the world would've *had to* muster some kind of protest, some kind of resistance.

That hope was gone, the moment had passed. China had taken a card. Fred Eiffrich, the same US President who'd compelled the English government to accept Ax as Head of State two years ago, had given the rape of England his blessing. And for their next move the Chinese would take over the world. The whole, entire planet. It was horrific, a nightmare, your brain couldn't take it in, yet it was going to happen. There was nobody left to stop them.

But I am here, thought Dian, watching the seconds. With the Commander in Chief . . . Wang had been the public face of the invasion; the sexy one you saw all the time. He was tall and handsome (a man's height was important to Dian). He looked just as good out of uniform; and the Four Commanding Generals were supposed to be equals, but it was obvious that Wang was top dog. The so-called General of the Capital, Hu Qinfu, was nowhere when Wang came to town.

As a journalist she was dead meat. It didn't matter how close she'd been to Ax Preston once upon a time. At the end, Dian'd been the willing servant of the ruthless occult *junta* the Chinese had deposed, and everybody knew it. She couldn't get a job as a toilet cleaner . . . But I can still follow the money. It's what I do best. Recalibrate, recalibrate (that's such an Ax Preston word). Survival is the new success.

Time's up. Most of her make-up was permanent: the face in the mirror above the basin looked back smooth and bright, thank God. She added a dash of gloss to her lips and adjusted the neckline of her glittering tunic, worn over narrow quilt-stitched trousers, Allie Marlowe style. Looking good. No man can resist a superb pair of boobs . . . A row of photos on the wall behind her. Was that Fiorinda again? She turned, in the narrow space, with a strange tug of dread: looked closer, and saw a child in school uniform. It was Fiorinda, but she was about twelve years old. The room was differently decorated, but it was the one Dian had just left.

'Oh my God,' she whispered. 'Oh my God, where am I?'

The space capsule walls pulsed, black waves rippled across her vision. She found herself sitting on the side of the bathtub, clutching the silver charm of the three locked in congress; that she kept on her keychain. She stuffed it back into her bag, horrified. I must chuck that. My God, why haven't I thrown that away?

Now she must go back to Wang. It felt like the most terrifying thing she'd ever done in her life. But food and shelter were at stake, comfort was at stake.

She didn't hesitate.

The gold-curtained windows of the little living room were shimmering lamplit screens. General Wang made shadow puppets: a dog, a rabbit, a butterfly pursued each other into oblivion. He experimented quietly with the different tones, each with its specific meaning, of the most English of all words. Aggressive: *Soh*-ri; humorous, Soorrree; inquiring, So-ri?; and the incessant, barely audible whisper of social lubrication: *s'ry, s'ry* . . . Mechanical fluency in a language is nothing compared to the power of one perfectly natural sound. Dian was taking her time. He wondered if she had spotted the *other* photos, the ones he kept discreetly out of sight.

As soon as she reappeared, he knew she had.

'Ah, Dian. Have we finished with the food? Shall I have it cleared away?'

'Sorry about that, I suddenly felt ill. I'm not used to such rich dishes.'

'You're all right now, though? Good! I was wondering, while you were gone, what exactly is the meaning of that Western expression *heart of darkness*?'

She stared at him, her command of the situation shattered.

Wang nodded. 'I'm curious, because, of course, in a deluded sense, the "heart" of England's "darkness" could be right here where I am sitting.'

General Hu had taken possession of the Triumvirate's modest home on Brixton Hill. That was his prerogative, and the best he could do, since Buckingham Palace had been gutted by fire when the siege was broken. Wang, with a different brief and more imagination, had located a more potent shrine. An orderly silently cleared the dishes. Wang waited until the man was gone. He sat upright now, relaxed but stern, his authority emerging from behind the playful indulgence. 'Yes, Dian, you've guessed it. This flat was the love nest where Rufus O'Niall, a brutally successful old rockstar, brought his young girls; and the last of them was Fiorinda Slater, his own twelve-year-old daughter. Whom he believed could bear him a child with "magical" powers.'

'Oh my God. You can't be living here. This is *horrible*.'

'Close the door on the past, Dian. It's only superstition that makes you afraid of a place where something ugly happened to one of your rockstar royals. Rufus O'Niall was an unpleasant lunatic, and a war criminal. He's dead; that's all.'

'I'm n-not superstitious! I kept away from all that. I *hated* all that.'

'Good.' He watched her, with a gentle, urbane smile. 'This is re-education, Dian. This is how it works. First you will learn to feign indifference, because you are an intelligent woman, you understand your position and you want to live. Then indifference to these delusions will become genuine, and your self-made troubles will be over. Why don't you sit down?'

Dian sat down.

'Now then, let's continue our conversation. Dilip Krishnachandran, although by far the senior, was Aoxomoxoa's disciple. Were they also lovers?' He laughed at her expression. 'Speak freely, I'm not easy to shock. Actually I'm thrilled by all the Reich's Bohemian couplings. Life must have been so exciting.'

She fled into the past. It was Boat People Summer, a year of disasters overcome: which had begun with the monster hippies in charge, and Islamic Separatist war in Yorkshire; and ended with the country at peace, storm and flood defied, the Rock and Roll Reich established. But this was a night in June. A tv studio, as glamorous as such places ever are: a cluster of prefabs in a Wandsworth car park. Dian had interviewed Aoxomoxoa and the Heads on her live show; Fiorinda and veteran rock critic Roxane Smith also appearing. He'd waylaid her after the show, in a makeshift corridor of a room that smelled of carpet glue. He was eating hothouse grapes, tossing them into the open gullet of the living skull mask. Most rockstars are sad munchkins in the flesh. Dian was six foot, but Aoxomoxoa was easily six foot six, and *bench*. His shoulders in that fuck-you white singlet, sleek and massive and perfect. His nearness was making her head spin, and he knew it.

Possibly the hottest rockstar *on earth*, and she could feel his body heat.

'London's so different now. I love the anarchy but I miss the neon—'

'How about a fuck?'

'Augh! *Sage!* You can't *do* that. It's outrageous. You can't just, just—'

'I jus' did,' he said, reasonably, in that slow, insolent Cornish surfie accent.

'You're such a clown.'

'Not many people realise that.'

He took off the mask and smiled, with the bluest eyes. His naked face wasn't such a prize as it should have been. Sage and his brother Heads had taken off their skull masks on the show, a rare treat for the punters. But my God how *sexy*. She'd imagined this moment with better trimmings, she told herself the hearts and flowers would come. He wants me, possession is nine-tenths of the law, he thinks he's smart but I'm smarter. No way she wouldn't get the rest.

'Your place or mine?' she wondered, with a bold grin.

'Yours. I don' like sharing my own bed.'

The band came trooping by, with a few mates. Big George Merrick, Sage's second-in-command, cast a disapproving skull-grimace of a glance, and the blond bombshell moved in like a firestorm. His crippled hands, that she didn't like to think about, were all over her. Everything blurred, the sharp edges of reality vanished—

She had to recall the scene at the studio exactly as it had happened, down to the sting of George's little disapproving look, or she didn't get the shock of his first kiss, her most reliable sex aid, an aphrodisiac that *never* failed. Now she was free to improvise. Sage whispered tender things, how he'd dreamed of this moment, how he longed to spend his life with her. They went back to his place, after all, because he really loved her. He didn't even want to do it on their first date, he wanted to wait, but his passion was unstoppable, he was feverishly undressing her—

Wang had no occasion to resort to fantasy. He was in bed with a splendid, willing amazon, in the capital of the most romantic country in the world; which he had recently conquered. Sometimes the moment is enough. But when she was sleeping he put on a robe, and sat looking out between the golden curtains (the bedroom had the same décor as the living room) into the quiet of Chelsea. He had visited London before the Crash: a sad disappointment, all bling and guns and the most repellent spiritual poverty. He preferred Ax Preston's version, albeit ravaged by grandiose 'green' redevelopment; and Hu's somewhat careless treatment. He liked the *darkness* of these English cities. The frugality of street lighting that mapped human movement, little networks of fire, ever-changing—

The courtesan slept like a baby in the haunted shrine; which allayed his own nagging disquiet. Disquiet? Call it fear and dread, if you must . . . But fear made this distasteful address worthwhile.

She would be his litmus paper; her responses would be his test-bed.

'And if there's any secret gold in these clouded hills,' he murmured, with bravado to match Dian's, 'it's Chinese gold now.'

Ashdown

I

One Rainy Wish

The festival stages were going up, in the midst of a picturesque heathland known as the Ashdown Forest, some forty kilometres south of the 18th October Line. Scaffolders mounted the mainstage towers, with a merry clangour and hammering that sang of better days; of the Reich in its glory. Around the margins of the broad hollow that formed the arena rolls of doubled baling plastic were being stapled down, in the shelters for tentless campers. The big tents for smaller stages had been raised, the designated campground was filling up. Word had gone out and the faithful had made their way to Sussex, from raw battlefields and freshly occupied cities, some with Chinese permissions, some travelling on the underground; some from as far away as Yorkshire. They drifted, watching the crews, buying hot drinks and pies from concession stands, clotting into groups; meeting the locals.

No motor vehicles. True to its code, the Reich wouldn't have sullied the protected heath with chicken-wire track, also they had very little fuel to spare. A line of roustabouts, backs bent like Egyptian slaves, laden like donkeys or hauling great obelisks on handcarts, stretched from mainstage away out of sight, towards the road. Dogs and lost children fretted; ancient shopping trolleys ran aground. An enterprising local could be heard roaring out his wares, '*Skids! Get yer skids here!*'

Up on the stage a team of sound and light engineers were taking stock, reading the prospective 'scapes on gadget-belt screens, discussing their difficulties in a private world, oblivious of the scaffolders' row. A lanky individual in scarecrow jeans stared out at the arena from under the hood of a shabby grey fleece. He was looking, without much hope, for a man called Doug Hutton – last seen several months ago, on the night Ax Preston and his partners had been arrested as they tried to leave the country. But the crowd itself caught his attention. They had finally lost it, the indefatigable ravers. They had lost control, they were falling-down helpless, not a leg to stand on. They'd come here to be found, uprooted children clinging to the familiar "traveller's joy" logo on battered marquees; to the shards of the Reich's liferaft, flotsam and jetsam on the grey waves of the heath—

'Was' that rubbidge Caro?'

'Appropriate, healthy, social and political comment.'

'Sounds like arsing *culture* ter me,' complained a hefty fellow with a mane of curly black hair. The tall engineer in the grey hoodie shivered and gobbed into a nasty-looking rag, causing the team to yelp and gag, clasping their ears.

'SAGE! Don't fucking DO THAT! That's DISGUSTING.'

'Carn' help having a cold, can I?'

'It's the "Slaves' Chorus" from *Aida*,' admitted Caro Letwynd, a pigtailed woman with a serene broad face, long-time chief lighting designer for Aoxomoxoa and the Heads. Her colleagues jeered. Ooh, art-for-a-cause, the old Italian connection. Ooh, she's an intellectual in't she. If Caro was such a suck-up, someone inquired, did she have 'The East Is Red' in her catalogue? 'You bet I have. Coming soon.'

The event, barely a month after the ceasefire, was sanctioned. The Chinese had dealt harshly with the suppurating sore of delusion: they wanted to make the point that they had no quarrel with the English people. Or with England's legendary Rock and Roll solution to the global crisis, apparently. They called the Ashdown Festival 'an appropriate and healthy resumption of cultural life'. The Commanding General of the South East, Lü Xiaobao, had expressed concern for the well-being of the masses. He'd donated six truckloads of straw, to be collected from the October 18th Line. They're a predictable lot, our conquerors. They wanted to be liked.

But it might be a trap.

And yet here they were, like fish in a barrel—

A piercing, amplified voice invaded the engineers' private world, *no camp fires and you cannot cut down any trees . . . May* not, muttered Caro, defender of the arcane beauties of Native English. A bearded hippy, a grizzling toddler in his arms, crossed and recrossed the Breughal foreground, getting the headshake from everyone he stopped: no, haven't seen your loved ones. He was one of many, and he wasn't the only raver in proscribed Countercultural dress. Chinese had fucking better be in an understanding mood, when they look around here. A chunkily built black man in obsolete British Army uniform had collided with the despondent hippy. He recoiled and blundered on, groping his holstered pistol—

'Fuck.'

Sage retreated behind the desks, making a feeble attempt to disguise his height by stooping down and hunching his shoulders. Fat chance. The wild-eyed soldier charged for the stage, those in his path swiftly getting out of the way. This was Richard Kent, the former British Army major who had created Ax's barmy army: hero of the Islamic Campaign, commander of the Reich's armed forces. He should not be at Ashdown. Chinese goodwill didn't extend that far. He'd been warned (make that *begged*) to stay away. But of course he'd turned up, with his chiefs of staff. They were telling anyone who would listen that they were here to organise the Resistance.

The roustabouts gave Colonel Kent a boost, they weren't going to argue with an armed lunatic. He marched smartly to the trestles, where Sage was hiding behind his visionboard. Richard had lost weight, and there was a thick close growth of beard around his jaw. Deep-gouged lines of strain scarred his cheeks and brow, red rims to his hollow eyes; but he stood foursquare and belligerent.

'I want to talk to you . . . *Sage*, look at me when I'm speaking!'

The engineer sighed and shoved back his hood, revealing gaunt angelic beauty, sketchy blond cane rows; and a vivid pair of blue eyes.

'It's good to see you, too, Richard.'

'What the fuck's going on? Not a *word* from my leaders, all through the invasion, and we knew you were free. We were in contact with the Scots who sprung you out of jail. But not a word from you three, *nothing* . . . I suppose it was impossible. I held a meeting of the chiefs of staff, we decided that Ax meant the lads to lie low. We have to talk. I've been out of my mind. It was hellish, hellish, watching the regulars fall apart like wet toilet paper, and doing nothing—'

Abruptly, Richard lost conviction. 'Are you *listening*? Are you on some other fucking plane? Are you playing dance tracks in that private little world of yours?'

'I c'n hear you,' said Sage. He tipped the soundbead from his ear anyway, and looked at the pistol butt. 'Did the Rangers say you could carry a firearm?'

Richard made an impatient gesture, breathing hard.

Lowly electricians, who'd begun to cable-up the antique monsters, could be heard complaining. The patching of bizarre connections, the lack of gaffer tape—

'I couldn't find you! We arrived and no one would tell me where you two were, it was as if I *didn't exist*. What the fuck was that about? All right, forget it, forget it. Listen, it's not over. IT'S NOT OVER. Half the country is unoccupied, the Celtic nations are untouched. We have matériel, far more than they know. We have soldiers, few maybe, but harder, more experienced than they have any idea. We can have bases, here there and everywhere, we can *harry* them—'

'Oh really? You're gonna show the People's Liberation Army how to do guerrilla warfare?'

'I *know* it's been hell, I *know* what happened to you. But you have to get on, back on your feet, we have to pull ourselves together, and *strike hard*—'

Shouldn't say a word, except silence was going to make the man worse. 'Nah, you see, tha's where you're wrong. We're the pacifists—'

Richard's eyes bulged dangerously, he exploded in fury. 'So it's *true*. I didn't believe it! You're bottling out. You were an outstanding officer once, Sage. I was proud to serve with you in Yorkshire. But for you that was several lifetimes ago, that's the problem. Before your trip to see God, before the fashionplate years at the court of King Ax. Frankly, I liked you better when you were a loutish, sex-mad, drunken teen-idol in a ridiculous digital mask.'

'Thanks a lot.'

'Put not your faith in rockstars, they reinvent themselves every season.'

'Rich, I'm serious. This isn't somethen' we should fight, iffen we could. It's our share of a mighty disturbance in the force, bro. It's neither good nor bad, an' violence is not the way to meet it.'

The soldier curled his lip.

'I'll wait until I hear the dreamy mystic line from Ax, Aoxomoxoa.'

'Suit yourself.'

Someone who had quietly come up behind Richard crossed into view, with a guitar he'd taken from a stagehand: tucked a bead in his ear and sat on a cable drum beside Sage, head bent, a wing of dark hair falling. He wore a ring with an incised, red bevel on his right hand; a band of red and white and yellow braided British gold on his left. He picked the strings, one welling phrase of single notes, and looked up, tossing back the hair to reveal a keel of Celtic knotwork around his left eye.

'The Chinese invasion's a mighty disturbance in the force, Rich. It's neither good nor bad. And violence is not the way to meet it.'

Like his Triumvirate partner, the President (technically still President of this vanquished nation) looked as if he'd been sleeping rough since his last known whereabouts. His brown jacket was stained and muddy, his sheeny hair unkempt.

'I'm fucking glad you're okay, but I wish you'd stayed away from Ashdown. If you have to be here I wish you'd turn in that gun, ditch the paramilitary look, and tell your cohorts the same. We're holding this gathering on sufferance, you know. I can't protect you guys, and I won't try.'

Richard was distracted by the knotwork, dark blue against skin the colour of milky tea; which he had not seen before.

'What's that on your face? Did the Scots *mark you* like that?'

'Yep,' said Mr Preston, shortly. 'They did. Price of our ticket out of jail.'

'It doesn't disguise you. But that doesn't matter. The Chinese don't know if you're alive or dead. They have no idea where you are!'

Ax let it pass. 'Yeah, well, maybe, but that doesn't make me your secret weapon. I'm not going to join you this time, Rich. It's not tenable.'

The leader of the Resistance stood nonplussed, his face working. 'All right. I've been shooting my mouth. We'll discuss this further.' He turned on his heel and marched, ramrod straight. He got a hand to the ground, and forged away into the mill of the lost. Ax looked at Sage. They went together to the front of the stage, Ax still with the guitar shipped, to watch the wild man's progress until he vanished.

'Where d'you think he's going?'

Sage was overtaken by the need to fill his dirty rag again, sneezing out great gouts of bile-coloured phlegm. He was no longer togged into the engineers' space, so it was only Ax who got the benefit. 'Looking for Fee, of course. See if he can convince our little tearaway to pick up her AK and git some.'

They laughed: but it was painful. They could only tell themselves that if their friend was in his right mind the reality of the situation would be blindingly obvious.

'That's a problem,' said Ax.

The people had spotted him: Ax Preston with guitar. They drifted uncertainly forward, dirty faces upturned, dark eyes, dark eyes, what a ragged, ramshackle bunch of orphans. Ax looked to the side, and sound-system ruler George Merrick nodded: go ahead, why not? What are we saving it for?

Gold and rose, the colour of the dream I had . . .

Not too long ago, yeah . . .

Fiorinda had been walking around all day being visible, between bursts of vital conferencing with the stewards. The mood was eerily cheerful, eerily familiar on the surface. Could have been any daft, outdoor winter fest of the old Reich. But the dead stood in the eyes of those who'd come from the occupied zones; and the gut-shot misery of defeat was in them all, beyond reason. The fact that the Chinese had deposed and executed a junta of vicious monsters made no difference. Late in the afternoon she was in the backstage canteen, hiding from friends, lovers and the bleeding crowd alike; warming her hands on a mug of sweet, scalding black tea. Fragments of festinet chat scrolled across the tabletop. The lonely hearts photos, row on row, inescapable. Fuck, I can't stand much more of this, why doesn't the tech break down for a while? Has anyone seen . . . ? Any information . . . Any information . . . Have you any news of . . . ? Biff . . . ? Are you here? Biff is nine years old, here's his picture, we haven't seen him since—

Poor Smelly Hugh Raven, baby Safire in his arms, searching for Silver and Pearl, who had been missing since the Reading Massacre. The Few's token addled hippy geezer, earnestly hopeful; in the dignity of his grief—

'They'll know to come here, won't they, Fio? They'll turn up, won't they—?'

What, all my pretty chickens and their dam?

Smelly's old lady, Anne-Marie Wing, was definitely dead, as were his two little boys, and his oldest daughter. Dilip, confirmed dead too. No additions to that aching personal list yet, as far as they knew. Sage's dad hadn't even been arrested, in spite of his closeness to government circles. Ax's family was okay, hostages again but okay; if you could trust any information from the South West. Sage's son had been with his mother, safe in deepest Wales, since before the invasion . . . The Wing kids preyed on her. Prime girl-flesh, and worse: prime targets for interrogation. What is happening to those children now, have they died for me?

How many died for me?

Got to get Smelly out of those clothes.

She heard Mr Guitar striking up with some gentle Hendrix and stayed put, fighting her demons. Get a grip, live with it, nervous breakdowns not allowed. Chip Desmond and Kevin Verlaine peered into the tent and spotted her. Chip's round black cherub face broke into a grin and they zipped straight over, unimpressed by *leave me alone* vibes. Verlaine, very pale, his brown cavalier curls scraped back, dragged up two more plastic chairs.

'Any chance of us snagging a hit?' wondered Chip, inhaling tea fumes.

'The urn's over there,' said Fiorinda, jerking her chin in the direction of a press of bodies. 'Try your luck. I think they've run out of sugar, though.'

They stared like puppydogs. 'Oh, all right. Don't bogart that caffeine, *mes amis*. I'm unspeakably glad you're alive, but I have refugee needs too.'

'We're unspeakably glad you're alive, as well,' said Chip. He sipped deep, sighed, and passed the mug to Verlaine. 'Okay, behave naturally.'

'Act as if we're, say, squabbling over a set list—'

'Bad-mouthing a stupidly successful boyband.'

'Whatever rockstars normally do. We've forgotten.'

'What the fuck are you on about, idiots?' Her heart thumped. Someone else she knew must be dead or worse—

'We have something to tell you,' said Verlaine, handing back the tea, not badly depleted. 'Don't worry, it's good news. Excellent black! Where do they get it?'

'There's a bloke called Dave, a poacher. *What* do you have to tell me?'

'Dave Wright? He's a legend, isn't he. Did you know he does stand-up?'

'Yeah, only unfortunately I can't stand stand-up. If it's good news, why couldn't you tell me last night, when you all got here?'

'It's probably better if the folks don't know.'

'Maybe better if Ax and Sage don't know, either,' added Verlaine. 'For now.'

'I don't like the sound of this.'

While their leaders were quietly hiding in the Forest, the Few had been in the midst of the invasion. At the close of official hostilities they'd been holed up in the Tower, last stand of the Republic of Europe partisans; except for Dilip, who'd died in the firestorm at Buckingham Palace. The Chinese had taken out the partisans in a hand-to-hand fight (trying not to damage anything mediaeval), and the Few had been held by Hu Qinfu, until they'd been given special permission to join this festival.

Only Roxane Smith, veteran music critic and the Reich's post-gendered court philosopher, was unaccounted for; but s/he'd been seen on tv once, looking okay.

'The debriefing last night was a pinprick,' said Chip, sternly. 'Layers upon *layers* of things happened to us, that we haven't told you yet.'

'This particular thing is about how the Republic of Europe Desperantos had robbed the Jewel House—'

'They did? I suppose that makes sense.'

'It hasn't been reported,' explained Chip. 'We reckon Hu cut a deal, let a few top partisans through the net, and has most of the loot squirrelled in his own kitbag.'

The characters of the Four Generals were established. Wang was articulate, smooth and ruthless. Sheng of the North East was an effective soldier, political lightweight. Lü, the 'little brother', Commanding General of the South East, seemed like a kindly old geezer (unlikely!). And Hu Qinfu was bent as a safety pin.

'Anyway, it happened, and we knew there was a bag of loose stones hidden in a bedroll, in the room where we'd been assigned.'

'All non-combatants had to sleep with the soldiers. They'd split the Few up, into different dorms, we didn't know if the others were still alive—'

'It was horrible, but listen. We saw our chance—'

'Battle was raging. Panic-stricken Chinese were trying to skewer Desperantos without denting the sacred holy ancient stonework, it was an opportunistic thing.'

'We should just *show* you.'

Ver unslung his daypack, burrowed inside and pulled out a dirty sock with a lump in the toe. He rolled it down, circumspectly, under the rim of the table so nobody around them could see. She was scared it would be some grisly relic of Dilip, that was how her loopy mind was working . . . Icy, scintillating light sprang up. A white diamond, stellar brilliant-cut and bigger than a baby's fist, sat in a nest of soiled Argyle knit – catching rainbow fire from the ATP patches on the tent's walls.

'Jaysus fockin' God,' breathed Fiorinda. 'That is a *pretty* thing.'

'It's the Koh-i-Noor,' whispered Chip.

'I thought it might be,' said Fiorinda softly. 'Put it away.'

Verlaine buried the sock again.

Fiorinda rolled her eyes. 'You're right about not telling the folks. They'd go mental, we're supposed to be on our best behaviour. What were you planning to *do*?'

'Er, we weren't planning. It just seemed too good to miss.'

'We're bound to need funds, and diamonds are always negotiable.'

'Not that one.' She put her chin on her hand. 'Okay, well, I don't know what to do with a famous national treasure right now, either. For the moment, you keep it.'

They grinned at each other, the young queen and her beardless counsellors, an alliance reforged, survivor guilt briefly vanquished; the future irrationally illumined by that stolen blaze.

The socially cohesive rock concert was happening tomorrow, with non-Few bands bussed in from London, tv cameras and mediafolk. Tonight was Reich for the insiders, local heroes and radical rockstars on equal terms; a raw and consoling ritual. A girls' *a capella* group from Uckfield, singing ethereal, chilling post-modern madrigals. Rob Nelson and the Powerbabes and their big band sound, teenage guitar outfits from lonely villages; an ancient folkie with an accordion. More Sussex folkies, top of the range, playing for their own tonight and for the tourists tomorrow. Chip Desmond and Kevin Verlaine, the notorioso Adjuvants, far away in leftfild. Haywards Heath Operatic society's *Joseph and the Amazing Techni-coloured Dream Coat* highlights. The retro-Eurotrash duo from Maresfield (in their sequined catsuits). Aoxomoxoa and the Heads with a guest guitarist, and a guest punk diva—

The dreamers stood in the rain that had set in at twilight, water running off their binbags as so many happy times before. They cheered, they sang along, they got into stupid arguments with the Heads' snot-gobbing frontman. They eagerly accepted invitations to come up and have a go; they embraced Fiorinda, and other stage divers, most tenderly. The lights shorted and darkness engulfed the hollow, as mud engulfed the heather roots, but nobody left. At the end Ax gave them a bonus set – the President of the Invisible Republic, in a stained brown jacket and mismatched suit trousers, his fine-drawn profile sober and serene, making that guitar weep like nobody else alive. And then everyone, musicians, engineers, security crew and babes in arms, trooped back on stage for the traditional finale.

The Chinese approved of the English National Anthem. They had made it the theme tune of their Joyous Liberation tv channel (essential viewing, these days). And that was fine, no problem. A fuck sight better than the Second Chamber bastards using 'I Vow To Thee' to promote their Slave-Camp, Occult-Horror-Weapons Neo-Feudalist State. But tonight the Reich's leaders had elected to use a different song. It was a poem by Catullus, 'Ave Atque Vale', translated by Aubrey Beardsley; set to music by one of the survivors who'd got out of Reading before the bloodbath.

Ax sang in the original language, with minimal guitar.

> *Alloquar? audiero nunquam tua verba loquentem?*
> *Numquam ego te, vita frater amabilior,*
> *Aspiciam posthac?, at certe, semper amabo—*

then Fiorinda read the English poem.

> By ways remote and distant waters sped,
> Brother, to thy sad grave-side am I come,
> That I may give the last gifts to the dead,
> And vainly parley with thine ashes dumb—

No encores, no singalong. It would be their only act of defiance, their only solidarity with the dead. Brothers, sisters, for all time hail and farewell.

The babies were taken off to bed, the support crews left in search of false cheer. The backstage tent, marginally waterproof, dimly lit by ATP patches, was soon deserted except for the Triumvirate, the Few and their closest friends. They wanted to tell tales, bonding with each other in the strung-out exaltation of reunion . . . Sage's brother Heads hadn't been in the Tower. Lucky they'd been in London, because of the cognitive scanners affair: if they'd been caught down in Cornwall or Bristol they'd have been stuck. What exactly happened to you guys? We haven't had the details?

'It's a long story,' said Peter Stannen, without enthusiasm.

'Does anyone think Beardsley's a great poet?' asked Bill, gloomily.

'No,' said Ax. 'I'm not mad about Catullus, either, tell you the truth.'

'It was appropriate,' said George. People nodded, silence fell.

Sayeed Muhammad Zayid al-Barlewi, leader of English Islam, heaved a sigh. His wife, his brothers, his daughters and his sons-in-law were in Bradford/Halifax, in Chinese custody; he was free because he'd been somewhere else. He stood up, shook out his sober raingear, and clapped Ax gently on the shoulder.

'Come on, lad, on your legs. Let's find the bar: I'll buy you a pint.'

The young Islamics, Muhammad's unarmed bodyguard, laughed.

'Call it medicine,' said one of them.

'Call it what you like. The Prophet himself (peace and blessings of Allah be upon him, added Muhammad, automatically, tenderly) wouldn't forbid it tonight.'

The tent emptied. But Sage had copped a *look* from Rob Nelson. He stayed where he was, in fear and trembling, and the bandleader stayed too. The last gophers trolleyed away the tea-urn, calling goodnight. Rob stooped and rubbed at a splash of mud on the turn-up of his sharp yellow trousers; Armageddon would not get Rob on stage without a sharp suit. So what's the damage? Not my dad, unless the Chinese telecoms controllers had me talking to a Joss Pender voiceprint the other day. My sisters wouldn't rate this treatment, and Mary's safe in Wales—

Oh, no, please—

'Rob? What is it? C'mon? Please?'

'It's nothing bad, not terrible.' Rob shrugged deeper into his borrowed parka, and ran a hand over his nappy skull. 'It's, er, Marlon's gone missing. Apparently he vanished, and left Mary a note saying he'd decided to join us.'

'Oh. Right, I see. When . . . when was this?'

'The week after the ceasefire. The first we heard was a few days ago, we couldn't get to speak to you. Mary's okay about it,' Rob added quickly. 'I spoke to her. Naturally she's freaked out, and, you know, ancient history—'

Sage nodded, unable to speak. His relationship with Mary Williams had been an evil thing. For years she hadn't allowed him near his son, and she'd had a right.

'She's more angry than scared. He's sixteen, he isn't a child. She thinks he's with you, an' she thinks we've been a lot more organised and in the Chinese pockets than is the case. I didn't tell her any different. She said, er, "Steve was a bastard to me, but he's turned into a good father. Tell him to do the responsible thing and get Marlon back here, don't care what strings he has to pull . . ." I told her I'd be seeing you soon, and you'd get Marlon to call her, and not to worry.'

Stephen was Sage's original name.

Missing means dead. Sage leaned forward, slowly: elbows on his knees, hands clasped. The dim light caught on his yellow lashes, making them glitter.

'I haven't heard from him.'

'I didn't think so,' said Rob, compassionately. 'How could you have? Listen, there's a ceasefire, he's your son. We can ask the Chinese to help us trace him.'

'Is there any record of him crossing the border?'

'It's closed, man, and Scotland too. Officially nobody's crossing, but you know that border, it's a sieve. I'm sure he's okay, but I thought you'd want to hear news like that without the folks straight at you—'

'You were right.'

Rob had two children himself. Little children can make a world anywhere, but they get bewildered, they get scared. Every hour of every day you blame yourself, and you pray you can get them safe through, to a better life.

'Kids. It breaks my back, thinking what we've brought them into.'

'Yeah.'

There'd been a time when Rob Nelson had regarded Aoxomoxoa with quiet loathing, and resented his ascendancy. That big muscle-bound, swaggering ex-junkie, with the intimidating body-language, stupid fucking mask, and a past record of beating up his baby's mother? How could you really trust him? There had been a time when Aoxomoxoa, perfectly indifferent to Rob Nelson's opinions, had seen the bandleader as a liability: stiffly righteous in the head, won't pick up a weapon, apt to fall apart in physical danger. A *bad* combination in the hellish situation that had closed over them all, on Massacre Night—

So now they looked at each other, two thirtysomething veterans of Utopia in a cold leaky tent; remembering a lot of past, reflecting on human changes, sharing in silence a thought that need not be spoken. *You'll do, mister. You, I trust.*

'Let's we get along to the bar, bodhisattva. You need a whisky for that cold.'

Sage was attacked by a bout of gluey sneezing.

'I'll be along in a minute,' he said when he could speak. 'Thanks, Rob.'

Plunged into memory. He was seventeen years old, fresh-skinned clean of his teenage love affair with the brown, still deep in hate with Mary Williams. That black hole obsession was going to drag him down for years yet. He was holding his baby son in his arms, so *small*, so very small, thinking *is this how it feels to be forgiven?* Missing means dead, gone for three weeks means dead. It was some comfort to realise that Rob genuinely didn't think so. Marlon's sixteen, he's not a child. He's not some little five-year-old, wandering along—

Oh, but he is to me. That's exactly what he is, and he always will be—

'Hello?'

Sage was wrenched from a vision of his tiny infant son, wandering alone in a warzone, by a six-foot blonde beauty, in pristine green wellies and a slim, black and gold padded coat. Dian Buckley had appeared before him.

Ah, *shit*.

Dian was the mediababe who had done the werewolf interview, prelude to the doomed cascade of events that had put them under house arrest; after Ax had punched the head of the Secret Police in the jugular, and broken the bastard's neck. She was widely regarded in the Reich, and in England, as the traitor who'd brought Ax down. She didn't deserve that: but she'd been lucky to escape being punished by the Chinese for the way she'd served the Second Chamber. He'd known she was untouched, and rumoured to be very close to a General (Joyous Liberation news had its scurrilous gossip). He could not imagine what she was doing here.

He had seen Dian Buckley looking well-groomed in so many leaky tents, he waited for a moment for the vision from the past to disperse: she didn't.

'Hey, Dian. Long time no see! How did *you* get out of London?'

'Wang Xili,' she said, chin up. 'He's a friend.' She stared at him, chewing her glossy underlip. 'I heard the single. The one George put out, and it got banned, when you three were in Wallingham. It was about me, wasn't it? "Hell Hath No Fury Like A Sandwich"?'

'I'm sorry,' said Sage. (Dian, you don't change.) 'You've lost me. George did a protest song, I know. I was touched. I expect it had stupid words, they always write stupid words when I'm not there to guide them. Don't worry about it . . . Dian, I don't care what was in the charts last June. What are you doing here?'

'I told Wang I wanted to be at Ashdown because something important is happening, and it's true. I care, passionately, about the Reich, whatever anyone thinks. I don't expect you to believe that.'

'I'm sure you care as passionately about the Reich as ever you did.'

Dian looked around. She sat her pretty coatskirts on a plastic chair that at least had no puddle in the seat. 'All right. You've decided what to think of me. But I – I have to talk to you, and this was the only way I

27

could get near. It's not about me, it's about you, you people. Something terrible I've found out, and I have to tell you.'

'Go ahead. It's karma night.'

She braced herself, with fearful intensity. 'You know that Hu Qinfu has moved into Matthew Arnold Mansions, your place in Brixton?'

'Of course we know. He couldn't very well move into Buckingham Palace, could he? So, what?'

'Wang has done better. His *pièd à terre* in Chelsea is the flat where Rufus O'Niall used to take Fiorinda. I sleep there. In that bedroom.'

Sage blinked at her: pulled out his current rag, found a relatively unused patch, filled it and carefully looked around for a binbag. Nope. All been cleared away.

'Oooh, tha's ingenious of him, if true . . . Is Hu pissed, is it a competition?'

'You don't get it, Ao-*hahaha*, Sage. He has photos of her when she was twelve, photos Rufus must have taken. Everyone knows Rufus took pictures, no one's ever found a trace. Wang has them on the bathroom wall, where he can see them from the shower; *know what I mean?*'

Sage cast another leisurely glance around for somewhere to dump the rag; sighed and returned it to his pocket. 'Is that the terrible news? Dian, aside from I'm not sure I believe you, this is Fiorinda you're talking about. Grow up, mediababe. Using a rockstar as wank-aid: not a crime. Not unless it leads to the fantasies getting invasively acted out. It's a hazard of our employment, I'm sure Cliff Richard did not escape. Fiorinda is anybody's. Ax too. An' even me, eh? You think?'

Maybe she blushed: difficult to tell in the dim light, with permanent make-up.

'It d-doesn't concern you that he took great pains to find the shrine of the evil magician, and he's desecrating the image of our lady there? Doesn't that scare you? The Chinese claim they don't believe in magic. So why would he do that?'

Sage seemed at a loss for an opinion. 'What did Wang say? Have you told *him* where you think he's living?'

'It's not like that . . . I saw the pictures in the bathroom. Then he told me.' Dian shivered. 'He says he's making me live there to re-educate me; he's living there to re-educate us. To teach us that the story of Rufus's magic is nonsense.'

The Minister for Gigs thought it over. 'Maybe he's right . . . It's a piss-off if he's making a big thing of a place we'd rather forget, but he's got the right idea. Dian, take my advice and ditch the evil magician, lord and lady shite. Paganism's the religion of the Counterculture. No matter how close you are with the General, you can't afford to talk like that.'

The mediababe looked very sick for a moment, and he wondered exactly why. 'I could be useful,' she blurted out. 'That's what I really came to say.'

'What—?'

'Look, I don't want to do this, I want to survive. But I'm more afraid of what, *what might return*, than I am of s-starving. I'm sleeping with the enemy, that's my business, but he's off his guard with me. Wang uses me as a source of information, but he talks. He talks about immix, about the Zen Self experiment, using those words. These are forbidden topics, supposed to be treated like they never existed, but he doesn't care with me. I could tell you things, find out things.'

Fer fuck's sake, he thought. You could go back an' tell your General we're not quite as dumb as we look. But he felt her desperation. He believed she was sincere, in her own eyes, at this moment; and he pitied her, dangerous as she might be.

'They'd kill you,' he said, bluntly but not unkindly. 'Don't you understand that? And they'd take their time, *know what I mean?*'

She held her ground, chewing the glossy lip again.

'He keeps asking me about Dilip. Why would Wang need to know about Dilip? He's a m-minor figure, believed to be dead. You know that no bodies have been recovered from the State Apartments?'

Sage had not been in London since before the invasion, but he'd seen the news coverage of the breaking of the siege, and he'd had eye-witness accounts. The Chinese were refusing access to the heap of sodden spoil that had been the Insanitude, on some atavistic theory that this would humble the English. And in some atavistic way they were right. But there were no *bodies*. When the human remains search teams were allowed in, they'd be sifting the ash for teeth.

Dian stared at him, insistent; he refused to be drawn.

'There never will be. What are you getting at, Dian?'

'I don't know. I don't know what I mean. But there's something going on. If they're lying to us, if they are adepts at Black Art, anything's possible. I get a sense that Dilip may be in their hands. They may have called him up. Not alive, but—'

Sage stopped her, shaking his head.

'You have a lurid imagination, did anyone ever tell you that? Dian, you're giving yourself nightmares. Lay off, think better thoughts. The Chinese are our liberators, we needed to be liberated, let's live with it.' He stood up. 'Are you on your own? You know, you don't have many fans at Ashdown.'

'I'm with friends.'

'I'll walk you back to them.'

The late bar was in one of the Reich's prefab sleeping bag shelters. From the outside it looked like a sagging cowshed; with a front wall of layered marquee membrane that heaved like something alive in the dark. Inside it was warm and bright, full of bodies, and the draughts were welcome. Many of the defeated Utopians had been living without regular showers since September. The Few had scattered themselves through the throng, working the crowd. Fiorinda and Ax sat on stools at the counter, elbow to elbow, talking to anyone who accosted them; telling Reich-and-local mediafolk they were exhilarated to be starting from nothing again.

They would not be meeting the mainstream press. The situation was far too uncertain for that.

Fiorinda got into a conversation with Areeka Aziz, rising star of the Reich's second generation, that began with medium-term strategy (slightly premature) and degenerated to Ashdown catering. The concession stalls weren't running out of food, but too many ravers had turned out to be penniless. Wristie numbers were past five thousand, spot estimates on the ground already well over that, got to boost the free meal provision. If we can do pease porridge and beer, they won't starve—

'I'm on to it!' cried Areeka, 'I'll check the stores physically, it's the only way, festinet is *so* fucked up—'

Away she darted, burrowing between bodies, overjoyed to be back on board. Time was, they'd said that vivid London teenager was "the new Fiorinda". Areeka, you are *nothing* like me. You have loving parents, who taught you to believe in things. You have A-Levels, or whatever they call them now. So caught up in the events of your time you couldn't care less what you're doing to your career, never mind that you're risking your life: and how you shine—

I want a daughter like that . . .

(Her hand drifted to touch her belly, but she caught herself. *Absit omen.* Baby, what baby? Nah, silly idea, go away demons, no baby here.)

Ax's kitten, who'd been left behind the bar all day, crawled from Ax's knee to Fiorinda's and hustled to be allowed inside her hoodie. He was a good little homeless persons' cat, unfazed by anything as long as Ax was near. Ax glanced around and they grinned at each other, snatching a break.

'Still up for blowing the lovely Rosamund out of the water?'

'Rosa*mond*,' said Fiorinda. 'Get it right. She'll think we don't care.'

Ax and Sage would be lying very low tomorrow. Fiorinda had a solo set, unpublicised except by word of mouth, in one of the tents. Rosamond, a much-touted singer/songwriter, was the top female act on the official line-up. They'd discovered that the rumour mill (Ashdown had a rumour mill in London; apparently, amazingly) was billing this 'collision' as a catfight between the senior nation's sweetheart and the young contender. A bizarre concept to deal with when you're testing very murky water, not sure whether or not you have a price on your head. And by the way, Rosamond's *older* than I am—

Ah, poor Areeka.

'I don't mind blowing people away,' said Fiorinda. 'I used to do it all the time when I was a teenage superstar. The worst is when you blow someone away without knowing they existed, that's when they get really pissed off.'

'We could quietly cancel your tentshow—'

'Nah, I'm fine. It's these blackberry crushes, they make me quarrelsome. One more and I'll be on the canvas. D'you ever envy them, Ax? The normal rockstars?'

'Hahaha. I had my time in the sun. I'd only be embarrassing myself by now.'

'Me too. I was born to burn out young, it's what makes me so romantic. Art for a cause is such a mug's game. We aren't even good at it. The real icons of the revolution get shot, very quickly. The rest of us are just wannabes.'

She was twenty-four. I will see your name in lights again, he thought.

'Why *are* we still alive?' he wondered aloud. 'I can't remember.'

'No one can say we haven't tried—'

They raised their glasses, in silent accord, to the friends in this long struggle whom they would never see again. To all the *stupid* rockstars, who'd got involved, when anyone could see all you had to do was talk the talk, in Crisis Europe and beyond. To every melodramatic fool who ever dared to be something other than a dumb pop idol. And the roll call stretches back, into the dim history of the twentieth century—

Hey, compadres. Long live futuristic Utopia.

The bar crowd saw them toasting each other, which raised a cheer. Then Sage walked in, immediately followed by the huge and awesome Gintrap, with entourage. The amiable metallers were not supposed to be on this site. The official acts were supposed to stay in their trailers, until they were bussed to the special area backstage. But the Trap claimed it was okay, the Chinese were cool. Thrilled with themselves for being at Ashdown, and rubbing shoulders with the rulers of the Reich, the non-Few rocklords prattled happily, a daft ego boost. Boje Strom trashed Rosamond at length. Dessy Foumart, the Trap's old-style girly frontman, *spectacularly* hammered, needed to know what the Minister for Gigs had thought of 'Save Your World (Why should I try to?)', an ancient and punishing Heads track which the 'deliberately crude' ones had mined, in the creator's absence, for its buried lyrics, and an unsuspected jolly tune.

''S *fine*,' growled Sage, folded onto a barstool, all arms and legs; downing his second pint. 'I couldn't give a bugger, Des, an' I hope it goes platinum. But I tell you what. If you ever give that shite treatment to 'Colour of Stars', or 'Arbeit', I am personally gonna have to invade your stage an' kick your fucking head in.'

'Oh fuck, I would be honoured. I'm selirious, Sage. I *would* be honoured. That would be the greatest, *greatest* moment of my life.'

'What happened to you?' murmured Fiorinda, as the flood of clean shiny hair, clean shiny clothes and *clean fingernails* dropped the two of them and swirled around Ax, fucking ace the President was still alive, and hey, fuckin' great tattoo—!

'I got waylaid by Dian Buckley.'

And Marlon is missing, he thought. But that'll wait until we're on our own.

'*Dian Buckley?* You're kidding. What the fuck's she doing here?'

'Tell you later.'

'Is it bad?'

'Of course.' Sage's glass was empty: Mrs Brown from the Anchor at Hartfield immediately delivered another. 'Thanks . . . Oh, I don't know. She's having problems adjusting, as aren't we all. Her General fixed her up with permits, she's with the press corps, but she was wandering around loose on our site. It's okay, I walked her to their gates, she's safe. I need a kitten to hug, lemme have Min. Can we go home soon?'

But they stayed, joining the outlaw revelry, getting used to being with people again; cravenly reluctant to go out into the wet dark, where who knows what might be waiting. It's karma night, there are demons abroad, clawing around.

Demons, daft music biz spats and Dian Buckley, we must be in business again.

II

By midmorning on the second day of Ashdown, illusory peace and calm prevailed in the Reich HQ. The marquee, meant for workshops and meetings at summer festivals, was impossible to heat; but they had battened the hatches, lowered the ceiling sheets and were making liberal use of blankets. The Triumvirate had arrived early, lured by the promise of hot showers. Cats and babies were tucked away in the security of an inner section. Off in their own space, Muhammad's Islamic youngsters sat in their neat corral of bedrolls, having a religious discussion with their *shaykh*.

Who could have foretold, a hundred years ago, that the creation of wealth would lead to utter destruction? Are the infidel not justified in reproaching GOD?

It needed no foretelling for us to know that profit amassed by the oppression of the poor was a transgression—

In the Few's living space, Sage was getting his rows reconstructed by Dora Devine's expert hands, while Ax worked on embedded tangles in Fiorinda's curls. Call it superstition, but it was important that he didn't resort to scissors. Desultory conversation passed around. Thank God they'd given up storing the tour gear at the Insanitude, before the last disaster struck. Their roadshow had been discovered and impounded, but Hu Qinfu had handed everything back, lacking only the forbidden tech. So he's not a total crook. Thank God you're such a hoarder, Allie. The admin-queen had never allowed obsolete hardware to be thrown away—

Nathalie Que, the Vietnamese ceramics artist who'd been Dilip's last squeeze, and ended up trapped in the siege, was still with them. She sat close to Allie, by the brazier (the other brazier was with the babies), and kept reaching out to charge it. 'Don't be dumb,' said Allie, catching the girl's spider-fragile hand. 'You'll pass out.'

As an alternative energy source, ATP was doomed. A gene therapy that allows you to turbo your own chemical energy production, and even add it to the local grid, only works when people have a lot more food than they need—

Nathalie had lost her terror of ending up in a Guandong re-education camp (a real danger for ethnics of the New Autonomous Regions, the countries that used to be China's neighbours). Her current dream was that Ax would use his mighty influence to get her repatriated to Hanoi.

'I have relatives, I can prove right of citizenship, if my case is opened—'

You inherit your boyfriend's clueless little babe. You hate her, but you get attached to her. As if she were his old coat . . . Then she leaves you too. Allie, arms around her knees, rubbed her cheek against the sleeve of her beloved Gucci jacket.

Fuck it. I will have love-affairs with my clothes—

'Natty, you know, Ax might never be able to help you.'

'Oh, he will. I hear the way they talk about him on Joyous Liberation news. The Chinese hold Ax in the highest respect.'

'They don't say much.'

Nathalie smiled, with irritating confidence. 'Wait and see.'

Fiorinda talked to festinet with an earbead and a throat mike, ignoring Ax's labour of love. The pease porridge for the free meals had been made with garlic, and the poor didn't like it. 'Tell them it's boosting their immune systems . . . What's *wrong* with garlic? . . . Oh, all right, how much garlic? . . . Okay I *will* come and taste it . . .'

Can't compete with that.

'There, all done. The miracle of hair conditioner.'

The Spartans on the sea-wet rock sat down to comb their hair. Where's that from? Ax had a feeling he wouldn't like the ref if he could place it. He twisted up a handful of springing, shining copper silk, kissed her nape and went to look at the 18th October map, which was spread on a flexible broadsheet on a table of boxes.

The occupied zones made an irregular butterfly bow, from the south-west to the north-east; leaving Cumbria, Sussex and the whole eastern flank untouched. He knew that shape, aside from the anomaly of unoccupied Sussex (and we know why they did that . . .). The Chinese had subdued the Reich's heartlands, and then stopped. Did that mean they believed they'd done all they needed to do? Or what? Cumbria had been isolated for a long time, and there'd been no-go areas in the east, Essex to the fens, long as Ax could remember—

He flipped back to that graceful, ominous mission statement.

在 城 市 的 花 园 里, 在 乡 村 的 田 野 里

In the cities, flower-gardens, in the countryside, cultivated land. That's easy to read. The government the Chinese put together will be made up of acceptable public figures, looking pretty but walled in Chinese authority; food production will be a priority.

'I think they mean to keep the damned camps.'

But the biggest agricultural labour camps were in unoccupied territory.

'Maybe your fifth General's going to turn up,' said Sage. 'To finish us off.'

Ax believed there was a fifth General, who had not yet appeared. His friends weren't sure whether to take this seriously; his reasoning seemed bizarre. But Ax was the one who had studied China; their knowledge of the vast superpower was vague. Capitalist Miracle, Expansion of Asian Economic Sphere, and what else—?

'I'm sure there's someone. Four is not a good number, and the invasion was a phenomenally high-profile operation. They wouldn't do that.'

'There,' said Dora, with satisfaction. 'All done.'

'Terrific.' Sage tried to admire the effect in a tiny make-up mirror.

The murmur of the *tafseer* grew on them, a sad and sonorous music, with occasional bursts of English . . . Dave Wright the poacher, who had dropped by for a brew, reviewed the wild harvest Cherry and the Adjuvants had collected before the rain. Ax watched the process idly. Parasol mushrooms were approved, and the spiny puffballs. The poacher's sinewy, earth-coloured hands hovered over some little purplish 'shrooms, and set them aside. 'It says edible on *First Nature*,' said Chip diffidently, crestfallen. 'Non-psychoactive, but a useful protein source.'

'Ah, well, that's the website. I'm the man that's been living off the land.'

What about the handsome penny buns? Dave sucked his teeth. 'Ooh, *my lord*. Which of you mad little louts picked these fellers?'

'It was me,' confessed the junior powerbabe. Eye-candy Cherry was looking thin and wan, her poreless chocolate skin grey-tinged. She needs feeding up, thought Ax. As don't we all. 'Found under oak and beech, edible and delicious.'

'I hope you washed your hands before you et anything after. Lucky you showed me. I better take these and get rid of them—'

They'd talked it out. The Few were in full agreement with the plan their leaders had devised in hiding. But already they faced a challenge that might wreck them. Right now they were waiting for something to happen, and hoping it wouldn't. Fat chance. 'With mushroom poisoning, by the time you're sick it's too late, did you townies know that? Rush you to the hospital, there's nothen' they can do except watch you die in 'orrible disgusting agony—'

It needed no foretelling for us to know that this world is a mosque, and we walk here answerable to GOD—

'Here we go.' George was liaising with site security, a bead in his ear. 'He's been sighted. On his way, with a fuckin' mini-army.'

'Good,' said Ax, getting up. 'That's good. Sooner we get this over with the better.' The Few crowded round the broadsheet, switched to the outside camera feed. Ax went to talk to Muhammad; stooping on the way to break off a piece of boletus cap and shake his head at the comedian.

'Wanker.'

'Heheheh.'

Colonel Kent came into view out there, with the barmy chiefs of staff and a troop of other-rank paramilitaries. Reich security and uniformed Forest Rangers were escorting them, heckled by a minor rabble of rubber-necks and fight-fans.

'How d'you want to do it?' asked George. 'Have the ring-leaders in here, or we go out to them?'

'Have them in here with the walls up,' said Ax. 'We can't be out of sight with the paramilitaries. This has to be done in public, but in our control.'

'Let's have some dignity, aye,' agreed the leader of Islam.

Ax went to warn the baby-minders. George told the escort to stall for a few minutes; the main space of the marquee was swiftly re-organised. Richard and his company marched in to find Ax and his friends, with their Islamic allies, ranged in a hollow square, the Triumvirate at the back, crosslegged on a camp-bed *divan*. Crew persons started cranking up the walls, supervised by Bill and Peter: letting in the cold grey day.

'I've come for that meeting you promised me, Ax,' said Richard.

'Are you sure you're in the right place?' asked Chip, who had not found his coat, and sat cloaked in a multicoloured blanket. 'This is the non-violent solutions tent. Anger management is somewhere else.'

Velcro ripped, and a frantic child came shooting out of the crèche. He saw the guns and began to scream, racing for Dora, holding up his pudgy little hands.

'Mama, mama come inside! Don't shoot my mama! DON'T DARE!'

Rob came after, grabbed Mamba and swept the kid up in his arms. Smelly Hugh followed, hugging Safire. 'I'm well sorry,' said Smelly. 'I sed you can't go out, there's men with guns, an' Mamba went berserk.'

Rob glared at the barmies. 'You'll have to excuse him. My kids don't like guns.'

'They've seen *enough* guns,' cried Felice, appearing behind Smelly, with Ferdelice clinging to her hand. 'We all have. Are you fuckers out of your *minds?*'

Safire began to howl very quietly, hiding her face.

'I wasn't planning on a meeting,' said Ax. 'I've told you how I feel. But if you guys want to talk things over, that's fine. Hand your weapons to security, please, for safe-keeping. F'lice, cool down, it's not necessary.'

Richard relinquished his pistol. Cornelius Sampson, the old soldier, another British Army veteran and Richard's long-time lover, ignored the instruction. He was not searched. The rest of them disarmed fairly willingly, under Felice's baleful eyes.

'See,' murmured Rob. 'See, nobody's going to shoot anyone. C'mon, good boy, let's go back in the warm.'

The children and their minders retired. Richard noticed for the first time that the tent walls had been raised, and that there was an audience looking in, held back by a cordon of Rangers and security crew.

'What's going on—?'

'We think this should be in the open,' said Sage. 'Don't you agree?'

'All right,' said the Colonel, with a deep breath, and a shine in his eyes. They saw they'd made him hopeful, but they couldn't help it. 'All right, that's all right.'

Chairs were brought for Colonel Kent and for Cornelius. The rest of the deputation sat easily on the floor, chiefs of staff in the front row. The history of these dozen or so eco-warrior vets, including one woman, went back to the original green rampage, when Pigsty Liver had been in charge of the revolution. Richard Kent had tamed them by appointing them as general staff: but the discipline they'd acquired in Ax's army only made them more of a threat now. And each of them was a chieftain, commanding hundreds, perhaps thousands of hardcore, volatile followers.

'I'm here at Ashdown to organise the armed resistance,' announced

Richard, as if he were doomed to repeat this line until somebody answered him.

Ax looked at Cornelius. He'd been hoping Corny might be a voice of restraint, but he saw the tough old man's expression, and his heart sank.

'I think everyone's heard the message, Rich. And I told you, it's a bad idea.'

'I can hardly believe I'm saying this, but that sounds like cowardice, Ax. And I can't believe I had to come and find you hiding behind the non-combatants—'

'I love the way that's become a big insult,' snapped Dora.

'We're not here to insult your womenfolk, Ax,' shouted one of the chiefs. 'We just want to know, are you for or against us? Don't waste our time.'

'We're *staybehinds*!' shouted someone else. 'We'll *stay*!'

'You talk about non-violence,' cried Richard. 'Is that going to impress these people? My God, where *were* you during the invasion? Did you ever turn on the tv? Do you know what happened at Reading? Or do you hope they'll give you a piece of their pie, is that it? You think you can *negotiate*? You're dreaming. Human lives *are like grass to them*. They spare the work of hands, but they have slaughtered men and women and children, mown down anyone who stood in their way— '

'Richard—'

'It was a bloodbath at Glasto too,' shouted the Hawk, a handsome young man in a rawhide jerkin, black hair in a braided scalplock, tattooed arms and throat naked to the cold. 'But they never touched the Abbey. They want our mediaeval shit intact, they're gonna turn England into a fucking theme park. I followed you once, Ax, and brought my men behind me. I trusted you when you converted to Islam. I'll follow you again, to the death, but I won't stand by and see my nation exterminated—'

'They're gonna dynamite *our* sacred sites, may ruin fall on them.'

'Reading's gonna be *their* capital, walled city, no English allowed.'

'The Counterculture lives. Death or glory, man!'

The crowd outside gasped. The soldiers in the back rows of the seated company, some of them in regular forces uniform, started protesting. They weren't fuckin' hippies. They were decent citizens, they wanted this quite clear. One of the young Islamics, outraged beyond endurance, cried out, passionately—

'The Great Chastisement is rightful and merited! It has fallen on us from God, the Chinese are only instruments. No hand should be raised against it!'

A hejabi girl grabbed him, and hissed at him in spanking Punjabi to shut his big fat mouth. *The Great Chastisement* was a term the Chinese liked about as much as they liked *Counterculture*—

A Forest Ranger shouted for order. 'Let Mr Preston speak! Show some respect! This is deplorable! Who do you think you all are?'

But it was Richard who plunged on, the words spilling out of him, lines that he'd obviously been repeating to himself, over and over. 'What are you going to tell me? That we were the pariah of Europe under the Second Chamber, and no one's going to help us now? That we stand alone? That half the world lives under Chinese rule, and the USA has gone belly-up, so why shouldn't we? That we should be *grateful* for this forcible invitation to join the fucking "Great Peace Sphere"?'

'It's an idea. Richard, listen. We have contacts in Pan-Asia—'

'You mean *virtual* Asia,' shouted a chieftain wearing battledress, a chain-mail coif and a repro Norman steel cap. 'That stuff's not real, Ax. The datasphere is a globalisation fairytale. I believe in earth and stone, trees and rivers, flesh and blood.'

'Yeah, right,' growled Sage. 'And the world was created five thousand years ago by Noggin the Nog; or no, sorry, was it Galadriel? Bertram the Bold, you've never been a great argument for the rationality of yer cause.'

'Please don't stick your wires in my brain, Aoxomoxoa.'

'Why didn't yu do an immix set las' night, Sage?' yelled the only woman among the chiefs. Not all of them were Pagan Fundamentalists: she was a techno green. 'Why the Robbie Williams singalong? Are yu and the Heads running scared?'

'We didn't do immix because immersion code is *PROSCRIBED*,' roared George Merrick. 'That means not just we're in trouble, Looise, but all our crew, and all their families. What the fuck kind of employers do you think we are—?'

'As I was *saying*,' Ax broke in, still patient, 'until trouble that had nothing to do with the Chinese stopped us, we were talking to Pan-Asian Utopians, and what we were hearing from them gives me hope. Not proof, but hope.'

'Hope of what?' breathed Richard, a grey shock rising in his face.

'That we can live with this. That we can come to terms with them.'

'Oh my God, oh my God.'

Ax pushed back his hair. The mark the Scots had put on him stood out, precise and midnight. 'Richard, do you think it was national pride that made me pick up an assault rifle, in Yorkshire, long ago? *Not fucking guilty.* I was fighting to keep things together. That was why you were fighting, too, when we first met. The sane people versus mob rule, *do you remember?* That's why I got into this, whether I was playing guitar or trying to talk sense to the wreckers in the streets. I haven't forgotten what the green revolution was supposed to be about. It was about saving the living world, and that's a true and worthy cause. But I want more than that. I believe in a future that can still be ours, and I believe *this is not the time* for guerrilla warfare. This is a time for teaching and learning, building bridges, saving what we can. I *will* fight, yeah. For hospitals and schools that work, sanitation and power, and people who can be good to each other. Who can read and write and *handle simple arithmetic.*'

'Oh my God.'

Was the little mob out there behind the cordon listening? Not likely, thought Ax. Anyone with a brain cell or two wouldn't be anywhere near. He could not shift Richard. He was preaching to the dogfight fanciers, but he went on with it, anyway.

'Remember what I said in the Commons debate on violence? I've finished with the killing game. Whether I'm right or whether I'm wrong, I stand by that—'

'You don't have to do the dirty work, Sir!' shouted a regular soldier. 'Just point us in the right direction, we'll handle it!'

There was a burst of laughter.

Ax grinned, and shook his head. 'Thanks, but that doesn't work for me—'

Colonel Kent sprang to his feet: suddenly, obviously, a man over the brink.

'Oh God, I didn't believe it. I didn't believe it could be true—'

He looked wildly from side to side, baring his teeth. Ax stood up too. He took his old friend, brother-in-arms, by the shoulders.

'Rich, listen to me, *listen.*'

'I'm listening, I'm listening, I'm listening. I can't believe what I'm hearing—'

'They came three-quarters of the way around the world, in ships, and using fuel, so far beyond us that they might as well be flying saucers. Leave aside their massive technical superiority, they brought two hundred thousand troops, at our best informed estimate. That's twice *the entire standing armed forces* of the three British mainland nations – last time I

41

looked, a few months ago when I was President of England. And d'you think they haven't more at home? Okay, I'll stop trying to convince you that what you want should not be done. *It can't be done.* Use your head. They've been moderate, so far. They'll destroy us if they have to.'

'You think they have *magic*?' cried Richard, pulling away from Ax's hands, his eyes bulging, bloodshot white all round the iris. 'Is that it? Oh, God, is that it?'

'No,' snapped Ax, beginning to lose hold. 'I think they're Venusians. *No*, I don't think they have magic. No way, absolutely not. Magic is the delusion.'

'So you refuse. You refuse, you're not going to lead us?'

'I'll lead you to peace,' said Ax. He noticed that the barmies showed no unease at Richard's hysteria. Fuck; that's a bad sign . . . 'I have a plan, I know what I'm doing. I can get us out of this, and I will.'

'They're at the end of their reach,' announced Cornelius suddenly.

This was the wise old soldier, distinguished military analyst, China watcher for a decade of his long career. The chiefs straightened, paying attention and *shit*, thought Ax, that's it. They don't care that Rich is nuts, this is Corny's show—

'There will be cracks in the régime at home by now, it's a law of nature, after such rapid growth. The expeditionary force is far from the centre of power, and it can be harried. Each officer here can raise a thousand seasoned troops, and there'll be more. We'll have in the region of twenty thousand actives. Oliver Cromwell showed what can be done with numbers like that. Shi Huangdi is an energy-auditer. Wherever he has met determined resistance he has abandoned the difficult ground. There is no Chinese authority in Free Queensland, or Irian Jaya. Or Tamil Nadu.'

'There are plenty of regions where there's no direct Chinese rule,' countered Ax, though he knew it was useless. 'The Big Nine, the Sphere nations, are not ruled. They're partners in the Great Peace. But leave that aside: this isn't Queensland, Corny. This is their beachhead in Europe. Shi Huangdi will not be defeated here.'

'I believe resistance is possible,' said the old soldier, with finality.

He got to his feet, moving like a much younger man, and looked Ax dead in the eye, with a cold smile. He was lying. The old man was bare-faced lying, they both knew it. But he wasn't going to back down, and that's the end of this conversation.

Fiorinda sighed, pulled her boots out from under the camp-bed and began to put them on. Against suicide warriors the gods themselves contend in vain.

'What are you doing?' exclaimed Richard.

'I'm leaving. I have a gig soon.'

'But, Fiorinda, *you* can't just walk out, *you* must have something to say—'

'Must I really? Okay, if you insist, I'll say something. We're going to work with the Chinese, Rich, the way we've always worked with whatever government. We're going to make love not war, keep the home fires burning, play our music and secure the best deal we can for the people of England in a Chinese world. Now I'm off. I don't belong in your counsels. I'm a non-combatant.'

'Goes for me too,' Sage unfolded himself. 'Non-combatant.'

'Sorry, Richard,' said Ax. 'They're right. I have other sessions to visit. You and your people are welcome to come along, unarmed. You might learn something—'

Richard was not listening. He was staring at Sage Pender's hands, at present engaged in pulling on Sage Pender's muddy boots. Nothing special about these hands, except that they were beautiful: weather-tanned, honed by use, with broad-tipped artist's fingers. Nothing special, except that until Sage completed the Zen Self experiment, and became the first person to break the barrier between mind and matter, his hands had been crippled paws; destroyed by infant meningitis.

Forbidden science, forbidden topics. Did those things happen, those events that have been wiped out of history? Does England have appalling secret power at her command, a weapon too terrible to use? Or was it all delusion, as the Chinese have decreed—?

A change came over the Colonel's face. He looked from the queen to the Minister, and they returned his gaze, the grey eyes and the blue; impenetrable.

'I suppose you'll turn the Scots against us,' he said, slowly, in a voice that cut Ax deep, because it was *Richard* speaking, not a raving automaton. 'Your new allies.'

Ax shook his head. 'The Scots have made up their own minds.'

So the great confrontation ended. Ax refused to lead the guerrillas. He argued for non-violence: when the barmies wouldn't listen, the Triumvirate and the Few walked out, and the Islamics went with them. The armed resistance party was left in possession of the field, bewildered, bereft; but utterly determined.

Sage watched Fiorinda from the dark side of the stage: the national sweetheart in a drab rainjacket, a tattered skirt that took colour, soft purple, under the lights, bare brown legs and army boots. His throat was raw, his head was thick and ringing, the face-off with Richard adding misery to a terrible helpless panic about Marlon. The faithful in the mosh cried out her name, like lost children found. She gave them her calm little wildcat grin, and he felt the same—

A voice murmured, *How's that for Sugar Magnolia, Sage?*

In the corner of his mind's eye a slim figure turned. He caught the gleam of dark shining eyes, the Mixmaster General's teasing smile of fellow-feeling—

Dilip, that was *Dilip* . . . He looked sharply around, but of course there was nobody there, his friend was burned to ashes, months ago. And this is mourning. Your dead will flicker on the edge of vision, recalled by the nets of fire; by an angle of light, a shadow, a tone of voice. It's natural, it will fade all too soon.

Allie and the Powerbabes detached Fiorinda from her hulking minder – that's Sage – and took her out on the town, to celebrate her triumphant comeback. They fled the adoring fans, which was not too hard, and swanned off to Anansi's Jamaica Kitchen. Rupert the White Van Man had been obliged to leave the van offsite, but he had his bbq fired up, dispensing hot corn patties with jam and dandelion coffee with optional cognac; for its medicinal properties.

The Powerbabes' bright winter coats, yellow and green and blue, Allie's red Gucci jacket, made a brave blaze in the November gloom. They talked about the Fox Force Five, a fantasy band the Babes and Allie had made up to comfort themselves in the invasion; including Fiorinda, of course, although they hadn't known if she was alive. Allie would learn to play bass, Fiorinda would do keyboards and sing; two saxophones and a trumpet, hey, that's a proper little band.

'D'you really think I could learn to play guitar?' said Allie, wistfully.

The four professionals looked at each other, and decided not to tell bassist jokes. ''Course you can,' said Dora. 'All you need is three chords.' Cherry began to draw sketches on her notepad. We'll have jackets with FOX FORCE FIVE in silver glitter on the back. Or dayglo pink. We'll have neon-coloured cowboy boots—

Dandelion coffee starts to taste okay after a few years, though not so great with no cognac. I worry about Ax, thought Fiorinda. Sage is strong as a horse, but how long can Ax live like this? His mother was a refugee, she nearly starved too often, and it's maternal nutrition that counts. If people get stressed by underfeeding, the hidden problems surface . . . You get to know these things, working with the homeless, and then you can't switch them off. She was worried about Cherry too. The rest of them seemed fine, but Chez had a weary little cough, and *no* energy, though she was trying her best. Unpremeditated, Fiorinda reached out and squeezed the junior powerbabe's hand. Bless you, she thought, same as she'd been blessing the crowd all day. It does no harm, wishing people well. Cherry smiled, and the moment passed.

'Let's get another round in,' suggested Dora. 'Maybe skip the coffee, have the straight brandy, if Rupert'll do that. Could I tempt you to another patty, Fio?'

'You bet.'

Another fantastic hot golden blob of maizey goodness, oozing something sweet and red. Rupert, you are as a god—

'Fio?'

Suddenly they'd all turned serious. Felice leaned across the table. '*You got to come in from the cold*, baby. Even if it means leaving your guys. You can't go on sleeping under a hedge. You're three months pregnant.'

'Oh, no, that's okay.' The rock and roll princess quickly brushed off this threat. 'You should have seen me when I was pregnant the first time. I was a string bean with a football on the front, and the baby was fine, he was big and strong.'

'Until he died at three months,' said Felice. 'It was pneumonia, wasn't it?'

Dora and Cherry drew in their breath. Allie looked grave.

Fiorinda took the cruel blow, and felt her mouth begin to tremble.

'T-that was because I was thirteen. He got ill, and I didn't know what to do.'

Allie and the Babes did not blame anyone. They knew how desperate Fiorinda had been to have a baby, and how stubborn she could be. But without laying blame, you have to wonder what the fuck those two beautiful guys had been thinking of, to let this happen. Felice compressed her generous lips, a frown between fine-arched brows (an expression which caused her fellow-babes to quail, just a little bit). Fiorinda is a living goddess, no lie, but sometimes, swear she behaves as if she's four years old. She produced a treasure from the rose-fur lining of her parakeet coat.

'What's that?'

'This is a bottle of Guinness. Hey, Rupert, you got an opener?'

Rastaman came over, with his beautiful wide smile, and cranked off the cap.

'But, but that's *alcohol* . . . I know it's carbs, but—'

'No alcohol is an old whitey-man wives' tales. A pint of stout a day is good medicine, for a woman with a baby to build. Your mama isn't here, so we are going to look after you, like it or not. Down it, baby.'

Rupert's stand was far from mainstage but it was on a thoroughfare, and the Utopians streamed by, some newly arrived. You peer into every face: looking for Charlie Middleton, Allie's personal assistant, missing since the day of the invasion. For Charm Dudley's dyke-rockers; or anyone at all from the North East. You know it's useless but you can't stop. Everybody was doing it, all the time. Fiorinda stood up, the Guinness bottle in her hand, doubtful and then transfigured—

'*Marlon*—? *Silver*—? Silver and Pearl!'

A boy of about sixteen, medium height, with black hair in stubby silver-bound braids, emerged from the crowd, two girls in tow. The smaller of the girls had a dirty shawl wrapped round her head like a turban, the taller girl was crying hard.

It was Marlon. It was really Marlon, and really Silver and Pearl.

'Mum's dead,' sobbed Silver. 'Mum's dead, did you know our mum's dead?'

'They shaved my head,' announced Pearl, matter-of-fact. 'I dunno why. They were going to cut our eyes out, so we wouldn't get sent to Guangzhou. We have Chinese eyes, you know, like Mum. So we ran away, and Marlon came and found us. Silver just cries all the time, she's all right. Is our old man dead too?'

'I left my mum a note,' said Marlon. 'Is Dad about?'

The Chinese had taken the elementary precaution of blocking access to the airwaves and the datasphere, from any location on the Reich site. There'd be no bootleg broadcasts, no Ashdown coverage except through their censorship. Sage had to lurk around the trailers and snag a good-willed VIP (*not* Dian Buckley, no thanks), who allowed him to make a vital call to his ex-girlfriend. At nightfall he sat with his son outside the Stanger's Farm Cider stall, and heard the whole story. Or some of it, who knows. It turned out that the parents were to blame, of course—

'I thought Silver was dead. *You'd* sent her back to Reading camp-ground, to her mum's bender, when you sent me back to Wales. She had to be dead. Then I saw a programme about bounty hunters, and hippy kids who'd got away at the last minute. They were sleeping in ditches, being rounded up by the bounty hunters, and sent to China as slaves. So I had to try and find her.'

'Why did you tell your mother that you'd come to find me?'

'I thought it would make less trouble. You both hated me being with Silver.'

Silver Wing's daffy parents had wanted Sage to take her as a concubine a few years ago, and the child had been willing and eager; if Fiorinda didn't mind. But let's not get into that morass, post-civilised hippy culture, augh—

'I didn't hate you being with her. I just think you're both very young.'

'Well, Mum did . . . I don't think you've any right to talk, either of you. *You* were only seventeen when I was born. Anyway, I got to England but I didn't get as far as Reading. I ran into some soldiers, English soldiers who were helping the Chinese to mop up. Then I realised they were the bounty hunters, so I went with them to Newbury. There was a detention centre, not a building, a kind of camp, and the girls weren't there but they'd *been* there, so I cast around until I found them. It was easy. People were heading for Ashdown on the underground, I got on that trail, and I kept asking for two English girls with Chinese eyes, one of them with a cracked head. They'd been with some fucked-up Counterculturals before the bounty hunters got them, who tested them for magic and were going to cut their eyes out. I think that's the part that broke Silver, more than anything. She's usually so incredibly tough.'

The girls had been checked over. Pearl had suffered a fractured skull at some point, but it was healing. Silver had bronchitis and a fever; they were both anaemic, and full of roundworms. Neither of them was exactly lucid, as yet, but they were re-united with their father and their baby sister, and clean, and warm: it was a start. Two hours ago Sage had been sure he would never see his son again. He could not stop staring at the miracle beside him; the gleam of golden-hazel eyes, the Welsh accent that was a constant reminder of their separation. Not a five-year-old. A young stranger capable of incredible feats, a reserved, enclosed, private knight-errant.

'D'you think she'll be okay?'

'Yes I do,' said Sage. 'You have done excellently, Marlon. I am very proud of you, and the girls. Your mother'll be proud too, when she knows the whole story.'

'I'm, er, really glad you two are getting on better.'

'Mm, yeah.'

Sage had decided to take responsibility for not getting in touch sooner, rather than tell Mary that her son had been wandering in the hellhole of Occupied Berkshire. Maybe this had been a mistake: the détente was in tatters. Ah, well. He drank cider, from a paper cup. He didn't like cider, but Marlon detested English bitter, so there you are. To be with him, just to watch him breathe—

'What's going to happen now, Dad? Is England going to be okay? Can you guys come out of hiding after this, you and Ax and Fiorinda?'

'I don't know. We're still non-persons at the moment. But they know where we are and what we're doing, and they seem to approve. The Chinese are keeping their options open, best way to put it . . . Do you love her? I mean, Silver?'

His son gave a little start, like a wary animal surprised—

Fuck. *Why* did I say that?

'I don't know,' whispered Marlon. 'It's deeper than love.'

The truth, which would have horrified Richard beyond apoplexy, was that Ax was already talking to the Chinese. He'd been approached, overtures had been made. He expected to be approached again at the fest: he didn't know exactly when, or where. Both parties had every reason to keep the negotiations secret. He watched Dave Wright's debut in the comedy tent, from the side of the stage, and saw the Chinese agent in the front row. He walked away from that venue, his knitted cap pulled well down, a scarf around his face. The sky was starless, thick with cloud; Gintrap were in the middle of their set. He went into a booth selling hot fruit wines and joined the people getting warm by a charcoal brazier. Shortly, the agent came up with two steaming, fragrant pottery beakers.

The two men didn't drink their wine. They left together, heading for the Reich's site fence (not much of a barrier), and crossed a stretch of heath to the old tourist car park; which was the VIP Hospitality Area. Ax was afraid they had company, and he was supposed to be alone: but thankfully the shadows kept their distance. He was very scared. No question the Chinese knew about that confrontation with Richard Kent; no idea how it would affect this. He was taken to a parked car, in the darkness away from the trailers. The agent, who was not Chinese, just someone working for them, motioned Ax to get into the back.

Soft light showed him a tablet lying on the seat. He opened it: after a second or so Wang Xili looked out. A head and shoulders shot, you couldn't see much of the room he was in. The handsome General of the South West was in uniform.

He smiled, disarmingly. 'Mr Preston, good evening. Please imagine that all the proper salutations have been made. I know you'll want to keep this short.'

'You're right, and likewise. This is my answer. One day, the ruler of Chu sent two high officials to ask Zhuang Zi to assume control of the government. They found him fishing. He asked them about a famous sacred tortoise, which was kept at the capital in a jewelled casket and had been dead three thousand years. Wouldn't that tortoise rather be alive and wagging its tail in the mud? The officials had to agree. "Clear off then!" shouted Zhuang Zi. "I, too, will wag my tail in the mud here." General, you are not asking me to assume control of the government, nor offering me death in a jewelled casket; but my answer is the same. I will wag my tail in the mud.'

'Hahaha! That's very good! Is that all?'

'I'm afraid you overestimate my importance.'

The tablet screen winked out. The agent, who had not spoken a word, opened the car door. Ax left the tablet on the seat and walked away. That was it.

He kept walking, not caring much where he was headed. A frieze of slim tree boles loomed up, twigs stung his face. He was on the brink of one of the heath's plunging wooded valleys and he knew the self-appointed bodyguard close to him now; the familiar presence like warmth in the cold dark.

'Sage? Is that you?'

'Yeah.'

'That's not very fucking clever,' said Ax. 'Suppose something had gone wrong? You like the idea of Fiorinda left to cope on her own?'

'Insh'allah. You shouldn't be alone out here.'

They had been living outdoors since September. They had the night vision of wild animals, they were changing into foxes. Or wolves, timid and savage. Ax sat on a log in the rustling dead bracken under the birches. Sage sat beside him.

'How d'you get on with Wang Xili?'

'I played hard to get, it was brief. Who else was following me?'

'It was the Islamics, I've sent them back. They're good, aren't they?'

'Yeah, but it won't do . . . We'll have to talk to Muhammad, I can't have those kids following me around. Thank fuck *Rich* isn't onto us. That would be hell.'

'Rich is in a world of his own. He thinks the Chinese don't know you're here.'

'*Corny* knows the score. And he knows fucking well what he's leading those damned fools into, and he doesn't care. He wants it.'

'Carn' argue with a man in that state of mind.'

They thought about the irregular army they had joined as rockstar officers, in that long-ago baptism of fire. The idealistic ruffians, the psychos, the villains; some lasting friends. Cornelius had said twenty thousand, he could be right. The Chinese didn't tolerate recalcitrance, and they were *thorough*. All those men, and women, were going to die: abandoned and betrayed by Ax Preston and Sage Pender.

'At least they can't muster many rock bands between them.'

'Not funny, Sage.'

'Sorry.'

The Rock and Roll Reich had spent a decade using the music as a tool of social control, taming the beleaguered English with free concerts; selling Ax's Utopian manifesto with stirring anthems and spectacular futuristic tech. They had forged rock and roll idealism into a national religion, a passion that made hard times sweet, and it had worked. They believed they could do the same again. But the Reich would lose all value to the invaders, awful prospect, if the barmies started using the same tricks.

'They wouldn't do it,' said Ax, after a pause for anxious thought. 'They're heartbroken death-wish idiots. They're not malicious. Well, not much.'

'Mm . . . In ways it's going to be worse talking to Muhammad '

The leader of English Islam had been Ax's sponsor in the Faith, and a major force in bringing the separatist war to an end. Immensely tolerant, yet respected by the most conservative of his own people, he'd been the Triumvirate's most valued ally in this endless, fearsome rollercoaster ride. He knew *everything*. But Islam was a connection they could no longer afford. No baggage, no allegiance except to the new masters. Stand or fall alone, it's the only way to do this; if it can be done at all.

Something about, goodbye forever. Something about, cancel all our vows—

A wave of desolation swept over them. Everything must go. They must be ready to sever themselves from their families, from the Few—

'Remember when we were going to get married?' said Ax, at last.

It was bizarre to recall, but a royal wedding, Fiorinda in a cloud of tulle, had once seemed like a good idea; when Ax had been trying to live with the Second Chamber. Really it would have been hateful, worst aspects of the gilded cage, but—

'We weren't. We were both going to marry Fiorinda,' said the bleak shadow beside Ax, somewhat distantly. 'I was never asked. Too New Agey.'

Fiorinda I know thought Ax. We can fight like hell, we *do* fight like hell, but she's part of me, I can't lose track. I will *never* get a handle on this big cat.

'Well, I've changed my mind. I'm asking you now. Will you marry me? And please don't fucking laugh. I'm desperate.'

'I'll think about it.'

'All right, spurn me then . . . Where is Fiorinda, anyway?'

'Took Min and went home. She gets so hellish tired. Ax, what am I going to do about Marlon? I very stupidly swore blind I'll send him back to Wales, but he's way past that. I can't tell him what to do.'

'I bet you can. You can be very intimidating . . . Let him stay with the folks, and lose Mary's number. You'll probably never see her again anyway.'

The cold air smelled of leaf mould; disembodied bass from the arena was like the roar of distant traffic, on a winter's night in a lost world. They sat in silence, the darkness restoring intimacy, the thrill creeping up on them: is he going to touch me? What'll I do if he touches me? Standing up together, they managed to cross that ever-perilous border-line; into each other's arms.

'You okay, babe? I mean, fuck, you know what I mean. Are we okay.'

'As long as you never let go,' mumbled Ax, face against Sage's shoulder. How gaunt he feels these days, but strong: long bones strapped together with ropes of steel. 'I'm never *sure*, big cat. A day in the public eye and I'm thinking, fuck, can I possibly be lovers with this bloke? If I touch him he's just going to belt me one—'

'Me, same. I don' know where I get the nerve to hold you, Sah.'

They returned to the arena, found Muhammad, and had the conversation. It was not as bad as they'd feared. Sayeed Muhammad made it easy on them.

Slight Return

Fiorinda dreamt that she was sleeping in the annexe, the army-surplus tent pitched beside Sage's van in Traveller's Meadow, on Reading Festival site. Oak leaf shadows danced on her eyelids, she could hear the distant blur of the music. In her dream she knew she was pregnant, and it puzzled her that it didn't seem to matter which of them was the baby's father. It was Dissolution Summer, Ax and Sage were deadly music biz rivals, and the country was falling apart—

. . .

The oak tree was gone. The annexe was gone, and the meadow by the riverside. There was nothing left. The hazel bothy was pitch dark, and very cold. She crawled halfway out of the blankets to light a candle stub in the tin lantern, and lay down again, checking with her eyes the battered hard case of a cherry-red Les Paul Classic (never called the Classic, always 'The Les Paul', or 'The Gibson'). The case that held Sage's visionboard, which Ax and Fiorinda sometimes called *Rho*, the name of the model, but Sage referred to only as 'my board' (as in, my arm, my leg). And the tapestry bag that hid Fiorinda's saltbox, the wooden apple that was the talisman of her magic. Min sat on the end of the heather bed, blinking at her sleepily.

We have to stop clinging to our little gods, what the fuck happens to our morale if we lose one? But refugees can't help it—

The missing years returned, filling her mind with a dense, blurred volume of information, horrors and beauties, mainly irrelevant. I am pregnant, I am not sixteen, we are starting again from nothing; that seemed to cover it. She remembered a garret in Paris, a cabin on a cold beach in Mexico, and here we are again. Our house of sticks, this destitution, to which we keep returning, it feels so right. We're desperate to declare ourselves bankrupt, crawl out from under the mountain of debt that fell on us. Fucking global crisis, wartime with no human enemy, we are so sick of it . . . Someone coming. She sat up, pulling the blankets around her. Min padded up the bed, burrowed into her lap and set his front paws, which were like plates of meat (he's going to be a huge cat) on her knees. The two tall men came in, making very little sound as they flowed like smoke into her space.

'Fiorinda?'

They were holding hands, a rare gesture with them. Brother-enemies, she thought, the annexe dream still her reality. 'You're holding hands.'

'Yeah,' said Sage, holding Ax's hand up to his cheek, kissing the knuckles, Ax leant his brow against Sage's shoulder. 'Something wrong with that?'

'Wang Xili must be a terrific date. What happened?'

'I said no,' said Ax and let go of Sage's hand to scoop up the kitten.

Min burst into rapturous purrs, pummelling his chest with razor talons. 'But nicely.'

'No repercussions about Richard's performance?'

Ax shook his head. 'None at all, it wasn't mentioned. They've made it clear, by everything that's happened, that they want the Reich. I've made it clear we're interested; but that we don't want to seem too eager—'

'A proper, decent reluctance,' remarked Sage, taking off his boots. 'Very maidenly collaborators, us. Is there anything to eat? Any offerings at the shrine?'

'Yeah, there is. A Dave haybox with a chicken stew in it had appeared when I got home. It's *extremely* tasty.' She watched them settle. They stow their boots, they touch their totems, they casually brush a hand against my bag; they sniff out the food and tuck in. Like two big simple animals, my tiger and my wolf.

'Where was he speaking from? Was he in the flat?'

An uneasy glance between them.

'I don't know,' said Ax. 'Head and shoulders, I couldn't tell.'

'Don't worry about me,' said Fiorinda. 'I couldn't give a toss.'

'Dian probably made the whole thing up,' Sage passed the spoon, 'to see if she could get me to take her on as Mata Hari . . . Either that, or Wang is occupying Rufus's love-nest for exac'ly the reasons stated, to exorcise the pernicious delusion.'

He was keeping the photos in the bathroom aspect to himself.

'He's a cool customer, then. The chances that he *really* thinks my father was just your average unpleasant megastar with dodgy politics are very slim.'

'We don't know what they really think,' said Ax, around a savoury mouthful of chicken and wild mushrooms. 'Don't know what's going on there at all.'

The ugly rumour Dian had offered as tradegoods troubled them. It had the ominous, unlikely ring of truth; and that was very bad. But if Dilip was somehow in Chinese hands, alive or dead, there was nothing they could do. They dared not use Dian as a double agent. They had to buy some power first, this had to be their primary objective, and it wasn't going to be easy.

'Just keep Dian away from Allie,' said Fiorinda.

Agreed. Allie doesn't need a bright idea like that to add to her mourning. They reverted to issues within their reach, while the stew got finished. What to do about Smelly? Marlon, Silver and Pearl, the next steps for the reborn Reich.

'And he asked me to marry him,' Sage confided. 'Finally. He tried to brush it off as a joke, but I think I screwed it out of him.'

'I did not! I said *please don't laugh at me*, you bastard.'

The splendours and miseries of Fiorinda's teenage life were clinging to her—

'I think you should exchange rings.'

'Tha's a good idea. But I'm holding out for Hawaii on the beach at sunset.'

'Don't be crass, Sage,' said Fiorinda. 'Just do it.'

Sage was six inches taller in old money, and heavier in the bone. But the guitar-man had big hands, the exchanged rings fitted; which seemed a kind gesture on the part of fate. The men went outside, barefoot, to rinse their mouths and take a piss. They lay down together, without undressing much; Fiorinda in the middle, you notice she's stopped complaining about that? 'I keep thinking it'll be nice when the fest is over,' sighed Fiorinda. 'It's tiring me out. I want to get back our nice life of eating stolen chickens and picking slugs out of our hair.' Body heat soon builds up, but never quite enough. Got to do something about the winter insulation in here.

'That's not going to happen,' said Ax, resolutely optimistic. 'Brace yourself. Something different and much better is going to happen instead.'

Winter Wind

I

Snow had been blown off the helipad, the blowers were still going. As he stepped down into white-out, white noise, Ax glimpsed through dancing powder the railway bridge over Richfield Avenue, at the western boundary of Rivermead. The windows in the rear section of the machine – captured from the English, no relation to those fantastic airships – had been blanked out. He wondered why he was being allowed to get his bearings now; then he saw the wall, rising from frosted winter pasture about a hundred metres away, pale and sheer, a bewildering affront to his senses. He had seen this development on tv, but the reality was something else. He was going to spend the day reading signs and gestures: would they all be writ so large?

'This way, please, Mr Preston,' said the Australian sergeant. People's Liberation Army insignia cannot always be trusted, but Ax didn't feel he'd been given an honour escort. Not a visiting dignitary, not a prisoner, the soldiers marched him to a giant Chinatown arch (weirdly stripped of its natural, vibrant but scruffy inner city accoutrements): creamy pale, with a few courses of indigo, and dark red inscriptions. The wall was not so huge as it had seemed at the first shock, but it was twice Ax's height and *growing*: he could see movement, a constant stirring; just perceptible, very disturbing. Was the material alive? Maybe.

总的来说，当长久的分离后，这个世界变得更加统合。

The inscription on the lintel was the opening sentence of the Romance of the Three Kingdoms: *In general, the world must unite when it has been long divided* . . . They liked that quote, he'd seen it often. Profound vertigo went through him. I know you, you fantastic monster. I heard of your birth, long ago, in the Utopian chatrooms of Pan-Asia. I wasn't afraid of you then, I'm not afraid now, this feeling isn't fear . . . and he'd been looking at the characters too long, he didn't want them to know he could read.

Ceremonial guards, very smart in olive-green with scarlet belts and shoulder boards, stood to attention on either side of a pair of huge doors, the same creamy, quivering material as the wall, but shaped into hinges, studs and bars; an imitation, no, a *reference* to ancient bronze. The doors opened majestically, Ax and his escort passed into the gatehouse, with no halt, no greeting, no perceptible security scan. They waited in a blank sideroom. The air was chill; the only furniture creamy, naked couches with scrolled ends, set against the walls. The soldiers stood face-front. The sergeant was a ginger-haired individual with a prominent nose, the private soldiers looked like Han Chinese. Ax wondered if he should try whistling *Waltzing Matilda?* Start a conversation about cricket? No . . .

No romancing the help. He'd decided not to play that game.

A flat screen in a scrolled frame, about three metres square, hung on the wall to Ax's right. Never stay where they put you. He walked over there, no one stopped him, and watched a huge kaleidoscope of Barnard cells. They switched from disorder into order in intricate combination; a single pattern took over, and colonised the whole. It broke down, the process started again, subtly different in detail. The piece was called *Simplicity As A Result Of Complexity*, or that was how he read the characters; there was no translation.

He was beginning to wish he'd been more Ax Preston with his soldiers, after all, when a tall figure burst through an inner door (also pale, also moulded of a piece); incongruous as something leaping at him in a nightmare. A shock of stiff, contrived ringlets around a celebrity face from the international music scene: an olive fatigue jacket cast over the shoulders of a mandarin gown with rainbow striped sleeves. 'Ax Preston!' cried the newcomer, pumping Ax's hand. Under the gown he wore yellow trousers, and a sarong with a fat Japanese rising sun print. 'Delighted! Delighted!'

'Pleased to meet you, too,' said Ax. 'I'm sure.'

'You look amazed! Did nobody tell you I'd be here? I'm working with the AMID, the expeditionary force. It's absolutely wonderful!' A suspicious glance. 'You do *recognise* me? We haven't met, which is a crime, but you know who I am?'

'Er, yeah? You're Norman Soong, the, er, rock show director, aren't you?'

'*Lieutenant Colonel* Soong.' Striped sleeves whirled, Norman Soong thrust his shoulder board at Ax. 'See my stars? All my people have ranks. It's a great joke.'

'But you're still in the music business?'

The great man frowned in reproof. 'Rock is more than music and more than business, as you above all should know!' He released Ax's hand and glanced around. 'You don't have a guitar with you?'

'Sorry.'

'Well, well, never mind. We'll be meeting later. Enjoy your tour.'

Lü Xiaobao's men didn't get past the gatehouse. An HQ officer showed Ax around, a young woman who gave her rank as lieutenant, and spoke English with a bland US accent. He guessed she was something fast-track, aide de camp. She told him that the wall enclosing the festival site would extend to surround the ancient city of Reading, which was to be the new capital. Outlying built-up areas would be razed, the waterways would be securely managed against flooding. Temporary measures had already been taken to culvert the Thames at the Rivermead site itself.

'It was very impractical to live under permanent threat of inundation.'

Ax was wondering what the hell the presence of Norman Soong meant, and why there'd been no mention of him, ever, on Joyous Liberation news—

'They were thinking of making Rivermead into a Laketown.'

'That's culturally correct, and we did consider it.'

Rumour had it that there were no actual women in the invasion force, only trannies, but as far as he could tell this was a real girl beside him: a serious, professional, girl-soldier.

'You people move very fast.'

She nodded, with a shy smile, as if at a personal compliment.

How long does it take to 'conquer' a country the size of England? A matter of days, if you have overwhelming military superiority and no outside intervention. You trounce the regulars a few times, occupy a few cities, execute the ruling junta, and announce that it's over. Then you just have to crush the recalcitrants, and convince the silent majority they're better off accepting their fate. These may be related tasks.

It was near the end of December, three months since that dawn when the airships had come zooming out of the Atlantic like a swarm of UFOs. Chinese forts were sprouting throughout the Occupied Zones, putting the definitive stamp of Sphere Instant Architecture on the

English landscape; while 'life returned to normal' for the masses. The rest of the country was 'quiet'. So much for Joyous Liberation news. Ax knew things were uglier on the ground, he didn't know how bad. Unofficial sources said Richard and Cornelius had their base in East Anglia, and actives were crossing the ceasefire line at will, inflicting casualties; inspiring occupied-zone terrorists. But no single event had caused him to accept the latest approach from Wang Xili, he'd just felt it was time. He'd tried to raise his value by reluctance; he hoped he hadn't held out too long.

He'd frightened himself imagining the unburied dead, the charred marquees, but of course it was all gone. No trace of the massacre of thirty thousand righteous campers, who had lived here like Bangladeshi peasants for a decade. Purple domes, instant buildings all on the same pattern, stood in rows. They looked like upturned boats. Teams of soldiers, with shovels and with heavy machinery, were at work in the open spaces. Lieutenant Chu talked about gardens, how the English and the Chinese both love gardens, and recounted harmless facts about the invasion. The airships were classified as amphibious, for historical reasons. The invasion force was made up of *amphibious mechanised infantry divisions*, hence the English expression: 'AMID' which Mr Preston would often have heard.

'In English we are the 2nd AMID army.'

'The first AMID being the army that didn't need to invade Taiwan?'

She smiled and nodded, pleased with him. Ax continued to air a limited fluency in *putonghua* (which delighted her), covertly read the notices that identified various sections, and tried to stop himself groping for vanished landmarks.

Now we must be in the Arena. Here the Zen Self tent stood; where Olwen Devi's labrats trained their brains for techno-mediated nirbhana. Maybe right here I parted from that extraordinary little babe Fiorinda, one morning in July, and went off to the Roving Presence tent, to visit the Pan-Asian Utopians. We talked about the fall of the old powers, the mandate that was passing into our hands—

The hope of a new dawn.

Yesterday's snow lay on the bare earth, wherever it wasn't being dug; nothing rested on the purple hulls. The wall was ever-present, obliterating his old horizons.

'Who were you thinking to keep out? The Mongol hordes?'

'No,' she said, with that unexpected frankness, their secret weapon.

'These kind of walls aren't for defence. We use them to impress, to awe the people.'

'Right.'

He knew he was being observed. This is where the Counterculture died, Mr Preston. We penned them here, we moved in and cut them down without mercy. We have planted our HQ on their heartland; which was also yours. Do you accept our judgement? He thought of Silbury Hill demolished, Avebury and Stonehenge levelled, the White Horse scraped from the side of the vale at Uffington. Waves of useless fury drained through him, and he let them pass. Accept. Five thousand years isn't a bad innings, everything tainted must go, what must be, must be—

At last the aide de camp brought him to the Palace of Rivermead, where the Countercultural government of England had made its last stand, after the fall of London. The gaudy, crumpled, lo-rise Palace had been built for Ax, out of mulched cars and other mad scraps, but it had no sentimental associations. Too many bad things had happened here, long before the Chinese arrived. He'd heard the place had been burned down but it seemed intact, except for one wing hidden by hoardings.

'A fine, unusual post-modern building,' said Lieutenant Chu, approvingly.

As they mounted the steps he glanced back, bad move. From this vantage the campground rose through the alien overlay, full of its dead. Horror shook him—

'One more thing you should see before you meet General Wang, Mr Preston. This is the Memorial Hall of the September Offensive. Please step inside.'

He stepped inside. There was an antechamber, with a display of the first relics he'd seen of the invasion. Newspaper pages and printed emails from that day, behind glass. The wild reports of a UFO fleet, the panic in London, recorded on crystalline touch screens. Blackened fragments of domestic objects; clothes and weapons.

please no, don't make me see—

They moved on, into the Memorial Hall. Now they were not alone. Grave-faced Chinese of varying ranks, all in uniform, were studying the exhibits, in groups and singly. The atmosphere was hushed. 'We intend this display to be permanent,' said Chu, quietly. 'The public will be allowed to visit, soon.'

They'd have to be bussed in. Reading had been cleared of English civilians.

Ax inclined his head in acknowledgement, and said nothing as he walked from one image to the next: he didn't linger at the little movie theatre, but stood for a while in front of each huge, analog still photograph. There was no soundtrack but the one that was playing in his mind, don't make me see, don't make me see . . . But he must see. The dirty naked bodies piled on plastic sheets, shattered and whole, the glimpsed faces tug at you from under anonymous slack limbs, men he'd known and talked to, friends, acquaintances, enemies. All of them seemed to have been subjected to the Chinese form of castration; probably after death.

'Why were they mutilated?'

He thought she would say, in her calm young voice, *to impress the people*.

'I don't know. General Wang may be able to tell you.'

'I see.'

They had reached the end of the room, and double doors stood ahead. He looked at them with terror: are you hard enough for more of this, Ax Preston? She ushered him through, and they were back in the foyer. The drab décor of the original Leisure Centre had returned, all the neofeudal colour stripped out. There was a nostalgic, utilitarian smell of fresh carpet glue.

'Why were there no women in the pictures?'

She blushed. 'That's a different room . . . You're a Muslim, Mr Preston. We didn't want to insult you with the sight of naked female bodies.'

'Thank you,' he said. 'That was considerate.'

Wang Xili had been sitting in on the press conference arranged for Norman Soong: assessing the English music journalists, those *not* mired by collaboration with the deposed régime, of course. It was strange work for the commander of an occupying army, but there was no denying the importance of the music these days, and Wang was not an ordinary soldier. He had found the discussion fascinating – though he did not like Soong; who struck him as humourless, grasping, and absurdly vain. He left the meeting before it broke up and lay in wait, in the great solar, for the journalist who had struck him as most sympathetic and promising.

'Come over here, Joe—'

The toughness of honest mediamen! Joe Muldur came to join General Wang by the huge west-facing window, a cheerful smile on his face: perfectly convinced he was about to be flung into a cell, heaped with abuse, raped, mutilated, shot.

'It's a beautiful view, isn't it?' said Wang.

Rivermead site was bare of any feature except for instant buildings, heaps of naked frosty earth, and the wall. Joe nodded, not quite capable of speech.

'Potentially beautiful,' Wang conceded. 'There will be beauty here, Joe. There will be flowers, fountains, groves of trees, rocks and dells. I wish I could tell you the river will run free, but that doesn't make sense. Tell me about the Triumvirate. How do they get on with the media? Your own impressions, and please speak candidly.'

'They each have their different ways,' said Joe. Wang smiled encouragement. 'Sage, I mean Aoxomoxoa, was never *mean*, he would make you laugh, but we all used to dread him. He's just stupidly, stupidly clever, it was easy for him to make any poor journo feel like a squashed bug. But he was amazing copy.'

Aoxomoxoa's unpleasant taste for public and domestic violence, Wang noticed, did not get a mention. Sensible mediaman! 'Was? You use the past tense?'

Joe had just been told that the three great English stars were to resume their musical careers. 'He's changed, since.' He recoiled from deadly danger. 'Since he and Ax . . . The tiger and the wolf, you know they're called the tiger and the wolf?'

'I've heard that.'

Joe glanced at the soldiers, Wang's bodyguard. He nodded: a gesture that got away from him, and went on too long. 'Better together, they're better together, they, how can I put it, they earth, mellow each other. Sage is kinder to us these days. Ax's style is something else, he's in charge of the interview, he's looking at you like, *how can I use this person*. Not for his own benefit, for the agenda, but always. Fiorinda, well, different again because she was born in the business.' A genuine, involuntary smile illumined the journalist's fear-cramped features. 'She's brilliant. She knows we're family, she's Rufus O'Niall's daughter, her father taught her a lot. She won't stand no nonsense, but she cares, she looks out for us like a big sister—'

'Her *father*?' Wang raised his eyebrows. 'The same father who got her pregnant when she was twelve, whose minion made her his sex-slave during the green nazi régime; and whom she and her male concubine later murdered, having pursued him to his private Irish island?'

'Er, yeah.'

'Remarkable.'

Joe nodded uncontrollably again. 'Rock and roll, er, General, er, Sir—'

Wang reflected that he could do anything he liked with Joe Muldur. Jump out of this window, Joe, and he would jump . . . or at least bump his rather awkward nose badly against photovoltaic glass. He flattered himself that the abuse of power held no attraction. Only tell me the truth, Joe, only fear to deceive me, and I will do you no harm. He considered saying this; but reassurance would terrify the man further.

'Ah, well. Family affairs forced into the open often look very strange. Thank you, I'm glad we've had this chat.'

Flee, Joe Muldur, still nodding like one of those toy dogs that used to be a Western joke, in the back window of a private car; in the long ago.

Ax was delivered to Wang Xili's office straight from the Memorial Hall. Lieutenant Chu took his greatcoat, revealing him in a suit from Hollywood, dark red with gleams of iridescence; cleaned and brushed but distinctly worn. A dress-uniformed guard, or secretary, who sat at his own desk, stood up and saluted. He sat down again as Chu left: he did not speak. Every single one of them wears uniform, thought Ax. Add that to the equation . . . A smaller art screen hung behind Wang's desk, the same style as the one in the gatehouse, perhaps the same artist. This time it was a map of the Chinese world that changed through the iterations; from close detail to a China-oriented projection of the globe. The capital was marked at Xi'an, ancient Chang'an, not Beijing, although many of the changes shown predated that shift. He couldn't read much secret history, he didn't know enough about China's internal affairs, but he watched until his eyes were tired, because it was beautiful. Then he paced about, sneaking a look at the message Chu had left in full view on the General's desktop screen. *Watch out for this one*, he was chagrined to read. *He's literate, and he thinks like a Chinese.*

Damn.

Wang Xili breezed in, his uniform cap under his arm, accompanied by a private soldier, clerical grade, with an armful of folders. He beamed, tossed his cap and offered his hand. 'Ah, Mr Preston, we meet in the flesh.'

A scholarly face, unlined, broad square high brow, regular features; humorous eyes and a quick smile. His screen image doesn't lie, he's a good-looking bastard, and he has instant charm. They shook hands. Wang dismissed the clerk. The General and the fugitive President sat down together. The courtship's over, thought Ax. They've got me now.

Better be ready for intimidation, and it could be **crude**. They do it by numbers, they're experts, they know it works.

'You saw the exhibits in the Memorial Hall?' said Wang.

'Yeah.'

The General nodded slowly, sombre-eyed. He was a five-star general, Ax was able to confirm now, by eye; a marshal of China. They piss around with their badges, but say that makes him one of the top ten military: which figures, the invasion was a showpiece. And Hu was another of them, yet seemingly subordinate to this man. But who would be Wang's superior? Maybe scratch the fifth element theory.

'I have some information I'd like you to glance at.' Wang handed the folders across the desk. 'Everything's in English.'

Ax took out documents, slick e-paper. He assumed the interview was being recorded, possibly transmitted live to some Department of Conquered Countries in Xi'an. He did not know how many eyes were upon him as he steeled himself for hideous news. There was nothing about England, it was all about China. Good God. True or false? He could see nothing that suggested the statistics weren't genuine.

'You are privileged, Mr Preston. You're one the few, one of only a small number of non-Chinese in the world, to have been shown those figures.'

'My God.'

Wang nodded. He leaned back, touching that humorous mouth with his fingertips, watching Ax. 'Yes. We have suffered, Ax; may I call you Ax?'

'Sure.'

'Thank you. Blow upon blow, like the rest of the world. The Crash. Horrific environmental degradation; plus the more insidious damage of climate change, and two, ah, very large-scale industrial accidents. We have grown great among the nations while absorbing an almost frightening net population loss. This is a terrible time for humanity, Mr Preston. Do your losses match ours, by any measure?'

'Nothing like,' said Ax, with a straight look. 'Our floods and storms have killed very few. Likewise the civil unrest, and famine isn't biting yet. So far the extra deaths have been attrition of the vulnerable: old age, infants; major league disease that we can't treat any more. Our worst problem is a generation lost to Cultural Revolution, and I think you know what that means. Did your grandfather, the distinguished novelist, ever recover from what he went through?'

'He did not. My beloved grandfather died insane, several years ago now.'

'I'm sorry.'

Wang's grandfather, a notorious Red Guard, had survived that débâcle and lived to become a distinguished literary figure in the Deng Xiaoping reform years. He'd suffered a psychotic breakdown in the late eighties, the price catching up with him at last. The grandson's rank, and his presence here, were indications of the state of play inside China's current power structure. Ax wanted the General to know he understood this. No babytalk, okay? I'm not entirely ignorant. They measured each other, the dead standing between: the millions on millions of Chinese swept away like dust, versus the mutilated bodies of Rivermead's Counterculturals. Intimidation by numbers, with a vengeance.

'I am a soldier,' said Wang, 'not a wanton killer. This country has been identified as a human treasure, first class. I am here to preserve it, not to destroy it. The Counterculture's foul delusion was wrecking England and spreading its filthy rot through Europe. They had to die.'

'They had to die,' agreed Ax, statesman to statesman.

'All Counterculturals will have to die, wherever they are found.'

Abruptly Wang changed the mood, looking around with a little moue of apology. The furnishing in here, apart from the fabulous art screen, was military basic. 'I wish we could have met in cosier surroundings; my London flat is charming. In official quarters I favour austerity, it's good old-fashioned practice. Do you happen to recall what function this room served, when Rivermead was your palace?'

Ax shook his head. 'Sorry, I've no idea.'

'Pity.'

'We never lived here, you know. Rivermead was a showplace, conference centre, assembly rooms. I don't think I slept under this roof more than once. I'm afraid I don't like the place. To me this is where Fiorinda was held prisoner, in the worst episode of our short history—'

The General raised his hand to interrupt. 'You refer to the "green nazi occupation". Tell me, what do you make of the story that Ms Slater's father, Rufus O'Niall, came to England *disguised in the body of a dead man*, to lead those villains; when you were being held by the drug-cartel in Mexico, and believed dead?'

'I think you can regard it as metaphor,' said Ax, unperturbed to find himself discussing forbidden topics. 'Fergal Kearney, an Irishman we thought we knew, had insinuated himself into the inner circle. I was on a mission to Washington when I was taken hostage – I'm not proud of that, I was a fool to get caught – whereupon Kearney showed his true colours. O'Niall was certainly running Kearney, while he never left Ireland. As you know, he was in league with the Extreme Celtics of mainland Europe. Their plans were damnable, the rest is—'

'Metaphor.' Wang smiled. 'Very good. I'd love to have your personal account of the jungle hostage affair one day . . . Hm. As self-made dictator of England you were titular leader of the Countercultural party. After you had vanquished the "green nazis", when you accepted the Presidency at the instigation of Fred Eiffrich, you retained the post. This looks like intimate association. What is it that makes *you*, and your people, something other than Counterculturals, Mr Preston?'

The fact that you want to use us, thought Ax. But he talked the talk.

'David Sale's government, our last legitimate government, recruited me as Green Head of State, as a popular leader. The Counterculturals were forced to accept me; they didn't like it. Later, when the Counter-culture had outright power, Mr Eiffrich convinced me I should try to work with them. I know I was wrong even to try.'

Wang accepted the formal submission with a nod: and moved on. 'What about Stephen Pender, he of the ridiculous nicknames? How did "Aoxomoxoa" come to be the ringleader of the pernicious Zen Self experiments?'

'Neurological experiments were carried out, here at Reading. I can't deny that. They were misguided, but innocent. Aoxomoxoa is guilty of being a rockstar who sought spiritual truth in a scientific fantasy. He's over it.'

'In your view the "Zen Self" had no relation to the experiments in the US, at Vireo Lake, where the project was to create a so-called "occult superweapon"?'

'None whatsoever.'

'Good, very good.'

Eighteen months ago, at Vireo Lake in California, a small group of neurologically altered psychics had broken the mind/matter barrier together, and willed the destruction of all supplies of crude oil; incident-ally wrecking the other fossil fuels beyond recovery. This was not the task they had been set. The 'occult superweapon' had been intended for use against the oil-powered might of Islam (might which had vanished like a dream; hard to believe it had ever existed). The A-team had acted for the best, and died in the act. They had plunged the world, in recovery after years of crisis, back into chaos.

The Chinese had taken their time, and then tackled the situation with masterly efficiency. The two countries where the 'so-called' occult weapon had been invented and developed were in Chinese hands. The novel and wonderful technologies associated with the mind/matter barrier were under a global ban, backed by staggering military superiority, and the A-team event *had never happened*. To believe otherwise was the 'pernicious delusion' Wang Xili had come leaping round the world to suppress. Ax wondered what was happening to Fred Eiffrich right now. Fred, who had fought the Pentagon's Vireo project tooth and nail, but had not been able to prevent the single, catastrophic, successful test. Did you fence like this, Fred, when the Chinese arrived: trying to find the bottom, trying to guess what you were meant to say? He dared not express the slightest curiosity about the President of the United States. Who was alive and well, of course, in this Chinese world: he could be seen on tv, making speeches in support of his new allies.

Wang had turned his wrist and was consulting a small screen he wore there. Clock watching? Getting feedback? Maybe he was checking his list. Dead Counterculturals, Rufus O'Niall, Sage and the Zen, what next? Be ready.

'What's your opinion on the Welsh problem?'

'The Welsh problem?'

And Ax was caught, after all, off guard—

'The people of Scotland and Ireland have welcomed our intervention. They are co-operating fully with Chinese inspectors in stamping out forbidden technology. The Cardiff government has made good resolutions, but can they be trusted? They may be harbouring suspect characters.' The General cast a dismissive glance over Ax's knotwork, which said he had friends in the north. 'Scotland and Ireland are sovereign states, we have undertaken to respect their territories. The case of Wales is different, as you know. What do you think? Should we go in, and cleanse the running sores?'

At the Dissolution of the United Kingdom there'd been a rush for Welsh assets. The little country had ended up substantially owned by Japan, whereupon Japan had vanished into China's maw. It had all seemed so far away, so harmless, like the corporation that 'makes' both your breakfast cereal and the car you drive. Now the Chinese were here, and why hadn't he been prepared for this threat? Caer Siddi on the Llyn

Peninsula, where Olwen Devi and her team had fled, was the last, secret refuge of mind/matter tech. What did Wang know, what was Ax supposed to say—?

He had a moment of total fugue.

He was in the Zen Self tent, cool light through the planes of the geodesic, with the woman whose genius had provided the tech for his dreams of green Utopia, spin-offs from her great experiment. He was a penniless rockstar warlord; Olwen was saying, with the force of prophecy, you will pay me by looking out for Wales, Ax, when you come into your kingdom.

It's not the past, there is no past, when I was there I was here—

Wang's office looked very strange, as if it shouldn't exist.

He shook his head. 'I can't advise you. I'm not a political leader.'

'Well then, we'll put the Welsh question aside. Running sores should clear up of their own accord, when the system has been restored to health . . . By the way, we intend to handle the so-called "Pagan sacred sites" of England very carefully. They should be preserved, if possible, for their ancient beauty, and they could be booby-trapped. Do you think that's likely?'

'I know nothing about it.'

'Good, very good. Now, to business.' Wang opened a drawer, and produced a cigar-shaped tube, popularly known as a blunt-case. He set it on the desktop, with distaste. A pink, penis-shaped rocket rose perpetually, on Monty Python clouds and attended by tiny wriggling spacebabes, from a flattened ball of virulent green; possibly representing the earth. 'You persist in turning down the government post? This looks like resistance to our mission, Mr Preston.'

'I want to help, sincerely. I'd be no use as your appointed President, because I am called the Just.'

Wang brightened, the scholar intrigued. 'That sounds like a quotation.'

'It is . . . The people of Athens decided to banish Aristides, who was called the Just. The citizens cast their votes, in cases of the kind, by writing the name of the person they wished banished on a shard of earthenware. An illiterate peasant fellow came up to Aristides during the voting, without recognising him, and begged him to write *Aristides* on a shard. He, surprised, asked what harm "Aristides" had ever done to the peasant. None at all, replied the other, but I'm tired of hearing him called "the Just" all the time. Aristides made no reply, he simply inscribed his own name, and handed back the shard . . . . The story's from Plutarch's

Lives. Like Aristides, Wang, I have a tired old reputation for virtue; it annoys people. You need fresh faces.'

'You're too modest,' said Wang, with that disarming smile. 'But I like the quotation.' With a lightning change of tone, he pounced on the blunt-case. 'So! You have the insolence to tell me that your "virtue" would be compromised and useless to us in an official post. Very good. And you wish to be a rock musician again. What do you call this *excrescence*? An album?'

'It's called a rez,' said Ax. 'Short for residency. It's what replaced "albums", when downloading finally killed the cd. Sort of a music-video compilation, usually purporting to be a candid diary, like reality tv. That one's called *Wood Court—*'

The Triumvirate had made *Wood Court* on Sage's visionboard, when they were hiding out in the Forest. They'd sent it to Paris, where their friend Alain de Corlay, the French techno-green leader, had produced it for them. It had just had its underground 'launch' in Europe. Excrescence was a mild word for the packaging, and they'd probably never know why Alain had shafted them—

'It will be banned. There is nothing patriotic here, nothing inspiring. Every song celebrates a degraded lifestyle smeared with the filth of the Counterculture.'

Ax nodded. 'Fair enough.'

They'd used forbidden immersion code: three per cent direct cortical stimulation for the emotional triggers, stronger for the qualia. They must have been out of their minds to think they could publish. Yeah, easily: those pure and naked crazy days, hiding in the undergrowth, building their house of sticks, he could feel the madness now and he wanted to be back there.

General Wang glared. 'I know what you're thinking. Your work cannot be banned, it is in the datasphere; we will only add to its filthy notoriety. You are mistaken. We decide what is propagated, and what is deleted from the record.' He squinted at the case, unable to find the angle that would make a list of tracks blossom. Briefly the commander-in-chief became a fortysomething undone by youth-tech. He didn't lose his temper. 'Why *do* the kids buy these things? Pop videos are freeware.'

'I've no idea. They say it's the romance of owning an object.'

'Ah. There it is. What does *this* title mean?' Wang's finger stabbed the air, where Ax couldn't quite see anything, his tone venomous. ' "The Doctor Came"?'

'The Eighteenth of October is the feast of St Luke,' explained Ax. 'One of the Christian Evangelists, held to have been a physician. It was the day you had chosen for the ceasefire, and your executions. Sometimes medicine hurts.'

'I see. But you are a Muslim.'

Ax shrugged. 'Got a lot of respect for the prophet Jesu. Sayeed Muhammad would have taught me that, if my mother hadn't. The English like "old". Christianity is older than the so-called Paganism of the Counterculture by a very long chalk, and it preserves the only genuine relics of animist religions older still.'

'Ingenious.' Wang leaned back, touching his fingertips to his lips again. 'Hm.' Do good to them that hate you, thought Ax. Sometimes it works, bizarrely enough. But you have to be sincere in your good will, or the enemy will sniff you out at once. He waited as General Wang, flattered despite himself, puzzled over the enigma that was Ax Preston's attitude.

'I think you should say, "The *Teacher* came".'

'Well, good luck. I've been trying to get the English to respect education for years, it's an uphill task. Doctors are better liked.'

'Hmph.' A leap back to venom. 'The song called "Hard" is crude repellent filth. *Something hard, shoving through* . . . It's about rape!'

'I believe it's more complex. You'd have to ask Fiorinda.'

'No woman was raped in the operation I commanded; nor man. Chinese soldiers do not commit rape. NO non-combatants were harmed.'

Counterculturals who refused to recant were classified as combatant, down to babes in arms. Ax thought of sights in his own past that he wished he could forget, things he'd been unable to prevent on the first rampage of green violence. And times he'd chosen to put his own life and fragile authority first, tell the absolute truth—

'You can't be everywhere.'

'*Wood Court* will be banned,' repeated the General. He tossed the case back into his desk drawer. 'Your music lacks focus, it lacks energy. You've lost direction. We'll see if the track called "Lay Down" can be rescued, stripped of foul, deluded technology. Its pacifist message separates you from the active recalcitrants. They need to know that you have abandoned them to their fate.'

'Yeah. I want them to know that.'

'Good.' The General rose to his feet, indicating that Ax should do likewise. 'What d'you make of Chu? A remarkable young woman, she'll be jumping over my shoulders soon. Don't you think?' No answer seemed required. The secretary, who had been silent in the background all this time, hurried to open the office door. 'My intention is that you and your partners, and the Few, will resume your role as cultural icons. First you three must be rehabilitated. You'll have to work hard, take direction, be humble, win respect. Become better artists, you can set your sights no higher.'

They left the rooms that had been Fiorinda's suite, heading for the spectacular main stairs. 'I'll see you again before you leave. Now I want you to meet the mentors under whose direction you'll be working.'

The great solar, with its nineteen sixties-style wall of glass, echoed with memories best forgotten. It seemed to be dead space in this incarnation, a strip of utilitarian carpet making a pathway through. Ax's 'mentors' were occupying a small huddle of chairs in front of a mobile display screen. They stood up as Wang and Ax approached. One of them was Norman Soong. The other two were Joe Muldur, rock journo in a different mould from Dian Buckley, and Toby Starborn, a digital artist who'd been the darling of the Second Chamber: whose presence here was astonishing. Soong grinned, and saluted the General with relish. Toby Starborn, wearing the olive-green uniform over a red shirt, sketched an odd bow. Joe, in civvies, tried to copy Soong's salute and made a mess of it.

'Hey, General,' said Norman. 'Did you convince the prince?'

'I believe so.' Wang looked at Ax: the charming smile had a hint of devilment in it. 'Enjoy, Mr Preston. You'll be excited by the plan, I'm sure.'

Toby Starborn. How the fucking hell does that work?

Toby's amber, tip-tilted eyes were fixed on Ax with a disquieting, shallow intensity. His nappy brown curls were dressed like Norman Soong's in a stiffened aureole. They looked, the big gaudily-wrapped impresario, the faunlike artist, as if they'd made their heads into fright-masks to ward off demons. Ax's stomach was hollow, he had been offered nothing to eat or drink and he'd been hungry when he arrived. Bodies piled on plastic rose from where they'd been suppressed through the interview, threatening to overwhelm him—

There was a gear-changing pause as the General strolled away. 'Hi, Ax,' quavered Joe. 'I'm, I'm incredibly honoured to be invited to join this.'

'This is the turning point of your career, Axl-baby,' said Toby, the shallow stare replete with malice. 'No more sad pseudy self-referential lyrics about the fab threesome, endlessly up yourselves in a garret. No more smug fucking protest song hit singles. This will be concrete, this will be beautiful. We'll make you famous.'

Soong patted Ax on the arm. 'Ax, what a privilege. Did I say that? Love your music, guitar-man, the toast of the world and the jam on it, in the words of our native guide here, I mean Joe. Toby's being tactless, but he's right, we're going to commit fantastic things! He's a genius, I *love* the themes he dares to tackle.'

Ax looked at the hand on his sleeve. 'May I speak to you for a moment?'

They walked to the other end of the glass wall, Joe and Toby Starborn left awkwardly standing together. 'Norman,' said Ax, electing the man his instant buddy, showbiz culture's got to be good for something. 'Who the fuck set this up?'

'Everything we say is heard,' intoned Norman, unctuous and alarmed. 'Everything we do is seen, and it's good. It's *good* to live like this.'

Ax gave him a disgusted look. 'Of course. We all live in the same household, it's the human condition, we all watch and listen. One day I plan to be boring, it's my dream, meanwhile I'm *fine* with being under surveillance every moment. What are you trying to do to me? Toby Starborn is a professed Pagan.'

'He's recanted.'

Toby Starborn was obsessed with Fiorinda. His celebrated portraits of her, created with forbidden tech, betrayed a sinister, dangerous subtext. Ax wasn't going to tolerate having him around. 'For fuck's sake . . . excuse my rockstar language. He was the Second Chamber government's favourite artist, their digital laureate!'

'So were you,' said Norman. 'You were their darling. They made you President, didn't they? The Second Chamber wanted you for team captain, Fred Eiffrich brokered the deal. And *you* are back from the brink, look at you.'

Ah.

You forget it's there and then the hellish stress trips you up when you least expect it, *after* the difficult passage, over something you should have handled easily. His blood ran cold, shit, what was I thinking—

Norman mistook silence for resistance.

'What do you *really* want to do right now, Ax? Don't tell me, let me guess. You want to strip the dreadful actives of their support, and convince them to give up the struggle. Am I there or thereabouts?'

'You are there,' said Ax, grimly. 'But I've recanted, Lieutenant Colonel Soong. I know that's somebody else's job. I'm just a rock musician—'

'And I'm a music director. Every job is our job now, we are the liturgy of history, and *you* helped to make that so. What would you say if I told you stripping the actives of the support most crucial to them is exactly our project? And we will do it with the music. And the way we get there will be strange and difficult and mysterious, but you and I, and Toby and Joe, and Fiorinda and Aoxomoxoa, will reach a momentous, epochal, rock apotheosis—?'

Ax lost his grip on time. Past, present and future became one, as in that moment in Wang's office. Simultaneity took him in its sway: the intense feeling that all this had happened already, the hammer-blow of inexorable destiny, almost knocked him to his knees. He knew that Norman Soong's plan, whatever it involved, was a disaster, but he saw the white light. No fighting it.

'Tell me more.'

Eventually Norman and Toby took themselves off. Ax and Joe were left in the solar, waiting to be collected. Joe was heading for Reading Station, Ax would be returned to the Line. 'You couldn't make it for the press conference?' said Joe.

'Too early for me,' explained Ax, hazarding a guess. Press conference, what press conference? 'How was it?'

'What d'you think? Selected media persons get invited to Rivermead, and find out that the weird and wonderful Norman Soong is here. He's been here all the time, and the Triumvirate are going to work with him. We were fantastically excited.'

'I'll bet you were.'

Joe swallowed, and nodded. 'I didn't get a chance to say, at Ashdown: it's so great that you came through, you three. So great to have you back.' He had kept his coat on, he huddled deeper into it, dug his hands into his pockets and shivered. 'I never expected this . . . How's Fiorinda? I kind of got an inkling, from the teetotal thing. If I'm right, many many congratulations—'

Mr Preston stared. Everything we say is heard, Joe.

'Oh fuck,' breathed Joe. 'Oh, *sorry*!'.

Happily Wang Xili appeared before the silence that followed could become embarrassing; with Lieutenant Chu, who was bearing Ax's greatcoat.

The General walked Ax through the foyer, very pleased with himself. All that you want you can have, Mr Preston; as long as you accept you are our creature.

'Do you have any *ideas*, Ax? Anyone I should know about?'

'People you should appoint?'

'Yes. As outgoing President, who would you favour for the next PM?'

Ax thought about it, he took a woman's life in his hands. 'Lucy Wasserman.'

'Ah. Is she in this country at the moment?'

'No. She could be contacted, ask around.'

'This is the bio-fuel crops in underground car parks with grolamps woman?'

'You're well-informed,' said Ax. They walked out into winter dusk, and the contours of Rivermead tugged at a grief he must not show. Pray God he would never have to come here again. But there's always another turn of the screw. 'It works. I mean the grolamps, in a small way; a net gain. Piecemeal solutions suit us.'

'What's your best overground crop?'

'I don't know that we have a *best*. Grain's a big issue. Cash-crop wheat-farming soils here in the south just gave up on us. We have superb grazing in the Midlands; we do well on meat. Could be self-sustaining on dairy, root crops, market garden, with more cuts in housing and more urban farms.' A car was waiting, he didn't have to walk to the helicopter (an upgrade on the return trip, good sign). 'The real problem is space for biofuels, which we have to find because H just is not the answer. You Chinese don't seem to use any ethanols, or H. How do you manage?'

General Wang laughed heartily. 'Don't be afraid to ask a bold question! There's no mystery. China started to prepare for the post-petroleum age when the Burma Road was closed, in 1942. We were far ahead of the game. When our lower-grade fossil fuel stocks proved worthless, a perfectly natural phenomenon, we turned to safe, powerful, sustainable alternatives, it's as simple as that.'

The Burma Road, take that last word away with you. It was supposed to be Fred Eiffrich who had started the World War Two refs, a code identifying and uniting the people who understood that the Crisis was a global war, against no human enemy. A fight for the survival of civilisation . . . Put that into the equation, it's surely not an accident, along with, *human treasure, first class . . . my beloved grandfather . . . they could be booby-trapped . . .* (shit, that's a bad one). Through the long cold journey home to his lovers he ran the permutations, the volume of his mind trying to hold a whole world, like that art screen in the gatehouse; reforming, reforming, reforming forever.

II

The Few were in London, well-treated apparently but back in General Hu's custody. The Reich-in-Hiding had been on tour around Sussex villages and small towns since Ashdown; very low profile, but practising for a greater destiny. Their base was a derelict racing stables on the flank of the South Downs. No running water indoors, most of the ground floor uninhabitable and few ceilings that didn't leak. Crew and roadies, engineers, techies and performers slept in bed-roll dorms. At least they were eating well. In a cluttered kitchen, stacked with tour hampers, the walls smoke-stained by vagrant fires and papered with rags of horsey memorabilia, Fiorinda cut slices of yesterday's oatmeal for Marlon, Silver and Pearl, and fried them in cinnamon-sugar ghee (from the same dry-goods store in Uckfield that had rendered up the dried peas for the infamous garlic mush). She'd done two shifts of breakfasts already; this afternoon she'd be giving a performance. Did it occur to the *jeunesse dorée* that they might lend a hand? It did not. Silver took her plate and stared at the food in dumb misery. Pearl picked her nose, frowning. 'Has Father Christmas come yet?'

She was behaving like a child half her age. Wish we could get her to a neuro unit. George's first-aid box said her skull was doing fine, but it didn't do brain scans.

'No. Eat your breakfast: here, have some condensed milk.'

'Is it organic?' asked Marlon. 'I know the oats came out of a *packet*.'

'Of course it's not fucking organic, it is Nestlés. It's what we have.'

Marlon spoke *sotto voce* to Silver: *it's the Fiorinda Slater miracle diet, you can eat what you like, as long as it is called porridge and tastes like sheep shit.* He used their secret Welsh-English pidgin. Silver ignored him, too sunk in her personal despair to make trouble. Fiorinda caught the drift.

'Marlon, there's something we need to straighten out. It was your dad and Ax who took the non-violence pledge. *Not me.* Do not push your luck.'

'I'm eating it. Look at me, diwl, I'm *eating* it, for—'

'Father Christmas might bring me something,' Pearl began brightly; but lost the thread. 'Might bring me something, might bring me something, might, might.'

Augh. Out of here, before one of them ends up sliced and fried.

Sage found her in the stable block, grooming one of the pack ponies. He propped himself in the doorway to watch his living goddess. When she was off guard like this he could see the scars left by the green nazi time, drawn around her lovely reckless mouth and shadowed eyes. *Nazi* hardly covered it. The games her father had played with her, using that animated corpse, his instrument, had barely been matched at Auschwitz, Belzec, Sobibor. Where did she find the brute courage to survive that sojourn in hell? – and not only to survive but to outwit the bastard, to save lives—

You're knocking on an open door, Chinese persons. You *could not* be worse than the fate we were circling around, helpless to escape, when you arrived. You would not believe how eager we are to help you stuff that fucking genie back in the bottle. The pony dropped its head, eyes half shut, as Fiorinda's curry comb worked on the cusp of its shoulders, where the scraggy black mane ran out into winter coat.

'That horse is going to be your slave.'

She glanced round, shrugged and went on working. 'A lot of people seem to like me now. It's funny, nobody ever did when I was on my way up.'

'You're not so terrifying as you were when you were fourteen. We've resigned ourselves, we're no longer thinking, God, why do I even bother.'

The pony tried to shove its big head under her arm. She shoved back. 'Don't flatter yourself, sunshine. I'm just doing what has to be done.' Fiorinda did not see horses as romantic, she saw them as a marker on the descent back to the Stone Age.

'They never ask themselves whether *I* like *them*. I fucking don't. I'm as self-obsessed and cold-hearted as I ever was. I just cover it up. You ought to be in bed.'

'It's not a tempting prospect.'

Sage had pneumonia. It wasn't a dangerous kind, but his liver was a re-gen, the original having been a casualty of the assassination of Rufus O'Niall. They were having trouble finding drugs he could tolerate, to hold the disease down while he threw it off. Meanwhile Sage functioned under the influence, performing stupid feats.

'You're not,' said Fiorinda. 'You're leaning on things.' He quickly stood up straight, the clown. She sighed in exasperation. 'You need bed-rest and real antibiotics, which we don't have.'

'Nyah. Antibiotics are bad for you. *You* should be resting.'

'Can't.'

Ax had gone to Reading, and they were not afraid for him, not much; but they were raw with his absence. *I need you always to be there* had stopped being a pious exaggeration in this relationship several hideous separation episodes ago. Fiorinda ditched her comb and walked into his arms in the horse-smelling gloom, frankly burrowing for bare, heated skin. 'Mm . . . nice. Would you like a fuck, pregnant lady?'

Privacy was hard to come by. The Triumvirate shared their dorm with three deranged teenagers, George and Bill, and sometimes others. Peter had a cubby-hole of his own, but that was fair: communal bunking would be very frightening for him.

'In here?' said Fiorinda, without hesitation.

'Sod's law, some fucker would walk in on us.'

They went around the back, to a yard where snow crusted the shattered puddles, the tumbledown walls; the ivy tangled in the trees leaning crazed branches over them. An icy breeze bit their cheeks and teared their eyes: he stooped, trying to mould his height to her body, tried to be even with her the way Ax could be.

'Are you too tall, are you feeling too tall, my baby?'

'Too fucking tall, *hate* being so tall. Oh, I want Ax.'

'Me too, whisper to me about him, *please*—' She jumped him, legs locked around his waist, trying not to dig army boots into his spine, snow on her hair and melting down her back: oh but it was still good, stone age sex for stone age royalty. Body heat and slick inside surfaces clumsily shared, the infinitely reassuring smell of each other's musk. *My little pony*, he mumbled, wondering when he would see her naked again. *I hope I didn't hear that right*, growled Fiorinda, *I do not find that idea erotic;* but she did. Close your eyes, get up a sweat together, reach a peak and float—

They slid down the wall, back to earth. Sage tipped his face to the sky, relishing her warm weight in his glassy, fevered world; his cock melting into her like contented candlewax, my girlfriend, my girlfriend . . . and

79

the baby moved between them, a tiny stir; someone talking softly in another room. Fiorinda pushed herself away from him, and crouched on her heels, arms wrapped around her head.

'Babies are like aliens,' she said. 'Unreal until they arrive.'

Sage zipped up. He didn't touch her, he knew better than that, been with this damaged, amazing Fiorinda long enough. 'I've always wanted to meet an alien.'

'When I was pregnant before, that time in Paris when I only managed to stay pregnant about ten days, it was like a wormhole from my belly to another universe, now there's a worm in the hole, oh I didn't mean to say that . . . I have these creepy thoughts, they come into my head and I deal with it, I'm okay.'

'I know you are,' said Sage, and she came back to him.

'Will you say, *everything's going to be all right?*'

'Everything's going to be all right.'

He soothed her, murmuring nonsense, thoroughly alarmed.

The trains were running, a mad survival in this mad world. Berkshire was only hours away. Get home on time, Ax. Please.

The pews and cross-stitched hassocks had been removed to safety; the altar was screened by a green stage curtain. Probably in mediaeval times they'd left His Lordship presiding over the drunken commons, but the set-up crew had decided to err on the side of decorum. It's not a mosque, but you wouldn't want to risk committing sacrilege on Ax Preston's manor. The bar was in the foot of the tower at the west end, with a burner for mulled ale. Brass and wood had been polished, stone and tile scrubbed. Boughs of holly and ivy had been raised to the rooftree by tackle formerly used in the mighty spectacle of an Aoxomoxoa and the Heads gig.

No mistletoe, because that's Pagan and you can't be too careful.

The crew had departed to the pub. Dave Wright and Mrs Brown sat on the sanctuary step, in the lull before the storm. Dave had a new skit in his head, Caro Letwynd and the churchwarden . . . Mr Shaun Hammerpot, self-important fat lad from another age, busting the buttons of his yellow waistcoat. The *Saxon quoining!* Caro looks at the long and short work, looks at Hammerpot. She becomes possessed, suddenly she's two metres plus, thin as a rail and solemn as an owl, big baby blues and yellow curly-wurlys good enough to eat: an' she says, in that voice, you know: *Tha's all right, moi dear, we'll make fuck-sure we don' go an' fuckin' hurt yer pet rocks* . . . They're all a clone, you know. 'Cept Bill, of course. The boss buds them. Ooh, we need a new roadie? I've seen it happen, like a carbuncle, which is a giant inflamed pimple, if you haven't met the word before: squirt, squirt, an' out the bugger comes, like a blob of pus, only partly formed. My arse in butter!, picture what it looked like when *George* came squeezing out—

There's a way of being funny where you do nothing at all: except treasure the trivial things and play them back with a little nob on them. This was the art that Dave aspired to perfect. You start with a small world like this one, the Reich-in-Hiding, that loves the smell of its own in-jokes (the tag *'cept Bill of course* had them FOF by now, failsafe, instantly); and then you take it to the big time. He could dream.

'I love Norman churches,' he said. 'I'd go looking for the ancient village church, with me little assault rifle in me mitts in case, when we were in Yorkshire.' Dave had been a barmy army squaddie, before he took to life in the woods. 'But there was nothing like this. They're nowhere in the world but here on the Downs, and they're a human treasure first class, as the tourists would say.'

'I never knew you were religious, Dave.'

'I'm not . . . I just like Norman churches. The quiet. Maybe it's some kind of place where suffering is over.'

'I like the atmosphere,' agreed Mrs Brown. 'It's the peace that time forgot.'

'*That's* gonna change. Who's on the door? It might get rough.'

'The snow'll keep troublemakers at home.'

'We hope. Is Alison coming?'

'She might.'

Maybe he shouldn't have asked. He'd had the daughter just once, one night stand; he preferred older women. Now he was getting his marching orders from the mother. He could feel it coming. Maybe she was doing a pre-emptive, suspecting Dave was about to move on to greater things . . . Shelley Brown went on gazing calmly down the nave, a dark-haired woman, fearlessly going grey, in good shape for the far side of fifty. 'D'you ever think about getting her out, I mean, out of England?'

'Me, I love the little birds,' she sighed. 'The garden birds, they mean a lot to me: sparrows and robins, chaffinches, great tits and blue tits. And wrens; I like wrens. I've always fed them. But they'll be feeding us, we'll be eating them next winter, at this rate. I hate the thought of that . . . I think about getting Alison out all the time, Dave, thanks for asking. Her dad's family's Spanish. But we're not in touch.'

'They call tits "chickadees" in the US. It's a prettier name.'

'I'll stick with the English.'

The north wind sighed. The immemorial stillness was illusion, the peace of exhaustion, there was blood on these stones. The Reich-in-Hiding was a whirlwind that had swept them both up and was about to blow away again.

'One day the king of England came to my pub's kitchen door like a beggar, and ever since it's been like a magic carpet ride. I'm scared for Alison. I'm sitting here thinking, what if Ax never comes back? What if we're all rounded up tonight and tortured to death? But it's been the peak of my existence, this has.'

'Our lives have been *touched*,' remarked Dave wisely.

They decided they'd better go and haul Hammerpot out of the Yew Tree. The boiler still had to be fired up, and the fat tit was bound to make a jobsworth of it.

Sage and Fiorinda arrived and retired at once, megastars that they were, to a closet which held shelves of dusty vases, a defunct harmonium and a white enamel sink. An antique CCTV screen gave them views of the nave; and of the churchyard, where the fans on the whisper network of this rave were gathering. She smudged out the violet shadows under his eyes, added blusher and wiped most of it off again. He was dressed for the stage, in clean black jeans and a white tee-shirt; and running a high fever, but mentioning that would only piss him off.

'You look like an archangel with a *bad* hangover.'

'Tha's appropriate. We should do your carol again.'

'Fuck, fuck, fuck, I hate that fucking carol, oh all right.'

Sage built them a soundcone, as the closet was not soundproofed. So here we are, back to where it all began. Crisis Management gigs for a government we don't trust in a country that's fallen apart. Free concerts to keep the peace—

'And once more,' said boss, inexorable. 'Up, up, sweetheart.'

'I wish you'd speak English. I don't *get* this music.'

'You're coming in flat on the descant.'

Fiorinda glowered. 'That's better.'

Collection buckets were going round outdoors, shaken by crew persons in Santa hats. No gallant Norway spruce had been slaughtered, or shackled in fairy-lights, perish the thought; but Caro had lit the yew trees. Every red fruit, in the darkness of the foliage, had a star in its heart; drops of ruby quivered on the snow. If we see olive-green uniforms erupting into that pretty scene, will we have time to get out by the back way? They believed it wouldn't happen, they knew it might. The lesson of the invasion lingered. All we know is that they give no warning—

CCTV everywhere, a reminder that the sacred twentieth century wasn't as good-natured as all that. The stars and crew in the communal dressing room, aka vestry, had the gratifying sight of a standing crush in the nave. VIP seats in the tiny chancel – for those with small children, and ravers who'd been young when the Beatles were playing the Cavern – were packed too. Big screens in the churchyard for the overspill (Big Screens were supposed to be forbidden, but Lü Xiaobao often sent a helicopter to fly by their venues, and he'd never complained). Snatches of Dave's warm-up routine reached them, between waves of laughter. *Don't worry, they won't rip your ears off but they might take the piss seeing it's a* chamber *concert . . . Now don't start . . . My arse in butter, imagine when George came squeezing out?*

'Story of my life,' Sage propped his head on his hand, stacking coin; 'fifty, sixty, are the Swedish euros any good at all?' They called all the micro-currencies 'Swedish euros' for the good reason that the Swedish Euro isn't money. '—fuck, I lost count. Everyone picks on the way I look, an' I know they are jus' jealous.'

The bucket collections were almost worthless financially; but it was a Reich ritual. A coin in the beggar's cup signifies acceptance of the beggar, and it cuts both ways, we like to touch their money, it's an intimate contact. 'If he does the Cornish Meths Revival riff agen,' growled big George, 'I'm goin' out to kick the fucker's head in. That ought to be good for a chuckle.'

'Now, now. The jester has licence. It's true, though,' mused Fiorinda, as she rolled old 500 notes and cinched them with one of her precious hair bands. 'The rest of us get off lightly. 'Cept Bill, of course.'

Sage, George, Fiorinda herself, the sulky teenagers and the stage crew, instantly leapt up and fell about. They leaned helplessly on ecclesiastical panelling, wiped tears from their eyes, imitated dying ants, propped themselves, shaking, against a moth-eaten banner of St Pancras, rolled in ecstasy thumping the floor; all in voiceless, scuffling dumbshow. Bill Trevor looked down his aquiline nose at them.

'Fuck off. It's not my fucking fault.'

Peter Stannen had been searching chill, frankincense-scented crannies for a pen that worked, he found one and wrote a note to Fiorinda, *did you rehearse the carol?* Sage's immix collaborator, known as 'Cack' for ancient laddish reasons, had Asperger's and was often puzzled by the world. He had not joined the silent laughter. He believed, quite simply, that you weren't allowed to talk in a church.

'Yeah, it's okay,' she wrote. 'We did it in the flower hole.'

The Reich, Unplugged

No satellite link, no tv cameras or radio pick-up. No mediapack other than the reporter for the Long Man Villages intranet. A guest list of local heroes, an audience of around three hundred; counting the overspill. The Heads, bereft of immix, were trying a different sound every show. This time it was West Coast seventies: Bill and George romping on guitar, Cack boldly pasting the drums, the sick archangel energised, bouncing around the tiny stage-space in a knees-spread heel crouch, *me and you, nothing to do, what am I going to do with you?* Good old romance, no pants dance – The VIPs loved it: aged hands clapping, aged feet stamping, two swinging eightysomethings getting up to cut the rug; a rocking riot going on in the nave.

Fiorinda walked onto the blue carpet feeling intimidated, and took her mellow Stephen Hill electro-acoustic to the waiting stool: a donation, she'd lost all her own guitars. Why make me follow Sage? Not fair, I am not in good voice and I feel boring. On her left, a canopied fourteenth century piscina, on her right the Norman lady chapel. It was four in the afternoon, deep dusk outdoors. The church ales are a smart move, Ax. I don't *like* these places but they're beautiful, and a palimpsest of national history. Also, bleeding heart goodwill sold here, which suits us . . . She gave them back catalogue: 'Stonecold' and 'Sparrow Child', 'Wholesale', 'Rest Harrow', 'The Lady With A Braid', 'Love Is Like Water', and this is 'Hard', with its soft, deceptive intro:

> There's less that I want now I know
> That the things I need can't be had by wanting
> If it's true that you reap what you sow
> Then I spill my seed for the birds and leaves
> No return, no return

> *When something hard*
> *Is coming through*
> *Despite of me*
> *Despite of you*
> *It hammers on the days before, it breaks my body's open door—*

Commonsense for the comprehensively trashed; and something she'd been wanting to put into music since the green nazi time. Ground into the dirt and the world rolls over you, but you're part of it. Mouth full of earth and you're part of it. When I was a pushy kid I used to think the meaning was in the words and the notes, now I know that, scream or whisper, it's in the *shape* you give a lyric line, the *exact* weight and speed laid on these strings. I suppose now you think I'm telling you to accept the Chinese invasion, three hundred of you at a time, not v. efficient, but I'm not. I'm chasing perfection; elusive in this song; that I will still be learning ten years, twenty years from now—

She looked up when the applause burst, and caught Sage with an expression in his eyes that frightened her.

The Chichester and Arundel group parish priest read a lesson, and spoke movingly of how the Chinese word for good, *hao,* is written *nü zi,* signifying a woman and a child. On this night, of all nights, let us remember our humanity, the symbols that we share. Rock music and the Christian message aren't so far apart, all we need is love . . . etc. Stained-glass windows black as midnight. *In the bleak midwinter,* sang Fiorinda, guest soloist with the Long Man Parishes Choir, *frosty wind made moan.* A sheepskin gilet over her green knitted dress (Heart Foundation, Lewes), hid the slight round of her belly. George Merrick at the onstage sound desk, ready to catch her should she fall (she didn't), found himself thinking, there's one secret we can't keep much longer.

Curfew was nine p.m. It couldn't be enforced beyond the Line, but *they will give no warning*: the Reich didn't presume on anything. The show ended at six-thirty, with Sage's 'Winter Song', that he'd written after Ashdown; which had become their regular finalé. Crosslegged on the chancel steps, he chanted the lyric into a hand mic, the way he used to chant Aoxomoxoa lyrics on the live stage. Behind him, under the transparent flow of words, the Reich Chorus harmonised a dark, earthy beat—

85

Black frost grips the waters, binds the drifts and hangs in daggers
From the drain and silent culvert, and the sun is ringed in vapour
  larks and finches lace-stitched starving, print the snow among the
  reedbeds where the tide uncovers only bone and empty sockets, gazing
Under the glassy sweep of wind, that breaks the backs
  of beasts in pasture, swans turn hollow down the searoad past the Crow
  Neck, and the beating of their silver is the only bird that flies . . .

But we who lost our brothers and our sisters in the hunger, will live to
See once more Antares burning, low and red in the southern sky—

The detail varied, mysteriously. Sometimes he led his audience down-stream to the sea, some nights it was over moorland or through lichened, crouching oak woods. There might be red mice, foxes, badgers; even human interest. There was always some clue, for those who knew, that he was singing about the south-west, the lost heartland; the end was always the same, Antares like a beacon fire in a summer evening sky. Tonight, as the singers held their last chord, there was a murmur of delight. Flowers had sprung into existence: rose and gold and violet, painted in light on the air; over the ancient walls.

We expect no return on our investment, what happened to us just happened. Down in the information, the ocean of os and 1s, there is no cruelty. No courage, no justice, only silence. But you have to give the punters *something*.

'It's a promise,' whispered Sage.

The lightshow vanished, the entertainers joined the crowd. Sage propped himself against a pillar and made as if he wasn't falling over. Fiorinda sipped homemade sherry and chatted to the priest and family, while her ersatz teenage family (augh) hung around moping. Dave Wright reverted to his other persona: a dour woodland creature, seeking the shadows. Suddenly Pearl let out an ear-piercing shriek: *it's Dad! It's my Daddy!*, and there was Smelly Hugh Raven, in a damp parka with bulging pockets. Smelly had vanished after Ashdown, letting the Few take Safire to London; accepting his outcast fate. 'I won't stay,' said the old hippy, shamefaced; while Pearl plundered his coat, radiant with greed, and Silver hugged a parcel of bright, trashy paper; that she never wanted to open because then it would be gone. 'I just thought, since I was in the district, I'd drop by an' see the girls—'

*

The doctor checked Sage's temperature, and said she'd seen worse. She listened to his chest, examined his lungs with a pre-Dissolution medical imager, and the face in her voice fell. No comment on the shark-attack scars that roped the patient's right side. Min the kitten sniffed for rats in a pile of empty seed sacks. Fiorinda stood at the window, and watched lights move in the dark of a lambing fold, on the white slope of the downs. If the ewes gave birth in February, as in the old days, they'd be in poor condition, and too many would die. Tendrils reached out from her to the post-gig party at the vicarage, and to the Few in London. But not to Reading or points between, she dared not touch that direction. Entrails laced across the landscape, trailing blood and mucus, a track the Chinese would have to be blind not to read. I am entangled, 'Hard' is about entanglement: wickedly tangled with this baby too, which gets more vulnerable as it gets bigger . . . They were in the loft above a farm supplies yard, a good gaff, clean sheets on a real bed. They had a supper tray, a chamber pot for Fiorinda, toilet in the yard for the men, water in a wash-stand jug; and an early warning system, just in case. Every comfort, except that Ax was late.

The doctor departed, leaving a Thermos of febrifuge. 'Not bad,' said Sage. 'Not bad at all,' said Fiorinda, automatically feeling that Sage ought to have only superb reviews, and the doctor must be rubbish. She checked a mug of the pungent mixture, with an LFT test-strip from George's first-aid.

'Well, it's no worse than paracetamol.'

He held the mug, fixing her with a fevered blue glare. 'You are *not* to worry about this, brat. Me, bodhisattva. I'm on top of it.'

'Don't worry about me then either,' said Fiorinda. 'Get into bed.'

'Better keep an eye on that kitten,' said Sage. 'He might find a way out.'

Appalling if they lost Ax's cat. 'He's not an idiot, it's freezing outside.'

The candle lantern stood on the floor, making haloed shadows. Sage got into bed with his clothes on, Fiorinda walked around, and the kitten scampered. 'I thought they were going mental,' she said. 'Poor kids, they were pining for tinsel. It never crossed my mind I was supposed to do Christmas for them—'

'Nor me. Why should it? Christmas is fer punters. It'd be like eating cat food.'

'I hope this loft is not bugged by the *East Sussex Gazette*.'

'New Year's Eve, that's the one I *really* hate. But you can make good money.'

'Whores that we are.'

She joined him under the quilt; bringing Min, who kicked himself free and ran off, chirruping indignantly. They put out the candle and moonlight, suddenly brilliant, flooded the dusty floor. Old dreams move in the unreal space of fever, she's mine, we live in Alaska, Ax Preston, who he?; but this dream was consumed by a black hole at the centre. 'He's got a phone on him. Shall we try it?'

They block your number, and no matter how many identities you have they nail them all. They use a voiceprint and fake whole conversations. Telecoms under the Chinese was a paranormal phenomenon. It worked sometimes and you had no idea why, but you knew a million demons were listening.

'If Ax is in trouble,' said Fiorinda, as to a small child, 'phone in trouble too.'

'Okay.' I will go for a piss, he thought, an' try my luck.

The drone of an engine entered the silence out there, grew, faded, and grew again. Someone was let into the yard, footsteps crunched on the loft steps. Fiorinda leapt up as the door creaked open, and zoomed across the room—

'She thought you'd been eaten by bears,' said Sage.

'Nah, just mildly masticated by National Rail. Wrong kind of snow.'

Ax had got a shock. He'd held her only this morning: but for the first time he felt the change, indisputable. This was a pregnant woman he was holding, full breasts, curved belly; and my God, I'd forgotten this problem, but she feels so *wonderful*—

He bent to kiss Sage's brow, Fiorinda still twined around him.

'How are you, my big cat?'

Sage grinned, but did not attempt to sit up. 'Okay, just knackered.'

'Yeah, I heard, you lunatic. According to my driver you were almost as knock-out as Fiorinda, and *she* was nearly as good as Dave Wright.'

'Excellent . . . How about you, Scheherazade? What's the damage?'

'Still got my head.'

Ax methodically removed hat, coat, gloves and scarf. He lit the candle, and sat on the side of the bed, staring at the trembling flame. 'What did you see?' whispered Fiorinda: because he looked like someone returning from a place of fearful visions.

'I have seen the first rays of the new rising sun. Is there anything to eat? There was nothing on the trains, not even hot water. Where's Min? Min?'

The kitten came belting over, quivering with joy. Fiorinda got out the extra blankets, and the malt whisky the priest had given them. She wrapped one blanket around Ax and the other around herself, scooped the supper tray of mince pies from under the bed, and poured the Muslim warlord a healthy dram.

'What the fuck's in this?' Ax peered at his pie's dubious interior.

'I detected mutton, suet, beet molasses, calf's foot glue, perhaps one sultana, and a *soupçon* of currants. Please, do not ask me if the meat is *halal*.'

'I wasn't planning to . . . Those walls are really something, close up. Nano I assume, but it looks as if they're alive, building themselves out of thin air.'

Sage hauled himself up on the pillows. 'Any *details* on this grey goo?'

'Didn't see any grey. I saw a creamy white. Indigo blue, and a dark red. Mostly the cream, probably for the, the in-your-face albedo of it. They call it *di*.' He set down the pie and mug, and wrote the character on his palm, Min following the strokes intently. 'Meaning earth; which figures . . . What can I tell you? Their barracks look like upturned boats. I think it's true that the army's in charge. They can put anyone in uniform that they like. And I think Corny's *Shi Huangdi* exists.'

There was a theory, unsupported by anything from official Chinese sources or the Sphere partners, that the PLA had taken over at some point in the Crisis years; leaving a façade of geezers intact. Supporters of this scenario said the megapower was secretly run by a small group, a 'gang of four', who kept out of the public eye. But Cornelius believed there was just one man at the centre: whom he named *Shi Huangdi*, first emperor, for obvious reasons.

'It was in the way Wang talks, the whole set-up. I asked him the grandfather question, and other key words. They're Neo-Confucianists, yet Maoist in style—'

Ax saw the household gods, propped against the wall by the bed. It washed over him that they were INSANE to keep hold of those forbidden things, Sage's board, Fiorinda's saltbox, and the Gibson was a useless warrior, helpless to protect its proscribed companions . . . But that was the day he'd spent at Reading talking, a fog of confusion. It was Ax who was protected, and his lovers would be the warriors, if the worst came to the worst. But so far so good.

'*Shi Huangdi?*' prompted Sage. 'How does that affect us?'

'I dunno, maybe not at all. But Wang said "England has been designated a human treasure, first class. I am here to preserve it, not to destroy it".'

Sage laughed. 'That's out and proud.'

Put this in the equation: the Chinese might make it. It was now clear that they meant to take over the entire world, *the whole board*, and by this stage who was going to stop them? Rightly or wrongly, the prospect did not fill the Triumvirate with horror. A Chinese planet? Better than some solutions that had been tried. For a moment rockstar nature came to the fore. They hardly asked whether Shi Huangdi was a monster or a saviour. They hardly asked what kind of World State it would be, as they contemplated the sheer spectacle of this awesome fledgling—

'It gets to the point,' said Fiorinda, slowly, 'where you want them to make it just because it would be such an *amazing* stunt.'

'Yeah.' Ax sighed deep. The food and alcohol were kicking in, he felt steadier. 'Okay, start again. Lemme tell you what happened, in order . . . I was shown around. By a high-flying young woman, Fio, you'll be pleased to know. I was told they mean us well, but they don't care how many hippies they have to massacre to awaken us from delusion. And in China they count population loss by the tens of millions before it makes the six o' clock news, so don't bother begging for mercy.'

'Is that what Wang said?'

'In just about so many words, yes he did.'

'What did you tell him?'

'I made ritual submission.'

A moment's silence. They watched Min patting a bar of moonlight.

'He showed me figures. It's been horrible in China, if they were real. Then he walked a plan to invade Wales by me, mentioning that running sores of delusion might be lurking there, and told me they aren't going to touch our so-called Pagan sites. He said "they might be booby-trapped", I don't think he meant high explosives.'

'Fuck,' breathed Sage.

Fiorinda stared at Ax, absolutely still, her eyes wide.

'Right, that was about my own reaction . . . I near as fuck panicked. But you have to remember, *they know most of what really happened*. It's fucking hard to keep that in mind, when they're forcing you to lie all the time, but *they know*. They know that Rufus was a naturally occurring supernatural monster, they know that Sage had to achieve the Zen Self in

90

order to defeat him, and they know that the Zen Self way of breaking the barrier doesn't create an occult superweapon . . . Look at it this way, they know at least as much as US Intelligence knew, after our green nazi episode. And yet everything they've done says they still want to hire us. It's a mystery, but it's okay. ' He poured more whisky, necked half and offered the mug to Sage. 'Oh, sorry, are you allowed spirits?'

'I'm not pregnant. I'll just quietly pass out, no problem.'

'I think Wang was calling a deer a horse, making sure I knew the right answers to the questions on his check sheet. It was a warning of how we have to behave, the line we have to walk. I feel fucking *brainwashed,* but not threatened.'

Ax fell silent; looking at things they couldn't see.

'Calling a deer a horse? . . . You're bein' inscrutable, babe.'

'Oh . . . Zhao Gao, the chief eunuch, wanted to know if he had enough power over the officials at the court of Qin. He had a deer led past them, and announced it was a horse. The emperor said, hahaha, it's a horse. Most of the officials agreed with Zhao Gao. The idiots who questioned his judgement were purged.'

'But you knew the right answers,' said Fiorinda.

'It's not rocket science. Okay, we still don't know what we're up against, we still could be *hopelessly* fucked, but our first aim was to buy some power. No doors closed today. If I'm making it sound bad; I'm tired. The news is *good.*'

'Now you're softening us up,' said Fiorinda. 'You have your softening-up voice on. What do we have to do? Don't break it gently, please.'

Unexpectedly, alarmingly, Ax laughed. 'How d'you want me to break it? Okay, I met Norman Soong. We're going to work with him.'

Fiorinda struggled with this. 'You mean you had a video conference?'

'No, I mean Norman Soong, rock director-in-chief to the Great Peace Sphere, is at Reading in the flesh. He's been there all along. Between the lines, he was kept under wraps until they knew if we three would co-operate.'

'Good God,' said Sage. 'You're kidding.'

'I'm not. We are to be rehabilitated, and they've hired the great Norman Soong to do the job. He's taking us on a goodwill mission to East Anglia, which will be recorded view to immediate global release, with Joe Muldur, and—'

Fiorinda and Sage were grinning, bright-eyed, in relief and disbelief.

'Wait, before you start celebrating. And Toby Starborn.'

'*What*—?'

'You heard me, the one and only Toby Starborn, immix artist and Fiorinda-stalker. I don't understand it either. I was spinning out by that stage,' (he flashed on piled bodies, blots of dark blood, he was not going to share the Memorial Hall with them). 'I could have missed stuff, I dunno what his role is. We're to do concerts at a couple of the big camps, to win hearts and minds on the wrong side of the Line, presumably with plenty of safeguards—'

'Is that all?' said Sage, acutely. 'No, er, information-gathering on the side?'

'Spying on the Resistance?' Ax shrugged. 'Maybe. Except we'll be on a leash, and the actives not likely to trust us . . . So that's the offer. If we accept, and Norman gives us a good report, the Reich is back in business. I said yes, was I right?'

'Yeah.'

'Yes,' said Fiorinda.

Elation quickly faded. They sat in silence, collaborators in earnest.

'What's he like?' wondered Fiorinda, 'Norman Soong?'

The good malt bubbled in Ax's blood, he was overcome by her beauty in the moonlight, with her blanket cloaked around her. 'Colourful. Ebullient. You'll find out. He's going to put you back where you deserve to be, sweetheart.'

'Oh, come on. We have other things to think about.'

Sage looked at Ax, Ax looked at Sage. Her name in lights, that's on the list.

'Ax,' said Sage, earnestly. 'She's *pregnant*.'

'Oh my God. You're *not* going to leave me behind!'

'We fucking for definite are not,' Ax agreed, fiercely. 'I remember what happened last time you stayed safe at home. We'll think of something.'

Fiorinda took up the challenge. 'Do we have to tell them? When does this trip happen? I don't really show if I dress carefully, and I'm eating like a herd of pigs. I could get away with being just fat, for a few more weeks—'

Fat was a crazy exaggeration, but they kept quiet on that.

'Almost at once. Within the next month, I'm sure.'

'Then it can be done!'

'She'll have to skip the bikini pageant,' said Sage, grinning.

'Okay by me,' said Fiorinda. 'I don't like bikinis.'

Every time he came back to them it was a revelation. The responsibilities, the vows, the terrors are nothing: this is the only way we can bear to live. Your mouth, his mouth. Pass me between you. Kiss him soul-deep, while you are driving into me with that power-hammer hunger . . . Three in one; for once nobody stood guard except a tabby kitten; and the mysterious presence of an unborn child, watching from the shoreless silence of the os and 1s.

The tiger and the wolf slept in each other's arms. The three-quarter moon left their window and the winter stars looked in. Fiorinda lay awake, demons and entrails reduced to a scrabble on the edges of her mind, thinking of the eerie glow that Ax had brought back from Reading, which he had not explained; wondering if Shi Huangdi could really save her life?

III

The Triumvirate came to London from their rural retreat. Joyous Liberation did a special feature, in which it was implied – CGI – that they'd spent the duration chilling in an Elizabethan manor house on the Sussex coast, under the protection of the kindly old General of the South East.

How had they felt about the invasion, when it happened?

'Stunned,' said Ax. 'It was truly awe-inspiring. And grateful, frankly.'

'We knew at once we had to be part of this thing,' said Fiorinda.

Aoxomoxoa, is it true you were taken from detention and tortured by the Second Chamber junta's orders?

'It was a hideous experience,' said Sage. 'I don't like to talk about it.'

Sage had been tortured because the bad guys thought he knew where they could find a pair of realtime cognitive scanners, vital component in the making of an occult superweapon. What was he to do if this line of questioning continued? Okay for you, Ax, but for me it *is* rocket science. It disturbed him to be called Aoxomoxoa, but he wished he had the living skull mask to hide behind.

The woman (this one was a major, by rank) turned her back, and asked Fiorinda something. Chinese give Triumvirate nice house, evil deposed régime tortures them, point made, moving on. The front row of the studio audience was top brass. Wang Xili sat there smiling, carelessly elegant, one leg crossed over the other, his trophy courtesan beside him. Sage wondered how she felt about being there, on the wrong side of the lights. Was this part of her re-education, or did Wang simply like to show her off? His role in the interview was not taxing, Ax and Fiorinda were getting all the questions. Dian's white face kept tugging at him, as if she were trying to catch his attention. Stay away from me, he thought. We can't afford to listen to your nightmares, not now; not yet.

Norman Soong's Peace Tour launch was held at The Bays, Covent Garden, rockstar hideout of choice; where the Triumvirate and their kooky entourage were filling the gemlike rooms. Areeka had found out at the last moment that the salon was being filled with vases and vases of spring blossom. My God. How can anyone NOT KNOW that Fiorinda hates cut flowers? Fiorinda felt that the less the Chinese knew, the better, but she insisted the décor had to be changed to a winter theme. Bring chrysanthemums, witch hazels, hellebores, camellias, scented daphne, oh, you can leave the snowdrops. The result was very beautiful, but had a wayward, funereal feel.

The story got around. Norman Soong sought Fiorinda in the crush, and stood before her in a multicoloured business suit, one large fist pressed to his breast in salute. 'You!' he intoned, rolling his full, dark eyes. 'You!' He lifted a dark bronze chrysanthemum from the nearest display, snapped the stem and tucked it into his buttonhole. 'Superb!' He nodded mysteriously. 'Into the unknown!'

Norman walked away at once, fearing that the diva would break his mood by some banal response. By the buffet he was accosted by a large, solemn person who said. 'I am the Egg Man, you know.'

'The Walrus was Paul,' agreed Norman, bored.

'No, I'm the egg man of *now*. Happy hens free to roam, that egg man. In the shelter of the trees, playing with the bugs and bees. I'm in that song on *Wood Court*.'

'*Wood Court* has been erased,' said Norman, forbiddingly. 'You don't exist.'

Toby was ensconced among his very close friends, refusing to say a word to the mediapack. It was unwise, but Norman had decided to let him be.

Fiorinda wore a sleeveless fleece-lined tunic over layers of empire-line indigo taffeta; and grinned at Allie Marlowe across the room. Yeah, I look like a Tenniel chesspiece. Pregnant? I don't think so, just fashion victim. Oh, it was spooky to see their friends in the ascendant, the Second Chamber celebs swept away. There's Shelley Brown, already being courted for several Reconstruction Committees. Dave Wright, very big comic, chatting up Roxane Smith. The Chinese had only recently discovered Rox, and they loved hir. Transgendered, flamboyant doyen-oid of rock criticism, Oxford accent: right up the tourists' street. Ax hadn't forgiven hir yet, but he would come round . . . At the centre of attention, dazzling newcomer Areeka Aziz (where's Rosamond now, eh?) interviewed Ax and Sage, in suitably anodyne style; for *Weal*, Chinese approved futuristic-Utopian zine. Sage was telling her that the lyrics for 'Winter Song' had come from a kiddies' talking book.

'*Tarka The Otter*, Henry Williamson, you got that?'

'Is it really about otters, or is that just the character's name?'

'Real otters.'

'Cool . . . ! Did it hurt *stupidly* when you had your Celtic tattoo done, Ax? My mum says the pain is so bad people faint. She says I'd throw up.'

Ax took the interviewer's hand, kindly and sorrowful. 'Areeka, someone has to break this to you. Your parents, well, they tell lies.'

'Your feet won't fall off if you wear spike heels, either,' added Dora.

'You'll just get bunions,' said Allie, reassuringly. 'They're nothing.'

Chinese mediapersons in spruce uniforms crowded eagerly around this nexus: pointing their gadgets. Fiorinda leaned over Cherry Dawkins' chair.

'Must say, you scrub up nicely, outlaws.'

Here we go. Into the unknown.

Rivers And Lakes

I

Coppola In A Cold Climate

The personnel carrier was a big bugger. It dwarfed the two men who walked around it, staring at the track housing, the gun turrets, the armoured decks fore and aft. Traces of amphibious tank design could be discerned, and some relation to the purple airships. Maybe it *was* one of the airships, morphed into ground-covering form. Or a module podded from one of them, who knows.

Ax watched the *di* of the track, stirring like water troubled by hidden springs. Nanotech has no off switch, only stable iteration; running on the spot. That's what the Luddites used to scream about pre-Crisis, when the grey goo was barely real. Now it's here, everything scary is still true, and it doesn't matter.

'There are five directions. North, South, East, West and Centre. It may be something they worked out *after* deciding five was vital for numerology reasons, but it makes sense, you know. Without a centre there are no directions.'

'And this is your argument for the fifth Commanding General?'

'One of them.'

'You think numerology is *important* to them, in the twenty-first century?'

The purple snake was comatose, like a python replete, but these things could move like the clappers if they wanted to, he'd seen it on tv. He wondered how long the journey would take. Half an hour? That would be good, better get it over with: and a damned fine change, after the mediaeval pace of the Reich-in-Hiding—

'Don't numbers, the meaning, the feel of them, matter intensely to you?'

'Well, yeah. But Ax, I'm a geek—'

'They're a nation of geeks. China is geek heaven. There's a centre, to make five directions, and a nominal extra season, between summer and autumn, to make five seasons, to go with the five elements and the five phases. When a new dynasty was established the emperor announced a tutelary season, tutelary element. The Great Peace has done the same, did you know? This a Winter, Water, régime.'

'Mm . . . But surely that's a package dreamed up, for a trifling few billion yuan, by a Hong Kong PR firm. It's not the truth about China.'

'It's what they choose to say about themselves, and that matters. Water's obvious. Winter is,' Ax frowned, '*modest*, strangely enough. Say this was an emperor, he's calling himself a forerunner. The new beginning will come after him. It was a very good thing Fiorinda did with the flowers.'

'She's a genius.'

'Yeah.'

It was the second week of January, and they were inside a Chinese fort planted on derelict London sports grounds; waiting for the off. The snow and ice had taken a break, the air was wet and chill, the strange vehicles in this parking bay were shrouded in grey dusk. They'd be heading for Peterborough in the dark at this rate. Possibly for security reasons: rumour said the actives avoided night attacks, as they had no night-sight tech (they only had rumour to go on, recalcitrants barely featured on Joyous Liberation News). Count your blessings. At least they wouldn't be making their first progress as megastar collaborators in the exposure of daylight—

'I can see why they have to erase immix,' said Sage. 'The connection with the so-called Neurobomb is damning. But can they make a total, clean sweep? The whole virtual movie industry, all the medical apps, bi-location phones? Of course I mean "pernicious neurological division"—'

'I don't see why not. The Great Peace Sphere is in full agreement with the ban, and no outside nation is going to argue with the Chinese Inspectors. They don't have to threaten intervention, the economic argument is enough. It happens all the time, Sage. Your dad's probably killed a good few big ideas, in his software baron career; without compunction, eh? And without the excuse they were direct from hell.'

'Hm.'

They took another turn up and down. They'd discovered by trial and error that they were not to leave the bay. 'Will you be able to get on with Norman?'

'Oooh, I think so. Aoxomoxoa has turned over a new leaf.'

It had become clear during the last fortnight that the Chinese were going to snub Sage at every turn. It was a trivial punishment, considering this was the man who *invented* immersion code, and had flirted at length with deluded neuroscience. But grass cuts can be a refined torture, when they never let up—

Playground bully tactics. The Chinese are expert at them.

'Don't let it get to you,' said Ax. 'They know what works, just take the medicine. We could try asking if you could be called Steve?'

Sage had ditched the cane rows and looked like himself again, except without the muscle bulk of long ago. Raindrops clung to the golden lamb's fleece; he smiled very sweetly. 'Nah, no worries. I won't let you down, Sah.'

'I know you won't . . . "Sage" is a big concept in Chinese thought,' said Ax. 'The ideal emperor is a sage, a gentle, wise and morally superior being: and they know of you as a notorious yob. They'll find out who you really are.'

'Hahaha.'

A gunner stared down from the narrow deck. The Englishmen glanced at each other. Everything we say is heard. We could be bugged with the most exquisite surveillance devices, but that doesn't mean every private soldier isn't observing and reporting on us. This is rehabilitation, it's not supposed to be fun.

'There's a five-year plan missing,' said Ax softly. 'Speaking of numerology. We should be on fourteen, but we're not. I should have paid more attention to the documents Wang showed me, there must have been an explanation . . . This isn't the twenty-first century, Sage. Or the fifteenth, either.'

'You're right. It's the year of 0-1.'

A soldier came up, saluted to Ax, made sure Sage copped a dissing glance, and ordered them back onboard. Maybe something was going to happen.

The cabin was austere. Two blocks of hard seats forward, two blocks aft; between them a bare floor space. Utility carpeting, a drinks machine in a bulkhead. There were no windows, the lighting was drab and diffuse. Fiorinda and Joe Muldur sat on the floor, playing gin-rummy. Norman was examining the classic revolutionary posters that were printed or programmed onto the curved, indigo walls. Toby Starborn, wrapped in a large faux-fur rug, occupied half the front row of aft seats. Personal baggage filled the rest. Ax took off his hat, but not his coat as the cabin was unheated: dug out a towel to rub the rain from Sage's curls, and caught Toby's faun's eyes fixed on this intimacy with smouldering contempt. If you're acting a part, Toby, under orders to needle us to death; you deserve an Oscar.

Sage had been taking a Chinese synthetic keloide, which had cleared up the pneumonia like magic. (Not magic, some other word!) Think of that, and a decent hospital for Fiorinda when her time comes; and ignore the pricks.

'Any idea how long before we set out, Norman?'

The impresario smiled enigmatically. 'None at all.'

Ten minutes later a group of Chinese arrived, in religious robes and close-fitting dark caps. They were ushered into the cabin by private soldiers who stowed their bags for them, saluted and departed to their own segment of the snake. Norman had a chat in Chinese with the woman who appeared to be the leader of the group: all smiles but out of earshot, at the far end of the cabin. The robed men smiled and bowed, Norman returned to the rockstar end, looking positively exalted.

'A Daoist nun and her missionaries,' he explained. 'They are *wonderful* people. They have a part to play in my drama, you'll see.'

The nun and the missionaries took their seats, facing inwards, and locked themselves into the crashbar cradles. Norman resumed his perusal of sugar-candy Communism, Fiorinda and Joe resumed their gin-rummy. Sage stretched on the floor propped on one elbow, flipping the pages of Fiorinda's tablet. After a while Ax realised with a lurch in his gut that the landship was in stealthy motion, without announcement, without a sound.

'How long's it going to take to get to Peterborough, Norman?'

'We should be there by morning.'

A lo-rez map on the drinks machine bulkhead showed their inchworm progress. Ax watched the icon until he felt watched, and turned to see the nun and her missionaries gazing at him placidly, attentively. Playground tactics. He went to join Sage.

'What are you up to, big cat?'

'Oh, I thought I'd work on that song idea of yours.'

'Which one?'

'You know, "The Day Before the Revolution"? Isn't that what you called it?'

'Mind if I join you?'

Fiorinda quit the gin-rummy tournament. Joe played patience: the rockstars worked, like model revolutionary artists. Ax had a tune, a bridge and some scraps of lyric. Sage, as was customary, had the design. A forward-looking anthem, and a return to our core message. The liferaft idea was never enough for the Reich. Utopians, looking to a better world beyond the great dying; let's get back to there. Yeah, we want bold endeavour against the odds, the way we were in the glory days.

Don't make it sound easy, make it *profound*. Stir them up.

Ax's title was swiftly dumped, but allowed to stay as the first couplet—

Always the day,
Before the Revolution

Sage's contribution next, *Always the wave/Before the one to take*—

'I feel surfie imagery is too laid-back,' said Fiorinda the scribe.

'Nah, you're wrong. This is English surfing, and it's wintertime too. We're bobbing up and down in the freezing cold, crying with frustration, yet consumed by longing. We *know* that wave will come, listen to the chords.'

'I want more frustration,' said Ax. 'It hones our will to succeed.'

Always the way/and never the solution—

'And then we open it to the universal—'

'Not yet, Fee, not yet. We need the verse to end with a twist on what's there already. There's a wave, think of something else that breaks—'

'How about *always on the* something *save/of a story that is bound to break?*'

Fiorinda and Sage shook their heads. 'Too vague, Ax. Meaningless.'

'Meaningless has to sound deep, this does not sound deep.'

'I'm bringing in a football metaphor.'

'Yeah, like *you* know the slightest thing about football, Ax dear.'

Norman fetched himself a paper cup of green tea and came to lie on the floor. The sleeves of one of his multicoloured robes protruded like flippers from the cuffs of his padded coat. 'Red four on black five, Joe. When were the glory days, by the way?'

'From the September of Ax's inauguration as dictator,' said Fiorinda crisply, 'To the November when he left to broker the Danube Dams question.'

'A little over two years. How poetically brief. What was it like?'

Fiorinda, crosslegged Tenniel chesspiece, looked up from the scratch of notes and words on her tablet. 'It was hopeful, Norman. Europe was in ferment, terrifying things were happening, floods and storms, crop failures, vast tracts of poisoned land, but it *felt hopeful*. Governments believed in us, it was exhilarating. Especially in Ax, because of the way he'd turned things in England around—'

Toby's eyes were on her, a new brand of stalksperience, more personal, more rancorous. What the hell are we supposed to do with him?

'And then the "Celtics" turned on you, because you had not come to terms with the four olds, as we Chinese have done. Although now you are friends again . . .' Norman winked at Ax. 'They give you cool tattoos.'

'The Scots gave me this,' corrected Ax, touching his knotwork. 'The Celtic Movement was something separate from the three "Celtic" nations. In the glory days it was a streetfight. Gangs of mad lads roaming around Bucharest, Berlin, Amsterdam. Look! There's a Utopian! Deck 'im. Then it got nasty.'

'The green nazis and their final solution, led by a vile, devilish English Countercultural cabal. Rufus O'Niall, horrible fellow, was involved somehow?'

'My father was in it up to his neck.'

Norman looked from one to another, big eyes round with respect. 'You know, it really is a *miracle* that the three of you are still alive.'

No comment seemed advisable. Ax cleared his throat. 'Okay, are we agreed on this, partners? *Always on the desperate save, of a story that is bound to break*—'

'No!' Fiorinda swooped on the tab, which Ax had stolen. 'That's STUPID.'

'How fascinating to watch the artistic struggle. What a privilege—'

'Yeah, watch and learn, Norman,' growled Ax. 'This is the way it works. Any suggestion of mine gets ripped to shreds, happens every time—'

'If that's what you call getting ripped to shreds, Ax,' remarked Joe, folding his failed solitaire and shuffling. 'It casts a new light on those screaming fights you used to have with Jordan, when you were fronting the Chosen Few.'

Ouch, a wrong step. Ax's brother Jordan was a hostage in the South West with the rest of the Preston family, non-person status; he should not be mentioned. The rehabilitees trembled. Sage's father was in London under house arrest, the rest of his family was untouched as yet. Fiorinda had no blood relatives in England. Her grandmother the witch had died – thank God – in her secure nursing home, in the last days of the Second Chamber régime. But the Few were hostage—

Norman merely looked interested. 'I thought you never wrote lyrics for the Chosen, Ax? Weren't Jordan and Milly the wordsmiths?'

'Great myths of the Reich,' explained Fiorinda, 'Ax never wrote the lyrics, no, he preferred to *rewrite* them. It used to drive Jordan nuts.'

The nun and her missionaries paid close attention, like people trying to follow a soap opera in a foreign language. The icon on the bulkhead screen was in Chigwell, moving imperceptibly, as if time had gone into reverse and they were back in gridlock days. Imagine a black January sleet out there, the rivers of scarlet and white edging on their clutches, probably a tailback right around the M25—

'Hahaha. I was going to say how impressed I was with the speed of your agreements . . . How about a recreational smoke, my rockstars?'

Joe, Ax, Sage and Fiorinda looked at each other. This was unexpected.

'If you're sure that would be okay,' said Ax, cautiously.

'Oh, of course. Other ranks are not permitted recreationals, but we artists have a dispensation. It's my own blend of crystal and bud, with a *tiny* smidge of fine tobacco, from a very good firm in HK. You'll love it.'

'I better ask the holy woman, she might object.'

Before Norman could demur, Ax crossed to the forward seats and ducked down beside the 'Daoist nun' to ask permission: *jie-jie,* would you mind if we smoked some cannabis? The woman's seamed, serene face opened in a cheerful smile. 'Go ahead.' Daoism was an approved religion: maybe she was a real nun, a famous mystic, it would be within Norman Soong's style. But her 'missionaries' had an air that made him think of Secret Service minders. A fugitive memory tugged at him, he had called her 'elder sister'; what did that recall—? Gone again.

Norman produced a beautiful smoking kit, and fussed with cutting and lighting a green-skinned cannabis cigar. Fiorinda accepted it, blew smoke rings and watched them rise, auditioning verbs for the stately movement of this ophidian. It does not slither, it does not slide or glide, it surges like rock, at sedimentary speed, stops for a few million years, oozed majestically onward—

'You need to be ripped to shreds, Ax,' said Norman. 'Stripped naked. A chastening *artistic* experience, to nurture your maturity as a wild music legend.'

Fiorinda and Sage got the giggles. Rockstar, maturity, not in same sentence.

'All the mature rockstars I know,' said Ax, 'are solid bourgeois.

Conservative views, rather odd clothes, worrying about their kids' education—'

'This isn't the twentieth century, Norman. Rock music's respectable.'

'To be a legend you have to be a bastard,' remarked Joe, laying his cards. 'It's not like "power corrupts", it's more like the only way it can happen. Like they're marked, ruthless and nasty from the get-go. Trust me, I'm a journalist. Okay, Dylan, the greatest of all time. Was he a good man? I don't think so. Ax is too nice.'

'You're embittered by your profession,' said Aoxomoxoa, grinning.

'Nobody's good,' said Fiorinda. 'Not the way you mean.'

Ax drew in a lungful of fragrant smoke and thought about it. 'I dunno, count my off-stage activities, I might scrape by as nasty. I've killed people, Joe—'

He looked down at his hands, these bloodstained hands. 'And not gangsta style, either. In cold blood, for reasons of state; does that make me not a bastard?'

'You've had to make shit decisions, you mean. Sorry, that *is* different.'

The conversation expanded, Tardislike, four people in the back of the tourbus, ranking the bastardy of legends, disputing the nature of good and evil . . . Norman Soong watched them, his full dark eyes intent. Toby lay on his back, buried under faux-fur; maybe he'd fallen asleep.

'One pill makes you larger,' crooned Joe, under his breath, 'one pill makes you small, and a hookah-smoking caterpillar, has given us the call—'

'Okay,' Sage rediscovered the tab, '*Always on the desperate save.* Terrible. Ah well, something better will come to us on stage. I'm gonna wipe this—'

Norman gasped in horror. 'Give that to me at once, Aoxomoxoa!'

'Wha's the matter? We never keep our rough notes, what for?'

Norman secured the tablet and curled himself protectively around it, fishing bits out of the trash, a coiled, multicoloured, inquisitive bolster of a being. 'This is really rather wonderful, this lyric in process. So full of restless negation. You are empty, you are raw. You are ready to face the naked onslaught of the masses—'

Toby Starborn sat up. 'I'd like to ask you wankers something. I'd like to know if you call that CRAP art? Or is it propaganda?'

'Propaganda isn't a bad word, Toby.' said Fiorinda, cut-crystal. 'It's what we do, always has been. Spreading the word. Art for a cause.'

'FUCK you all! FUCK your drivel!!! I can't stand you.' Toby shot to his feet, kicked his rug across the floor, and stormed out of the cabin.

There was a startled silence. 'What's wrong with *him*?' demanded Sage.

Norman glanced at the missionary party, tapped himself on the side of the head and beckoned his rockstars and his mediaman to come closer.

'This is off the record, it's not a suitable topic, but I think Toby's wound is bothering him. It's healing well, but there's bound to be discomfort.'

'His wound?' repeated Ax (for some reason flashing on mutilated bodies).

Norman winced, and rolled his eyes.

'Quietly, please! You see, Toby's had himself castrated.'

'Had himself *what*?' cried Joe. 'You mean, actually—?'

'Sssh, ssh! This *not* a suitable topic. Yes, the full meat and potatoes chop. He didn't want me to tell you, but it's affecting his mood. You'd better know, so you'll be tolerant, but don't tell him I told you, and don't, er, *comment.*'

'That's extreme,' said Ax, quietly. 'What inspired the body sculpture?'

'Ah.' The rock director pressed a large fist to his lips and gazed at them over his knuckles. 'I really . . . well, if I have to spell it out, you told me yourself Ax, Toby was a professed Pagan, and the favoured pet of the régime. He's also a genius. He was, shall we say he was offered a choice. He chose to live.'

Jee-sus.

Fiorinda felt the shock that went through the men like hot cheesewire.

'I'm supporting him,' said Norman. 'I've been through my own changes, as you know: I can help him to adjust. I arranged for him to join us, he may not do much work but his name will be on the credits, that's the main thing.' Norman got up, a flustered caterpillar. 'I *love* your dialogue, by the way. All of you. Natural, relaxed; a little daring. You know this game *backwards*. I'm delighted with you.' He flapped a hand at them. 'I must go after him. Remember, don't you say anything!'

Norman's rockstars and his mediaman resumed their conversation, their ability to act naturally under pressure somewhat dented.

Towards dawn Ax woke in the same diffuse light, his partners asleep beside him; a sleeping Joe Muldur, a motionless heap of faux-fur rug that was Toby. There were berths on the landship but they were for private soldiers. Norman had advised against them; unless you liked being buried alive. The nun and her missionaries slept in their crash-cradles, as if still waiting for lift-off. He tiptoed past them to the toilet, took a piss, rinsed his mouth; washed, and slipped out onto the deck. Flooded fields gleamed, shock heads of leafless trees. The escort vehicles had drawn close, their riding lights like the lights of flying saucers, hovering over the sodden landscape. There'd been no explanation for the inchworm pace, but he could see the reason for this halt. There was a firefight going on, ahead and to the left: to the west.

He was alone, the crew must be up front. He had the choice of facing east, or space for prostrations. He chose to face the sunrise, and prayed for protection and mercy: with a remembrance, as always, for the Saudi prince and his household in Charles Street; who'd given Ax refuge when he was in a very bad place. Ah, glory days. The English Caliphate, enlightened, benign, multicultural. Ax had never bought that dream, but he'd felt the tug of it . . . The slow, helpless journey had released him; like setting out for Yorkshire, long ago. What do I want out of life? Me, myself? He felt within him an untapped capacity for simple happiness, somewhere, somehow.

Automatic rifle fire rattled, a mortar shell boomed. He realised, with a shock, that there were other big vehicles standing around him, at a short distance; bearing no lights. What the fuck? Have we got half a division for an escort? Suppose that might explain why this is taking so fucking long—

Ax hadn't been able to get hold of any decent intelligence in London (he hadn't dared to try). Was it possible that the 2nd AMID army had completely lost control up here? They had swept from Asia to the gates of Bucharest like the Mongol hordes, but the only plan the PLA'd ever had for subduing an offshore island had involved Taiwan and they'd never tried it, Taiwan having joined the Sphere without a struggle. You have to trash the resistance *quickly*, Wang. Be brutal. Or this will go on for fucking ages, and you will *never, never* win the hearts and minds war.

Richard Kent's bewildered face took shape on the bruised darkness, and Cornelius, the fearless old man, at Ashdown; with that terrible look in his eyes. They'd been made to look like fools, but they knew the truth, they knew that Ax had changed his allegiance. He didn't want to drive the invaders into the sea. He wanted the Chinese to win. Hands down, and soon, and why isn't it happening?

Thank fuck I have foresworn the path of violence, he thought. At least I won't find myself accepting an imaginary rank in the Chinese army, just to get my hands on the wheel. He made his way around the flank of the amphib, and stood in shadow. Lieutenant Colonel Soong was in conference with his officers, their faces lit by orange stutters of fire. He couldn't make out the conversation, it wasn't *putonghua*: sounded like Cantonese, which was probably Norman's native dialect. An occasional word came clear. The taste of tobacco was in his mouth, an awakened craving he could have done without.

Norman spotted him. His big head loomed, stiff ringlets framed in the snood of his raincape. Ax glimpsed the puzzled, bear-like woman the rock director had been, and it made the man seem more human. 'Ax! You came out to see the fireworks. It's perfectly harmless, we're just having a rest break here.'

Ax nodded, though it was obvious they'd taken cover to keep out of trouble.

'You slept, I hope. How do you feel this morning?'

'Like an artist of the floating world. Norman, do you happen to have a common or garden old-fashioned cancer stick on you?'

'Hahaha. The nicotine urge! That's my fault! No, I won't corrupt you further. Let's go inside. There's not a scrap of danger, but the soldiers want us inside.'

At daybreak the passengers were on deck to see the white walls of Peterborough Fort, flashing in the midst of a steel-grey mere. Shards of rubble, slabs of tower block rose from the waters, where urban sprawl had been demolished; as was the Chinese policy around their major bases. The convoy turned aside and forged its way to a mudbank above the Nene's winter domain, and the Peace Tour disembarked. Norman had arranged private transport to their first venue. Their military escort unloaded a heap of crates, boxes and airline cases; the missionaries cheerfully lending a hand. The amphibs reversed, churning ochre-coloured foam, and headed for the fort.

The soldiers surrounded the boxes, clutching rifles, infectiously uneasy. The nun and her missionaries spread a plastic sheet and squatted on their heels. The mudbank was featureless, aside from a ragged metal placard on a pole, which bore a daub of something like a blue Noah's ark, and a number 15 in red. The rain had stopped, clouds were scudding; an icy breeze tugged their coats and set Fiorinda's curls whipping around her head. Toby hugged his fur rug and stared at the distant nano-tech wall, as if the tough love of the Chinese occupation would have suited him better than present company: Norman made a phone call. Presumably he had the deluxe service, without demons.

In general, the world must unite when it has been long divided—

The water bus arrived: a flat-bottomed boat without sail or engine, drawn by a two big work-horses, a bay and an iron-grey, harnessed in file; guided by a teenage boy; or maybe girl. The Chinese officers had an animated discussion with the rock director. It sounded as if they'd expected a much bigger craft. The Peace Tour embarked. The boxes, and most of the soldiers, stayed behind.

'Now then, who's got the travel warrant?' said the bus driver, a stubble-headed bruiser in perished neoprene shorts, dive shoes likewise and a National Express jacket.

'I do!' Norman proffered a slip of coloured plastic, a little nervously.

The bruiser looked it over, selected a spot and bit it. He winked at Ax. 'Mind you keep hold of that, Mr Soong. You'll need it if an inspector gets on.'

'Interesting start,' murmured Sage. 'We spend the night dodging firefights in slomo, then we take off for hostiles' territory minus most of our safety net. Do you know where we are, Ax? Have we crossed the Line yet?'

'I think we're on the A15. The horses seem to have hard standing.'

'Why do I keep hearing "The Ride of the Valkyrie"?' muttered Joe.

'Telepathy artefact,' said Fiorinda. Norman was gazing eastward into the breeze, the hood of his raincape tossed back, chin up in a mad, martial pose.

'I just hope he doesn't expect us to go surfing in these temperatures.'

Norman, the human camera (he had eye-socket tech, obviously) panned around slowly to face the four of them, his back to the horses. His gaze checked over the Gibson's hard case; glanced off Sage's visionboard, and grazed the tapestry bag that Fiorinda held on her knees. 'You look like children,' he remarked. 'Clutching the teddies you snatched from your burning house.'

'It would be cruel to part us from them,' said Ax. 'We're trying very hard to get better, but we still feel more like refugees than megastars.'

'I understand, and I won't snatch. I *want* your homeless vibe. You are the cultural icons of this refugee time. The most famous rockstars in the world, though hardly for your music – at least not at the moment, I'm going to change that. I want to combine, to *fuse* the naked, bereft humanity that I see with your immensely high profile. I won't take the teddies, but metaphorical bones may be broken, wounds torn open, it will be superb. You'll love what I make of you, I promise that.'

The refugee icons nodded, warily.

'The labour camps were established in the dictatorship?'

'Some of them,' said Fiorinda. 'We had a big problem with the people we call the drop-out hordes, the lost souls who gave up and took to the road—'

'Itinerant workers, ah yes, the global issue.'

'More like a redundant underclass. At first we moved them around, wherever gang labour was needed; which was mostly on the land. It wasn't sustainable. You can only do that with seasonal volunteers, who have lives to go back to. The drop-outs needed security, so the permanent camps went up. We tried to make them into communities, and claw back the children—'

'Under the neo-feudalists this became a system of reform through labour.'

The horses plunged into a deep pool. The teenage jockey whooped, the boat rocked, the draft animals became swimmers. Ax glanced behind him. A couple of small landing craft had left the fort, and were headed for the mudbank bus-stop. The soldiers and that mountain of boxes would travel less romantically.

'Nah,' said Fiorinda. 'The Second Chamber police state rounded up so-called political criminals, but not enough of them to change the mix. The camps are what they always were, the post-modern version of an institution called the workhouse. Containment for the people who can't, or won't, take care of themselves.'

'They are sheltered, they have useful work. It's a moral solution, enlightened capitalism. Why do you object?'

'I don't. I'm the one who set the camps up.'

'Oh,' said Norman, taken aback. 'I, ah, I didn't fully understand that.'

'I don't like the armed guards and locked gates, Norman. Policing doesn't have to be like that. And I objected very seriously to the Second Chamber idea that the homeless had become property; and could be sold into private ownership.'

'Hm. Well, this is supposed to be about the *music*, Fiorinda.'

'Sorry. It's been a hobby of mine, the last few years.'

The guitar-man and Aoxomoxoa, on either side of their lady, said nothing. But Norman could see why they were called the tiger and the wolf.

The whole countryside was under water. The route they followed was sometimes marked only by a double line of leafless hedgerow, bristling above the flood. They saw nothing moving except the squalling gulls that crossed overhead, beating away north to the Wash. Norman turned around again, and resumed his *Apocalypse Now* pose. The bus driver left his mate to handle the steering oar, and came and sat by Ax.

'Mr Preston?' he said quietly.

'Yeah?'

'The guys want to meet you, at Westberry, Sir.'

'Oh really? Which guys?'

The driver tugged on the gold hoop, traditional National Express décor, in his right ear; and jerked his head in Norman's direction. 'Don't worry about the luvvie. He knows bugger-all, an' he'll come to no harm, nor will the military. We know that would be fuckin' counter-productive.'

'What's your name?'

'Tucker. They call the jockey Frosty, she's my kid. Me mate's called Ed.'

'Tucker, tell your guys Ax is here strictly to win the peace.'

Tucker grinned, revealing a gold tooth to match the earring; a sign of considerable status. 'As long as we're winning. I like winning.'

'We'll win,' said Ax.

The white light was still with him. Some of the time.

The camp stood on an island above the flood, surrounded by the birch scrub that provided priming for their biomass generator. The last time the Triumvirate had visited here, the spiked stockade and the watch-towers had been new. They'd seen Auschwitz planted in the fens, and they'd been frightened. Today the gates were open, and a crowd had come to the landing stage. The campers – motley in Volunteer Initiative clothing supplies, virulent in Second Chamber-issue green overalls – waved homemade streamers, and cheered as the water bus came in. The teenage jockey pulled off her baseball cap, releasing a mass of hair white-blonde as a dandelion puff, sprang onto her hands on the grey's shoulders, and back-flipped to the ground.

The crowd hooted, the male warden took a swipe, yelling, 'Get out of it, Frosty, ye' pushy disrespectful—' He recollected his dignity, and bowed.

'Welcome to Warren Fen, Colonel Soong.'

'Delighted, delighted,' said Norman. 'You must be Warden Fisher, and this will be Madame Warden Flagg—'

'Commandants,' corrected Jack Fisher. 'We prefer commandants.

Wardens was what the Second Chamber fuckers called us, couldn't take a joke, that lot.'

Norman frowned. 'You are wardens. I don't appreciate ugly humour.'

'Right, of course sir,' said Hester Flagg, seeking the eyes of the Triumvirate; and ducked a little curtsey. 'An' we'll make sure the disruptive element stays out of shot, *we* know 'ow to do this. Now, where's our inductees?'

'Ooh, I'm not having that lanky yeller-hair,' exclaimed Jack. 'We know 'im, charge sheet a mile long, had 'im under me before. He's a right troublemaker—'

Cousin Caterpillar drew himself up, shocked. 'Aoxomoxoa *has already been an inmate?* I was not fully informed of this—!'

'It's okay, Norman,' said Sage. 'Jack's referring to very ancient history.'

The landing craft had caught up and the soldiers were unloading. The crowd made a rush, correctly identifying a bounty of Chinese aid supplies, and were repulsed with reversed rifles, panicky vigour. The Triumvirate saw this out of the corner of their eyes, and kept smiling. No shots fired, thank God—

'Oooh yeh. Long, *long* time ago, he used to come up here with the barmies. It was when we were burning out the monocultures: we lived on this isle, it were an eco-warrior camp then. We'd cook up a big tun of napalm, you know that stuff? Burns like fuck. An' this great tall mad rockstar lad was a pilot, on the crop-spraying.'

'Ah, you were rooting out the blight of western globalisation agribusiness, good, that's different. Did you say *napalm?* Hm . . . Oh, but I'm afraid Aoxomoxoa cannot have been a *pilot*, that's quite impossible—' An expression of pure panic assailed Norman's broad face, over the brink of a dreadful *faux pas*, unable to recover.

Sage came to the rescue. 'You're thinking of my hands, before I got them surgically fixed, in the glory days? Nyah, tha' was never as bad as I made out, I could do stuff. It was more of a metaphor, me cack-handed fuck-up, see—'

'Fuckin' shame. We uster love 'im for the ugly mitts, it made him one of us: screwed up, useless an' couldn't give a fuck. But they all sell out, rockstars, get their snaggle teeth fixed and fuck, the muckers.'

'Didn't know you cared, Jack.'

'We should get on,' said Ax. 'No offence, Norman, but I think your soldiers would be happier if we were inside.'

The boxes were piled on wind-up sleds, the crowd eagerly followed them. Norman stood gazing at the vast sky, the shining waters. '*Napalm*,' he murmured. 'What a scene that would make! We could CGI it, Aoxomoxoa has a flashback—'

Sage nodded. 'It's in *Rivermead*. Harry did a big sea of flame sequence.'

'Oh.'

The virtual movie about the Reich, by Harry Lopez, decadent Hollywood charlatan, was an item Norman could consign to the airbrush of history with no regrets at all. 'Please tell them not to script themselves,' he snapped. 'No unsolicited memoirs, no teenage acrobats; and no female staff *curtseying in boiler suits*. I'm not here as a talent scout, but I can see I'm going to have endless trouble.'

'I thought the curtsey was a neat satirical touch, me,' ventured Aoxomoxoa.

'You thought wrong. I am the director. Let's keep that in mind.'

Name: Axl Preston.
Address: None
Age: 34

Flying cams, a little buzzing team of them apiece, followed Ax and Sage through the induction process. Do the interview. Hand over possessions, strip, get deloused and shampooed, pick up your ragpaper gown, submit to the medical – including body cavity search. Measured, weighed; dental exam, finger and toenails tended, tested for addiction and transmittable disease, vaccinated; and biometrically tagged into the system. Issued with clean underwear and green overalls; Warren Fen wellies steam-heated to size on their feet. All this with Norman hopping around, framing his shots, crying *be more brutal, treat them the same as you would any lowlife vagrants* . . . (mortally offending the staff: who had been trained to be gentle, and wished to be depicted on their best behaviour).

It wasn't so bad.

When they came out the other side a silent, uneasy crowd had gathered, despite strict instructions to the contrary. The camp inmates did not know what to make of this stunt. Perhaps the invasion hadn't meant much to them, probably they had enjoyed the spectacle of the bad guys getting executed. But they weren't sure they should put up with this. Maybe they should do something? Make a protest, throw stones, give that Chinese wanker something to think about . . . ? 'Wander off,' shouted Sage. 'We're fine, it's make-believe, you're messing up the fucking video.' The people drifted away; the stars retreated to sit on a doorstep, between the end walls of two round-shouldered, turf-roofed housing blocks.

The murmur and shuffle at the end of their alley was like static from the past. The open spaces of the camps had always buzzed, especially in winter when gang-labour work was slack: but they suspected that Warren Fen was overcrowded. Maybe it was okay, just the camps representing security to the rural populace. Or not—

'Hey, detritus of history. How was it for you?'

'Hey, other detritus. I've been handled worse.'

'Me too,' said Sage, with feeling.

Ax shook his rings out of his baggie of personal items. Right hand, the carnelian seal Fiorinda had given him; left ring finger, Sage's Triumvirate ring. Thankfully, the manicurist had had the grace to spare his picking fingernails. He'd bummed a half-pack of cigarettes in the haemo clinic. He sparked up, and they passed the cancer stick between them, although Sage disliked tobacco.

'Glad it's not a slaphead camp.'

'Mm. Yeah.'

The induction had been an unexpected obstacle. They'd had to insist that Fiorinda must be excused: Ms Slater doesn't do nudity, and video-making in the female induction rooms is going to offend the Islamic community—

Norman had taken it fairly well. He seemed a little scared of Fiorinda.

They were supposed to be 'on a break', so they lowered their voices and never glanced at the flying cam which had tracked them; and was now watching them with its faceted eyes, an exotic insect perched on a breathable, wattle-and-daub wall. They were not afraid to be watched. They could channel the sight of Chinese soldiers rifle-butting English concentration camp workers, and look as chastened as Norman's dreams could desire . . . So far, so predictable. Don't ask if Norman's propaganda rock show, for global release, is *really* going to include the body-cavity probing.

We know what's going on. Speak to the audience.

'What d'you think was getting to the masses?'

'I suppose they thought we were being humiliated, somehow.'

'What about you? Do *you* feel as if you've been humiliated?'

'*No*,' said Ax, passionately. 'I do not! I think this is what we should have done ourselves. This is where we ought to have been last year, when we first knew how the Second Chamber were treating people. Instead of staging our fucking Lennonesque bed-in "labour camps protest"—'

Sage took a pull on the cigarette. 'No thanks, babe. The Chinese I b'lieve I trust. They make us take the medicine, but they mean us well. If we'd walked into one of these places in the bad guys' hands, we'd never have been seen again.' He lowered his voice further, soft and deep; deceptively carrying. 'D'you think we'll be able to do anything on the side? For Wang Xili?'

'Dunno. Mustn't push it. We'll make ourselves available, see what happens, follow any leads.' Ax shook his head, and half-laughed. 'I hope he likes the concerts. I'm not sure the General is convinced about rock music as the liturgy of history.'

'Hahaha, nor am I, Daddyo; nor am I.'

Fiorinda looked into the alley, and came and sat down. They stank of disinfectant, but she felt that morale was good, in spite of the telltale cigarette. Wound tight; but good. 'How did it go? Did you get tattooed?'

'Penned, not inked.' Ax turned his wrist, to show her his National Insurance number on the inside. 'We get inked at our monthly review; if our neighbours give us a good report. I knew mine,' he added proudly. 'Sage they had to track down.'

'Fuck off. Can I help it if I've never had a proper job?'

'I hope Norman understands it's only in jest. Some people find the English sense of humour *difficult* . . . The Second Chamber made these places hateful, but really Warren Fen's okay. Not at all like a nazi concentration camp.'

'They don't mean anything by it. What's happening now?'

'Norman and Joe and Toby skipped the showers, which I think is *disgraceful*. They're at the guesthouse, where our bags have been taken. The soldiers are guarding the loot. They have piled it in an outdoor market near here; I think that's a poor idea. The nun and her missionaries seem to be keeping an eye on the soldiers.' Fiorinda wrapped her arms around her knees. 'Ax, Sage, may I say, formally, I'm sorry I wimped out. I feel I've missed an opportunity. I should have done it.'

'No you shouldn't,' said Ax. 'Allow us to be the pin-ups, for once.'

'We are proud. We're definitely buying the tee-shirt.'

They laughed until they choked.

The relentless north-east wind of the fens had found their hiding place. It lapped them in raw, wet cold, fingering all their bones. Two little girls in short frocks with bare blueish legs scampered by; the smaller of them clutching the choke-chain of a large Alsatian dog. A woman in threadbare jeans, and a nylon puffa jacket sprouting down from every seam, came hurrying after them. She smiled uncertainly, hesitated and seemed about to speak: but she passed on.

'What do we do now?'

Ax mashed out the cigarette on the sole of his wellie, and pocketed the fag end. There was not a scrap of litter on the coloured-pebble paving of Warren Fen's alleys; let's keep it that way. Got to get some more of those, he thought. 'Touch base with Norman, then go walkabout. I've a feeling there's a lot of people in here who haven't been through the showers. Let's see if any of them will talk to us.'

Speaking Bitterness

Lieutenant Colonel Soong had rather liked the statement of the aid supplies, sitting out there in the open, protected by nothing more than Chinese prestige and a few honest common soldiers. But after a discussion with the Daoist nun he took Fiorinda's advice, and the loot was shoehorned into storage. Freed from guard duty, the soldiers went on a minor rampage; having spotted signs of delusion and even Counter-cultural belief. A lucky horseshoe was torn down, there were several incidents of corn dollies and dreamcatchers being ripped from front doors; and obsolete coins scooped from congealing water fountains. The officers were ordered to put a stop to it, while the Triumvirate made a swift appearance on the camp public address tv, saying the AMID soldiers were under their protection. Happily these measures seemed to work.

Hester and Jack reported that most of their security staff had vanished as soon as the invasion news broke, and it had been a good riddance. A lot of them had been right bastards, brought in by the Second Chamber régime. Warren Fen had been made an Open Access camp, as a result of the Paris Protest. They'd closed the gates at first to protect their charges, but they'd had to compromise, or they'd have been besieged. They'd replaced the guards by deputising useful inmates, but that was a problem too. You have to recruit the hard nuts, or they'll make trouble anyway—

They would not hazard a guess about the overcrowding. Everything had been upside down. They didn't know who was in the camp that shouldn't be.

'Long as they keep the peace,' Jack reasoned, 'we're better off ignoring them.'

Hester, cadaverous where Jack was lean, serious where her partner was chirpy, put it more directly; while avoiding the term 'actives'. 'We're forced into it, Sir. We're not *supporting* them. But we have to live here!'

Stel and Mackie might be thirty-five, maybe older. They'd never been hippies, no idea of nomad freedom. They'd just been in debt when the Crash came, failed to climb the slippery pole back to safety; ended up on the streets. So here they were in the learning resources common room, Badger Close, Westbery, Warren Fen: warm and dry, surrounded by the best in human culture, telling their tale of woe to a tall curly-headed blond, who used to be a scrapping, ugly-tempered drunk; a red-headed woman who was once a street kid, her baby dead, on the run from her abusive father; and a coloured lad from a Somerset sink estate, ex-soldier, hard bastard—

'They held me down,' said Mackie. He had lost an eye at some point, the empty socket gave him two faces: half death's head, half weather-beaten old lag. 'They beat me up and held me down, while they raped the wife.'

'I let them get on with it,' said Stella, 'in the hope they'd leave the kids alone.'

'Six of them. I dunno, six or ten.'

'But they didn't,' whispered Stella, bowing her head on her gnarled hands.

The neighbours, crowded round to hear the details again, freshly told in this august company, murmured in pity. *Bastards. It's th' Gaians, they hate families; breeders they call us. It's the yobs, the young men, they get hold of hard liquor and they revert to animals* . . . Mackie and Stella used to have five children, two of them together, three from other partners. Now they had three. Maybe nothing to do with the invasion, no reason, necessarily. Some campers are predators, that's all.

'You think these men were strangers, not inmates?' said Ax.

'I dunno,' whispered Stella. She looked suspiciously at the crowd, and decided on defiance. 'I know they weren't fucking Chinese, though. You can stick the fucking Resistance. It warn't any Chinky soldier that killed my little Fio.'

'What the hell do we want with a war?' drawled Sage. 'It makes no sense. Haven't we got enough trouble?'

Tucker the bus driver sat in the background, listening and saying nothing.

*

Fiorinda took a break. She found a toytown, miniature labour camp: turf mounds, communal spaces; the doe-eyed helpless creatures popping in and out of a multitude of little dark holes. At least the rabbits hadn't been trashed, good sign. She felt that Warren Fen was still functioning, just about. But there was trouble, they were harbouring suspect characters; and nobody would talk. What a life we all live, and there's no answer except to pay off the biggest bastards, and look as if you like it. Fuck, fuck. Helpless irrational hatred of Norman Soong and the Chinese soldiers—

Frosty Tucker the boat-bus jockey, sturdy young aristocrat of the waterlands, came up shyly and leaned on the fence. Her dandelion-puff hair, the colour of gilded silver, tumbled rich and loose in a drizzle that was turning to sleet. Frosty's hair was her delight, she wanted the living goddess to see it. She had a monkey face, whey skin and snot-coloured eyes, but fuck it, the hair was fantastic.

Bastards, bastards, bastards, muttered Fiorinda.

'Why don't you ill-look the bad lads, Miss? I wish you *would.*'

The Daoist nun, who had been strolling around, indulging her curiosity, had also followed Fiorinda. She waited, out of sight, to see how the rockstar would deal with this perilous and disgraceful suggestion.

'If I could, I'd be worse than them,' said Fiorinda. 'Wouldn't I? You don't want that. And other bastards would go on bashing babies' heads in, anyway.'

'I s'ppose. Two wrongs don't make a right.'

Well said, blue-skinned, jade-eyed child.

Dada daDA!
Dada daDA!

Some minutes into the stomping, hand-clapping start of the gig in Westberry Stadium, Norman Soong realised that he knew what the words, when they came, were going to be . . . He understood that he'd been gently *wound up*, as the English say. But he really couldn't blame himself. Who in the world outside England knew the Triumvirate's whole catalogue? It had often been *impossible* to get hold of their music.

The stadium was a roaring cave of darkness, the cantilevered rain canopies drawn together overhead, the precipitous tiers of seats packed. The only point of reference on stage was a tiny glowing core of red, the cigarette tucked into Ax Preston's guitar strings . . . No one had fully explained to Norman that the established camps had every provision for rock concerts. He had not believed Allie Marlowe when she said there was nothing to arrange; she'd ended (insolently) by failing to return his calls. The stars had been equally off-hand: now he understood. Westbury stadium was a temple of the Reich, the sacred machinery had rolled into action. There was nothing for Norman to do but sit in the director's box with the Peace Tour personnel, and his fractious, redundant artist-technicians; while the stadium's own flying cams, digital pick-ups, editing desk, ministered to his every need.

Lights. And there's Ax in his mulberry-red suit, Aoxomoxoa in a sweeping black-and-white kimono over white jeans and tee. Fiorinda wearing Chinese London's New Look, one of those hieratic, high-waisted tunics; in cloth-of-gold. Just the thing to delight the labour camp's feminine tendency, both female and male—

> *Always the way*
> *And never the solution—*

Always hearing 'bout that rising tide, roared the campers. But we're still stuck here UP THE CREEK! Joe grinned, shameless. Toby had presumably been in on the joke, but no point in nudging him, his mood was worse than ever.

The 'Daoist nun' and her missionaries made no remark.

> *Outside looking out*
> *Fate locked the door behind me*
> *Can't fit back in those old clothes*
> *I'm naked to the dream*
> *The road from truth to doubt*
> *Has led me on to blind me*
> *The freedom of the rose tree*
> *Is just a fitful gleam—*

The evening took a worthy, social enrichment turn, after that smashing start. Norman captured it all meticulously, paying special attention to the crowd, but nothing excited him. SWAMP MC were evidently the home favourites. They came on stage dressed in sacking, do-ragged heads and masked in white; and danced crouched down like potatoes. One of them had an arresting voice: it turned out to be the jockey from the bus, the girl with the silver hair—

No name
He had a sock over his head
No name
He said I'd soon wish I was dead
If I scream so I only cried
and then him rip me up inside
No name
Names are only for the free

Not exactly original. There was something tame and suburban about the whole line-up, this was not the raw and bleeding rock-flesh that Norman sought; not yet. But the Triumvirate, who had never been far away, returned with a generous set of Reich standards, very much what was needed; interspersed with what could only be called broad comedy. A gymnastic dance routine that collapsed, because Ax only had little legs . . . An episode where Fiorinda and Ax taught Sage to play guitar, which involved a very small man on a very tall stool, who came on to arrange a raspberry-pink Stratocaster around Aoxomoxoa's neck – and concluded with them playing a bravura 'Apache' together. The inmates found it all hilarious.

Highly commendable, thoroughly enjoyable, deeply mystic—

Ax, who had shed jacket and shirt during the 'how to be a guitar god' sketch, came loping forward, sweat gleaming on his copper-coloured, lean and chiselled torso, guitar slung low, hands above his head, slow-clapping back at the crowd. The lights caught the shine of his eyes, the spray of drops from flying wings of dark hair, and it was the last song, third encore, an old Jamaican reggae number (better known for the decadent Blondie version)—

The tide is high but I'm holding on
I'm going to be your number one
I'm not the kind of guy, who gives up just like that—

Norman saw the statement he had been brought to England to capture, and was suddenly, intensely moved. The rock revolution is complete, the rude boys have blown away the rhinestone cowboys, the docile profit-puppets. *This* is the truth about the music: one man, one figure, small on the wide stage, facing an ocean of humanity. One with them, inspiring them, because he is *the best of them*. Superb, patriotic, universal. He worked like a mad man, struggling to get it all down, seamless, before the light of actuality faded. The crowd was in a religious frenzy, even the soldiers in the director's box were on their feet, carried away, red-faced in delight—

What impressed Norman was that he knew it was not Ax Preston's ego he saw strutting there, singing his love song to the masses. The guitar-man keeps his formidable ego on another plane, he doesn't crave adulation. This was iron-willed humility, submission to the greater good. He is the father of his people.

Backstage in the communal dressing room, SWAMP MC were the only Warren Fen stars who'd had the courage to join the A-List party. They fell voraciously on the luxury snacks, and asked Fiorinda and Joe shy questions about Ashdown: which was their *Woodstock*, and they had missed it. The starvation, the danger, the mud—

'Only very picky people starved,' said Fiorinda.

'What was it like being on tour in Sussex?'

'Mental. Haywards Heath one night, Eastbourne the next.'

'Fuck. *We're* going to do a tour, all over Anglia, when we can get permits.'

The luxury snacks comprised a slab of reformed 'ham', turned out of its tin, glistening with yellow jelly, a dish of sundried tomatoes, artistically scattered with greying silverskin onions; a tin of withered chocolate biscuits, and a bowl of peach slices. An array of barrel-scrapings all too familiar to the founder of the Volunteer Initiative, but you have to feed the drop-out hordes on *something*. The alcohol was a jug of cloudy weak beer. No one touched it except Norman, who sipped crossly at a plastic beaker.

The great director had just discovered that when he'd arranged the onward transport – negotiated for him by the Unoccupied Zone Intelligence Office at Peterborough Fort – he had in fact hired SWAMP MC. They owned a 'gang' of fenland lighters, for which they had great dreams; but in the meantime it was a source of income. Norman was not pleased, he felt conspired upon by wannabes.

'It's too late to change my plans, but these tricks do not impress. I am not a talent scout. I need a crew for the boats, obviously, but *that's all*.'

'We have a floating studio and everything,' Frosty Tucker, young in hope, tried to talk it up. 'An' we know our way around, we'll deal with the tolls, and the accommodation. We can sleep on the boats if you like.'

'Never mind that, just tell me how long the trip will take?'

'About four or five days——?'

The tiger and the wolf, it was understood, had gone 'to see a man': camp code for a hole-in-the-wall serving illicit hard liquor. Norman hadn't commented on their defection: Fiorinda guessed he'd been briefed to pay no attention if the collaborators disappeared sometimes. But he seemed nervous, under the irritation. He was not so sublimely unaware of Warren's problems as he made out—

'Four or five *days*?' she repeated, suddenly noticing what was wrong with this sentence. 'What happened to Issit?'

They were supposed to be leaving Warren, tomorrow or the next day, heading for a camp called Issit Farm; further east, around twenty kilometres by water. It was private sector, a Second Chamber build, and likely to be a much rougher ride.

'Ah.' Norman frowned on her. 'There may have been a misunder-standing. Issit was no good, we need contrast. We're visiting Rainbow Bridge in Suffolk, instead; where the inmates have taken over. What could be better?' Cousin Caterpillar wore a fur-lined robe this evening, wide peacock-blue sleeves trimmed in scarlet. He spread his wings, metamorphosing into a plump-bodied butterfly, with a big-eyed death's head. 'Did I say the show tonight was *wonderful*? Pure pleasure! Wholesome entertainment, subtle, profound. I see it as a graduation.'

'I see it as Norman changing the subject.'

'Fiorinda, we will be perfectly safe. The Unoccupied Zone Intelligence Office assures me that there's no recalcitrant activity in the area we'll be crossing. We go in peace, we have been *invited*. The Executive Committee welcomed our overtures.'

'Rainbow Bridge?' exclaimed Joe, 'I didn't know there was a camp called *Rainbow Bridge*. A Hendrix-themed people-farm! Who the hell thought of that?'

'The campers,' Fiorinda told him, distracted. 'Camps start out with just a number, unless the place already has a name. The campers decide what to call them.'

'What a blast, wait 'til I get onto my editor—'

Norman glared. 'You will not "get on to your editor", Joe. I won't allow it.'

The Chinese artist-technicians sat in glum silence, in their military uniforms; each of them holding a paper cup of diluted orange con-centrate. Toby had not made an appearance after the show. 'What happened to the staff?' said Fiorinda. 'When the inmates took over. Did they join the wild rumpus?'

'More likely killed and eaten.'

One of the MCs had made himself a sandwich, two slices of pink meat enfolding a rich layer of dried tomato, peach slime and onions. He munched, uneasily. The Swamp kids looked from face to face, sensing conflict; like dogs trying to understand what's going on with the humans.

'That was a remark in poor taste, Joe. You know I don't like ugly humour. Fiorinda, I *told* you I would take you into the unknown. I expect your trust.'

Fiorinda and Joe made their excuses, leaving Norman to get down to business with the Swamp crew. They walked arm in arm to the guesthouse.

'Oooh, fuck,' breathed Joe. 'I'm going to make that call.'

'You won't get through.'

'Someone's got to know what's happening to us. This is insane.'

'The People's Liberation Army knows what's happening to us,' said Fiorinda. 'Isn't that enough for you? Joe, listen, for all we know, it's safer than Issit Farm.'

Joe was shaken beyond caution, although the air has ears. 'Norman says whatever comes into his head. I'll hook into the Warren callpoint frequency, I won't use an ID, how will they know to stop the call? Fiorinda, I have a bad feeling—'

She grinned at him, and kissed his cheek.

'Fear not. We *specified* we don't do cannibalism.'

'Live cockroaches?' asked Joe, with a shaky grin.

'Definitely nada. I always make sure there's a no cockroach clause.'

Tucker was waiting for Ax and Sage outside the stadium after the crowd had cleared. This was not the meeting with the Westberry 'guys' which he had promised Ax. This was a side-issue. He wanted to show them something, they knew no more than that; except that the bus driver, by his attitude, felt he was taking a very serious step. The rockstars wore their induction overalls, with anonymous parkas from the guesthouse cloakroom; hoods well down. 'Come on,' said Tucker. There'd been a curfew extension in honour of the concert, but no one lingered outdoors: they were alone in the alleys. About half a kilometre east of the stadium, between the sweeps of the watchtower searchlights, he let them into an access tunnel at the base of the stockade.

The tunnel was dimly lit by bulkhead lights; the slabs underfoot had a resilience that muffled sound.

'Why are you living at Warren, Mr Tucker?' said Ax. 'You're not a drop-out.'

'We live several places, Frosty an' me. Warren's a good gaff. Who wouldn't live here, as long as the gates are open? That's why it's stuffed.'

'What about the commandants?' asked Sage. 'Are they coping well?'

'You want my opinion? There'll be a warlord for every camp, and Jack Fisher's on his way. Don't trust him. Hester's awright, but she's sick, got some kind of malaria the vax doesn't catch an' it makes her weak. Don't trust her, either.'

'What happened to the guns? The security guards' armoury?'

A shrug. 'They took 'em. It's not important.'

Through the dull thud of their footsteps they could hear water rushing, somewhere below. Tucker stopped, and drew a breath.

'I'm comfortable on this side of the Line, Mr Preston.'

'I think I understand you.'

The man was plunged into dark doubt. Their maña felt paper thin. Almost certainly Tucker was armed, he could have friends close at hand, they could just vanish. He sighed, squatted down and peeled back one of the floor slabs to reveal an observation hatch: took a clutch of bent metal rods from inside his jacket, assembled the key, fitted the spider into place and tightened it.

'Give us a hand, it's a bugger to lift.'

The plate came up, they rolled it aside. 'Eight 'er ten grips to the east, on the bottom,' said Mr Tucker. 'See what you find. You decide to turn us in to the Chinese, well, fuck you. I'll get the keys back off yer tomorrow.' He pressed the access tunnel keycard into Ax's hand, and walked away.

Sage shone a pencil-light into the hole. There was a ladder, and a circle of black, moving water.

'Toss you for it.'

'Will I fuck. You just had pneumonia.'

'Walked around with pneumonia, doing fine. I'm fitter than you, and I dive.'

They tossed for it; with a ten p coin Ax kept as a souvenir. Sage won.

He stripped off, strapped an ATP flashlight his wrist, left Ax the pencil-light, and descended. A minute passed, by Ax's watch. Sage rose silently, gripping the ladder, a white seal with shadow eyes, a shadow mouth.

'Well?'

'Fuckingunbelievablycold, can'tseeathing, try again.'

Could be worse, could be sewage: can't smell it but it probably is dilute sewage when the floods are this high. Keep mouth shut. He discovered metal handholds screwed to the wall below water level, and now the instructions made sense. He counted, eight, nine: down, kick, touch a sharp corner, up again. The depth was about three metres, moving moderately fast. Down, grope, okay, yah, there's contraband in the drain. What the fuck's that mean? He leaned his forehead against the black, wet wall, thinking: and kicked back to the observation hatch. 'Ax, do you have a chisel, or a jemmy, or a heavy knife on you?'

'What'd you find?'

'Boxes, long and heavy. Arms cache, at a wild guess, long-term. You'd need two blokes and diving gear to get at them in a hurry, where they are now.'

'Okay, get out, and let's think how to handle it.'

'Wait. We know there's a Resistance cell at Warren, it's fucking obvious, if the *Chinese* don't know, it's because they've decided not to see. Tucker wants us to know something else. Maybe an oxyacetylene torch?'

'Oh, hey, I have got something—'

Ax pulled the hatch key apart. An arm of the spider was a squared bend of chisel-ended steel, about a centimetre thick. Sage took it down.

He tackled the job methodically: working the plate behind the hasp until the screws loosened, going up for air when he needed to. The current was a problem, but nothing he couldn't handle. Why'd you hand us this, Tucker? Big decision, and yet I felt you were recalcitrant to the bone. He shoved the lid up, and groped inside. What is it about these guns? He collected a trophy, and took it back.

No longer a lung-infected crock, practically ready for the decathlon, he hauled himself up the ladder, spat out the rifle bullet, handed it to Ax without a word, and began to scrub himself with the parka: desperate to be dry, to get some protection over his aching, freezing flesh.

'What denomination is that?'

'NATO.'

'Narrows it down, tuh. What kinda NATO? Is it old, is it new? Is it strange?'

'It's Russian, and it's brand-new.'

'That's bad news. Could it be from a garage sale?'

'The Feds will sell anything. But this is a box-fresh hollow-tipped 6.65mm RCAR round, cool designer ballistics, nano-guided stopping power, mashes up the enemy's insides a treat at 300 metres plus. It goes with the 2018 AK-74, which is still officially held to be a secret weapon.'

Sage finished scrubbing and dressing, gave up trying with the overall zip at half mast, and came to sit by Ax against the tunnel wall. He took the deadly little beauty clumsily in one hand, vivid pencil-light in the other, and confirmed Ax's report. The cold seemed to bite deeper, big blunt teeth clamped on his bones . . . Oooh shit. It's always the trouble you don't expect, then you see it was obvious. The Chinese have insurgents, the Feds will soon be along to help out.

'I know what this is,' said Ax. 'This is privateers. They're not working for the government of the Russian Federation, no, no, no. They just have access to the same weapons as the armed forces, what can you do, it's a grey market—'

'You got something against Russians, Ax?'

'No . . .' Ax slipped the bullet and torch into his pockets, and stared ahead of him, muscle knotted at his jaw. 'Nor personally, not really. How much down there?'

'I counted ten cases. No idea how many caches there are.'

'Or how long they've been here. Let's get the hatch back in place. I'm going to see Mr Tucker. Now.'

'*Hey!*'

'You have delusions of being my bodyguard, but you are not.' Ax fastened up that stubborn zip, ah, my big cat, owe you so much, wrecked your life and you never reproach me. 'Look, this is Warren Fen, model farm: we are with the fucking Chinese army. Tucker wants to talk, I know he does, the way he handled himself. I'll be fine, you are freezing to death, what will I do if you get sick again?'

'I s-should have let you do the diving.'

'Yeah, well, too late. Tell Fiorinda I'll be back really soon.'

He traced Mr Tucker without difficulty, at the drinking club to which he and Sage had been invited. The venue was in a learning resource centre: locked after curfew, but you knocked, and the night watchman let you in if you were okay. He knocked, he was admitted, and directed to the meeting room. The bus driver was there, with his mate Ed, and eight other men, no women. Ages from twentysomething to fiftysomething, ethnic origins, at a visual guess, Fenland, Pakistan, Afro-Caribbean and one Desperanto: all of them looking guilty as sin.

Ax took a glass of rot-gut, and told them what he thought of them.

He had a slight, dizzying idea of what this meant to the men sitting looking at him. He didn't know but he expected most of them had been in the stadium, and never underestimate the rock god effect, albeit reduced to family entertainment. They lived in Warren Fen, a house the Reich built, and here was Ax Preston, a pacifist Ax, but well able to talk the talk. You damned fools. You dog-stupid, pig-ignorant damned fools. And chapter and verse. But though he was calculating, from moment to moment he didn't give a fuck, he was angry enough to raise blisters on the air.

They were like children, so repentant they were distressed to the point of wet eyes, although as far as he could tell they were none of them drunk. Ax started to calm down, which meant he started to review what he'd just been saying: inevitably there were things he wished he hadn't, but fuck it, they won't remember, people don't, this kind of situation: and if they do, too bad. This was a job that had to be done. Rage leaving him, he told them he could see how resistance had seemed like the right option, in Anglia. They were naturally independent buggers, and all the camps were here. He didn't say a single positive word about the Chinese, he gave them only the idea that he might be able to negotiate a way out. No promises. Just hope. Another round of rot-gut was poured, this time in great relief of mind. The learning resource centre cat had been asleep on one of the chairs. It woke, stretched, stalked around, and came and curled itself on the skirt of Ax's parka.

The talk became dialogue, winding down to laughter. Ax was thinking that Anglia was a tinderbox full of cannon fodder. He could turn these men, they'd already made the wild leap of imagination it took to realise that the Feds were a BAD IDEA. But if the Triumvirate could do the same in every camp (and bearing in mind blokes like this will sing along with tears in their eyes, five minutes later they haven't a fuck of a clue what the song was), the task was *impossible*—

Swear to God, Ax, it was none of our doing.

We're small fry, we just knew the stuff was down there.

They told him things, no longer in a spirit of confession, that they thought he ought to know. As they'd thought he ought to know about the Russians . . . The cat's warm, impersonal presence was very comforting, like someone holding his hand, and he thought it was time to leave. He should leave now.

He said he would go, looked at the sleeping cat: transferred the contents of the parka's pockets to his overalls and shrugged out of it. Goodnights all round. Someone, not Tucker, escorted him to the doors of the building and keyed him out. He walked fast; eventually found himself leaning against a floor-length window, staring at a garden. Should I have got their names?; too bad. The sky was thick and starless but there were nightlights among the shrubs. He could see the guesthouse, across a lawn where mature trees had been preserved. Someone was walking towards him, a figure that seemed familiar, but puzzling. It was the Daoist nun. She carried a small lantern, a glowing red cylinder on a string or a chain. She saw him, and came over.

'We are breaking curfew, Mr Preston. A winter garden is beautiful at night, I intended to explain I was not planning to leave this courtyard. What's your excuse?'

'Drinking club.' It was hard to keep his teeth from chattering.

'Good heavens, where's your coat? It's freezing out here.'

'Left it indoors, *jiejie*,' said Ax, making a futile attempt to turn up the collar of the overalls. 'I had to do a bit of theatre in there, over something. There was a cat, it had fallen asleep on my coat, I c-couldn't disturb it, wrong message.'

Maybe he was making assumptions, speaking to her like that, but he'd seen the way she related to Norman (and the heavy glow of those 'missionaries'). Whoever she was, she was not out of the loop. Anyway he felt like cutting the crap. You know who I am, I'm a collaborator, renegade native, working for your side.

'Ah.' The nun laughed, softly. 'What shall we call this situation, where a tiger becomes a rat-catcher, and a wolf is forced to retrain as a sheepdog?'

'Civilisation.' Ax took out his crumpled cigarettes, 'Er, do you mind?'

'Yes I do,' she said, sternly. 'Cannabis is medicine for the spirit, those things are pure poison. Goodnight, friend Mohammad; peace and blessings.'

He smoked half a fag, defiantly, letting her get out of the way, and returned to the room in the guesthouse. It was warm in there. Fiorinda

129

and Sage sat in lamplight, on the wide bed. She was holding Sage's crooked hands to her breast to warm them, a very ancient gesture. He joined them, and pushed the hair back from his temples. Their room was spacious and simple, gold-stained bentwood furniture and willow-pattern hangings, walls in grey and cloudy green. Was it listening?

'Can we talk, is it okay?'

'We can talk,' said Sage. 'Fuck it, this is our house.'

Surveillance is a metal bar in your mouth, it gets existential, you can *never* relax. You can bear it, but you just have to let yourself off sometimes—

'What happened?' breathed Fiorinda.

'I told them they were damned fools, and they agreed with me. Turns out Tucker wasn't acting on his own, the cell was with him. The arms caches have been here for months, intended for an offensive against the Second Chamber. They're campers, not good at dates, but definitely long before the invasion.'

'*Fuck.*'

'Yeah . . . Seems like the Chinese interrupted other plans. That's the easy part. They told me something else. Richard and Corny didn't like it when they found out about the Feds. They've been court-martialled, and condemned to die slow. They're being held in a coffin-cell, in a place called Rainbow Bridge.'

He had the feeling that he had been away from them, further than the day he'd gone to Reading. Where was I just now? I was out of their arms. He wanted to say *where's Min?* But Min was in London, staying with Sage's dad, along with Marlon. And Silver and Pearl with the Few. Another little world broken—

He looked up, wondering why they seemed to be struck dumb.

'It's a camp in Suffolk. I'd never heard of it. But you have?'

'Rainbow Bridge is where Norman is taking us next,' said Fiorinda.

Ax was struck dumb himself. 'What happened to Issit Farm?' he asked at last.

'We don't know, but Rainbow Bridge has a health certificate from the Unoccupied Zone Intelligence Office. There's no recalcitrant activity there.'

'Oh, really? Same as Warren Fen had none?'

'There's a wild party going on,' said Fiorinda. 'The lunatics have taken over the asylum, Norman thinks it sounds *wonderful.*'

If two gangsters come offering protection, which of them do you pay off? Simple arithmetic. But leave aside the overwhelming might of China, they were Crisis Europeans. They feared the Russian Feds worse than the plague.

'You think we should report to Norman?' asked Sage.

Ax shook his head. He had a handle on the Peace Tour now, he thought he understood it. 'Norman would like us to believe he's making this up as he goes along; but he can't be. He has orders to take us to Rainbow Bridge. I'm guessing that means the Unoccupied Intelligence Office has the place filed as another Warren Fen: a marginal seat where the actives, or sympathisers, will talk, and we can make a difference—'

Ax took out the rifle bullet, and examined it thoughtfully. Fiorinda and Sage had been afraid he wouldn't be able to stand the level of surveillance. He had a horror of *always being watched* that dated from the year he'd spent as a hostage in the jungle. But since he'd come back from that trip to Reading Ax had been more like Ax they'd known in Dissolution Summer, who had convinced them the impossible was possible. Tonight he was the old Ax, completely: cool and certain, eyes on the prize.

'No, we don't report. This is where we stop being collaborators, and start working for the common good on our own terms. The guns are real, the rest could be a fairytale. Let's say nothing, go to Rainbow Bridge, and see what we find.'

Norman sent for them twice, around midnight. He was looking at his rushes and would value their opinion. They returned their apologies.

II

The Water Margin

Norman's personal orderly rapped on their door before light, and brusquely told them to prepare for an early start. They breakfasted with Joe in the guesthouse dining room: hemp-seed cereal, shrivelled blackberries and rehydrated skim milk, dried tomatoes and the rolled patties of rabbit-mince known as 'campy eggs'; dandelion coffee. Around ten, Norman appeared in a seedy dressing gown, hungover. He announced he was off to have a bath, and to get his hair dressed.

'My bowels,' he complained, 'are behaving very strangely.'

The Triumvirate retired under the covers, leaving Joe to fend for himself. Fiorinda could not get online (surprise!), but she found Rainbow Bridge in her cached VI registry. Founded in Fergal Kearney's reign, built in an out of town shopping centre, associated with a defunct village called Eyot. Named by the inmates, who had a reputation as party animals, in camp-world. On the Waveney, moated, hard to reach in winter except by water or helicopter, twenty klicks or so from the Suffolk coast—

'Ouch. That's a *long* way from here, in modern money.'

'Wonder how they'll get us there if the waterways freeze?'

The tablet screen glimmered in their cave of blankets: they noticed that Sage had withdrawn from the discussion and lay curled on his side, brooding.

'Are you okay, big cat?'

'I'm fine. What if this turns violent on us? Do we have a policy on that?'

Now that's a question . . .

'I'll pick up a weapon,' said Ax at last. 'If I have to, in self-defence.'

'So will I,' said Fiorinda. 'I'll defend little shoot with lethal force.'

'Thank God for that,' said the bodhisattva. 'Tha's a relief to my mind.'

'D'you want to get sorted *now*, maestro?'

'Nah, that would be dumb. Wait 'til war's declared. We are *so fucked* if we're caught with weapons by our mentors. Jus' wanted to know.' He hugged Fiorinda, arms and legs, attack of the giant cave spider: 'How long do we have to go on calling this baby Shoot, my brat? Ain't you afraid a handle like that might warp a child?'

'It's a small green thing, growing.'

'*Green?* Oooh, that'll cause comment around the font.'

'If you're determined not to commit yourself as to sex,' reasoned Ax—

'Although we know you know,' said the spider, nibbling her throat.

'Fuck off, I *do not* know.'

'Well, anyway,' said Ax. 'What's wrong with Jocelyn? Or Hilary, or Esmé?'

'You think you're so funny. Listen, it's MY baby and—'

Sage let her go. Both warm bodies retired, Fiorinda was left abandoned.

'I didn't mean that.'

'That's okay,' said Ax, distantly. 'I know where I stand.'

'Me, I've never been in any doubt.'

Ouch, fuck. Fiorinda trembled, terrified.

'I didn't mean it, I didn't mean it, you know I didn't, please, please—'

'Hahaha.'

'Heeheehee.'

'You bastards!'

Someone knocked. Sage went to open the door. A real soldier, not Norman's orderly, stood there. 'A call for Mr Preston,' he announced in English.

'Well, do come in.'

The soldier, junior lieutenant by his insignia, marched smartly into the room, laid a tablet in a slipcase on a small table, saluted, and marched back to the corridor.

Ax took the slipcase over to the windows, noting the protocol. He couldn't have anything placed into his hands by an inferior; we're getting very formal.

'Ah, Mr Preston,' cried General Wang. It was a different office, not the one in Reading: might be Whitehall. 'I wanted to consult you about my free range sheep farming. This is surely wrong. Wouldn't the animals be *happier* in cosy barns?' Inscrutable as fuck.

'General Wang, I'm not the expert. I'm repeating what I've been told in Select Committee. Soil fertility in the south and west of England has been strained past recovery, the sheep are muck-carts; they may win us back some arable, at the moment they're the best use of the land. I know it's hard to recognise local expertise. Africa and India are littered with fine-tuned farming and drainage systems wrecked by the British, meaning no harm, just convinced they were in Norfolk—'

'Ah yes. Your little loess belt, the fertile bulge. The east *must be* recovered, or England will starve. This becomes very clear to me.'

'It's very clear to me, too. Since you ask, General, we're doing fine but I'm not sure it's a safe idea to go over to Suffolk.'

'Nonsense. Recalcitrant activity is on the Line, not in the hinterland. We are watching over you, rest assured. At the least sign of trouble we'll have you back in Peterborough in half an hour.'

'I'm glad to hear it. But—'

'It's out of my hands, Ax. Ah, a call waiting. I must take this, excuse me.'

Blank screen. Ax returned the tablet to its slipcase and set it down: the lieutenant recovered it and departed. Sage and Fiorinda were staring at him—

'Shit,' he said. 'I didn't get onto the climate change crop shifting.'

It was two in the afternoon when they were summoned to the street. In a chill drizzle, soldiers were piling baggage onto the wind-up motor sleds, and arranging photogenic inmates for a happy farewell. Other soldiers, out of shot, held a rabble at bay; Toby Starborn stood aloof, hugging his fur. 'My God!' howled Norman. 'There you are! This is intolerable! Where's Joe? We should have been away by first light!'

It was petty, maybe, but a rockstar moment seemed called for.

'Excuse me. Remembered something I have to do.'

Mr Preston glanced at his partners in apology, and strolled away.

He found the learning resource centre, couldn't remember how to find the drinking club venue. He chose a door labelled 'book library', and walked into a big, quiet room. A group of primary-age kids were muttering; around a table scattered with paper and coloured pens. Grown-ups in a row, plugged into the Warren Fen datasphere (hey, no fair, that's not *books*—). Older children browsed the stacks or sat reading.

And there was the black cat, curled on a chair. He squatted down to stroke it, looking around at the battered paperbacks, coffee-table remainders, musty bindings (the Volunteer Initiative's not proud); feeling the presence of a lonely little girl for whom books had been a refuge. Fiorinda made this haven.

'Can I help you, Mr Preston?' The learning resources manager had come out from behind her counter and was hovering beside him.

'Er, yeah. What's the cat's name?'

She bent for a careful look. 'That's Monty. His brother Winston will be around somewhere: they're both so black it's quite hard to tell them apart.'

Ah well. Winston or Monty, thanks. One of you did me a good turn.

The cat tucked its paw tighter over its nose. The woman, neither old nor young, waited there smiling. Something in her stance brought a puzzle to the front of his mind: *jiejie*. When Ax was at Reading, right at the end of that ordeal he'd heard Wang speak to Lieutenant Chu, the young aide de camp, calling her *jiejie*. The sliver of memory, lost and found, tugged at him unaccountably. Was that a joke? A convoluted family relationship that put her in a senior generation? Who does Wang Xili, Marshal of China, address as 'elder sister'?

'Is there anything else, Mr Preston?'

'No; no, thank you. You, er, you're doing very good work here.'

'I hope we can continue,' she said, biting her lip. 'I'm proud of our library.'

The lighters, linked together bowsprit and stern by rattling chains, made their departure from Warren Fen Quay an hour before dark; with four members of the Swamp MC as crew and native guides. Swamp's bright-painted gang of five lead the way. The gang Swamp had hired for the military escort followed behind. The night was cold, uncomfortable, but not too bad. There were hooped shelters, that could be raised like tents over the open boats. The Triumvirate and Joe bunked together, Norman and Toby had secured a boat to themselves. Pity the soldiers, their boats were working freighters: no provision for passenger comfort.

Over breakfast there were transports of fury, as Norman finally grasped that the journey of a hundred or so klicks was going to take days. This had not been fully explained! It wasn't in the least *obvious*! Joe Muldur's phone call villainy was revisited, and the Triumvirate's intolerable, insolent delay; but the kids got the worst. By noon they'd reached the Great Ouse basin, and the tow-horses had to swim for quite a distance: Norman, vengeful, refused to believe they could be taken onboard.

At the first dry halt Swamp MC jumped out and strapped rope around the braking posts, without waiting for permission. The gang jostled to a standstill: there were yells of panic from the PLA, coming up too fast behind—

Not much harm done. Fenland's lighters, river barges with sail and oar, modern take on an ancient design, were built for rough treatment. Fiorinda decided to stretch her legs, while the collision was post-mortemed. The river was higher than the flooded land, water on both levels; an eerie effect. Water over water, that's *K'an*, *K'an*, The Abyssal. What does the superior man (huh!) do in this situation? Something poetic and unintelligible . . . Large soft flakes of snow began to fall, vanishing when they touched. Frosty and her best mate (not boyfriend), a very hench black lad called Nel, former street kid from Nottingham, had also escaped, they were giving the horses a feed and a rub-down beside the halt-hut.

Rusty, the bay who pulled the soldiers, was a working stiff from Warren's horse labour pool. The iron-grey mare, known as Gator, belonged to Frosty; or at least, she *would* be Frosty's in a year or two, when Frosty's dad had finished paying for her. Not untrammelled property, since Frosty was not free, but good enough, and a much more reliable earner than the boats. She was the kids' pride and joy; money in the bank, liquidity on the hoof.

'Is she okay?'

'She shun'ter had to swim that far,' muttered Nel, eyes down.

'Miss.' Frosty was anxious to unburden her mind. 'We *did* tell him. We told Cyril Mao from the Unintelligence Office, an' we told Colonel Soong. We said four days, minimum. They *paid* for four days, in advance. It don't make sense!'

'People hear what they want to hear,' said Fiorinda, soothingly. 'It must be linked to a survival trait, because everybody does it, all the time.'

'Uhuh.' Frosty stared at a line of sails that moved along another waterway in the distance, pale brown winter butterflies. Silver-gilt hair escaped like froth from her parka hood. 'I'm getting out of this. I don't believe in God, I swear by *you*, Miss. I'm getting out of the camps, an' out of fenland, it's a dump. No one's going to speak to me like that. I'll have respect.'

(Maybe you should think twice about the music biz, kid—)

'Never mind, he was really yelling at himself, not you. Hang your head and say very sorry, it's the Chinese version of smile and nod.'

Nel removed the feedbag and rubbed Gator behind the ears, almost cracking a smile, not sure he was allowed to laugh at a joke against the conquerors.

They were too young to have spotted that Norman had been furious because he was scared. The flooded emptiness was intimidating, health certificate or not. Read between the lines, it's the insurgents who dictate the terms for things like this Peace Tour, and Norman knows it. That's got to be hard on the nerves.

She looked up into the falling snow. 'Hey, what if it freezes hard?'

'It won't. The thaw's good for another week, my dad says.'

Nel rolled his eyes. 'Your dad don't know. It'll be okay, Miss. Mr Colonel Soong will send for a landship. I mean, this is for a video, innit? It's not *real*.'

Along a straight cut on the Little Ouse, Gator plodded the towpath, steady on the beat. Nel walked by her head, Frosty slouched astride, singing to herself, bare blue sections of leg swinging, between her baggy shorts and her wellies. Loryan, the oldest of the kids, maybe seventeen, stood in the bows of the lead boat with a long oar, which she occasionally poked at the bank or into the water, apparently at random. The nun and her missionaries sat up front, as of right, enjoying the marshy vistas. Sage and Fiorinda were taking turns to steer: the top job, and they were proud.

'What's that one?'

Fiorinda had the bird book, a veteran of their travels.

'Common reed bunting.'

'You're kidding, it's blatantly a cock sparrow, 'cept it can sing.'

'It says here sparrows *are* reed buntings, country boy. That went to town.'

A flight of ducks rose from the reeds with a superb rush of wings and a violent burst of quacking. One of the monks looked round, beaming, to share the pleasure; his pleasant face ageless under the dark cap, with the earflaps like turned-up wings. They had never been known to speak English; they rarely seemed to speak at all. Fiorinda and Sage beamed and nodded back.

*

Swamp MC bunked in the lead boat, Toby and Norman in the second; Toby had hardly been seen. They insisted on keeping their shelter up day and night, which was a grievance with the kids. If Gator had to pull harder she ate more, and spoiled her audit for the trip. The crude expedient of cooking the work-horse's logbook had not occurred to the kids, and God forbid Ax Preston should suggest it. The third boat belonged to Joe and the Triumvirate, also used as daytime common room. Joe and Bone, the fourth Swamp MC, were in there, feet up, eyeless, locked in some virtual game of blood-spattered hide and seek. Hey, c'mon, lads. Here we are surrounded by Mother Nature . . . He let them be. The tail boat was where the missionaries bunked; if they ever slept. The fourth was the one with the cabin conversion. The Daoist nun shared it with the Tour's baggage.

Ax ducked inside, and looked around. The low-roofed space was painted in peach and blue, glass windows along the sides above cushioned lockers. The famous 'floating studio' was choked off by Norman's airline cases: an old Behringer mixer, a cannibalised Conjurmac; other components worn to anonymity or homemade . . . A curtain concealed the nun's private quarters. He counted off the company in his head, making sure he knew where they all were. Why was he here? To see what he could find out . . . Who is she? Why is she with us, and what's her relationship to our Norman? Face and hands are readily disguised by tech: gait and silhouette not so much—

He drew back the curtain. The space beyond held a neatly rolled sleeping bag, and a small rug, smaller than a prayer rug, laid in front of a camphor-wood travelling desk; that had been set on one of Norman's cases. The desk was antique, eighteenth century? The rug was a work of art. A slipcased tablet lay where the blotter would have been on a European desk. It looked familiar. The nun was also a calligrapher. A fine inkstone stood by the tablet: a brush case inlaid with flying birds and 'reed writing' in silver, a jade brush rest; and several sticks of vermilion ink. Ax looked at these things from where he stood, getting a strong intuition that he should take this no further.

He let the curtain drop.

Back in the third boat the game had broken up. Bone had gone away: Ax sat down by Joe, who was staring gloomily at the passing reeds.

'Hey,' said Ax. 'Did any of the monks take notice, when I was out of sight?'

'No,' said Joe. 'They're in the front. What have you been up to?'

'Spying on our masters.'

'Fuck!' Joe thrust his hands into his hair, so it stood up in greasy brown spurs. 'Are you crazy! We're already between the devil and fuck—!' The mediaman went pink. 'Uh, shit, sorry Ax. I, um, didn't mean to speak out of turn.'

'It's okay. I got scared and decided not to bother.'

Doorflaps of their shelter tightly laced, the Triumvirate held a birthday celebration, having banished Joe to sleep with Norman and Toby for a change. They presented Ax with a mink-lined parka, loving gift from Warren Fen; and a willow-weaving from the children, appliquéd with animals and birds. Sage gave him a little hare, carved from a hazel root (in Chinese astrology the big cat was a rabbit; or hare). Fiorinda gave him an amber and gold dragon, no bigger than the first joint of her thumb. It was ancient, Inner Asian, and undoubtedly plunder. (The battered streets of London were littered with plunder-sellers; how else do you spend your Chinese pocket money?) They dreamed they were in Sage's cottage in Cornwall, a fire burning low in the hearth, sweet lost things. 'One day it'll happen,' said Fiorinda, darkly. 'There'll be no more hell dimension. We'll settle down to live happily ever after, and we'll *really* fall apart.' The baby seemed to be trampling itself a clearing in the forest of her belly. 'Will somebody please, please take a piss for me?' The brutes would not stir, though Sage sleepily offered to fetch the pot into bed. Eech, I have my standards.

She crept out wearing Ax's jumper, touched the visionboard, touched the Gibson's case, clutched a handful of her bag to feel the saltbox. Ah, civilised values, a pisspot with a lid . . . Out there in the cold, a glimmer attracted her. She groped to the doorflaps and made a peephole. One of the missionaries was sitting outside their shelter, serene bulwark against a frieze of burning stars. He seemed to be reading a scroll, by means of a tiny light fastened next to his eye. Maybe that was a Chinese martial arts telepathy headset. Wonder what kind of weapons they keep under those robes? What if Ax is right, about who they are and why they're here? What the fuck would that imply?

The monk turned and looked her way: his head was Ax's head, a long dead Ax, with a hole in his dry skull. *Nonsense*, murmured Fiorinda, and crept back to the warm burrow. The inside world invades the outside; so what, I'm not impressed.

*

They passed through the broken road bridge on the A10, left the empty quarter and entered a populated countryside above the floods; where ordinary people were trying to live normal lives, and the Chinese invasion was a distant disaster. Swamp MC divided themselves between the gangs. The passengers and the military stayed out of sight: the soldiers crouched like potatoes under stretched tarps, Peace Tour personnel barricaded behind boxes in the night shelters. Norman handed over wads of money, and bitched about it. The Triumvirate reminisced about Volunteer Initiative labour on managed rivers like the Little Ouse; the waterways rescued from neglect. The Flood Countries Conference. The great sea defence works of David Sale's government, embattled by Gaians who wanted nature to take its course . . . Brandon and Thetford were traversed, with no worse trouble than a few free enterprise 'checkpoints'. At Rushford junction they joined the Redgrave Cut, another Reich Years project, the missing link in the all-England navigable network. Ah, glory days.

Maybe the Chinese listeners were impressed. The Swamp kids, when they popped in for a warm, were indifferent. They lived in the world of now, where water was the normal way to travel, ten klicks an hour was racy, and energy audit was the unalterable law. 'Did you know,' said Nel, importantly, 'we're comin' up to a weird place where, when you get close to it, Diss appears.'

By the fourth nightfall they had reached the Waveney River. The kids strapped the lighters to the dead stumps in a stand of alders, made the horses comfortable as possible, and consulted earnestly with Chin, the pilot of the soldiers' gang. They had only a few words of common language, but he was a river man. Their almanac for distances, times, tides and marks had no entries for Rainbow Bridge, though the camp was there on the map. Norman and Toby hid in their shelter to eat delicacies (it was presumed). The rest of the company, including those monks, messed on ancient tinned food, heated up and served with sweet black tea: almost relaxed with each other in the camaraderie of the shared epic.

Sage went out to stretch his legs, not an idle expression on this trip. The long hours of being squashed like a bug in that shelter had driven him nuts. In the gleam of light from the boats he saw Toby, with his fur rug, crouched on a shelf of roots above the water. He would have retreated, not to intrude on a desolate privacy, but the attraction between the unlucky genius and the river was palpable. He went down and hunkered on his heels under the tree. I'm sorry, he thought, and I don't pretend I can help, but right now it would be fucking awkward if you went over the side.

'Hey, Toby.'

Toby looked round. 'What do you want?'

'Nothing, really. Mind if I join you?'

'I don't know why I'm here,' whispered Toby, his profile traced by the polished blackness of the water. 'Immix is all I lived for, I should have died.'

'You don't need immix. You can still be a digital artist, tha's not banned.'

'Fuck off. What do *you* know?'

You're absolutely right, thought Sage. He stayed where he was, however, offering a couple more inane gambits, until Toby grasped that he was not going to be left alone with his thoughts, gathered his rug around him and returned to the boats.

In the middle of the night, or so it seemed, Swamp MC were shaking everyone awake. No, bad guys had not arrived. The tide was about to turn, with a breeze off the land. There was a free ride! The kids' urgency infected even Norman and Toby. Shelters were stowed, belongings secured, space cleared for the horses. Masts were shipped, tackle freed, lanterns hoisted; snowflakes blundered like moths into the light. Gator was led on board, and undertook the manoeuvre with calm. The bay resisted, soldiers hauling and yelling at him in Cantonese and *putonghua* that he surely didn't want to be left behind; he gave way in the end. Frosty cast off, Nel steered for midstream, the kids and Sage raised the square sails in the first two lighters; the soldiers were doing the same. A red sun rose in an ochre sky, scattering the veil of snow. Suddenly the river was alive, no longer passive as asphalt. They flew along, maybe breaking the ten klicks barrier, in a cacophony of rollicking chains.

Rationally it wasn't much of a return for the upheaval and the loss of sleep, emotionally it was a fine charge—

'Do they know how to stop?'

Norman was hopping at Ax's shoulder in the lead boat: hands tucked into his cuffs, the scarf wrapped round his raincape snood giving him a head the size of a pumpkin. 'What?' yelled Ax. 'Nah, the only way to put the brake on these things is by leaping onto the bank and hauling backwards, haven't you noticed?'

'But, but what are we going to do? We've passed the marker!'

'What marker?'

'*There it is!* There's another one! We'll miss the creek!'

Someone had installed a sign by the side of the Waveney: a hoop of coloured bands rising high above the reeds. Ax laughed. 'Far out, man! I don't know. I've no idea, Norman. You better talk to your native guides.'

Swamp MC had spotted the rainbows. Loryan galloped to the back of the gang, waving and yelling at the soldiers, some distance behind. The sails tumbled, Nel swung the lead boat broadside, Bone and Frosty raced up and down, clearing the thwarts like hurdlers, fending off.

The teenagers raised a cheer when the turn was made. The boats kept on moving fast, there was a current. The landscape had blurred into white. 'How far is it along?' shouted Frosty. 'Where can we strap, what do we do?'

Norman shook his pumpkin head.

'Oh, shit, there's a lock, the gates are open, fuck, it's a fucking *weir!*'

The lead boat tipped and fell as if it was falling over the edge of the world.

Nothing to do but fling yourself down and hold on, praying that nothing precious had been left loose in that pre-dawn scramble. A thundering, elephantine, white-water rafting moment, and they had survived. Shadow fell across them, the soldiers' gang poured down the weir: engulfing them, the boats sloshing with icy water, dismasted, fouling each other. The lower level of the creek was a fast-moving drain, and right ahead this drain was rushing under a raised barrier in a wall of concrete. They barely had time to register a painted rainbow, springing from cloud to cloud, or the merry welcome message looping over it: MAY CONTAIN NUTS. Darkness engulfed them. A clangour of metal and the light behind was cut off.

Haha!

HAHAHAHA!

Giant laughter grew and echoed, disembodied faces bobbed about, luminous green and orange, flickering red eyes and mouths. Lights leapt up, big blazing white electric lamps that had to cost a fortune. They were in a channel cut through the floor of a blood-stained concrete cave: set with pillars, decorated with faded numerals. Ax took hold of his Gibson, and caught Sage and Fiorinda doing the same, getting a grip on the household gods. He glanced towards the tunnel entrance, yeah, the barrier had been dropped into place.

Monks, rockstars, teenagers stared at each other.

Masked revellers, directed by roars from a loudhailer, gaffed Swamp's lighters to the side. Chin's gang had not been so lucky. They had two boats capsized, the other two in confusion; soldiers struggling in the water. But the crowd was all over the Peace Tour, there was nothing they could do for their escort. 'Thank you all!' cried Norman. 'What a wonderful entrance, superb, we thoroughly enjoyed the whole thing. Let's all calm down, *briefly*—' His attitude was a credit to him, but it was far too late. The mad crowd seemed friendly, but they were in charge. Gator was led off, despite Frosty's frantic protests. Boxes and cases were tossed from hand to hand and vanished. The last that Norman's company saw of their soldiers, a huge character in a scarlet tutu, leather gaiters and a gimp mask was taking a fire-axe to Chin's bowsprit chains, his strokes guided by a screaming, giggling posse of gauze-winged fairies.

Rainbow Bridge Q&A

Where is the Arena?
The Arena's on the top floor

You get on stage naked or not at all.
You will NOT be sky-clad, decorations will be worn
If your décor looks like clothing you won't get on.
If you aren't stupidly cool you won't get on.
If you don't go on stage you are nothing.
Nobody will listen, nobody will believe in you.

Sage and Fiorinda had left Ax and Norman negotiating over the fate of the soldiers, changed into rockstar finery and were checking out the populace. Rainbow Bridge, if this floor was anything to go by, was more crowded than Warren Fen; and the campers liked to be out and about, in their bedraggled indoor world. The stars edged through a *Dawn of the Dead* crowd: flashing smiles, fielding personal questions, pressing flesh, signing anything thrust at them; mainly anatomy. The advertising hadn't lied, it was permanent party time. Fiorinda's cloth-of-gold, Sage's sharp suit, half-hidden under winter coats, were matched by jumble sale pizzazz on every side: lurid feather boas and glitter bodypaint. Codpieces, penis gourds, tasselled pasties; ghoulish adornment for slack flesh and booze-scoured faces. Somehow it didn't help that the temple of consumerism had been ruthlessly knocked out of shape, the wide malls overwhelmed by clumsy partitioning, the acres of plate glass vanished. The floor was sticky and thick with evil wastes, the chill, stuffy air smelled of a defeated municipal swimming pool: disinfectant, faeces and urine.

You had to be glad there were very few kids around. Unless there was some really hideous reason for that . . .

'It's functional,' said Fiorinda, thinking positive. 'They have light and power. And they don't seem to be starving. I wonder how they're supplied.'

The Chinese military authorities had been co-operating with the Volunteer Initiative to get basic provisions to the state camps. But Rainbow Bridge had been private sector, and it was a long way from the Occupied Zone.

'I could hazard a guess . . . How were they supposed to support themselves, I mean originally? What did they do?'

'Nothing much. My father didn't expect his camps to be viable, remember.'

They had reached a food court. They bought black tea at the counter, found a table, and looked at the flyer that had been handed to them, very earnestly, by a sagging Miss Whiplash. They couldn't figure out what it meant. All they could do was stare at the drop-out hordes problem, in its intractable ugliness. So many people, millions of them, over the whole of Europe; who had fallen out of the world in the Economic Crash came, and could not find their way back. Scholars of these years compared the phenomenon to the scourge of the Black Death. Utterly different from the tides of flight, south to north, east to west, the drop-outs weren't struggling, they were lost. No nation wanted them, no state needed them, there was no teat of cheap food and finery for them to suck at anymore; and maybe never would be again. No model of recovery had the surplus coming back.

Warren Fen seemed like Toytown from this vantage.

The tea was sweet and foul. Nihilism rose up, hard to resist. 'Maybe this is what *we* looked like to the suits,' mused Fiorinda, 'back in Dissolution Summer, when we were running around trashing fast food joints, hooked on rebellion.'

'You could be right.'

'At last I understand why they were *scared* of us.' She smiled for the faces, the eager hungry faces, the demons she couldn't feed, doomed hecatombs of them. 'You know what I'm thinking, Sage? Why the fuck did we stop him?'

'Yeah,' said the bodhisattva, with a grin worthy of the living skull. 'We should have just let Rufus get on with it.'

who would have thought death had undone so many . . .

Joe Muldur appeared, seeming like an optical illusion, as if all the faces that stare at you so avidly start to look familiar. 'My oh my, you two look cheerful.' He joined them, dragging up a chair. The food court was stuffed, but Sage and Fiorinda were getting respect, they had space. 'What a place . . . I met an old-timer who told me it's never been right. It's built on an old native graveyard, you know.'

'Could be true,' said Fiorinda, remembering the plans in the registry file. 'There's a village buried under here. What's happening upstairs?'

'Sorting out accommodation. You three have a suite, the nun and monks have a suite; the soldiers have detention. So, it was worth bringing them, after all. They've distracted the bad guys, while our *real* muscle floated by on a cloud of incense . . . I'm happy, because I get a single. You three won't be able to force me to bunk with Norman and Toby whenever you, er, have something private to discuss.'

'Hahaha.' Sage frowned, remembering his exchange with Toby under the alder trees. 'How *was* that, Joe? Did anything strange happen?'

Joe burrowed his hands into his pockets and shuddered. 'If you mean did either of them make a pass, no. Sleeping with Norman and Toby, okay, the breakdown. Toby lies staring at the wall. Toby mutters, and stares at the wall. Sometimes he cries, more like whimpers, like a sick baby, and that's *grim*.' Joe reflected. 'Grimmer for Toby, of course, poor bastard.'

Fiorinda tried her tea again: still disgusting. 'What does Norman do?'

'He snores like a pig: well, you knew that . . . Stares at me, for no reason, for ages. Takes off his dress nails and uses them to poke wax out of his ears. Bites his real nails. Fiddles with his rushes: meaning he stares into space, watching eye-socket tv, and talks to himself. Asks me Reich pop quiz questions, hard ones that prove Chinese superiority. Like, who was the Chosen Few's little-known first drummer?'

'That's a trick question, there's only ever been Milly.'

Milly Kettle, long ago Ax's girlfriend, now married to Ax's brother Jordan, had been a founder member of the Chosen Few.

'Wrong, there was a lad called Rafayel Sticking. According to Norman.'

'False,' said Sage. 'Ray was the drummer with Mulan, when Ax was their guitarist, before the Chosen Few existed.'

'Okay, next time *you* can sleep with Norman.'

If truth be known, Joe had found sharing with the Triumvirate intensely reassuring. Just being near Sage and Fiorinda, talking bullshit, made him feel he might get out of this alive. Pride barely kept him from clinging to their coats.

'Oh, shit, I forgot. You're wanted, I was sent to fetch you. We have to drink 'shroom tea in the Executive Bar now. It's a symbol of good faith.'

The Executive Bar was on the sixth floor. Lights were low, acres of murky purple carpet disappeared into the beery shadows; oil-film colours squirmed on the white backdrop of a disused stage. The lunatics who had taken over the asylum slouched in booths, or relaxed at their ease on bean bags around knee-high tables. Young women in homemade Playmate outfits carried trays: one of them welcomed the new arrivals and led the way, her cottontail jaunty in the gloom.

No attempt at concealment. The Executive Committee and their cronies wore traditional dress, and displayed their weapons, guns and knives and exotics, like body décor. The ambient music was Aoxomoxoa and the Heads' proscribed early immix album, *Bleeding Heart*. Presumably they'd have been running the immix itself, if their sound and vision system hadn't been so crap. It was like walking into a room full of dead men, the slaughtered corpses of Reading campground, up on their legs and haunting a dirty old drinking hole; oblivious, defiant.

Lieutenant Colonel Soong, splendidly robed, sat beside Mr Preston in the midst of this den of iniquity. He was holding it together, but barely. His fright mask aureole seemed to be standing on end of its own accord.

'Ah!' he cried, waving his vivid wings. 'The hero and the diva! And our mediaman! Isn't this a *wonderful* place? So bold, so wild. Aren't you glad I brought you here? I'm *humbled* by the ideas these crazy people have—'

The hippy war chiefs thumped their glasses, grinning like mad dogs.

'Time warp,' muttered Sage to Ax, as he folded down.

'Yeah,' murmured Ax. 'Still don't know what the fuck's going on—'

They'd walked into scenes like this in Yorkshire, long ago, and survived. But they'd had novelty value then. Rockstar maña wasn't going to help them here.

'Let me introduce Gola, Sage,' said Ax, dryly: indicating a big man, slaphead, many piercings, lardy and pale, as if he rarely saw sunlight. 'The Anglian chief exec.'

Gola nodded across the table, stone-faced, through the wreaths of smoke.

'Harvey of course you know.'

'Hi,' said Sage. He was looking at one of Richard Kent's chiefs-of-staff, baby-faced, dreadlocked; mixed record in action, immensely high opinion of himself. There would be other familiar faces: he didn't look, he didn't want to know.

'How's it going, Harve?'

'It's goin' great,' Harve reported, expressionless. 'Fuckin' *perfect*.'

'The two of them are sharing power,' said Ax.

A Playmate knelt by Sage's side, brave bunny ears a little worn, fishnets with a run in one knee. 'Wha'th your poi'on, Fage?' lisped Gola. 'Or are yu off the boothe, your holineth?' He bared a ragged gap where he'd lost his front teeth.

'I'll take vodka,' said Sage.

The girl smiled shyly. 'I'm Eve, I'm your bunny. I'm so incredibly honoured to meet you guys. May I bring you something, Fiorinda?'

'Thanks, a Manhattan. And a glass of water.'

Fiorinda had left her coat in the suite. She shone like golden armour between her bodyguards, and Norman was *staring* at her. What are *you* looking at? thought Sage. Yer big overdressed luvvie, we're doin' our best . . . Norman caught his eye, and quickly wiped an expression of dawning consternation—

The Playmate took herself off; Gola and Harvey stood. 'Okay, Colonel Soong,' said Harvey. 'We'll take this from here, got things to discuss with our performers. Thanx for bringing these great artists along, on yer noble mission of intercultural understanding. The drinks'll come to the meeting table, superstars.'

Gola surged over the table and secured Norman's hand, before the Colonel could stop him: a condescending whale, in an embroidered kaftan and ammo belts. 'The girlth will look after you an' your boyfriendth. Wha'ever you wan', yuth athk.'

Joe seemed to be waiting with resignation for the wrecks to fall on him and start chomping. Toby watched the oil-film colours; very small without his rug.

'I suppose I'm to make the Manhattan vanish?' murmured Sage as they followed the new leaders of the Resistance; henchpersons closing up behind.

'Please. Ax is in a Muslim mood, I can tell.'

'Damn right I am. I need all the gravitas I can get.'

'Gagh, fucking disgusting drink. This is a hazard they don't tell you about—'

'Sorry. First thing that came into my head.'

They wondered if Ax could do a miracle, if the strange vibe they were getting could be some insane version of repentance; if Corny and Richard were still alive . . . In the depths of the bar, deep in the shadows, blood-red and bright blue candles had been lit along a table set with rows of chairs. The party animals stood up.

They hadn't been seen since that bizarre reception. The armed hippies had taken over, the revellers had disappeared, somewhere in that confusion. 'We *knew* you'd come to us,' announced a middle-aged woman with a stream of tangled dark hair and a raddled, handsome face. She wore a short gown that left her ample breasts bare, Grecian sandals and dog-collar of iron thorns; she glowed with exaltation.

'There's a condition,' said one of her companions, drag artiste; nervously. 'The Chinese Colonel Minder does not sit at the negotiating table with us, he doesn't have to be in our face. Can it work like that?'

'That's fine,' said Ax. 'That's just how Colonel Soong wants to play it.'

So the Triumvirate sat down with the two factions, hawks and doves, as if in their glory days, and heard the peace plan Rainbow Bridge had devised for Anglia; while the might of China waited across the room, in the person of fright-wigged Cousin Caterpillar. The hawks were not happy, but the party animals had come up with an offer that the Counterculture could not refuse—

'I have no idea what's going on,' announced Norman, when his rockstars returned, looking drained but smiling. 'I create situations, I created *this* situation, then I relinquish all control. There's a fascinating *edge* to Rainbow Bridge, isn't there?'

Sage grinned. 'You could say so.'

The mad dogs looked as if they'd been having fun. Cousin Caterpillar flapped his hands. 'We've heard all about the show! We've been talking it up over here, it's profound. Superb! You'll be headlining, of course, and we'll need to see the set-up, the stage, the lighting, later, when I've digested—' He tapped the side of his head significantly, 'digested the raw material in here, silkworm that I—'

Ax reached over and tapped the other side of Norman's head, none too gently. The hippies roared with laughter, the caterpillar reared up indignant; met a wry warning in Mr Preston's pretty eyes and controlled himself.

'I said I *digest*,' he muttered to Toby. 'The raw material. Why not?'

But Toby was staring at Fiorinda; between horror and utmost reverence.

The party animals had left after the conference; to them this bar was hostile territory. Fiorinda stayed a while; then made her excuses. The hospitality was just beginning. The tea-tray arrived. Eve the Playmate handed fragrant china cups; brought a tray full of bottles that had Stoly on the label and went to sit beside Joe Muldur. Conversation became antic, ebullient, spiced with the threat of violence; increasingly difficult to follow. . . . Some unmeasured time later Norman, Toby, Ax and Sage were alone. Joe had left with the bunny, the Counterculturals had vanished into the undergrowth of this snakepit wonderland. The teapot was empty, the level in the vodka bottles was low; one of Norman's dynamite smokes lay forgotten in an ashtray.

'I really don't *understand* recalcitrance,' confided Norman. 'What have they to lose? The nasty dreadlocks? Surgical removal of decayed Nirvana tees? I really *don't* understand recalcitrance . . . We will have to stiffen each other's hair, Toby, as my orderly is in detention. I'm sure nobody here knows how to do the liondog style. It will take years to train them. Shall we call them the Weird Stripes?'

'The Wavy Gravys?' suggested Ax. 'I find the colours have mulched down.'

Toby laughed until he cried. 'I didn't do it! I did not paste the paste. No Dead Seas were injured in planting the worms around my head.'

'We think you've made yourselves into *taotie* devils.' Ax rolled his eyes, puffed his cheeks and stuck out his tongue.

'Yeah,' Sage confirmed this, cackling. 'Devil-masks to ward the demons off.'

'Plenty of demons about.'

Toby wriggled on his cushion. 'Sage, I've been taking snapshot. What do you think of that, Sage? What do you think of that?'

'You mean Aoxomoxoa. I think we should put you in the teapot.'

'Don't you want to know where I got it?'

Sage laughed, and flashed Norman a jolt of wide-eyed menace. The reformed Aoxomoxoa had seemed such a gentle giant, it was a shock.

'In the teapot, dormouse. Head first, if you don't shut up.'

'DON'T YOU WANT TO KNOW?' shouted Toby.

'Who the fuck cares how you got ripped off, talc-snorting fan-boy?'

Snapshot was the nickname of the neurosteroid cocktail used in the Zen Self experiment, vilely implicated in the pernicious delusion. Anyone suspected of using, supplying or manufacturing the drug was liable to death by dismemberment, and the Chinese were not kidding.

'Oh yes,' Toby's amber eyes blinked rapidly, he ground his teeth and rubbed his hands along his thighs. 'Call me a fake. *They* gave me the snapshot, fuck you. I have filleted the wounds and bones of infinity, they want to know where my genius comes from so they sent me to hell. I've been to hell.'

Ax lifted the blunt from the ashtray, lit it, and tucked it into Toby's mouth. 'Now stop talking and breathe deep. Suck it down. That's right, and again.'

Toby took a long sick pull, but he couldn't let go. 'You can't bear to think I can take it and you can't anymore, that's your problem, oh bodhisattva. I had so much I'm an addict. I'm addicted, I'm gonna get some more and I know where.'

'Toby,' said Sage, 'you've been taking acid, you arsehole. Or ketamine.'

'Hell is ordinary,' said Toby, staring at him. 'This is hell, where I am now.'

The cigar took effect and he fell off his beanbag. They coaxed him to his feet – whereupon he vomited copiously, nothing this carpet hadn't seen before – and half-carried, half walked him to the VIP accommodation. Joe was not at home; Fiorinda had gone to bed. Three of the teenagers were still up, watching ancient videos. Nel seemed like a competent drug-related first-aider: they left Toby in his care. Outside the rooms Norman stared, pop-eyed, at the tiger and the wolf.

'I must to speak to Fiorinda! It is imperative I speak to her *now*.'

'You can't,' said Sage. 'Not possible. Sorry.'

'Let's go for a walk,' suggested Ax. 'Clear our heads.'

They found an emergency exit, hit the bar and walked out onto a flat roof dusted with new snow. A storm of clucking greeted them: there was a tarred chicken shed in a wire run. The sky was clear, the tattered scarf of the Milky Way flung across the zenith. Sage and Norman walked around with their heads tipped back, staring at the firefolk. Ax went to the edge to survey Rainbow Bridge by starlight: lesser buildings joined to this by walkways, frosted market garden tunnels. He wondered about swimming the moat. At last the stargazers came to join him: Norman brushed the snow aside and sat down. The tiger and the wolf just folded.

'Fiorinda is pregnant,' said Norman, in a tone of apocalyptic doom.

Ax chuckled. Sage drew up his long legs, giant grasshopper, and grinned at Norman sidelong. 'Maybe she just doesn't care for mushroom tea.'

'She's *pregnant*. My God, I don't know how I didn't see it before.'

They sighed, gazed into space, and offered no further prevarication.

'How – how far along is she?'

'We're not rock-solid on dates,' admitted Ax. 'Say twenty-two weeks?'

'*Twenty two weeks!* That's—' Norman's lips moved. 'Five and a half *months!*'

'Well done.'

Norman passed a trembling hand over his aureole. 'This was, this was never fully explained to me!'

'For once, Norman,' remarked Sage, dreamily, 'you have a right to say that.'

'My God. My God! But why wasn't I told? Why was it kept secret?'

'I don't know that it's been kept *secret*.' Ax thought about it. 'Her personal friends know, her doctor knows, our families know. We haven't yet made a public announcement, we're not ready for that.'

Norman scowled. 'That is not an answer! Please be serious!'

They glanced at each other. 'When we first knew, we didn't want the Second Chamber to find out,' said Ax. 'Since then, there's never been a good moment. Can you accept that? It's the truth. You know Fiorinda's history, it's a sensitive topic.'

'Oh God, I see. The poor brave girl. I do see.'

He wanted to ask them which was the father, but he felt inhibited.

'I think you're the one who's got some explaining to do,' said Sage, mildly. 'It looks as if your Unoccupied Intelligence missed a few points about Rainbow Bridge.'

Norman put his head in his hands, his dress nails spiking up like caterpillar horns. 'My God!' he moaned. 'I have *never* been so shocked. The Countercultural dress. Right in front of me! The weapons! Unbelievable! Shameless! It was all I could do to behave naturally.' He wiped his face, trembling. 'The situation must be a very recent development . . . *Of course* we had to venture into places where you three could encounter rebel sympathisers, and reach hearts and minds through constructive dialogue. I *expected* you would find sympathisers here. But this is unthinkable!'

Sage moved to the offensive. 'Yeah but you knew the rules in Rainbow Bridge Arena, didn't you? Don't bother, we know you did. "Naked" has been your favourite word since we left Hackney. You're asking us why Fiorinda didn't tell you she was pregnant? Why didn't *you* tell us what kind of gig this was? Why didn't you bring it up when Fiorinda specified no nudity, fer fuck's sake? You signed something, hm?'

'I DID NOT KNOW!' howled Norman.

'Calm down,' suggested Ax. 'You'll fall off the roof.'

'I had no idea. I envisaged nakedness in a pure way, the ultimate honesty!'

'Oh really?' said Ax. 'How original of you. I usually like to keep my socks on. I get fuckin' cold feet on those nude photo shoots. Leave it out, Norman.'

'I was plunging you into the unknown! Artists make conditions, I say yes then later I get them to do what I want, because they trust me. She's the punk-diva wild child of the rock and roll revolution. I had *not* fully understood what happens in the Arena here, I had no reason to think Fiorinda would not, would not come round—'

'You don't know her very well,' said Sage, staring ahead of him.

'You cannot deny that we created something wonderful at Warren Fen! You refused to view the rushes, I didn't understand that, but already I know I have a huge global hit, a masterpiece. I have been *good* for you!'

'Yeah,' said Ax, bitterly. 'Right.'

'But this is all nonsense,' Norman drew a breath: terribly defeated, shattered to the core, staring into a dreadful abyss. 'This is over. We have to get out of here, we must leave at once—'

'And how are we going to achieve that?' wondered Ax. 'Shoot our way out?'

'Of course not! I'll send for a ship, it will be here immediately. But if there were any interference with us,' Norman hesitated, looked from one to the other. 'This is classified, please, but as you may have realised, we're not entirely defenceless.'

Sage grinned. 'Yeah, we spotted that. Carn' say I like the numerical odds.'

'Norman,' Ax began, in a different tone, 'it won't do. If we pull out that means total loss of face for this mission.' Cousin Caterpillar shuddered and nodded, head bowed. 'That would be bad for us, same as for you. You Chinese believed in us, we're out here, we want the Peace Tour to be a success. We're prepared to do the gig, what do you say? To you it sounds grotesque, but it would win plenty hearts and minds in the camps. What do you *really* want to happen, right now?'

The rock director wrapped his robe closer around him. 'Why did you hit me, Ax? In front of those appalling hoodlums! I have an eye-socket cam, why shouldn't I allude to it? The so-called Committee invited me here, they knew I would be recording. It was negotiated.'

(You don't know the half of it, Norman.) 'You're here to record the show in the Arena, that doesn't mean they want you making a secret video in their council chamber. They may not have read the small print.'
. . .

'Very well, I accept your apology,' said Norman, stiffly.

They had reached a level of sobriety where the night seemed two-dimensional.

'Tell me one thing. Are they—?' Norman hesitated, afraid his fear would be evident in his voice, 'are they *Celtics*?'

'Nothing like,' said Ax. 'Anglians are a different brand. More like *Danes*.'

'Oh, I see . . .' He took a deep breath. 'You would *do* this? General Wang has the utmost faith in you, Ax, and so do others, more highly placed still. I feel you should be told that . . . You two are prepared to do this?'

'We *three*,' Ax corrected him. 'It's Fiorinda they want. Can you blame them?'

Norman pressed his fists to his breast, completely overcome.

'Hey,' said Sage. 'This is our culture.' He leaned over, and before Norman knew what was coming he had been softly kissed on the mouth by Aoxomoxoa: who drew back, mockery and affection in his bright eyes. 'Born an' bred in this drug-sodden briar patch, Norman. Born and bred.'

The stars, glittering and scintillating over the great arc of sky, shone down on waterbound no-man's land. Something cried out there, one desolate squeal, cut off.

Norman raised his voice, it came out in a register far above his customary basso. 'I'm concerned about Toby.' He cleared his throat and tried again. 'He's going through a difficult adjustment, and he needs to take more water with it, as you people say. We all know he is not responsible for his words or actions.'

'He has nothing to fear from us,' said Ax, gently.

'Yes, I understand that.' Norman heaved a sigh, and got up; carefully.

'You have responded very well to him. I have been favourably impressed.'

They saw that he was shaking from head to foot. The Chinese system is unforgiving of failure, but his relief struck them as extreme. Get a grip, Norman. How *do* they punish a fake Colonel for pulling out of a daft propaganda stunt?

'I'm going to bed. It's very, very shocking. I would be greatly in your debt.'

Rainbow Bridge after curfew was a beetle-infested basement. The crowds were hidden, scuttling in the shadows, teeming and scratching behind paper-thin walls; the sounds of someone being beaten up, round a corner somewhere. The young woman and the girl, in dark leggings and jackets, and hooded ski-masks, stared at graffiti; whilst their guide parleyed through a slot in the prison warden's door. Grimy rainbows, badly-drawn wedding tackle, crude flowers; tags. The partition wall was pieced together with filler; there was a ragged section missing at the top.

'I know where I was when this place was being converted,' said Fiorinda.

'I know where I was too,' offered Frosty, like a child. 'We were in a camp near Holbeach, that's in Lincolnshire, Miss, it's where Dad comes from.'

'I was living in the Palace of Rivermead.'

At random moments the touch of that dead flesh would come back to her; it was clay in her throat. They say nothing's too bad if you know why you're doing it, why you *must*. It's not true, but you do it anyway. For nothing, no return.

'I remember that time,' whispered Frosty fervently, taking hold of her hand. 'I was only a kid, it was well scary. You saved us all, Miss.'

Their guide, the worn-down sportsman in his peculiar tweed jacket, had agreed a price. He ushered them in to a room almost filled by the shaft rising through it. It looked like a brutal work of art, or a giant model of some alien musculature. Fiorinda saw chunks of hardcore under the black paint, broken girders, plastic timbers, lath and plaster, verdigrised piping; carved masonry that might have come from a Christian church. This was where the coffin cells were hidden; in this tower of waste.

'Who made it?'

'No one,' said the prison warden. 'I reckon it just happened, when they were converting. There was a hole through the levels, that they filled with junk, an' the junk kinder formed into a hollow nob. They found it when they were cutting back these walls, an' made it a feature. They got passages and secret rooms all over the place. If we were taken we could carry on for years, in the tunnels, harrying them.'

'You've been playing too many computer games.'

'It's deep water at the bottom, they say it useter be the old churchyard. There useter be a village down there, called Eyot.'

Fiorinda peered into the gap that had been hacked through the side of the shaft. The inner surface was as lumpy as the outside, grey shafts of light ran through the pit. 'We won't need the rope,' she said to Frosty. 'That's good. We'll take it down with us, in case we get stuck.'

'Here!' cried the warden. 'What the fuck? Look don't touch, little ladies!'

He was youngish, bedraggled, ragged black hair and an acned, burnt-umber complexion. He had a stool to sit on, a game-pod for entertainment, the remains of meals kicked into a corner. There wasn't room for much else. A gamma-lunatic, risen to this responsible position, unlikely to rise further. She peeled off her ski mask.

His jaw dropped, sweat bloomed. 'It was n-nothing to do with me. I wasn't a part of it. I have to do what I'm told, I didn't agree!'

'I see you know who I am.' She included the sportsman in a glance. 'Get out of here, both of you, don't come back tonight and don't tell anybody you saw me.'

Frosty handed over two more boxes of matches each, and then decided to pursue the men out of the door. My God, teenagers. Thankfully, she was quickly back again. 'For fuck's sake, what was that about?'

'I wanted to ask about Gator. She's got to be still alive. They won't have slaughtered a good strong young workhorse! That's just crazy!'

Finding Gator was the kids' first priority. The adults didn't have the heart to try and convince them the horse was *gone*. 'Well, okay.'

They bolted themselves in, and began the descent. The baby knew there was something up, it was very quiet. Better talk to her (not aloud, don't want to freak Frosty out), hey, little shoot, this is called *climbing*, it's excellent. More fun going up, but this is good. Down we go, easy as pie, great big hand and footholds . . . My silent words touch you gently. The shaft was never entirely dark. Dislodged fragments rattled and fell, the sound ricocheting; but no splash at the bottom. What if the whole thing collapses under our weight? she wondered. But the waste was rock solid.

'How far down do we have to go, Miss?'

'Orange Level.' Red Level was the underground car park. Orange Level was the basement of the shopping centre. There were no colours in the bird's nest pit, but a sweetish, gagging smell was getting stronger.

'How do they send them food down here, Miss?'

'They don't.'

There was something scrabbling, rats in the bird's nest? The climbers looked at each other, ghost faces. 'Richard?' called Fiorinda. 'Corny—?'

The sounds increased, as if something was trying to retreat deeper into the wall. Another two metres or so and their dark-adapted eyes didn't need the torch. There was an iron grille, set in fairly new cement. Fiorinda found a place to stand below it, and grasped the bars. The smell was bad, but something was moving.

'Richard? Corny? It's Fiorinda. We're going to get you out.'

Something lunged forward, a claw of a filthy old hand groped over her clutching fingers. '*Weers us weers us, nihao feeerrrinda eaah?*'

'Corny! Cornelius, we're here, we found you, you're getting out of this. Is Richard with you?'

'*Aw . . . eeeeh . . . Nahm, Nahm, uhuhu . . .*'

'*He doesn't speak English anymore,*' came a thread of a voice. '*He's lost his head, poor old Corny.*'

'Richard—!'

'*They don't feed us, but there's water dripping all the time, I get him to lap, enough. I'm holding up. Only thing is, when . . . fired on, shattered my shinbone. It's infected, I'm afraid it's not too good.*'

'I'm going to shine my torch, are you ready?'

She struggled out of the straps of the backpack and gave it to Frosty to unload. 'Hide your eyes, light.' Her torchbeam, shining into the horizontal shaft showed an uneven coffin, barely wide enough to hold two bodies; and some fragments of sodden straw. Rags of wet clothing clung to the tangle of limbs, they were chained together wrist and ankle. Here is the commander of Ax's barmy army; and his *eminence gris*. Here are the career soldiers who saved all our fucking hides, when the rockstars stole the glory. But at least we haven't forgotten. Richard had covered his face. The old man gaped at her, bewildered. She held the light steady on Richard's left leg. Below the knee it was a blackened mess, the foot hideously swollen.

'Rich, can you give me your hand?'

'*He keeps trying to get out. He never lies still. He can't understand when I tell him. Keeps trying to crawl out, and it fucking hurts me.*'

Frosty pushed pouches of juice, yeast concentrate strips, dried tomatoes, a pack of hempseed crackers, boiled sweets, hand-milled aspirin, through the bars. Hope they connect with the juice, thought Fiorinda, the rest's surely beyond them. She switched off her torch and looked into blackness, listening to the drip of water.

'Richard. You have to let me touch you.'

'How did you find us, who are you, how do you know my name—?'

She could put her hand through the grille. She got hold of his and gripped it. There was someone there, Richard himself, not the way he'd been at Ashdown, although he didn't know her. He asked her was she from the Red Cross? She reached for Corny's claw too, but that had no affect, nothing.

'We have to go. But you're found. You're getting out. It won't be long.'

Formless mouth-noises followed them, and faded under their feet.

Back in the prison-house Frosty crouched on her heels, head in her hands. 'I'm all right, Miss, it was the smell, just give me a minute 'case I throw up.'

Fiorinda crouched down too, and hugged her belly.

'Are they your best mates, Miss?'

'Not really, Ax and Sage know them a lot better than I do. Say it's a debt of honour, do you believe in those? We have to get them out, they chose a wrong path, they don't deserve to end like that. We will get them out.'

Frosty looked up. 'I'm okay now.' The young woman and the girl were face to face, very close to each other in this squalid cell, in the pity and horror of what they'd just seen. Love and trust blossom in your brain at such times, reliable as if you'd taken a pill for the effect. Frosty swallowed, and ventured, brave and naïve.

'Miss, there's something I wanted to ask you. Are you pregnant?'

And that's me caught, thought Fiorinda. I cannot hide little shoot any longer, it's been confirmed. The instinct to say *no* was very strong, but she resisted. 'Yep.'

The fenland girl did not yelp, she did not get appalled that Fiorinda had brought her unborn child to a fearsome place like Rainbow Bridge. Probably she understood that there are no safe places. She just nodded, and wiped her eyes again.

'Thought you were . . . That's lovely, Miss.'

'Let's get away from here.'

By noon the next day, when the prisoners of Rainbow Bridge came out onto the roof, the north-east wind had blown a grey pall over the clear skies of midnight. The rockstars and the mediaman huddled behind the chicken shed, and Joe was brought up to date. They felt he had a right to know.

'They refused to have the Feds on board,' said Ax. 'They were ready to surrender, rather than go along with that. Shots were fired, Corny and Richard were "court-martialled", and ended up here, walled up in a coffin cell and left to die.'

Joe nodded, straight-faced. 'How long—?'

'About a month,' said Fiorinda. 'They've had water but no food. Corny's off his head. Richard is better mentally, but his left leg is bad. It could kill him in days.'

'Shit . . . And the Chinese don't know?'

'I'm not sure,' said Ax. He lit a cigarette, more for the illusion of warmth than anything, and watched the glowing tip. 'I'm not sure they even know Rich and Corny have been deposed. But I'm sure they knew about the Feds. The Unoccupied Zone Intelligence Office isn't totally useless . . . They knew, or they found out very soon after the invasion, that our eastern flank had been infiltrated. That's why they've been so reluctant to tackle the actives. China doesn't want to take issue with the Russian Federation. The logic of the situation says they'll have to do it some time: but not here, not now. Ideally, they want the privateers to back down and go home, with no trouble.' He grinned. 'I tend to agree with that.'

Joe tried to take this in.

'Fuck . . .' he whispered. 'So this was your secret mission? To uncover the Fed connection, and discredit the resistance? And that's why we came here?'

'Not really,' said Fiorinda. 'We were winning hearts and minds, that's all they told us. Wang Xili expected us to do some encounters with Resistance sympathisers on the side. That's how Ax and Sage found out about the Feds; and about what had happened to Rich and Corny. Everything says the Chinese didn't know about Rainbow Bridge. They thought it was a soft option, another Warren Fen but funkier. And maybe it was . . . But it turns out this place is a kind of sacred city to the camps of Anglia; which is something we didn't know. So the recalcitrants decided to move in, and the party animals couldn't stop them. Now we're here, where we shouldn't be, and *we have to get out gracefully*. We can't admit we didn't know what was going on, anything less than smooth success would be an utter disaster. That's the Chinese point of view, and Norman is very grateful that we share it.'

There was snow on the wind. Joe blinked flakes from his eyelashes. 'Okay,' he said. 'Okay. But why the fuck did the bad guys *invite* Norman Soong? '

'Norman invited himself,' said Ax. 'The party animals said yes. They recognised the Peace Tour as a way to get hold of us . . . The hippies who are now running poor Rich's Resistance agreed because they are delusional alpha geezers, who do much drugs. They think they're a powerful armed opposition group. Why wouldn't the Chinese send a delegation? They've *no idea* what effect the sight of them had on Norman. They don't understand that they are proscribed. They yell about it, but they don't understand what it means.'

'We were talking to people who call themselves the Grand Council Of The Slave Camps,' said Fiorinda. 'I don't know about that, but they say they speak for a silent majority, and they want the Resistance out. They're using the Feds issue, which is a gift to them, because they don't want to sound like collaborators.' She smiled faintly, wryly. 'But their aim is clear. They've figured out a solution that the hippies have to accept. That's the situation. That's what we're being asked to do.'

Joe had heard the Triumvirate cheerfully discussing this gig. Going along with the idea, getting into the details. He'd known they were babbling. You realise you're talking to psychos: you agree to whatever they say, you swear eternal friendship, you neck their vodka, planning to run like fuck first chance you get . . . The mushroom teatime in between didn't help him to deal with what he was hearing now.

'Okay, all right. You, you do this . . . The doves get a royal charter, hearts and minds are won, and we can leave? Is that the way it works?'

'Plus they hand over Richard and Corny,' said Fiorinda. 'We brought them up, but the campers feel the same. I'm sorry, but to me that's the main point. The rest could be hogwash, we have to do this because Richard Kent and Cornelius Sampson *don't die like that*. We may not be able to save them, the Chinese may just shoot them. But they'll be out of that hole.'

'You don't think the Executive Committee will stick to the deal?'

'*No*,' said Ax, with feeling. 'Not at all. But I think they might be lonely.'

'D'you think—?' began Joe again. 'Oh God, forget it.' He tried to laugh. 'This is another of those great stories that can never be told, isn't it?'

' 'Fraid so,' said Fiorinda.

Sage, a windbreak beside her, leaned forward: peering through frosted yellow lashes. 'Hey Joe, what the fuck did you do to deserve this? Why did you ever take up with us? Can you remember?'

I was a cub rock reporter, thought Joe. I was chasing the nearly famous, the nearly famous got tangled up in a national disaster, so I did too. I rode in Fiorinda's tourbus through the Newcastle riots; I had a huge crush on her. I was *terrified* of you, Aoxomoxoa, I thought Ax Preston was the kind of arrogant, super-talented bastard that never gets anywhere and he wonders why . . . And even in that feral saloon, I was thrilled to be on your fabulous trail. I'm insane.

'You've always been f-fucking good copy.'

They stood up and walked around: sinister, hooded scarecrow figures in the white-out. 'You are a fucking heroine,' said Joe to Fiorinda, dead straight. 'As always. Does the Committee know you went prison-visiting? Was that in the deal?'

Fiorinda tasted snowflakes. 'No, but they won't say anything. We were asked to accept some very crap video-evidence that Rich and Corny were alive. We had a right to check. Anyway, I'm the girl. I can do bleeding-heart stunts like that, and get away with it.'

'I b-blame the Chinese,' cried Joe, throwing his head back and opening his mouth to the wind. 'Fucking Daleks! How did they end up dominating the world, if they can't do their own reconnoitring?'

'Oh, it evens out,' Ax answered, off on his own track. 'Good decisions, bad decisions, good information, bad information. I'm sure there've been cock-ups all the way from Xi'an, some of them spectacular, but the victories have been far greater.'

'Don't worry Joe,' said Sage. 'If it turns ugly, we have the fourteen most unstoppable buggers in the known universe on our team.'

'Can you promise me that?'

'Guaranteed,' said Fiorinda.

They struggled with the emergency doors, attained the drab, slightly foul-smelling corridor and went their separate ways. Joe went back to bed. He tried to sleep, to get rid of his hangover; but he had the horrors. There were things about this situation that had been censored on the rooftop: words that must not be spoken, not in any circumstances. This *ritual* (go on, think it—). He remembered thirty thousand people, ripped to shreds at Rivermead.

Sage pounced on Fiorinda, before they reached the suite, and nuzzled into her hair. 'How bad is that leg, Fee?' She turned in his arms, and snuggled in the same light-hearted vein. *Everything we do is seen, everything we say is heard*—

'Not getting worse right now.'

'Thought so,' he said against her mouth. 'Good.' *Oh, my brat, be careful*—

In a weird way they felt rescued. Better to go down in a colourful screw-up than find yourself pining for Rufus O'Niall's final solution.

He thought of the people, men, he had killed in Yorkshire. They came back to him very vividly, though there'd been others later. How many kills with the assault rifle? None, he thought. He'd taught himself how to deliver a controlled burst by the end, but in combat he'd been spraying air, just showing willing. Hand to hand, his strength and size had made the crippled paws invincible; and he had used a sword, the legionary's sword Brock the re-enactment nut had given him. Human flesh gives like butcher's meat. New to murder, he had felt nothing, it was just *you or me, brother.* Not until after the last battle, the bloody chaos at Yap Moss . . . *I was alone with Ax, in a derelict ballroom it seems to me; we'd heard the casualty figures. We stared at each other, then suddenly we hugged like mad, no sex in it, not until long afterwards, but the only way I can stand this is if you are beside me . . .* Richard walked in: *I can see his face. Oh, sorry, he says, kindly (totally mistaken). I can hear his voice.*

The dead time whiled away, the empty hotel-room hours when you have to stay indoors because of the stupid fans, and the thought of the evening's gig stales and dries. Sage and Fiorinda went to join Joe and the kids. Ax was alone, thinking about those fourteen unstoppable buggers, thinking about making these rooms defensible. When the knock on the door came he knew what was going to happen, and it did. One of the missionaries, placid as Buddha, bowed to him: deposited the tablet in its slipcase, and retreated to the corridor without a word.

'Ah, Mr Preston. Now, about the *prison service*.' Wang's fine eyes kindled with irritation. 'The numbers employed are *fantastic*. I see no rational explanation!' The office décor looked like Whitehall again.

Ax was getting the hang of this.

'General, have you ever tried to break up a fight on a dance floor?'

'No.'

'I suppose not. Okay, the rule is you may not use lethal force, the threat of lethal force; or even of GBH, grievous bodily harm, which is a legal term in this country meaning serious, lasting physical damage. The aim is to have everyone feel that the right thing happened; ideally including the sinners. It takes numbers, General, same as on a battlefield. You can win when you shouldn't by luck, but there are no short cuts to overwhelming victory; it takes bodies.'

'Bodies. I see.'

Something slipped: a very anxious man stared at Ax. Then the General was back, urbane and mildly annoyed, looking out of shot. 'We will discuss this further. Enjoy your wild rock festival, Mr Preston.'

The Abyssal

Norman had decreed that the whole party should disrobe, and don the short gowns that traditionally distinguished contenders. The cloakroom was none too clean, nor were the traditional gowns; the 'lockers' didn't have locks. 'I'll take my robe with me,' said Norman, expecting no argument. 'I'll fold it over my arm, see, like this. It's antique and rather valuable.'

'No,' said the cloakroom manager, with the immoveable confidence of the very fat. She was herself mountainously naked, except for her knitting, the tassels on her nipples and the tinsel decorations in her bouffant hair. The black-leather lederhosen bouncers looked hopeful. They'd been told this was for a video and they should treat the Chinese rock director 'the same as they would treat anyone'. Nothing a bouncer likes better than a celeb who personally *asks* for trouble. Ax took the Fu robe from Cousin Caterpillar's arm, and wadded it into his own locker.

'Into the unknown, Norman.'

The changing room was unisex, and not very roomy. Fiorinda stripped beside Toby Starborn, Toby's negative to her positive, each of them keeping their eyes to themselves. Two cloakroom attendants came in, with a special gown for Fiorinda: Toby swooped, and intercepted them. She realised, as he handed it to her (eyes still averted) that he'd known she was pregnant all along. He couldn't have missed the changes in this body, his obsession. Hey, compadre stalker, thank you.

The Triumvirate's special gowns were angel wings, cotton-waste dyed a vivid violet and teased into thousands of feather shapes, a labour of love. *Eyot Swingers Club* read the pulsing sign above the Balcony doors, *Over Eighteens Only.* Ten years and a hundred worlds ago, they used to arrive in their pretty cars, desperate housewives and scheming dentists, did any of them end up drop-outs? A piece of card had been tacked up, enforcing the sensible message.

Strick'ly No Under 8teens's.

They entered to a fanfare of trumpets. An attendant in a Grecian tunic, bearing Norman's mixing-desk on high, led them through the tiers where Rainbow Bridge's in-crowd thronged. An honour guard, their hair dressed in high, ribboned towers, tossed tinsel confetti. Someone decided to cast his garment at Fiorinda's feet; at once gowns started flying. *Make Love Not War!* chanted the crowd.

> *Abandon to the random!*
> *Make Love Not War!*
> *Abandon to the random!*
> *Adapt to the Triassic*

'Hope you're getting all this, Norman,' murmured Sage.
'Of course I am! Ah, is this your music—?'
'Nah. This is Gintrap.'
A section of the lowest tier had been roped off, a waiter showed them to their chairs. He wore a sequined codpiece, a glittery scalplock, a napkin folded over his arm; he took Norman's order for iced champagne (mind it's French), *ad lib*, with a straight face. The club was so clouded with condensation it was like a steam bath. Through drifts of vapour they saw the dance floor, startlingly close. It was already crowded, but the stages that made islands in the ferment were empty.

'How civilised!' cried Norman, staring around. 'What a splendid place! We could be in New York, don't you think? . . . I have a confession. I visualised Rainbow Bridge as a foetid bothy, worker artists from the dregs of society thronging naked to commit raw acts of music and concept, deep in cold stinking mud—'

'Ex'ackly like New York. You should'a told us, Norman. We could have done the naked foetid bothy thing in Hackney, with the AMID for a live audience—'

The director flung wide his arms, with perilous effect for his modesty in the shortie gown. 'I was *naïve*, Sage! I don't mind admitting it. But I was groping towards something, and now I know. This is the reality, this *is* my bothy!'

Toby was like a trapped bird, Joe a silent stoic. Norman had to talk.

'I imagine this must be very like the setting of the shit-fest, at the Festival of Dissolution. Did you really eat human excrement, Aoxomoxoa?'

'Yeah. Carn' exac'ly remember why.'

'Would you do it again?'

'No!'

'What strange music, is this *really* Gintrap? I didn't know one could dance to them. Didn't you write some folksong themes last year, Ax? Do you have them with you? What do English peasants and workers sing about?'

'Birds in the bushes,' said Fiorinda, smiling, feeling the night coming up on her, a bubbling in her blood. 'Pasting the French. Not many here we go a-winnowing songs, we don't really like work; but plenty of ghosts. We do good ghosts.'

The champagne arrived, with waiter-underlings bearing a tureen of amazing iced fruits, and another of teeny black frogspawn on crushed ice, my God, it's caviar.

'Compliments of the Committee,' said the waiter, laying silver forks, plastic dessert bowls. 'We can't find any lemons, we have lemon juice; it's coming.'

'Is there a card?' wondered Ax. 'Any message?'

'Look over the other side.'

Ax looked and there they were, on the other side of the Balcony. Gola, Harvey and entourage. 'The number one crop beside Gola is Yevgeny Ivankov, Mr Preston,' said the waiter. 'He calls himself "*Major* Ivankov", we think he's real military. He's the fixer. He knows where the caches are. The muscle man on the other side is Ospenko, he's a bastard, and he's a *suit*. They're like policemen, you can always tell.'

'What's your name?'

The man opened champagne, and poured deftly. 'It's Bottom, sir.'

The Feds and their protégés wore old-money big white towels around their waists, no gowns. Harvey and Gola raised their own champagne glasses. Hard to make out the expressions, but the malign insolence came across all right.

'Bottom,' said Fiorinda, quietly. 'Are you expecting trouble?'

'No, ma'am . . . I can vouch for the champagne. I wouldn't touch the rest.'

The recalcitrants could be planning a pitch invasion. The party animals were peaceable, and outgunned, but they could be here prepared to defend themselves.

'Change of plan, compadres?' wondered Sage; but not seriously. 'The music's a bit crap. Dunno, what say we go home, have an early night instead?'

Fiorinda shook her head. 'We're over the top.'

And there's the bell. A huge clangour, crude and compelling. The honour guard had reformed, time for the garlanded victims to be led to the altar—

'Oh my God!' cried Norman, smiting himself on the forehead. 'I must be *losing* it! What will you be singing? We have the sample from 'Hard', and then what! This is terrible, how could I have let this happen—!'

'We'll decide later,' Sage cast over his shoulder. 'CGI it.'

'I never do that!'

They were gone, in a wave of glory, tinsel and paper flowers—

Norman reached for his desk, struggling for the calm he needed.

'You'll never be able to publish,' whispered Toby, malevolently. 'You think you're touching the void tonight, but you'll be erased. Like everything of mine.'

'I know that!' snapped Norman. 'Of course I know that! Leave me alone!'

Red Stage, which was mainstage, was a fighting ring. It stood at the east end of the dance floor, like mainstage at Reading. Other stages, different conceits, rose like reefs from the sea of flesh. They were empty. The MC on her tall umpire's chair wore a towel round her neck and a ref's whistle on a chain. Is it always sex in here, or do they have other gladiatorial events? Food fights? Naked ballroom dancing?

And there's the bell again, tolling for the reckless, the abandon and forsake.

Nothing but this hard floor, no props, no bordello bed? Damn right: this is for athletes. Fiorinda saw a bentwood stool in the stewards' corner and went to sit there, disposing her cloak of feathers over her body, arms along the ropes, slim ankles crossed at ease. Her hair was a burnished storm, her skin like candleflame; she smiled on the crowd and thought of Dissolution Summer's bonfires.

Sage and Ax stood in the centre of the ring, arms loosely around each other's necks, hard on hard. They were not sky-clad. Breasts and thighs were bound in silver ribbons; catching light from the looping, interminable strings of coloured diode bulbs. The scars that sectioned Aoxomoxoa's white flank were livid. The crowd couldn't see the crease across Ax's copper breast, where a bullet might have ended his career at an early stage, except for Richard Kent's intervention.

'Hey,' said Sage. 'Forgot to ask, did you ever fuck for an audience before?'

'The datasphere's full of us in action, some of it looks real.'

They kissed, deep and slow. 'I did once go screwing with another guy for a while,' remarked Ax. 'We'd collect a few girls, we'd do them and the rest would be cheering us on, it was terrific. But we never touched each other, only the babes.'

'Yeah?' Sage had not known this. 'Who was the bloke? Anyone I know?'

'Hahaha.'

Oh, it was me . . . In Yorkshire, long ago.

One eye in the mirror of that crowd, and there's the bell—

'Fucking glad they didn't ask me to do this with a guitar round my neck.'

'Are we galley slaves, Ax?'

'*Yeah,*' whispered Ax, with intense satisfaction. 'We are slaves now.'

'Did you ever?' Norman adjusted his gown. The tiger and the wolf, erotically embraced, made a thrilling sight, and what a diptych this would be with Warren Fen, the two great truths of rock! The one man who rules the crowd, and the superb, male-on-male, homoerotic dance . . . 'Joe? When, ahem, when they threw you out of the shelter, did you wish they'd invite you to stay and make up a foursome?'

'It crossed my mind,' said Joe, staring at the fighting ring, transfixed. 'In a s-stupid way, but n-no. I couldn't have, I couldn't handle that.'

'Hmph. They're only human, you know.'

Norman thought of the emperor, and recoiled from the blasphemy. But it was time for his second entry. *Now*, for Fiorinda—

Frosty Tucker's powerful, raw soprano rose, apparently from somewhere in the Arena crowd, filled the air and took on immensity; infinite bleak authority.

I don't believe in anything, except the cold and the equations.

If God were a young girl, that's what God would sound like.

She let the feathered cloak fall, raised her arms and clasped her hands, silver ribbons bound between her breasts and above her thickened waist. The crowd gasped and murmured, and *roared* their appreciation. The homage shook her, but eat shit, bad guys. Not only a living goddess, a pregnant living goddess. You are *screwed*. She could tell that her lovers were covertly anxious, but come on. Far more of an issue if you two had stage fright! Ah, my galley slaves, I see there's no fear of that.

Thank God I'm pregnant actually. The only time in my life I'll ever have the tits or bum to be a porn star. She crossed the floor with a shimmy in her step and a smile like starlight, remembering what Wandering Billy said. Nor shrine, nor stone, nor sacrifice, we are a right place. Pictures of matchstick men and you, always.

Remember when we said we'd get married?

> *We stole and changed to keep us sane*
> *The dirty sweet, and hidden power*
> *To carry on*

And there's the last bell. Ax sat back on his heels, his cock still standing, feeling a weird rush of gratitude towards Norman Soong. Not that he'd want to make a habit of this: but something in him had been released, new pathways opening. The sexual figures we are, the *submission* of that explains everything. But the place he'd been, with his lovers and the crowd and the music, fell from him. He saw the Fed military advisers looking down, and leapt to his feet. He didn't know what he was going to say until he said it.

'Okay,' he yelled. 'You up there! Gunrunners! We've kept our side of the bargain; you'll find you're going to keep yours. Listen to me. Once before I asked the people of England to turn their backs on civil war; and they did it. I asked them to support the weak, feed the poor, welcome the stranger, dig potatoes, scrub hospital floors, and they *fucking buckled down and did it*, because they knew we were at the line, and we had to hold on or go under.' One of Norman's cams buzzed him, he batted it away. 'And *now*, I'm telling them to give you the push. We are spoken for. Get out of our house! Go home and take your gaspipes with you!'

The Balcony erupted, leaping on the simplicity of Ax's catch with joy. 'Go home Rasputin!' they yelled. Bodies swarmed over the leaders of the Resistance and their backers, in an unstoppable fleshly tide. 'Go home, Rasputin! Ra Ra Rasputin!'

Norman was a frantic sorcerer's apprentice, although he knew Toby was right and it was for nothing. Joe had joined a conga line. A band of revellers clustered around Toby Starborn, and led him away. Norman saw this happening, out of the corner of one many-faceted eye; he assumed that Toby left willingly—

They took him to the Arena. Between the drug-test counter and the condom machines they disrobed him, giggling at his healing wound, at the plug he still had to use, to keep open the hole he pissed through. Of course they assumed the body-sculpture was Toby's own idea. He ran away from them, and found his way to the plinth around the Pit. There was a joyous riot and a lot of fucking going on. The lifeguards were yelling GO HOME RASPUTIN, keeping an eye on Balcony divers, and craning for a glimpse of Ax Preston's cock. Nobody was paying attention to the abyss, where the mouth of the Black Shaft had been opened in the Arena floor.

Negative to Red Stage's positive, it was a suicide venue, the party animals accepted that; but in fact there weren't too many jumpers. A punter spotted Toby, crouched on the wrong side of the chain fence. Hey, he shouted (it was screaming-pitch). Are you okay there, nice-looking half-and-half kid?

Toby wailed, and made his leap into the unknown.

The Executive Committee had not planned to disrupt the ceremony. They feared a backlash among their supporters, and they weren't immune to superstitious dread. But they'd sent an execution squad to the prison-house. The squad had arrived to find their concierge outside, a limbless trunk, his arms and legs bizarrely knotted behind his back. 'Don't go in there!' he keened at them, through the pain. They went in, and found a single dark-robed figure, apparently at prayer. They got no further. Hours later, when the coffin cell had been opened from Orange Level, and Richard and Cornelius had been drawn out, the stinking, filthy bodies cut free from each other; the searchers were still looking for Toby. It was a formality, a decent ritual, observed without resentment. They didn't expect to find him.

Voices echoed in the wet dark under Red Level, smoke from rag-and-rape-oil flares trailed through lances of electric torchlight. If you don' find them straight off you never do; maybe they get washed out to sea, who knows where all these drains go? Sage was alone. He had waders,

but the cold was penetrating to bone, he was reeling from that performance; not in a bad way, just want to let it bleed awhile . . . He spotted the
body, caught in a mass of fibrous, floating debris; like a fish in a net.

'Hey!' he shouted. 'Over here!'

He strode through icy water, his torch beam showing vaults of small,
yellowish brick, gaping black mouths of other channels; slick mud
beaches. He was gripped by a conviction that he'd been here before, as
if he'd visited this moment in a snapshot vision. He'd been feeling déjà
since he'd talked to the distressed bloke in the tinsel breech-clout, the last
person to have seen the artist alive . . . Toby's body swayed in the
current like flowerstems. He felt for a pulse, expecting none.

'Over here!' he yelled, and took the weight in his arms.

Toby coughed water, his eyes opened, his lips moved, drowsily.

'*I have seen her whom I lived to praise. I lived for this.*'

Sage shouted again for the lifeguards.

'Hang on Toby, help's coming.'

'Sage?' The artist tried to lift his forearms, which were broken, his
drowned voice took on urgency. '*They know, Sage,*' something lost . . .
'*very . . . be careful . . .*'

He was left holding the body, waiting for the lights and shouts to
reach him. Toby was gone.

III

Sage had climbed a modest slope behind the Rainbow Bridge complex to see the countryside. So this is Suffolk. Newly frozen waterways slate-grey in the snow; disused access to the former shopping centre roping the quiet fields. Smoke rose from the chimneys of a town, beyond woodland; a vehicle or two crept, bright insects. At least England's still breathing.

Bet the neighbours hate that fucking camp like poison.

Richard's leg had been taken off above the knee in the early hours of the morning; Corny was cleaned up and under sedation. That's how it is, the way we live now. The cannibal meat stalls, next alley along from the clinic where dedicated staff are vaccinating babies, scrubbing up for emergency amputations, handing out leaflets on healthy eating. The Executive Committee and their friends had vanished overnight, which was tactful of them. Had been allowed to vanish, get it straight. But Rich would probably survive. He would wake to be told the amputation had been a success, and he was in amazing shape, considering. Later he'd find out that Cornelius was gone forever, and he'd have Ax telling him that *he must* co-operate with the Chinese, he must give them a formal surrender. We saved your life, Rich, aren't you grateful?

Ah well, cheap at the price. Four teenagers safe, military escort not badly dented. Two horses and the lighters written off, and a sad feeling that they wouldn't be seeing Joe Muldur for a while. Last night was a Reichsperience too far, he won't be on our fabulous trail no more and I'll miss him . . . A tiny purple dot appeared on the pale western horizon. He watched it for a moment, then he put the glasses away and left the hilltop: bareheaded, fists in his pockets, the collar of his greatcoat turned up.

And all the time it was Toby we should have been watching. We couldn't figure out what a mutilated genius was doing on our trip; and we've never liked him, so we ignored him . . . Now I believe I get it.

What did Norman say? *You have responded well.* Maybe showing no interest was our best option. What were you trying to tell me, Toby? Were you warning me that we're suspected of clinging to forbidden powers, same as you? Tha's okay, we knew that—

A robin followed as he tramped down the hill, along the margin of a field of snow-crusted turnip greens. At a break in the hedgerow it waylaid him, on the stump of a felled beech: let rip a burst of song and cocked its head, expectant.

'Sorry, mate, can't help you. No change.'

Humans give me food, said the little bird's indomitable glance. You are human, therefore give me food. Don't piss me around, just because I am small.

'Okay, okay, see what I can do.'

He came up with some manky fragments of chocolate biscuit.

'You talk to animals, Aoxomoxoa? Is this your magic?'

The bird whisked away.

The Daoist nun had changed her robes and cap for an elegant padded coat in dark silk, and a discreetly fashionable little hat. She still wore the serene, seamed face; but context is everything. This morning it was obviously a digital mask.

'Anyone can talk to a robin. They like people, dunno why.'

'You seemed to understand each other.'

The trunk of the beech, shorn of branches, had been left by the hedge. She brushed snow from the close-grained grey hide and sat down. Sage realised he'd better sit on the ground; to make this woman look up at him was not a good idea.

So he did that, and waited.

'They call you the Zen Self Champion. Tell me about that.'

'*Jiejie*, I don't know what to say, it's embarrassing. It was a daft adventure in rockstar spirituality, dressed up in fake tech, and I'm over it.'

'I have watched you,' she said, with decision. 'And I don't think so. Tell me the truth.'

'Hm.'

'Tell me about your fabled yogi powers, that would be a good start.'

Sage thought about it, studying the crystalline snow. 'There's a passage in a Zen text, about a master approaching enlightenment. I can't quote, but he meditates, and goes out of his house and looks around. He talks to animals, he sees demons and lurid monsters; the spirits within appear through the veil. Then he meditates again, goes out and sees the abyss of non-being opening before him . . . But having achieved enlightenment he goes out of his house and everything is as before. I don't know if the ancients wanted us to believe in yogi powers as literal fact; I do know they're a distraction. Wherever I went, *jiejie*, I'm back where I was. Except perhaps I reached a starting point, perhaps now I know how to live.'

He looked up. The nun studied him carefully, and nodded.

'That's a good answer.'

Rufus O'Niall's assassination hung in the air, he wondered what the hell he'd do if she raised the subject, but she decided to move on.

'Immix code is *extremely* dangerous. Don't think we don't understand it, we do. We know that an *immersion* is achieved by building the neuronal firings and fractional firings of a perceptual state in code, and delivering this fake to the visual cortex; where it is processed as if the stimuli were external. This is playing games with the stuff of reality! This is the highway to pernicious delusion, it CANNOT be permitted. Do you want the universe to dissolve into primordial information soup?'

'Well, no, but . . .' Somebody, maybe Toby Starborn's ghost, grabbed him by the scruff of his neck. Never say *no*! Think of your meat and potatoes! Okay, okay.

'It's a great loss to you, but you must accept it.'

'I know I must, and I do accept. '

'You have other talents. The lyrics of "Winter Song" are beautiful.' She laughed. 'But why a "children's talking book", Aoxomoxoa? Can't you read?'

Sage grinned, eyes down. 'Not exac'ly, not very well. Dyslexic, me.'

'Good heavens.' She stared at him. 'Were you *never* able to read?'

Fuck! Am I nuts, trying to score points off her? 'Nah, it's temporary, it seems to be the result of, of, er, the time I spent with the secret police.'

'Ah . . . you were tortured, I know. I didn't know there were lasting effects.'

He found the compassion coming through the mask disquieting, but he answered. 'They stuck needles behind my eyes, allegedly to retrieve memories I told them I didn't have. It was *bullshit* . . . It's settling down, better all the time.'

'You haven't had a scan of the damage? But you must!'

He could not stop himself from flinching. 'Er, no. I'm fine, really.'

And that's all on the torture topic. He felt a change, a steely edge.

'And yet, Aoxomoxoa! . . . *And yet*, despite these wise opinions, despite this courage of yours – in the face of the most terrible threat the world has known – last night the Triumvirate had the folly to perform a flagrant act of ritual magic!'

Thought you'd get to that.

He chose his words with care, not daring to look up, wishing it was Ax dealing with the rocket science. But she's not going to do this conversation with Ax. That wouldn't work, Ax must be above suspicion.

'We performed a live sex act, undignified but harmless. The people in the camps don't have much. At Warren Fen you saw what we've tried to do to rebuild, it's nothing like enough . . . Sex means a lot to them. *Make love not war* is a sacred principle to the Rainbow Bridge Council, daft addle-brains though they may be. We gave them our affirmation, on stage last night. We believe it'll win you hearts and minds, and rip the support from the recalcitrants, all over the eastern flank.'

He knew not to mention the Feds. Let's hope to fuck Russian intervention in Anglia goes into the official *this never happened* file, and stays there.

'Hmph,' said the nun. 'I think you are prevaricating.'

Damn right I am. You and I both know what that was. It was something misnamed a fertility rite, a 'magic' humans have performed since they were human, not meant to conjure, meant to *enact* the bond between us and this world of flesh. It has fuck-all to do with occult superweapons. Did I do okay?

'The other aspect of it was Cornelius and Richard. Loyalty impresses the English, but I won't say we did it out of cold calculation. They'd taken the wrong path, but we couldn't abandon our friends to that death.'

'Right action, perhaps,' said the nun, judiciously. 'But faulty reasoning. You must learn to consult with your superiors. You will fall into error if you take things into your own hands '

The robin launched a flight of silvery notes, probably advice to leave the biscuit crumbs alone. Her silence held no threat this time.

They looked down on Rainbow Bridge, a stain on the landscape, and he spared a thought for the poor bastards out in the cold. It was hard to summon up any pity for the Executive Committee, but they weren't the only actives. Sorry lads, you fought for our cause once, but it's change or die time—

'In the Dunhuang Caves in the west of China,' said the nun, 'a great cache of thousand-year-old scrolls was discovered, early in the twentieth century. It seems the Buddhist monks and nuns, a thousand years ago, believed disaster had fallen on the entire world. So they gathered all the books, the sum of human knowledge, and hid them where they might survive. In places like Rainbow Bridge Ax's England has stored away a treasury of appetites. A hoard of redundant consumers, whose life consists in preying on each other and indulging in the coarsest pleasures. The world will never again have a place for those people, what use are they to futurity?'

'You're asking me?' Sage shrugged. 'I dunno. What practical use were the lost Dunhuang scrolls, when it came to rebuilding after that other disaster? It seemed like a good idea at the time. It was an act of hope.'

'Another good answer.'

The purple dot had been growing. The landship was suddenly very close, coming to a halt with a silken, pervasive thunder. Like a fenland lighter, he thought, looks as if nothing's happening until you have to kill the momentum. A group of people had emerged from Rainbow Bridge: he saw two stretchers. Ah, that's bad. Richard and Corny will wake up in Chinese hands, we won't be with them.

The Daoist nun, aka Ax's fifth element, stood up. 'Your transport will be here soon. You must tell Ax, I found his performance last night *very* impressive.'

Of course she'd been in the Arena. She does whatever she feels like doing, this nun; with her unstoppable buggers and no safety net. What does that imply? I was there too, he thought. How about my performance? It's those pretty brown eyes. And the insane naked yelling at clandestine Fed military advisers—

'I will.'

She smiled through the mask, and left him.

Sage watched the Chinese embark, and let the ship clear before he set off again down the hill. This is how it will be, he thought. We'll chip away, solving their problems for them, in our crazy rockstar fashion. Ax will go on saying no to their kind offer of the Presidency, until it dawns on them that he'd holding out for one particular deal. Then eventually we'll hit the *real* problem, and all the ducking and diving, all the triage and betrayal will have been for nothing. Ah well, such is life.

Keep on dancing 'til the music stops. So far, so good.

Spring Moon

I

'Eating shit was a feat of jackass gross-out,' said Sage. 'But it meant something about the rape of the planet, greed-culture. I was very angry, those days.'

'I know. I didn't know it at the time, I thought you were just weird.'

The roadshow was in Yorkshire, helping to normalise relations between the Islamic heartland community and General Sheng of the North East; or rather his subordinate here, Yen Dawei. Something must have happened to fix the privateers and their arms caches (imagine, a covert operations suit called Ospenko hunted down, top-level secret exchanges, the Feds folding their cards); the AMID was efficiently crushing the last die-hard actives in Anglia now. It was not for the Triumvirate to know. They had turned the tide in the east with their bit of theatre, now they were being used for something else—

Sage and Fiorinda, walking beside a drear, windswept reservoir, found some picnic tables. Imagine Sunday outings. Rough-hewn recycled plastic 'wood', like the timbers of Warren Fen's watchtowers. A row of bins, a car park gone to seed; the grey-brown whalebacks across the steel water. Winter goes on *forever*. In the third week of March, up here, you'd kill for a mist of green, a bank of primroses.

'I'm turning in some shambolic performances, Fee.'

'Mm.'

'Hahaha. You're supposed to say, *oh, what nonsense Sage, you are invariably superb.* I'm in a disaster zone. I feel like a kindly uncle, I can't never do the stunts I did no more, I'm an arthritic ex-ballerina and I'm fucking *bored.*'

Ax Preston will never have no work to do, she thought. They may take his guitar, they may throw him in a concentration, sorry, re-education camp, he'll be hustling for the people's right to a better class of peelings

177

with his last breath. It's different for my pilgrim. But she'd known this mercurial character a long time.

'You never remember being depressed between times, it'll pass. I used to think you were like a kindly uncle when you were wringing your incontinence pads out over the mosh, Aoxomoxoa. You enjoyed amusing those dreadful children.'

'Fuck off.'

She took his hand (this crippled hand, holding mine). 'Listen. The barrier between information space and the information in our heads, between internal and external reality, did not become permeable a few years ago in a neuroscience lab. It became permeable the moment human beings were conscious.'

'Your point is?'

'I'll get there. When people today see ghosts, have visions, suffer psychic persecution, get cured by charms (and I know some of it's real, though most of it is just daft), it's aberrant observation validated, after thousands of years on the margins, by novel tech. Like the earth going round the sun.'

He loved the way she moved, carrying her gravid belly with embattled ease. He remembered her saying, at Warren Fen, *I will defend little shoot with lethal force.*

'More like splitting the atom.'

. . .

'No,' said Fiorinda, after a sharp silence in which he cursed himself. '*Not* like splitting the atom, that led to nuclear warheads as the obvious application, fuck that. So-called occult superweapons can be erased, thank God. Mind/matter tech itself is inevitable. The Chinese can't erase it, it will be back.'

'I'm sure. In a couple of thousand years, you think? When we've been down the dark ages a few more times; an' if we're still around?'

This is what happens in a threesome, you form secret societies. The Chinese had taken Sage's life when they banned immersion code. He could not talk to Ax about that, it would sound like an accusation. So he talked to Fiorinda.

'Finding it hard to eat the shit, my Sage?'

He grimaced horribly. 'It's nasty stuff to get down. Oh, I will be fine.'

Ax and Sage had been called away. They were to attend a vital press conference, a major step in the reconstruction. It was the end of a long drought. The fifth element had vanished after she left them at Rainbow

Bridge; they might have dreamed her. The Reich was in business, but there'd been no further Presidential overtures for Ax to turn down. They'd been getting worried.

'Will *you* be okay, sweetheart, if I go to London?'

He knew she was having tiny psychotic episodes. Sometimes he would see her pause, mid-step – in the middle of a room, on stage, in his arms – for a fraction of a second. No fear, just her toughness, seeing whatever she saw and thinking *how do I deal with this?* There have always been magicians, people with mind/brains so poorly protected by the censorship that they can shift the world of matter, a little, sometimes, according to their will. There was never anyone – in nature – to touch Rufus O'Niall, who indulged that vice with a global megastar's power over *millions* of fans. His frontal lobes must have racked up appalling damage. Fiorinda would not go down her father's road, but stress took its toll and now she was about to have a baby. They sat on a rough-hewn plastic bench. A pair of grebes came gliding out of the rushes, and began a stately dance with each other.

'I'm all right,' said the living goddess. 'I'm blissfully happy, somewhere in the midst of all this. Of course I'll be okay. I have Allie, and the Babes, and Chip and Verlaine, and your brother Heads. I'm not without support.'

He felt rebuked. The Few had been beside Fiorinda through the very bad time. Sage had not been there. 'I know you're all right,' he said, despondently. 'Sorry.'

'What for? Idiot.' She tugged his sleeve, butting her head against his shoulder. Sage wrapped his arms around her, and the baby was curled between them, wriggling. 'She's a horribly active child. She sleeps about half an hour a night. I hope she's not like this all the time when she gets out.'

'Bet she is.'

The prospective Prime Minister had come to London for a short trip. She was meeting the media, with Hu Qinfu, Wang Xili and their aides; plus the former President and his 'Minister for Gigs'. Mr Rob Nelson, who'd been representing the Reich in London, was also at the table. The traditional field of alternative candidates, recruited by the Chinese from the weed-growth of post-invasion politics, filled up the ranks.

Someone in the media pack expressed concern about the forts. Would the foreign military presence be permanent?

One of the also-rans (suck-up), expressed entire willingness to co-operate with the liberators for an unlimited transitional period—

The Four Nations International candidate gallantly risked his life by saying something inflammatory, and well-nigh anti-Chinese.

The New Green Party candidate sweated in silence. It was not a comfortable role, owing to the Countercultural associations. But the Chinese had insisted that a cleansed, right-thinking Green Party must emerge.

Wang Xili, smiling and elegant in his Marshal's uniform, watched the horses being led around the paddock like a world-weary Rothschild on a spending spree. Mr Preston and his Minister were nervous. They had set this thing in motion, but in ways it was moving too fast, with their own fate still unknown. In ways they'd be happier when Lucy, brave woman, was back in Paris—

'Did I tell you?' murmured Sage, doodling Terry Gilliam clouds and rainbows on his scrap-pad. 'I found out why Alain screwed us over *Wood Court*?'

The Reich was in approved software radio contact with like minds in Paris, Amsterdam, Lisbon, Oslo: Sage had taken the opportunity to yell at Alain, over the the Triumvirate's invasion rez. Okay, it'd deserved to be erased, it didn't have to look like that as it went to its grave—

Ax chewed the end of an AMID issue pencil. 'Oh yeah?'

'It was the Church Ales, Ax. He was *disgusted*.' Sage gave a cherub on a cloud Alain's crisp, Breton features. 'You, of all people, consorting with religion.'

'Huh? How does that work out? I suppose my own professed faith doesn't count? The White Christ is religion, what's Allah? Chopped liver?'

Two Chinese stenographer units stood on the table. They looked like semi-AIs, which was interesting, given the ban on weird science. The leaders of the Reich were convulsed by silent giggles: what do Chinese AIs make of the two of us whispering about Jesus? Hu Qinfu, the General in Command of Subduing the Capital, shifted in his seat and frowned. Rob nudged Sage. Okay, okay.

'I wonder if we should look on the 2nd AMID army as a foreign military presence,' said Lucy. 'We are already, in effect, a part of that great empire.'

Hyperinflation had raised its demoralising head. The rebel leader, Richard Kent, was receiving the best of Chinese medical care . . . Ax made a mental note that he must explain himself: he'd needed to invoke spiritual values, and Islam had been out of the question. He couldn't afford to lose Alain. Sage drifted off, watching Lucy Wasserman. She wore a vintage Chanel suit, combining style and austerity, that made her look like the only grown-up on the ballot. He remembered how Ax's eyes had kindled when he first set eyes on this woman, when all they knew of her was her whacko ideas about the fuel crisis. Appearance isn't everything in a PM, but it's got to be there. He thought of how he would code her, bring out the Central Europe in her face (a touch of Allie Marlowe there), the olive warmth in her skin. Make her look like yesterday, when all our troubles were so far away. Make her look like light on water. Hey, that's my future. I can turn a stateswoman into liberators' poster-girl—

'Sage, will you *knock it off*,' muttered Rob. 'This isn't funny.'

'You don't know what I'm thinking about.'

After the meeting, the leaders of the Reich were invited back to Wang Xili's Chelsea flat. Ax and Sage accepted. Rob made his excuses, and went away scared he should have said yes. But the President, his Minister and their only rep in town don't get into the same car, no matter who's holding the door.

So this is it, this gold-curtained shimmering casket. This is where the bastard wrecked her young life. They had known the address, they'd never been into the building. We can airbrush history too: this episode in Fiorinda's past had been buried deep. They saw the publicity stills around the walls, just as Dian had described, and felt that they'd been brought to London to be confronted with Rufus's love-nest: not for the press conference at all. Something terrible must be about to happen, and yet the signs were otherwise—

Dian Buckley was not around, nor any other servant. Ax and his Minister were alone with the two Generals. It was one of those strange AMID army occasions where you think they'll offer you a drink, at least a cup of tea; but they don't. Wang baited Hu about his failure to preserve Buckingham Palace, and his quarters on Brixton Hill. A little awkward for him now that the Triumvirate were back in circulation!

Ax felt that he should say something (nah, don't worry, you can keep the doss, we'd never get the smell of defeat out of the rugs.) 'It was a dull old blockhouse, tell the truth. The former Royals had cleaned out the artworks, such as they were. There was really nothing worth taking.'

General Hu, who seemed to Ax like one of those old soldiers whose chief talent is for survival, gave the President-in-Hiding a look of suspicion, and turned to Sage, inclining his gaunt body sharply forward, like a pecking bird.

'Aoxomoxoa, Cornwall is a very beautiful country, full of ancient treasures.'

Not any more, thought Sage. It's full of fuckin' tourists.

'You must be glad to know that your father has been exonerated. Haha. The cat who catches the mice will not be hung!'

Joss Pender had been under investigation for profiteering – trust him, the software baron had played a double game with the Second Chamber and come out richer than ever. He seemed to have got off: but this was an alarming topic. Maybe this is where we are offered a *hideous* deal, involving our families—

'Yeah, it's good news.'

A strained silence.

'You are probably wondering about the portraits,' announced General Wang.

'I was, in fact,' said Ax.

'I don't think you can possibly realise how important the stories of the Reich have been to us, in China. What an inspiration.'

'An inspiration,' put in rancorous Hu, showing horse-teeth in what seemed meant for an ingratiating smile.

'No, I didn't quite realise that.'

'Perhaps for you this apartment has painful associations. I see myself as the custodian of a shrine. Every hour of a great woman's life is worthy, her struggles and her triumphs are full of lessons.' The Generals looked at each other. 'But to the present. Today we are Elder Sister's emissaries. We have the gifts she chose for you, just gestures, as mementoes of your Anglian adventure.'

Wang left the room and returned with two packages wrapped in pale gold tissue; which he carried in both hands, bearing them before him like sacred treasure. One parcel was long, rigid, flat and slim, the other was small. The tissue was embossed in a pattern of intertwined dragons.

'We couldn't,' said Ax. 'We really didn't expect this.'

'Please. As I said, these are tokens, nothing special.'

They went the rounds like car company executives, Sage being no help, Ax finding it hard to believe he had to say these lines, and struggling with a dangerous rush of relief. No, no; please. It's the merest token. Really we couldn't: oh, well, if you're sure, we're very touched and delighted. He felt somewhat duped when he discovered that one of the gifts was for Aoxomoxoa, and one was for Ms Slater. Wonder what she's getting. It's a box, wonder what's inside—

'Elder Sister would like to present your gift in person, Ax.'

'I'll look forward to that.'

The Generals beamed. The tension in the atmosphere collapsed, as if a mighty challenge had been successfully negotiated. On the verge of laughter Ax looked at the pictures of Fiorinda, and was sobered.

'General Wang,' said Sage. 'May I use your bathroom?'

'Of course. It's through the bedroom.'

He crossed the bedroom, noting there was no sign of female occupation; suddenly remembering Dian's place long ago, just one night . . . Took a piss for verisimilitude, and yep, there was Fiorinda, twelve years old, in her school uniform, opposite the shower stall. He stared at the young girl, who stared back, chin up, cross and wooden. He immediately wanted to take the pictures, stick them under his coat and run off with them: because it was his babe, and he didn't want to leave her here (pub shots are junk). But at the same time he felt strangely relieved.

He couldn't believe that he and Ax would be in this flat, accepting gift-wrapped sweeteners, if Wang Xili was an occult monster. Who knows? Maybe the General really did have a crush; and innocent, as such things go.

I have seen her whom I lived to praise—

I will get hold of Dian, he thought. I'll talk to her again.

In the taxi back to Lambeth – they'd politely declined an AMID car – they looked at each other, shook their heads and laughed.

An inspiration, whoa! *Elder Sister*, invoked with open reverence by the two Marshals. All very mysterious, but we are getting somewhere!

'I don't know,' said Ax. 'History, distance. Say that was where a wicked celeb kept a legendary young beauty, and it was far away and long ago, in another culture. Maybe it would be a romantic gaff—'

'I can live with it. Rufus O'Niall, who he? A ghoulish tourist attraction.'

'Yeah, chase out the ghosts . . . The call of nature, what was that?'

'Nothing,' said Sage, indignantly. 'Can't I take a piss?'

'Are you going to open that?'

Sage opened his present. It was a board, Chinese make, new model. Designed to do only permitted tricks, no doubt. There was a message taped to the case, in graceful Roman capitals, black on red paper. The letters stayed put instead of dancing around; which was good, but he couldn't make sense of them.

'Wha's it say?'

'It says ALMS FOR BELISARIUS.'

'No wiser.'

'Roman general, sixth century CE, best man the late empire ever had. Retook Rome for Justinian; but he fell foul of some court intrigue, had his eyes put out and ended up begging in the shop doorways of Byzantium. It means, um, the most noble deeds don't always get rewarded, the greatest heroes can fall upon hard times.'

'Right,' said Sage.

'She's interpreting another culture's refs. It's a thoughtful compliment.' Like hell. Oh, I'm not forgiven, whatever it is that I did.

'I wonder what you're going to get.'

'She knows what I want,' said Ax.

They fell silent as the cab crossed Westminster Bridge; full of thoughts that didn't bear discussion, because a taxi can so easily be planted on you. But mostly they thought about hurrying back to Fiorinda. Soon the thread of her pregnancy would be broken, and it seemed all wrong. They felt they were about to lose a guiding light, a faithful friend who'd been with them since before the invasion.

'She'll want the Babes and Allie with her,' said Sage. 'It'll be natural if we feel slightly left out.'

'Don't *say* that.'

II

Weak Become Heroes

The Fox Force Five had a disastrous rehearsal, compounded by fiendishly tactless behaviour on the part of Charm Dudley, front-woman of the Charm Dudley Band; formerly DARK, Fiorinda's early associates. The professionals tried hard to convince their fashionista that what you do with something like that is you pretend it never happened: walk away, forget it, pay no attention. Allie wasn't having any.

There was a doomed post-mortem, in the back of her blue van.

They'd had such good times through the brief span of Fox Force Five's existence. They'd been having *fun* together. Allie had taken some coaxing but she'd loved being on stage, actual guitar round her neck, and the crowds had been immensely supportive, thrilled to have *Allie Marlowe* up there. Turns out that was all illusion. The whole thing had been misery. Allie had been hating herself, the Babes and Fiorinda had been *lying* to her—

'If the other bands are laughing at me, saying I can't sing—'

I'm banking them, Charm, thought Fiorinda; although she wanted to strangle Allie. One fine day, when I am not pregnant anymore, I'm going to come up to Lambton Worm HQ, invade your stage and fucking *kick your head in*—

The partnership between the dyke-rock queen and her teenage singer had been electric but volatile, physical exchange of views on stage not unknown.

'You can't take any notice of *Charm.*'

'What about Justin?' whimpered Allie, mopping her eyes.

Justin was the tactless sound guy. 'Oh him,' said Dora, rolling her eyes. 'He probably fancies you, he was probably trying to get your attention.'

This daft ruse almost made Allie smile, but she struggled and resisted.

'No. I'm sorry, I'm quitting. This has never worked. It's over. Could you please, all of you, find somewhere else to sit around? I have to clean up in here.'

Needless to say, Allie's mobile home was exquisitely clean and tidy, warm and civilised. Not a trace of dirt or mess dared to venture. Min – who was hiding in a bunk, upsets scared him – was tolerated, barely, for Ax's sake.

'You can't QUIT!' Fiorinda exploded. 'Fuck's sake, we've got a gig tonight, a really significant gig! You can't pull out! Where are we to get a bassist?'

'Ask Charm,' croaked Allie. 'I'm sure she'd help out.'

Felice glared at Fiorinda, and tried getting physical. 'Come on girl, you're on the handbills, the punters love you, you can't let us down.'

The senior Powerbabe's tall curves could often *intimidate* a person into cheering up, but Allie was made of sterner stuff. The hug was rebuffed. 'Leave me alone, F'lice. I'm a make-weight. You have to be five, you're the Fox Force Five, that's why you had to drag me in—'

'Hey!' cried Chez. 'Knock that *off*, girl. Don't you remember when we thought of this? In the Insanitude non-combatants' shelter, not knowing if we'd live through another day? We're the Fox Force *because there are five of us*. Me and Dora and F'lice, and you and Fio.'

'We're the Force because we've been through hell and high water together,' intoned Dora, wearily. 'We're celebrating sisterly love. Can I open some wine?'

Spliff was forbidden. Allie wouldn't let anyone smoke anything in here, and she'd decided cannabis made her paranoid. 'It's in the floor safe, corkscrew in the side pocket. Oh, Dora, not mugs, there are wine glasses. Harry can wear my jacket. You can still be the Fox Force.'

Harry Child was the Charm Dudley bassist.

'We are *tight*, we have *soul*—' pleaded Cherry.

Wouldn't go that far, thought the others, but there was Allie, refugee-huddled over the ATP brazier, her black ringlets in non-Allie disarray, clutching her Fox Force bomber jacket; the sequined appliqué stitched by her own hands. In a moment she was going to get onto *the Reich is all I've got*, which drove them all mental.

'*Listen*,' snapped Fiorinda, 'what do you want, a medal? You're not great, but you look good, you keep time and you usually sing more or less in tune. Plenty of talent-free female stars have made their fucking fortunes on less—'

Shit. Didn't mean any of that. Why did my voice come out like that?

'Sorry.' She pressed the heels of her hands to her forehead. 'I'm sorry, Allie. I'm really irritable. Don't know what's wrong with me.'

Her friends glanced at each other. 'Don't bite my head off,' said Allie, in a changed voice. 'Please don't explode, Fio, but could it be that you are thirty-seven weeks pregnant, and running yourself ragged?'

'Thirty-six weeks.'

Someone thumped on the van's back doors. Fiorinda, feeling her honour as a nice person was at stake, jumped up to answer it. She could still jump. Walk on my hands if I had to, I'm in terrific shape, it's just that people are so annoying.

It was Charm, accompanied by a strange woman with chestnut hair in braids, wearing a suit of fringed deerskin like an Indian brave. Charm herself was one of those women who prefers a timeless look. She'd cut off her mangy dreads, but the badge-spattered man's jacket, torn jeans and sloppy sweater could have been the same she'd been wearing in Dissolution Summer. The sight of her, aggressively *non babe*, contemptuous of everything Fiorinda Slater had done since she quit DARK, brought the boiling-head effect straight back—

Charm raised her hands, palms open. 'Before you start, this is Birch.'

'Whatever it is,' said Fiorinda, 'we don't want any.'

'She's a midwife.'

'I don't need a midwife. I'm not *stupid*. I have my operation booked, I had a scan two weeks ago, the whitecoats said everything was fine. Go away.'

'Often the ultrasound scanners in public hospitals are in poor repair,' said the midwife, gravely, 'or obsolete models. Or the so-called doctors don't know how to read what they see. Most private hospitals are no better.'

Fiorinda had felt slightly uneasy about that scan herself. Her silence was taken for consent. 'Aw reet princess,' said Charm. 'Force yorsel te be rational.'

The Fox Force gathered round, attempting to help Fiorinda to lie down. 'Fuck's sake—' snapped their young leader. 'Gimme some privacy.'

The midwife's hands felt kind and sure, her voice was smoky Yorkshire. 'She's strong and healthy. She's a big baby and your birth canal is small.'

''S okay, I'm having a Caesar.'

'Hm.' Birch sat back on her heels. 'This baby was not conceived at Rainbow Bridge . . . But we pray that she brings peace. My community sees the invasion as you do, Fiorinda. A hard blessing, a fertile disturbance; something that must be.'

Just the kind of bedside manner I need. 'Then you shouldn't dress like a Countercultural,' she said, too tired to be discreet. 'You'll get yourself shot.'

'What about her dates?' demanded Charm, poking her spiky head officiously over Birch's shoulder. '*She* says three weeks. I say she's ready to pop.'

'I can talk, Charm. Thanks.'

'Three weeks? Oh no, this child's coming soon. It could be anytime.'

'You're entitled to your opinion,' said Fiorinda, sitting up. 'Me, I'm going to have my baby in London, it's all settled. Thanks so much, Birch, that was lovely. Now excuse us, we have girly grooming activities to do.'

Charm and the midwife left. 'Did someone say wine?' asked Fiorinda. 'What about a strengthening glass for a pregnant lady with a problem temper?'

'Oh, God,' said Allie, 'd'you remember the Ribena tequila sunrises? I'm sorry I've been a pain. Okay, I'll do it, just tonight; if you really want me.'

The Babes instantly assured her, with fake intensity but sincere relief, that she was indispensable, that she was their star, the one the people came to see—

Of course the baby wasn't conceived at Rainbow Bridge. Wish I could get hold of whoever started that daft story. The underground success of their Arena performance was disturbing, it was everywhere. Surely the Chinese will go ballistic, but what can you do . . . Something shifted inside Fiorinda's head, like fabric tearing. Someone was looking at her, over there in the corner.

Nobody had noticed anything strange, thank God. She saw the straightening comb, which was charging on the brazier, and grabbed it.

'Hey, foxes, what if I straighten my hair? That might be cool.'

They wouldn't take responsibility for a sleek Fiorinda. My God! What if Ax gets back tonight? Horror, laughter; and the midwife's pronouncement, which only Fiorinda had really heard, was handily lost.

An hour before the doors opened she escaped for a breath of air. The evening was quiet and chill, the moorland still the exhausted blonde of winter; or peat-brown where bracken and heather had been harvested. Furzy branches rose from sudden valleys; like Ashdown but so dour. In the delicate bell of the sky one star was shining, to the left of the gravid moon: maybe Venus, Sage would know. There's the transmission mast, holy in legend. It wasn't the actual mast where Ax and Sage had met at the turning point of the battle, it was a replacement, but never mind.

At the Yap Moss memorial – a granite plinth with long lists of names, and an anchor symbolising Hope – she met a shabby, bare-headed bloke with missing teeth, who gripped her arm and told her he had not fought here, no fucking way, but he remembered coming out to see the dead.

'Your boyfriends were back for the burying detail, Fiorinda.'

'Oh, really? I didn't know that.'

'Aw, yes. We came out here, because we're ignrant you know, to see the spectacle of the dead bodies, an' it was *'orrible*. Sage was there – eh, he were a massive lad – and Mr Preston, digging alongside the barmy squaddies, an' laying down the dead with their own hands. They'd a mechanical digger for the trenches. And they were all buried, in two graves, either if they'd been left here or else brought back from the hospitals, separately but together, Islam and Christian.'

'You're a Muslim?'

'Aye,' said the ancient mariner type, surprised. 'How d'you know?'

Only Islamists called the heathen majority 'Christian'.

'Just guessing.'

'Any road, it may sound gruesome but it were a big day in my life.'

She left him there, and went to find the vehicle fleet supremo.

Roger was on his back, ministering to a hybrid Bluebird bus. The vans hardly ever broke down, but maintenance was constant. They machined their own parts, which was getting to be a hell of a job, these days. He rolled out, a veteran Reich crew chief, grey ponytail and receding temples, wiping his hand on a rag that had once been a yellow-flash security bib. The Reich had special provision, but they never had enough fuel. They tried not to sponge off the Chinese, especially not up here. General Yen Dawei (aka David Yen) was hardline. He would have had them performing under armed guard, to protect them from Islamic Terrorists, if he'd had his way. They lived from hand to mouth, rarely able to hook up to the remains of the National Grid; patching together bio-liquids, cells, ATP, for all their power needs; liable to be shipwrecked by unforeseen demands. Today they'd had to fetch a piano from thirty miles away, and the Yap Moss Barn's turbine was bust.

'About finished,' said Roger, cheerfully. 'We'll need every drop to fire the stage jennies. We get a liquid delivery day after tomorrow, sounds like good stuff. Other than that, it's horse power, Shanks's pony or the bus stop.'

Fiorinda looked up at the Yap Moss Barn: a stalwart, graceful, modern edifice, fat white bird with folded wings. The stained glass windows glowed, spendthrift in the dusk. Everything changes, a rock concert stays the same: wanton extravagance.

'Anything wrong, Fio? You need to drive somewhere?'

'Nah, just keeping track.'

She thought she would call the tiger and the wolf. But she hated talking on the phone, and the Chinese would be listening. She decided not to bother, and did not realise that this was a sign of her growing panic.

The public had rallied in force to all the Reich gigs; AMID squaddies would turn up 'on their own initiative' to bodypop and pogo in well-pressed uniform. Yap Moss was something else again, a huge night, maybe a thousand people. The Fox Force Five played a damned good set. The Babes blew their horns like women possessed, Allie kept tight hold of her three chords, and her slight but tuneful voice was beautifully managed by the repentant Justin. Fiorinda sat at the piano on lead vocals, glad she didn't have to stand up, her friends in the front row. Big George Merrick, jiving around like a kid, poor Marlon with his teenage despair (Silver had done him wrong). Her heart filled up with helpless love for this life, for these comrades; for their past. But she kept looking for Ax and Sage, though she knew they couldn't be here.

Why aren't they here? Don't they realise I need them?

The Adjuvants and Cherry Dawkins sat up talking, in Chip and Verlaine's yurt. They were a platonic threesome, keepers of the secret flame: sharing interests the Sensible Tendency (that's Allie, Rob and the two senior Babes) couldn't stomach. Everything we say is heard, but it was now okay to talk about the Zen, as long as you censored the hardware and stuck to the philosophy . . . That's the Chinese for you. Only show that you submit, use the approved words, and you can get away with murder. They smoked local weed and spoke of the visitation phenomenon. You know your spiritual exercise is getting somewhere when you hit this *flood* of joy, objective, measurable joy, penetrating everyone in the room—

Cherry had not been a neuronaut. Weird science hadn't been in her repertoire in the Reich years. Her repertoire had been the Babes' pink Cadillac and a flirty sax, the fantastic feeling of swanning around with Dora and Felice. She thought maybe the terror drew her, more than the joy. Going under the scanner would be a step into the dark, stripped of everything, measuring her unknown self—

'Sage told me he's always there,' Chip reported. '*Always*, in some sense. When the secret police were torturing him, he was t-touching the beautiful void—'

Chez and Ver were immediately very jealous. Sage was their idol.

'So George said, what about when you go into one of yer mammoth sulks—'

They stirred in relief. Aha, so you weren't alone with him!

'What did he say?'

'He said *yeah, then too*. George and Bill were disgusted.'

The yurt was more beautiful than practical. It had a furry hide, a conical dome, and no sewn-in groundsheet, just rucked plastic tarp. The cold crept through their rugs, the keepers of the flame sat close, barely short of touching each other.

'I can't believe the Chinese think Sage is ugly.'

'They don't appreciate white guys,' said Verlaine. 'They don't like blue eyes.'

'They don't appreciate negritude much, either—' Chip launched into a rueful anecdote about an AMID squaddie he'd tried to chat up.

Verlaine and Chez caught each other gazing, and looked away. You look at someone, he's looking at you, but it can never happen.

The spiritual quest, and it seems so real—

Allie lay awake, half-drunk, thinking no, I don't want another body in the bed. We weren't lovers like that, he was never my soft toy. For weeks, months, after the breaking of the siege, she had been literally haunted. She'd seen DK's face in dreams, and sometimes in daylight, blackened and twisted by the Chinese incendiaries; the eyes still living. Here at Yap Moss, where hundreds of people had died in an afternoon, she realised with a sharper pain, a sting of final loss, that she wanted to forget him. What she really wanted was to fall in love. With someone new, someone from outside the circle, someone who knew nothing.

Fiorinda was in the other bunk, with Min. She'd been sleeping in Allie's van occasionally through the tour; sometimes the Foxes had gone off to do a show on their own. It made her feel young again. Wherever I lay my sleeping bag that's my home. How I wish Allie could have a happy love song, what's going on with that platonic threesome (give me a break, *platonic*); how great to be with the Babes with no kids for a change. Hope Sage is okay in London, swallowing that anger he's not allowed to express. The anger we must none of us express—

A ripple in her belly. Three weeks, she told herself.

fell asleep thinking of Ax and Sage, burying the dead.

George woke to find someone shaking him, and sat up at once. He was in one of the astronaut bunks, in the kitchen in Sage's monster van, and he was not alone. The local girl squeaked and vanished under the covers.

'Oh, ah, G'mornin' Fio. What's up?'

Extremely disconcerted, he reached for his clothes.

'Are you all right, my dear?'

Fiorinda looked at a slim hand which had emerged from the duvet and was groping at the floor. She poked the tumble of hejab attire into its reach, with her toe. 'No, I'm not all right. I'm having real contractions.'

'Holy fuck.' George pulled his trousers on, sheet modestly bunched in his lap. George and Lauren, his wife of many years, who was a potter and at present living under the Chinese occupation in St Ives, had no children. 'Are you *sure*, love?'

'Yes. My waters broke, and I've had a show. George it's a *problem*. I'm supposed to have a Caesarean. I won't bore you with the details but I just read my medical notes again, which I am carrying with me, I'm not stupid. It's important I get a Caesarean. I've tried using willpower but it,' she frowned, and drew a sharp breath, 'it isn't working. I need drugs to stop this labour and I need a hospital.'

'Where's Allie? Did you wake the Babes?'

'I've been here before,' said Fiorinda, looking to and fro. She was holding Min, the young cat looked frightened out of his wits. Fiorinda's eyes were black stones rimmed in silver, sweat stood on her brow. 'Haven't I? Why aren't things flying around, we're in space, aren't we? Where's Sage?'

'He'll be here soon,' said George. 'You sit quiet, we'll sort this out.'

George knocked up Bill, who emerged with *his* bedmate, Clio, the young muso-techie from Jam Today; Areeka's band. Peter appeared, and then Marlon. The lacquer incense box of ancient memory, that held the

Heads' supply of endogenous psychotropics, was rifled for progesterone, without success. A number of brain chemistry recreationals on the inventory were eager to *promote* labour, none of the fuckers wanted to put the brakes on. Clio ran to see if any sister on the Jam Today bus had the herbal remedies that might help, dongquai, liquorice extract.

Peter Stannen sat with Fiorinda, while everyone flapped around. *I urgently need Sage,* she whispered, knowing Cack would understand. 'Tell yourself he's alive, somewhere in the world,' he suggested, in his serious little voice. 'That's what I do. And I close my eyes. I think, if the boss was right here I wouldn't see him. So it's okay if you can't see him, he's still somewhere.'

She closed her eyes, but immediately they flew open again.

Oooh, bad idea. Cack, will you look after Min, he's Ax's cat—

'I'll look after him.'

Peter didn't like to touch animals, but this was an emergency.

The Babes and Allie arrived, with Chip and Verlaine. There was no fuel. They had tried calling a taxi, they had tried calling an ambulance. It wasn't going to work. There weren't any buses today, either. The Chinese had waived motor vehicle restrictions for the Yap Moss gig, and the whole area had been cleaned out.

'We could take her in the pony cart,' said Chip. 'There's got to be a doctor.'

'She needs a *hospital*. Fiorinda, are you timing the contractions?'

are you timing the contractions?

Her father was in the corner, clear as paint, with his rich curling hair and his red mouth, looking at her. She knew no one else could see him, so she didn't bother telling them. The van windows were black as obsidian. God, he's trying to claw my belly open, oh, fuck it hurts, oh little shoot, *hide—*

'She was so normal,' breathed Allie, awed. 'She really fooled us.'

'Don't say that!' shouted George. 'She's not *fooling* anyone, she's in fugue, can't you see? Right, it's time to scream for help. We call General Yen, we call Ax and the boss, we get her to decent medical care right now, no messing.'

'You don't get it, George,' said Felice, low and furious. 'The Chinese can't hear about this. Forget the fucking big lie. They know what magic does; what it did to the A-team. They see her in schizophrenic fugue, they're going to *scan her brain*, how are we going to stop them?, and it'll be all over.'

So this is what happens. You get caught jamming with the people in the New Third World, just when you really need to be swanking with the bosses. Fiorinda was supposed to have her baby in Lambeth, at the Snake Eyes Commune, everything was laid on for a Caesarean home birth. The privileged don't go to hospital, hospital comes to them. This time a few hours ago they would have fought *battalions* to stop Fiorinda from being taken to a dodgy public hospital. They'd rather have rallied a Reich surgical team, used a lot of boiling water, and tackled the job themselves.

They were silent, minds racing, failing to connect with any solution.

'Thank God it's morning,' said Allie. 'At least we're sober. Think, think.'

'I was thinking exactly the opposite of that,' countered Chip. 'I was thinking: one of us ought to take something, I don't know what. Well, I know what would work (snapshot, of course), and try to join her where she is. To be with her.'

'You are out of your *mind*!'

Their rock and roll princess sat with her knees drawn up, head bowed. Her red hair looked like tight-coiled blood in the pearly ATP light. Her nightdress and her coat, her bare feet, made her look like someone fleeing from a burning building. But the black flames were inside Fiorinda, the petals of a black rose. They were afraid to touch her. They lived with Fiorinda without ever thinking of what she could do to them, but now she wasn't in her right mind. She would rather die than do harm, how close was she to that edge? They had never *dreamed* that they could be in this situation, without Ax and Sage.

Peter was afraid too: he'd put on his skull mask. The Heads didn't wear their skulls now, but Peter always kept the controller on him, in case he urgently needed to take cover. The expressionless death's head made them feel as if time had folded around. They were in the past, and they'd forgotten how frightening their past had been, until this moment. The green nazi time, the threat of the occult superweapon. Mind-bending fear, how quickly you forget; until you're in the same place again.

Fiorinda cried, not the way a woman in labour cries: like something inhuman. Ax's cat got down from the couch with his ears flat, and slunk underneath.

'I'm thinking Charm Dudley,' said Dora. 'She had a midwife.'

'What?' demanded George, distracted. 'Charm had a *what*?'

'She had a midwife with her.'

blank, in which no time passed and fearful things happened

then there was Cafren Free, DARK's milk-blonde English rose, wherever she'd sprung from: too close, bringing on such an explosion of memory, oh God, where is Sage, I need him, I need him, a bunch of pink roses with blood-red thorns, a hot violence in her head, clay in her throat, come away with me, child, to the dark, under the hill, let me break you open, let me have that baby.

are you timing the contractions?

Oh, someone's talking to me. 'Yeah, more or less. Where's Sage?'

'Fio, listen. Birch has fuel in her tank. Remember, the midwife who came to see you? She stayed on site, she had a feeling she'd be needed. She's going to take you to the Priory, they'll look after you.'

Bill's voice, suspicious and angry. 'The *Priory*? What, is it a rehab place?'

'It's a commune,' said Cafren to Fiorinda, her voice echoing along wide empty corridors, in a very lonely place, where no help could come. 'They have a cottage hospital, women only.'

'A hippy commune?' Felice, shouting. 'Are you *crazy*?'

'They're not hippies—'

Fiorinda heard them deciding who would join this party. Charm and the midwife, Allie. George's ladyfriend, who would help them if they needed local knowledge, and George and Bill, who insisted. The Babes would stay behind, the fort must be held, and there was no room. She would have said *I want Felice*, but she didn't know that she could speak to these voices, so far away. She didn't want to think about it, anyway. The back of the van had no windows, she craned forward to see out of the cab. A point of light grew smaller and smaller, while the dead roses crawled up behind her, squirming like the bodies in the red fighting ring, and the moment was coming when she would have to kill herself and the baby. A shadow fell, they were passing through some tall, ruinous gates. There were rampant evergreens and trees, she tried to see the ground under them. Not a living flower.

The Priory was a big neglected, Victorian house in its own bleak grounds: gables like frowning eyes peered through naked branches. Birch told them to wait.

'I don't like this,' muttered George. 'The Babes were right, this is trouble.'

'Countercultural's not a hate word, man,' snarled Charm. 'Wi just pretend it is, te satisfy the new bosses. They're not *witches,* it's a women's refuge.'

The deer-skinned midwife appeared again. 'George and Bill may come into the hall,' she said. 'They can't stay. Holy Mother's coming to greet Fiorinda.'

George got Fiorinda out of the little van in his arms; with the baby onboard she was still feather-light. It was like carrying a paralysed child, rigid and helplessly contracted, and he was glad her face was hidden, he didn't want to see those eyes. 'You'll be all right, love, you'll be all right now.'

'You have to be okay, Fio,' Bill stuck close, glowering at Charm Dudley, who might think she could muscle in. 'Or he'll kill us.'

'He can flay me alive,' said George. 'I'll hold his coat.'

The Heads had watched over this blazing girl since she was fourteen. They loved and honoured the woman she'd become more than any wife or lover. They would die for her, any time, but that's not going to fucking help now.

Allie brought Fiorinda's bag. They hurried into a wide, high hall, and saw the grey, weathered wooden figure of the goddess. Three metres tall if she was an inch, swathed in drapery, crowned with a wreath of dead flowers, dead birds, a face of sombre majesty, great dark eyes hollowed by mourning . . . it was the Grey Lady, the Floods Conference apparition, as she'd been seen in Amsterdam; attested by many witnesses, including Ax Preston.

(Tho' Ax'd never allowed himself to be drawn on whether she was a projection from the collective unconscious, truly supernatural; or what.)

She was supposed to be Gaia, mourning the death of the living world.

'Oh *fuck,*' groaned George.

They were in a house of death, Gaia worship was proscribed. They would have walked straight out, but then what? On foot?

Fiorinda stood where George had set her down, looking at the totem. A mass of women, dressed in unbleached fine wool or deerskin, poured into the hall. Some looked like nurses but others were armed, with knives in their belts, quivers of shuriken, metal-bound staves. One of these, a hawk-faced Pakistani, burn-scarred from brow to chin, strode forward and whipped off the hejabi girl's headscarf. An older woman, robed in grey, hair and throat hidden by a close, unbleached coif, came through the excited crowd, with Birch beside her.

'Ms Slater's gone into premature labour,' announced George—

'It's not premature,' said Birch, to the grey-robed woman.

Allie decided to ignore Gaia. The place was *here*, and it looked very clean.

'You have a women's hospital, do you have a, a maternity bed?'

'We want drugs to slow the labour doon,' Charm elbowed Allie out of the way. 'An' help te get hor te a non-fucking hippy-dippy maternity unit. Er, please.'

'The lady is safe in our care,' said the woman in grey. 'You women may stay or leave, except for the hejabi; that girl and the men must go.'

George and Bill looked at each other, and at the crowd of Amazon warriors, knee-high, but so many of the critters. 'Okay,' said George, breathing hard. 'But she needs a Caesarean, can your staff handle that, er, Reverend Mother?'

'It's in her notes,' said Bill. 'We've got them with us.'

'We are Gaians. We do not use the knife on a mother's body.' The woman raised her hands, as did many of the others, making the goddess mudra popularly known as 'the yoni with eyes'. 'The mother's body is Gaia.'

'But she *needs a Caesar*,' repeated George, sweat breaking out.

'And she's going to *get* one,' snapped Bill.

George was carrying an automatic pistol. It wasn't contraband. General Yen had required them either to assign a firearms officer, or have armed squaddies on their sites. It had been better not to argue. He'd brought it with him, thinking recklessly, *power is power*. He realised the madness of drawing a weapon, but that left him helpless as Gulliver, his hand sliding under his jacket of its own accord—

The armed women saw the movement. He saw their eyes flash with cool calculation, how many of them he could take down, and his heart failed him. All these years, unlike Ax and Sage, he'd often been carrying, never fired in anger—

The Grey Lady and Fiorinda looked at each other. The wooden totem opened her arms and stooped down to lay her hands Fiorinda's shoulders. 'Thank you,' said Fiorinda. Oh, fuck. Better do something, before George gets in awful trouble—

'Holy Mother.'

Fiorinda stepped forward, and gripped the back of a chaise lounge, solid piece of Victoriana. She was breathing short, her reckless mouth a tight line, her eyes fixed in concentration. 'I've got a brilliant idea. *Make an exception*. Just for me.'

The Holy Mother, thank God, consented. But they had to find their own surgeon, it had to be a woman, and she had to be brought here: Fiorinda wasn't going anywhere. Allie stayed with Fio. The van was handed over to them outside the house. George took the wheel. Charm was so knocked back by the trap she'd led them into that she didn't protest. It was starting to rain.

'They had no right to fucking snatch your scarf like that, Janan,' said Bill.

Janan was George's ladyfriend. 'They *hate* Islam at that place,' she said. 'It's not fair, it's prejudice, women-hating bastards can be any religion.'

(Whatever, they thought. Hatred isn't going to help—)

The gates were open. A few metres down the track that led to the road to Skipton, George pulled up. 'Okay, regroup, how do we tackle this?'

Rain smacked the windshield. He checked the fuel gauge, not bad, and made sure the Routemaster was up to date. Find a female surgeon, quickly. Does it have to be an obstetrics specialist, or will a fucking vet do? He was very shaken.

'Can you help us, Janan?'

'I hope so.'

'Can we use a phone?' demanded Bill. 'If not, we could be screwed.'

'What, and get overheard by the liberators? They're *Gaia worshippers*, mon,' snapped Charm. 'That's Counterculture wi' a bullet. She can't be in there.'

'Right, so we agree on a story—'

One of the warriors had followed them. She rapped on George's window for him to lower it, and stuck her head in. 'Whoever you bring back, better not be a Muslim. Don't care who it's for.' She glared at Janan. 'We only take Islamics if they've packed it in.' She withdrew her head, and hurried off into the rain.

'Great,' muttered Bill. 'Bet that narrows it down, round here, eh, Janan?'

'I've got an idea,' said Charm, doubtfully. 'But it's desperate.'

Allie waited in a birthing room. The Gaians brought Fiorinda, bathed, and dressed in a sleeveless grey shift. Her eyes were quiet, she was smiling. 'Fio,' whispered Allie, 'is this place okay? Are you going to be okay?'

'I don't know,' said Fiorinda, sadly. 'Maybe not. Maybe my little shoot is going to die, because she can't get out. But I'm sorry I lost it, I'm all right now.'

'I've got your bag here. Do you want anything?'

Fiorinda recoiled, her pupils flaring. 'Put that outside! Get it away from me!'

She changed her mind, she had to have the tapestry bag in sight, but as far away as possible. Allie had to move it a couple of times. The contractions slowed, but Fiorinda had no peace. Her body shook with useless pain, shook with useless pain. The midwives – a succession, as Birch brought her colleagues for consultation – examined her at intervals, and saw nothing that made them happy. Fiorinda's cervix was damaged; whatever the Gaians tried, it refused to dilate. They said *every labour is different*, and *it's early days*, but Allie knew they were scared.

The rain continued, beating on the walls and windows of the Priory, the bare trees and the grey dales. Allie had been her sister's birth-partner, she'd looked forward to sharing this day with Fiorinda. She was well-prepared, but she soon stopped asking questions. The midwives had a lot of skill, powerful herbal medicines, and not much tech. There was nothing they could do.

Fiorinda thought of going to look for a sharp knife, but she was so tired. Allie would stop her, the nuns would hold her down, let me keep some dignity. I cannot get out, said the starling . . . Shoot will not die straight away, soon I will think of something. Crouched at the head of the bed, nursing her rigid belly, she heard the scraping of Allie's chair. Hands coaxed her to lie down, as the spasm passed. A face looked at her, a Chinese face, framed between a military cap and a streaming wet raincape. Oh fuck, we're busted. She was past caring. The face said something in Chinese, went away, and there was Charm Dudley's triumphant mug instead.

'Who loves ye, princess? Here's the lady wi' the knife. We got hor frem Skipton Fort fre ye, affta gannin aal around the houses.'

'They don't have women.'

'They dee, man. People's Liberation Army lasses jus' don't bother dressing up in girl-suits. Ye dinna haveta, princess. It's not law.'

When she grasped that she wasn't going to be moved to a Chinese military hospital, Fiorinda was so relieved she got arrogant and reminded everyone she'd booked an epidural. She was frightened of a General, you woke up sterilised; or had that happened later? The surgeon and her anaesthetist said (in US English) no way, lady, you're going under. They assured her they would do it by acupuncture needles, which didn't sound too good. She held Allie's hand and watched them get ready, capped and masked, the sound of the rain.

'Elder Sister is not alone,' she murmured. 'What's your name?'

The knife-lady said, in English, 'Doctor Mao. My name is Mao Huafeng.'

'Hua means flower,' said Fiorinda, 'what character is Feng?'

'I'll write it for you. Now relax.'

She felt a change in her blood, a new mix of hormones, the sweet flowing oxytocin, which she thought she would call Sage, and something slippery, fibrous, darker, that's the prostaglandins, I'll call that my Ax. Oh, she thought, mutinous, I was just scared, I could have done it by myself.

When Fiorinda's friends poured out their epic tale, she found it hard to believe it had all happened in daylight. What she remembered was waking from the anaesthetic to find Huafeng and the anaesthetist gone, a Gaian midwife putting her baby into her arms, and a very confused dream about Sage's van in the middle of the night. Her father, a garden with no flowers; George being attacked by little demons, the Grey Lady . . . All right, she had been in a poor state, but *surely* it had been dark. She didn't argue the point. The Few brought gifts, warm clothes and food, toys the baby might like in a few years' time. The heroes gabbled about racing around the hospitals, and finally arriving at Skipton Fort. Turned out Charm had made a personal contact, and this contact had got them into the women's military medical team office. They'd explained how Ms Slater had been caught short, and forced to seek help at an unfortunate venue. Dr Mao had agreed to come along, no reprisals for the Priory. Charm claimed a victory for dyke internationalism. Fiorinda thought it was typically Chinese. They make the rules, they break the rules, as it suits them.

They were dancing in the rain, Charm said. All the Chinese, in their pretty uniforms, *dancing* in the rain, on a parade ground walled by the glowing *di*—

She had a neat wound across the top of her pubic hair, which reminded her queasily of Toby Starborn. She had a room to herself, and the grey-clad nurses left her alone a great deal; which was good. Between feeding and nappies, getting her wound dressed, and meals she didn't like, she practised walking about, holding her baby. She thought of the Chinese soldiers, dancing in the rain. Yen's troops were from the north, they came from country that was no longer habitable, oh, that's a problem.

She knew no one else had seen the statue come alive. The goddess stooping to touch her shoulders had come from deep inside herself, where there was an open door to the silent ocean; where her father, and all the demons that had been scaring her, vanished into nothing. Things like that would happen more often, to everyone. The aberrant observations had been validated, and their power would grow. Maybe we can erase the superweapon, but the genie's not going to go back into the bottle. She had sweated blood and fought with all her power against the rise of the magic world view – how irrational can you get? It was strange to let go. She lay for hours holding the baby's tiny hand, and learned acceptance, and made her peace.

The Few visited her once. Her boyfriends didn't call, didn't appear; when she braved the tapestry bag she discovered she didn't have a phone or her tab with her. The nurses said that she should treasure this sacred time alone with her baby. It was a few days before it dawned on her that she was (in a very mild way) a prisoner. She said nothing, she just stashed her clothes and money. Fuck it, I don't want to pick a fight. When I'm ready to leave, I'll simply walk out.

On the seventh, maybe eighth, night she lay awake, the baby sleeping in her cradle at the end of the bed. The room was on the first floor, at the back of the house. Every night the nurses closed her curtains: Fiorinda waited for the women to go, and opened them again. She watched the tossing branches and the dim, rain-filled sky; and listened to stealthy movement. The lock on her sash window shifted, as if it were haunted. The lower half moved upwards, a figure clambered in. Fiorinda didn't stir, until another had followed. It was thrilling to lie and watch, unsuspected; and yes, it was goodbye to a sacred time, no more just you and me, baby—

She sat up, struck a match and lit her bedside lamp.

'What did you do to the guards?'

Sage pulled off his balaclava. 'Nothing. What guards?'

'We came over the wall,' said Ax. 'From the moor, like foxes.'

'We've been in Skipton, trying to get in here. Finally we suborned a nun—'

'A pub-going nun, and she told us which was your room.'

'We were fucking scared, we thought she might be pissing us around, an' we'd find ourselves invading Mother Superior's boudoir—'

Fiorinda laughed. They were like little boys, bringing her the wild dark and the fresh night air and their delight in adventure. Then for a moment they didn't know what to do with each other; such a transition, they felt like strangers.

Sage came to the bed and sat down, taking her hands. 'I wasn't there,' he said. 'Oh, Fiorinda. I left you all alone.'

So the Few had talked. Can't I ever lose the plot without people telling tales? 'It was nothing,' she said. 'I was in no danger, *truly*. I was just scared.' She meant to brush it off, but his gravity invaded her. She felt the weight of his body in her arms, and heard the whisper of the tide, under the walls of Drumbeg Castle. 'You did not desert me. You are always with me, on the beach at Roaring Water Bay.'

Ax peeled off his own terrorist headgear, went to the bedroom door and turned the key in the ancient lock. Should give them time to hide under the bed if the nuns came. Sage head was down, Fiorinda was holding him and whispering. Ax wanted to join them, but he felt they had private business; he wouldn't intrude.

His attention was caught by the cradle, at the foot of her bed.

Oh, God. That's the baby.

A pair of candles stood on the mantelpiece. He lit one, and took it over to the cradle. That's Fiorinda's baby girl. That's what this was all about. She seemed big for her age, but he had never really *looked* at other newborns. She lay on her back, the dome of her head covered by a fine dark thatch, her little mouth snuffing at the edge of a knitted blanket. Insensate need to get closer, he set the candlestick on a stand that held baby-care things and knelt, brooding over her. *Hi, little shoot, d'you remember me? Good news, You can have a proper name now . . .* That blanket's getting in her mouth. He reached into her domain, very carefully, his hand seeming rough as a brick and enormous; and tucked it back. The baby opened her eyes and gazed up at him, without a sound.

'Hey, Sage—'

'Yeah?' Sage sat up, and tugged Fiorinda close in a fierce, frantic hug, making her yelp. 'Sorry.' He wiped his eyes with the side of his hand. 'What?'

She was grinning at him like starlight.

'Think I've got something of yours over here, maestro.'

Sage sat on the bed holding the baby, he had picked her up with an insouciant confidence that Ax envied. Ax, however, had Fiorinda, warm and pliant against his side, and thought it a fair exchange. 'Oh, hey, you have a souvenir from Elder Sister. A memento of our Anglian adventure.' He reached for his backpack and gave her the present, wrapped in rather battered gold tissue.

'It's not for the baby?' Only baby presents were interesting.

'She didn't know your baby would be born.'

The package held an envelope, and a jewellery case with a message taped to the lid, saying DECORATIONS WILL BE WORN. It was diamonds.

'Hmph,' said Fiorinda, and set them aside; 'very nice.' She opened the envelope and scanned the document inside, a wry smile dawning.

'What is it?'

'Unbelievable. It's your papers, Ax.'

Overseas Chinese were safe, judged citizens of the Sphere. It was the ethnics of satellite nations, and the Debatable Cases, who had the problem. How many mixed-race persons can *prove*, once suspicion has been raised, that they are ten generations clear of Chinese DNA? Not fucking many, given that 'Chinese DNA' is a meaningless punitive concept to start with. Not Ax Preston, with those pretty almond-shaped brown eyes; who has no idea what's in his dad's family tree. As far as they knew there had been no forcible transfers from England to Guangdong re-education camps; yet. But it was a threat the Chinese had used routinely in other countries.

'She's clearing the ground,' said Fiorinda, handing Ax his surreal permission to be English. 'Removing impediments. She's going to get you in the end.'

He put the envelope away. 'I don't want to think about that right now.'

'So what's been happening?' she demanded. 'What did the Gaians tell you?'

'They plan to keep you here until they've talked to you about your novitiate,' said Sage, grinning. 'They don't want to lose you, an' I can't blame them.'

'They can forget it. What about the Chinese? What's David Yen thinking? I've been scared he might wait 'til I've left, and decide to have a pogrom.'

'There's no risk of that,' said Ax. 'Things have moved on . . .'

They grinned at her, bright-eyed, full of themselves.

'How are you Fiorinda? How are you feeling? Are you doped at all?'

'Full of milk. Smelling of stale milk and baby sick.' She pulled a face. 'I hope you can get used to that, it's my signature for a while. Stitches melting nicely, I don't have to have them yanked out, I am glad to say. Not at all doped, just weak from lying in bed in this nunnery. If you hadn't come, I was going to shoot an arrow e'en from that very window, and have my outlaw band bury me where it fell.'

'Your outlaw band's in Huddersfield, playing to rave reviews without you, I call it shallow and ungrateful of them. Don't you call it shallow, baby?'

'Such is fame. You'll make her scream if you talk like that. She gets furious when people say things to her that she doesn't understand. It's more of a penetrating squeak than a scream as yet, but I warn you she goes for it.'

The baby did not scream. She was too interested in staring at her father.

'So, if we asked you to climb out of the window, could you do it?'

'Sure. You have a getaway car?'

'Fuelled up,' said Ax. 'We hope to kidnap you quietly without any discussion, but we'll brave Mother Superior if we must. What about it?'

'Two minutes.' Fiorinda scooted out of the bed. She tossed her nightie, the night bra, her pants and towel (bleeding already nearly over, thanks to Gaian herbalist), replaced that kit with fresh, dug out her stash and dressed in the clothes the Few had brought: every move nailed by a fascinated tiger and a hungry wolf. Yep, I'm back. Skinny as ever, except for the bosoms, it's my nature. Their gaze made her blush, hey, there's a small child with us you know.

'Where are we headed? Huddersfield?'

She didn't want to join the gang, she was guilty of wanting to be alone with baby, tiger and wolf, but where else? It felt extremely weird to be normal shape again, she cinched the belt of her trousers and looked up. They were smiling enigmatically.

'Further than that,' said Sage. 'Are you up for a long drive?'

'We're going home.'

To London first, in Ax's black Volvo coupé; which had been on blocks in a garage in Brixton, untouched by Hu Qinfu or other souvenir hunters. Then the roads to the south-west. A car that had been cramped for three, when one of them was Sage, was ridiculous for four, plus baby gear and a cat in a carrying-case. They didn't care.

They slept at roadhouses, and passed into Cornwall through a Chinese checkpoint at the Guinevere Bridge. They were welcomed with silence, and some tears; their privacy was respected. Better to have come back in triumph, but this is how we win. Piecemeal solutions, step by step. We'll live the way our people live, surrounded by the conquerors. Across Bodmin Moor, and up the lane from the Powdermill in twilight, hazel catkins shaken under the budding branches of the oaks; the little Chy rushing over its boulders. The stone at our turn, half-buried in red bracken, that says *Tyller Pystri*; which means the magic place. Up the hill and there's the twin beeches, sky-fingering crowns streamlined by Atlantic gales. Open the gates, park the car on the hardstanding under them. The back porch, where the spare keys are waiting, in the Dutch clog hanging from its nail. The cottage room, cold from long absence, the deep windows where night looks in.

They named the baby on Fiorinda's birthday, in a ceremony at the waterfall pool, under the holly trees. Sage and Fiorinda had seriously intended to dunk her bodily, where the water swirled and bubbled. Ax refused to countenance this, so they compromised with a washing-up bowl, and Chy water warmed by ATP from Sage's fingertips. Now you belong here, little one. Your name is Cosoleth, Sage's choice; and Huafeng, after the Skipton Fort surgeon. You'll obviously find this direly embarrassing when you are old enough to have an opinion, count yourself lucky we allowed you the veil of foreign language, Peace Flowers–Blown–by–the–Wind. Other rockstar kids have suffered worse, how would you like to be called Pit-Viper, hm?

No one need know, anyway. You'll be Coz, for all practical purposes.

They treated Ax's citizenship papers with respect: copied them, and filed the document carefully. The more idiotic something like that seems, the more likely it is to grow fangs and tear you to pieces. Fiorinda came across the diamonds again when she and Sage were sizing up the larger of the upstairs bedrooms, with a view to turning it into Coz's room eventually. The other upstairs room was Marlon's, though he rarely came here; and always would be.

The baby was on the bed in her basket, very gaudy in a dress made from a Hawaiian shirt by Ruthie Maynor, Sage's housekeeper, who lived nearby and kept Tyller Pystri in order. Baby clothes were a problem, they had vanished from the face of the earth, but the solutions were entertaining. Min the kitten – now a huge, dappled and spotted young cat – sat beside her looking touchingly devoted; actually watching for his chance to get in the basket, his main object in life. Sage was measuring walls with a metal tape, what a bizarre activity for Aoxomoxoa.

Fiorinda sat at the dressing table – a piece of furniture dating from when Tyller Pystri had been a holiday rent, before Sage's time – sorting through a heap of debris she must have tipped out of her bag, and dumped in here in a tidying fit. Strange things happen when you're looking after a new baby, items vanish and reappear in weird places. The jewellery case had shed that rather tactless reminder of the Rainbow Bridge incident. She couldn't remember what it was, opened it and got a face full of glittering light. She held the necklace to her throat.

Sage came over to admire the effect.

'Will you ever wear it?'

'No . . . The stones are good, though. I'd sell them if I dared. It's interesting that she likes diamonds.'

'Why?'

'Oh, no reason,' said Fiorinda, secretly thinking that she knew of a diamond Elder Sister would like to own. 'She gives us diamonds, she gives us sexy state-of-the-art videographic hardware. What do you think she wants in return, Sage?'

They looked into the threefold mirror where the back lawn was reflected, starred with spring flowers, blossom trees around it. Ax had been dead-heading the camellia hedge. He'd finished his chore and was playing guitar, sitting on a green bank, a basket of bruised red flowers at his feet. They could not hear the music, which made him seem far away, and infinitely precious. I will grow old in this house, thought Fiorinda. This is where I will grow old and die.

'I dunno,' said Sage. 'I suppose we'll find out.'

She looked up, they shared a faint, grim smile.

Tyller Pystri cottage had no outbuildings. Sage's twelve acres held one other potential dwelling, an L-shaped ruined barn by the track above the house; halfway to the boundary where the cliff top became National Trust property. Sage and Ax and the baby strolled up there one balmy day near the end of April. They climbed into the loft, and set Coz's basket down a safe distance from the drop.

Her eyes they shone like diamonds
We thought her a queen of the land
And her hair it hung over her shoulder
Tied up with a black velvet band . . .

She liked their singing. At her most alert she listened attentively, and opened her soft beak of a mouth to make her approval noise, eh, eh, eh. She was dozy now, where's the fun in being awake in the daytime? Fiorinda still maintained that Coz didn't scream, but Fiorinda had the knack of barely wakening, when she fed the baby at night. She was four weeks old, and the volume and variety of her yelling was coming on by leaps and bounds. In some lights her eyes were as vivid as when they'd startled Ax, but mostly they'd turned cloudy; baby blue. She had no hair at present, the dark thatch had fallen off. 'I fucking pray she doesn't turn out yellow,' said Sage. 'Yellow curly hair is an evil burden, bane of my life.'

'She has eyebrows. I don't think she'd have eyebrows at this point, if she was going to be a blonde.'

They walked around, kicking up mealy straw dust, squinting at the blue sky through the rents in the roof, which was partly intact over this loft; mostly vanished. 'She could have a grand piano, couple of them, and we'd still have rooms for visitors. It's no distance from the house, but it'd be her space.'

'You reckon you can get planning permission?'

'Oh yeah.' North Cornwall homeboy grinned sheepishly. 'I can swing it.'

'Ooh, I probably don't want to know about that.'

'It's more of a problem exac'ly where the money would come from.'

The Triumvirate had been very broke since a hostile government had decided that they personally owned the Reich. It was a hell of a mouth to feed, even in its reduced and battered state. They had no idea what was going to happen about all that, in the future that was still so uncertain.

'We have to sort out our finances. We aren't penniless, just screwed-up.'

Sage went to sit in the hayloft opening, long legs folded up, looking back towards the chimneys of Tyller Pystri. Ax sat by the baby basket; Coz slept. Sage's pathologically unreconstructed cottage had been the spiritual home they visited mainly in dreams. Brixton Hill, Ax's place, had been where Fiorinda had her music room. The wicked way men think, forever keeping score, forever wanting to put our mark on her. Ax knew what he was being asked. *I have lived in your house, will you live in mine, is that going to work?* Sage's averted profile, thick yellow lashes shielding the laser-blue, struck him as unbearably touching.

'Come over to my side, big cat?'

Sage came over. 'I love you,' said Ax. 'Don't you believe that?'

'Sometimes I think a threesome can't work long-term.'

Ax measured Sage's long fingers against his own, and kissed the palm. 'I'll never leave you. I wish I could say, I'll never let anything hurt you again—'

'Sssh . . . Ax, what makes you sure the offer you want is on the table?'

'I'm not sure of anything,' said Ax. 'But we keep going forward.'

He still had to collect his present from Elder Sister; delivered in person.

They sat thinking of changes, in this unchanging place. 'A building project will be good, tactically. It'll make us look—'

'Trusting,' agreed Sage. 'Yeah. I thought of that, too.'

III

Ghosts

When the Insanitude site was opened Ax went up to London alone. He didn't see why Sage and Fiorinda had to watch the sifting of those ashes; whilst providing photo-opportunities for Chinese mediafolk. The gesture was significant, the English finally being allowed to bury their dead. The event turned out to be lo-key; depressing as a poorly attended funeral. He did not feel much emotion, but it was eerie when they got to walking around inside the pavilion – no nanotech, just panels of translucent, rigid plastic – that had been erected over the ruins. The State Apartments had *vanished*. There were labels, as if on the site of some ancient city crushed by aeons: telling you in Chinese and English that this was where the Throne Room was, this was the Ballroom (everything at ground level, melded into the same charcoal porridge). The Met's Civil Disaster Squad was at work alongside Hu Qinfu's team, suited up and oddly identical, so as not to contaminate any human remains with their DNA.

The Few had stayed away, quite rightly, but Roxane Smith had turned up. Ax walked with hir at the head of the sad little procession, annoyed because he didn't want to talk to Rox. People thought he blamed hir for ducking out of sight in the invasion. He wasn't such a hypocrite. It was hir slippery performance under the Second Chamber that stuck in his throat: when the cunning old critic had turned hir coat, dissing the Reich from a great height . . . Neutral topics. They spoke of Cornelius Sampson, who had recently died, without recovering from his dementia. But he'd been kindly cared for, and he'd seemed to appreciate that, before the end.

'Richard thinks Corny knew him,' said Rox. S/he'd got hirself onto Richard Kent's list of approved video visitors. He ought to thank hir for that, Rich was in a very lonely position. 'And was happy to have him there. Though he never really spoke, or showed any sign of recognising his own name—'

'Yeah, he told me.' I'm on the list. Been talking to Rich myself, thanks.

'More like an old dog,' sighed Rox, 'than a human being. Old and blind, but still knowing master, and glad to be patted.' S/he stopped for a breather, leaning hard on hir ebony cane. 'I'm thinking of leaving the country.'

'Good idea,' said Ax, staring at the masked, Noddy-suited ash-sifters through one of the internal screens. Then he felt that he was being vicious. 'How long d'you think they'll keep it up? Find a tooth and lay some concrete, with a memorial slab—'

'I haven't a clue. It's a strange ritual.'

Ax was thinking of DK. Would he be reassured when he was told that some fragment with Dilip's barcode on it had turned up? Not really. A good part of Ax wanted to forget that doubtful story, and go with the positive things. Dian Buckley's appearance at Ashdown seemed so long ago, so irrelevant. But they'd discovered, when they tried to find her, that Dian was dead.

She caught pneumonia and she died; it happens.

An armed policewoman came up.

'Mr Preston, sir. There's a phone call for you.'

He had an earbead. 'Yeah? So patch it through.'

'I'm sorry sir, I can't do that. You'll have to come with me.'

Ax did not trust the Metropolitan Police. Of all the police forces in England they'd been the ones who co-operated, consistently, with whatever bad guys came along. They'd been supervising when Fiorinda was about to be burned alive. The woman was giving him the big-eyes, it's important but I can't explain.

'Okay, officer, lead the way. Excuse me, Rox, catch you later.'

She led him across the Courtyard, and through a door in the tall hoarding that hid the façade of the South Wing. In a charred ground-floor corridor, smoke-stains and Republic of Europe graffiti, grief suddenly choked him. Oh memories that have no home on earth, places where you can't return. The policewoman pushed opened a door that was still on its hinges and stood back.

'I'll be outside, sir. I'll knock if anyone comes.'

The heavy outer shutters must have been in place here when the fire raged. They'd been opened or removed since. In the dimness made by the hoarding outside he saw window-glass crossed by withered tape, familiar filing cabinets overturned; the trophy display cases empty. Broken screens, rifled drawers. He must be in Allie's new office, which he'd never seen; the Second Chamber refit had been completed when he was under house arrest. They'd moved the red voicephone, from the old Office upstairs. He looked at the handset for what seemed a long time before he picked it up. If the dishes were still on the roof, if the wiring in this wing was intact, the person on the other end would be speaking from Washington DC.

from a land lost as Atlantis

'Hallo?'

'Hi, Ax. Seems like you had a long walk, am I interrupting something?'

'No, no.' Ax sat down at the blackened desk, his blood thundering. '*Fred?*'

'Can you talk, Ax? I've things to tell you.'

'I'm good to talk.'

A deep sigh. 'I think I can talk. D'you remember the one time you were in the Oval Office? When we did the national broadcast, after the LA quake and the A-team event, and Fio and Sage refused to turn up? You said I should have the Civil Flag behind my desk, and I said, no, Old Glory is right, this is war, we are at war, against no human enemy. They're about kill me, very soon.'

'I remember. Fred, what happened to you? We know nothing—'

'You'll hear that I took my own life, or I stopped an assassin's bullet. I hope it's the latter, but scandalising my name isn't going to worry the guys running this administration. Maybe you won't hear anything. I'll be gone, but Fred Eiffrich will serve out his term, smile on the tv, retire to his dude ranch. It's a strange world now. I sometimes think that what Fiorinda dreaded has already happened, and nothing is left but nightmare. They were going to build another Neurobomb, I couldn't allow that so I let the Chinese in. I thought, hell, at least I'll have protection from the devils who screwed me over . . . I was wrong. I've been told the problem is the Chinese don't trust me. How can they trust a guy who betrayed his own country?'

The voice was strained and low, but he knew it. A vanished reality tried to reform, a *profound* dislocation. A year ago Ax's mighty ally had been gearing up for his second-term election, damaged by the same occult-weapons scandal that had engulfed Ax Preston and Sage Pender, and led to the Triumvirate's house-arrest—

No, he thought, don't do this to me.

'You still there, Ax?'

—Fred with his glass of bourbon between his hands, by the summer fireplace in the study at Bellevue, in the dying heat of evening, convincing me to come back.

'I'm still here.'

'And answering your phone. Remember when I sent you all those e-mails and you didn't answer a single one? Got Sage to seal them up again, and bounce 'em?'

'I'd resigned.'

'I knew you'd change sides,' sighed the voice. 'I left that door open for you, when we talked about China. You did the right thing.'

You warned me you might have to cut a deal, and I'd better go belly-up at once if that happened. I don't know that I *changed sides*—

But it's all over, all gone.

'Yeah.'

'You know what the Neurobomb is, Ax. You understand we've only had a taste of that literal hell. I saved the USA from damnation, the only way I knew how. And they call me an *opportunist*. That's a slimy word. The best thing I ever did will get me set down as a coward and traitor, but that's okay. I love my country. Love doesn't win you glory, Ax. Love is not a victory march, no parade, love is hard.'

'I know that.'

Who can refuse the dead, when they return? He'd have to hang onto this phone for as long as it took, or until the policewoman knocked—

'I guess you do. Look, this is not a social call. I've been racking my brains for how I could prove this is really Fred Eiffrich, but anything can be faked, so just listen. You know that Rufus O'Niall had a divorced wife and children, from his second marriage, the one after the liaison with Fiorinda's mother and her sister? They lived in the Seychelles?'

'Yes.'

'She's had them killed. The mother, the two teenagers and the youngest child, a girl eleven years old. The estate was a fortress, it was penetrated and the whole household massacred. Openly assassinated, my guys say, no attempt to disguise it, and the children's heads taken. This happened within the last month.'

'Okay,' said Ax. 'That's . . . news.'

'I remember the first time I paid attention to the rockstar Che Guevara. You were speaking at the Flood Countries conference, about the USA. You backed it with Thucydides, verbatim, in the original, and then kindly translated for us. *Of the gods we believe, and of men we know, that by a law of their nature wherever they can rule they will. This law was not made by us, and we are not the first who have acted upon it; we did but inherit it, and shall bequeath it to all time . . .* True words, fair judgment, and you loved the Classics: you got to me. So then—'

Silence. A hunted man, thousands of miles away, listened for pursuit.

'I have to sign off. Say hi to the big guy for me. And Fiorinda, well, you know how I feel about your gallant lady. Keep her safe, if you can.' A peremptory throat-clearing, and Fred was in the room with him, about to say something rash. 'I'll pray to Mary my Mother, and her Son the crucified, the servant king, that you guys come through. Will you pray for me, Ax?'

'Yes.'

He listened for clicks and whirrs; of course he heard none. He set the handset in its cradle. Was that a voiceprint talking? I don't think so. Athens has fallen, Rome's majesty is in the dust. I think that was Fred Eiffrich, and I think he's gone now . . . Took the children's heads, oooh fuck. So it's not over.

He thought of a tiny baby girl and her mother back in Cornwall; and the mysteries surrounding a person known as *Elder Sister*. But you don't know how we're placed, Fred (was that really you?). We didn't tell you everything.

The policewoman knocked. No one had come by, but she was uneasy. Mr Preston shouldn't be out of sight for so long. He returned to the funerary rites. He was ashamed now of how he'd treated Rox, and wanted to give hir a kind word. It was too late, s/he'd left.

The Shield Ring

I

Diamonds and Rust

The dining room struck a chill, the polished pedestal table invoking family meals of choking solemnity: mother, father and daughter lost in the wastes of mahogany. The sideboard, the ranks of wine-glasses, the dead stillness. Chip and Fiorinda exchanged a shudder. There was something here they had fled from, on different trajectories, suburban Manchester, haunted Neasden; terrible hours of childhood. Cosoleth muttered, sensing her mother's unease through baby dreams. Fiorinda rubbed her cheek against the baby's head, now decorated by a fuzz of black curls, ssh, ssh—

'I'll take her out in the garden,' offered Chip, undertone; with alacrity.

'You will not. I *need* this baby.'

Sage was getting the worst of it. Dian Buckley's father had monopolised him since they turned up at the door: giving out the life-story. Mid-rank professional golfer, second career in leisure management. Semi-retired with a consultancy now, getting by despite the obstacles the Occupation put in his way. It's no joke living within twenty miles of Ground Zero. By Ground Zero Mr Buckley meant Rivermead. There was no softening towards the liberators in this house. Sage listened patiently. He'd dressed for the occasion – they were all dressed up – in a dark suit, with the new long jacket look that flattered his rangy height. A month in Cornwall had warmed his white skin, the Reich's blue-eyed rock god returns. Then you see the difference, the lines around his mouth and eyes, it's this mission but oh, he's *older*—

Lance Buckley (they'd done the introductions, it was Lance and Mimi) talked as if he dared not stop. He needn't have worried. Nobody was going to mention Dian's fall from grace, how she'd served the Second Chamber régime; or criticise her personal way of dealing with the invasion. We've all been near enough to there, we're here to remember our favoured mediababe. Mrs Buckley came in, bird-legs buckling, with a large gilt-framed tray, which she set across a corner of the table. He was tall and fit, she was a soft apple on fragile little stilts. 'Excuse me serving you myself. It's Teresa's afternoon off.'

They sipped a scalding, greyish liquid Mimi called *real coffee*, and nibbled home-made biscuits that tasted of lard. Dian had come home on January the fifteenth, not having made it back to Rexborough for Christmas or New Year. 'She was ill,' said the mother. 'She was *very* ill, I knew that at once. I put her to bed, I called the doctor. She said it was a viral pneumonia, but I could tell she was puzzled. I said does that mean hospitalisation.'

Mr Buckley – Lance – snorted, and shook his head.

'Dr Pradesh said no, better keep her at home. I nursed her—'

'*We* nursed her.'

'Yes, love. We nursed her, and in a week she was dead.'

'It's suspicious,' put in the father, grimly. 'I call it suspicious, and I'm pursuing it. I will have justice. I don't think they knew who they were playing with.'

'You both knew about Dian's relationship with Wang Xili, Mrs Buckley?'

'Mimi, Mr Pender,' she reminded him. 'It's Jemima, but I answer to Mimi. Oh yes. She'd told us the General was her boyfriend. We didn't like it—' She glanced at her husband. 'But we knew she was lucky. Seemed to be lucky. She'd made some bad choices, but she'd got over it, and we respected that. She always wanted to get ahead, be at the forefront, whatever was happening. Our Dian was a survivor.'

'She would *always* get ahead,' repeated the father. 'She followed the money.'

The rockstars nodded, straight faces. Sage moved on.

'And when she died—?'

A sudden pall fell over the best china; a darkness over the accolade of this personal visit from the Reich royalty, whom Dian had once counted as friends. 'She died in her sleep,' said Mimi, through stiff lips. 'Not really sleep, it was a coma. We'd called an ambulance, but they didn't come, they wouldn't take her.'

'You have to notify a death,' said the father. 'I wish to God we hadn't. I wish we hadn't called the f—, the ambulance service. *That's* how they knew.'

'It can't be helped,' said Mimi, 'don't get upset, Lance.'

'We should have buried her ourselves, beside Budgie . . . Budgie was her dog, she loved that dog. They were listening on our line. I should have known.'

'They were here very quickly. They had papers, it was official. They took her away, they said it was a public health measure, an unknown strain. They took swabs from us, too. We couldn't say no. We haven't had any satisfaction since.'

'I'm pursuing it. I'll take it to the Court of Human Rights.'

The father was still fighting, they both knew they had no redress. Their daughter had come home sick from her position at the forefront, died in days from a mystery illness, the Chinese had taken her body away. End of story, as far as the 2nd AMID army was concerned. But, very strangely, it was not the end of the story of what had happened in this house. Cosoleth the unpredictable opened her eyes, gazed around with gentle calm, murmured eh, eh, and turned her head to gum the edge of the baby sling. The visitors offered the silence that was all they could give—

'Would you like us to see her room?' asked Fiorinda at last.

'If you would.' Lance jumped up, trim and active sixtysomething. They could guess how he would groom the garden, pursue his hobbies restlessly, while Mimi disappeared into her depleted kitchen; he would never have enough to do.

'She was very ill,' said Mimi, breathing a little quickly, as they went up the Crisis-shabby, achingly clean and pastel stairs. 'So I put her to bed. Nothing had ever happened before, not a cold spot. The house was only ten years old when we moved in, thirty years ago. The land was arable before that, back to mediaeval times, Lance has looked it up. She brought something back with her, that's all we can think.'

The room was a shrine to which the goddess had often returned. There were elements of childhood, pony rosettes, an unexpected and touching collection of china fairies, a long-outdated music centre; but there were adult trophies too, awards, a wafer-thin 3D PC on the desk, a bookcase where Dian's own works fought for space with pop-culture reference and her school textbooks. The bed was full-sized, for tall Dian, the coverlet a fashion item, metallic indigo; with a woven pattern of wheels and stars. She still *lived* here, they thought. It was a shock, something they had never guessed about the great Dian Buckley, maker and breaker of rock gods.

Fiorinda went to the window and looked out. An immaculate garden, a band of trees, the empty A-road, and the golf course tailored like velvet, as if nothing had ever changed; Didcot Power Station dominating the horizon, birds singing, the queen of all English landscapes in between, *Go, for they call you, shepherd, from the hill* . . .

Far too much fresh water is pouring into the North Atlantic, and the Feds' crazy attempt to turn the rivers around collapsed. Our winters will grow longer and summers shorter, the cold equations mount against us; eco-revolution came too late, the beauty our Victorian ancestors thought eternal is bound to die. But right now there's some sad kind of honey still for tea at the Villa Vallambrosa, and there are worse things than climate change. She felt nothing but mournful emptiness in this room. What did that prove?

'It was going to be a cultural icon, like Tate Modern,' said Lance, beside her, bitterly. 'I suppose *they'll* do that, now. We won't be off the beaten track, when they make Ground Zero their capital.'

He wanted them to tell him this would never happen, but they could not.

'No more incidents,' said Sage, 'since Dian died?'

Mimi and Lance shook their heads.

'You saw her *talking* to the apparition? You witnessed that?'

Mimi shook her head again, reluctant, knowing this was a demotion, a close encounter but not of the top quality. 'No, never. But I heard her, and I'll swear I heard two voices. Lance wasn't in the house.'

'I saw it. Oh, I definitely saw it. She was in bed, of course, propped up on pillows, her breathing was bad. It was eleven at night, the time my wife had heard the voices. I'd come up to listen, not to disturb her. We didn't sit with her, she didn't want that . . . I was looking through the door, like this.' He crossed the room, stepped out onto the landing to demonstrate, reappeared. 'If you look at the angle you'll agree she couldn't see me, which rules out a trick arranged for my benefit, you have to think of everything, although she was so ill. Between me and my daughter's bed was a figure with its back to me. There was a nightlight, a common wax nightlight in a glass bowl, on the bedstand, that was all the light in the room. The light went through it. It was male, I'd say, if anything. Slim, er, medium height or less, very close-fitting dark clothes. I didn't hear a voice. I couldn't tell you anything about the fashion, modern or historical, but I had the impression of someone enduring, or taking on, great pain—'

The detail and emotional colour gave something away. 'You saw the apparition just once?' said Verlaine.

Lance looked cast-down. 'She was only here for a week.'

'What did you do then?' asked Fiorinda. Cosoleth snuggled closer, still wide awake and quiet. She was a snuggling adept now. She could do all kinds of tricks, her body felt entirely different, very grown-up. Mimi Buckley smiled sadly at the baby.

'I went downstairs, Ms Slater. I didn't know what I was seeing, I knew my girl was very, very ill. I thought, maybe, it was Death with her.' He hesitated. 'I didn't want to disturb whatever was going on, and I was bloody scared, too. I told Mimi—'

'Did you go back upstairs with him, to see for yourself?'

'N-no. We thought better not.'

'Did you ask Dian about it?'

'In a way we did,' said the mother hesitantly. 'But she was very ill—'

'She didn't make any clear comment. Didn't really respond.' Lance looked at his wife, and she nodded. 'Should we leave you alone?' he offered. 'The Chinese will have searched, scanned, the room, I'm afraid. They had the opportunity.'

'There was no sign of a search after they'd gone.'

'I said *scanned*, Mimi. They'll have had non-invasive methods.'

'No,' Sage glanced at the others; no dissent. 'No, that's okay.'

'We'll go down again then.'

This time they went to the conservatory, passing through a living room as desolately formal as the dining room, into the extension where the couple clearly spent their time, although it must be hell to heat. Mimi's ironing board stood beside a grotto of hobbyist hardware; clean washing was piled on an old armchair.

'That's my ghostbuster rig,' said Lance.

They sat on rustic wheelback chairs, on the cold Italian-tiled floor, surrounded by straw-hatted donkeys, china animals, endless photos of Dian. Dian as a child on a pony, Dian hugging an Airedale terrier on the lawn. Dian at a VIP premiere, at her most inhumanly glossy. Dian on a beach with her parents, towerblock hotels behind, looking – at last – like the rock journo who'd been their camp-follower.

'I have every room in the house virtually mapped,' said Lance. 'I did that as an exercise when I first got my rig. I was ready to go, soon as Mimi told me about the voices. I started recording, but—'

'He's done a lot of this. He's quite an expert. Houses, barns, haunted pools, the library at Middle Clinton, where there were confirmed occurrences.'

'I was unlucky there. Just missed the psychic incidence, I think some of them are like a meteor swarm, we pass through them, on a cycle of some kind?'

Fiorinda had collected data on the Reich's explosion of supposed paranormal activity; for her own reasons. The Counterculture had ignored this project, they'd suspected (with justice) that Fiorinda was only gathering the facts to rubbish them. The bricks and mortar public had co-operated eagerly, and been hard to turn off. Lance Buckley was one of those who would have ticked the box for *curious sceptic*. He'd gone into it, bought the gadgets, taught himself the skills. He could talk the talk (I thought Death was with her), but he believed his hobby entirely rational, nothing to do with the Counterculture, blameless as metal-detecting; a perilous frame of mind.

The visitors had no opinion on ghostly meteor swarms. 'You found you hadn't recorded anything?' prompted Fiorinda, gently. 'It's nearly always the way.'

Lance nodded. 'Often the way, don't I know it, it's very tricky. Nothing that shows up on my humble rig, I tried everything. But you'll see what you can do?'

Sage accepted a button of solid state memory; and a small manila envelope, which her father had found under Dian's pillow and removed before the Chinese medics arrived. It was addressed to no one, but from the little she'd said when she was dying he knew it was meant for Mr Pender.

'Your baby came early,' said Mimi to Fiorinda, to cover a slight awkwardness. A young mother couldn't like to be reminded of her rock god's previous attachment. 'That must have been a shock. We were all waiting to hear the news from London.'

'I had my dates wrong,' Fiorinda mugged apology. 'I don't know how it happened. I was in prison when I fell pregnant, that's my excuse.'

'She's *lovely*. So good. Do you take her with you everywhere?'

'I don't know a safer place she could be.'

'You keep to that. You stick by that.' Dian's mother tried to smile, and had to cover her eyes with one hand, to hide the tears. 'I'm sorry, excuse me.'

Lance cleared his throat. 'I suppose you'll want to give the kit a once-over. Check my parameters—'

Sage, Chip and Verlaine had given the hobbyist corner a glance as they walked in. They shook their heads. 'No need,' said Sage. 'We can figure it out.'

The Buckleys looked at each other, crestfallen and alarmed. 'You *are* going to look into this?' insisted the father. 'There's got to be something in it.'

'Yes, of course. But the most likely explanation,' said Fiorinda, frankly and kindly, 'is transient psychosis, a symptom of acute stress. I know you don't want to hear that, but because what you saw was in your minds, that doesn't mean it wasn't real. Or it wasn't important. What you experienced was part of Dian's dying—'

'Did she seem to *know* the apparition?' wondered Chip. 'Maybe you needed to feel that Death came to her as a friend. How did she seem to be reacting?'

'Tense,' said Lance, with decision. 'She was tense.'

'We'll take the button,' said Sage, 'and we'll let you know. But if I were you I'd get rid of any copies, and get rid of the ghostbuster rig.'

'The Chinese don't know it exists,' said Lance, like a child told to smash his favourite toy. 'I'll swear they don't. They didn't search down here. They can intercept a phone signal, but if they'd been snooping inside my house *I would know it.*'

'He'd know it.'

'All the same, it'd be wise. What looks innocent to you might not look innocent to the AMID. I can't advise you to stop pressing for an investigation of her death,' added Sage, with appropriate gravitas. 'That's your right. But the Chinese say they can prove they acted properly, and viral pneumonia kills healthy adults all the time. Maybe you should accept the settlement they're offering; without any admission of fault.' He raised a hand. 'I know it stings, and it won't bring her back; but it'd be closure. Take the money. It's hard, but you should let this go.'

Mr Buckley read the warning in those famous blue eyes, understood that the words were censored, and staggered under a final blow. The Triumvirate, his last hope, couldn't do a thing. 'They'll pay us compensation? They send our daughter back to us dying, like a . . . like a cast-off servant, and they'll pay compensation! My Dian, an internationally famous writer—'

'It was good of you,' broke in Mimi. 'Very good of you to come.'

They'd picked up the car from the rank at Oxford Station, where Sage and Fiorinda had rendezvoused with the Londoners. No driver, no minders attended this visit of condolence, they were on the loose in the heart of the Occupied South West and it felt unreal. Fiorinda took the

223

wheel, after a brief discussion with her co-parent. Sage took the baby. They needed a proper car-seat for her, but where do you find one of those?

'What the hell was that about Death coming as a friend, Chip?'

'I was method-acting,' said Chip, gloomily. 'The clumsy juvenile sidekick.'

'Sorry, don't worry, you were okay . . . That house creeped me out.'

Last year at Ashdown Dian had told Sage a ghost story. The Triumvirate had kept it to themselves. There'd been nothing they could do, that dark November, about the sinister idea that DK – dead, or alive – was in Chinese hands. Now they had their freedom, to an extent, and it was a different world. The Chinese seemed decent enough overlords, peace was breaking out, Ax had hope. But then you find that Dian is dead, her body missing, and there have been unexplained psychic phenomena at her childhood home . . . Sage leaned back, soothing the baby's head as if she were a kitten. She spluttered ominously. Trust you, Coz. You liked the haunted house, you're not hungry, what's wrong with the nice National Rail hired car? And how does your mother always know exactly when to dump you?

He thought of the hollow woman at Ashdown, offering to be Mata Hari.

'I'm glad we went to see them, anyway. Thanks for coming along.'

'No problem,' said Verlaine.

The splutter segued through a bridge passage of grizzle to a piercing, repeated shriek. 'If she isn't hungry, she isn't bored and she isn't sleepy, she probably needs changing,' said Chip. 'That's the rules. Babies rarely break the rules.' Chip and Ver had notched up much experience over the years, what with Anne-Marie Wing's brood, and the Snake Eyes kids. They liked to think they knew their stuff (suckers).

'Pass her over,' offered Verlaine, 'we can do her back here.'

Sage and Fiorinda glanced at each other. 'She does stink a touch.'

'I'll stop.'

They were in Ground Zero's shadow, the road surfaces eerily smooth, no traffic at all. They had not intended to leave the car except at Villa Vallambrosa. But Fiorinda pulled off at the next lay-by, and they stepped out into the Thames Valley, the Reich's lost holy ground. Under new leaves, in a riot of birdsong, Coz waved her dimpled legs and reached for sky-brimming speedwells, piercing-green grass blades. She beamed gummily at Chip, who'd taken charge of the front end, mood maintenance. He touched her nose with a fingertip.

Eh! said Coz, rearing her head like a little stranded tortoise without a shell.

'Eh!' said Chip, and thought of Verlaine wanting to have a baby. Easy enough. You pay for the boy-on-boy IVF, hire a kind lady who will lend her womb, and of course you'd have to get nearer to Sphere-central. But the child was a stalking horse. It was something else Ver wanted, and Chip didn't know what.

Sage took out the envelope, looked inside and shook the contents onto his palm. A lock of ice-blonde hair, coiled and sealed in a small plastic baggie, another baggie holding lint and cotton-buds. There she is, all that's left of the green-eyed Valkyrie, one of those women I touched, and never knew it, really hurt her, and I never felt a fucking thing. But these were not sentimental souvenirs.

'Tissue samples,' said Fiorinda. 'Good for her. She had plenty courage.'

'Bugger all we can do about it, unfortunately.'

Fiorinda turned the baby over on her belly, so she could practise her mini-push-ups and improve her immune system by gumming soil. The rockstars sat round her, in the cool sunlit shade. Can we talk? Never trust a hired car, but out here we think so. Sage held the data button on his palm.

'The question is,' said Verlaine, 'could Dian have had a b-loc phone?'

The description of that 'ghost' had been so suggestive, so familiar.

'It's a big leap,' said Fiorinda. 'But I'm with you.'

Nothing's for certain, but these four thought they'd know, and they did not believe anything so-called supernatural had happened in that room.

'She definitely had a white label pair,' said Sage. 'She was on the testbed list. I can't prove it, can't remember ever seeing her with it, but I'm sure she had a commercial model as well. They were must-have.'

The first bi-location phones had been packaged in pairs. There wasn't much point in owning one unless you knew someone equipped to receive.

'Would she have *kept* something like that?' Chip imagined it. 'The Chinese are here, she's been working for the Second Chamber, all mind/matter tech is proscribed. She's going to throw it in the river. Isn't she?'

Sage shook his head. 'Dunno. She had a thick skin for personal danger. Like her dad and that highly contraband ghost-catching rig.'

'If there was a b-loc in her room, it's in Chinese custody now.'

'Not necessarily, Ver,' said Fiorinda, eyes on Coz, her mind (for once) distinctly elsewhere. 'Say the bodysnatchers were ordinary medics, who didn't know they were part of a cover-up. Say General Wang had been forced to off his trophy courtesan, but only the secret cabal could be allowed to know the truth—'

'You think we ought to go back and search?' asked Chip, doubtfully. 'No!'

'What secret cabal?' asked Verlaine. 'Who's in it?'

Fiorinda hadn't got that far. 'I don't know. I'm groping.'

'What about DK?' wondered Sage. 'It takes two.'

The Few's b-loc had disappeared. 'We had a pair in the siege,' said Verlaine. 'We took turns to carry them, in case we got separated. They weren't in our stuff when we were taken into custody by Hu, and that's all we know—'

'Any *idea* what might have become of them?'

'It's all a blur, what happened, what order things happened. We can go into it, someone might remember something, maybe Allie.'

'DK expected to die,' offered Chip slowly. 'I remember that. When we were trapped in the Insanitude, after the "Republic of Europe" nutcases took over, he was convinced he was not going to make it. The rest of us maybe, but not him. So, it was any moment could be the last goodbye—'

Dilip came back to them then: the veteran mixmaster, free spirit; their friend himself, not a piece in a tantalising puzzle. He had been HIV positive for nearly half his life. He'd been living for the moment, partying in the shadow of death, for as long as any of them had known him. DK expecting to die, what does that mean?

Grief, fresh again, flickered through them and was gone—

'What are we saying?' asked Verlaine. 'They snatched him from the burning building, he somehow has access to b-loc, and he's been calling *Dian Buckley*?'

Cosoleth failed to roll over, remained good-humoured, and tried swimming through the grass instead. Three weird scientists and Fiorinda looked at each other. Something had happened at the Villa Vallambrosa that hinted of utterly forbidden tech. Don't say a word, don't hazard a guess. Don't *whisper* that we may have found a chink in the world-conquerors' armour—

Chip couldn't see it. 'Why would DK send his virtual self to call on Dian?'

'Because she'd made contact,' said Sage. 'And we hadn't.' He pocketed the button. 'We don't know if this has anything at all to do with Dilip. Leave it. Lemme interrogate Lance's virtual bedroom, see if there's anything in there.'

Fiorinda went with Verlaine to the recycle bins, where they deposited the scrapings from the nappy in one orifice, the nappy itself (a nasty one, let the Occupied Rural Council sterilise it) in another. 'It's like having a dog,' she said, as they washed their hands. 'The scorn and pity I used to feel for dog-addicts doing the pooper-scooper, I am chastised. Ver, do you two still have that diamond you showed me?'

'Yes,' he said. 'D'you want it?'

Some choirboy rockstars go to seed; or their faces change completely, so you can't see how they were ever cute. Kevin Verlaine becomes only more grave and luminous as his bones get stronger; with his light-brown curls combed back and tied he looks like an Elizabethan poet, who? Philip Sidney? Someone like that.

'Not right now. Keep it safe.'

Notch by notch the brutal grip of the Occupation was stepping down. The Triumvirate were able to take Cosoleth to Somerset for Ax's mother's birthday, to introduce her to her Preston family. A few days later Ax was back; for a celebrity cricket match that marked the official return of Civilian Freedom of Movement (terms and conditions apply). Crowds gathered on the slightly fake village green of a suburban 'village' outside Taunton. Bonded servants served breakfast out of the backs of big fat Country Living hybrids. Cooler rurals, not in the neo-gangster class, left their horses and their pony-carts with the stablehands in pub yards. Common folk arrived by bus or on foot, and gave the swathe of soldiers around the AMID top brass a wide berth. Mr Preston sat with his mum and her tutor from Bristol Uni, on the deck chairs, among the neighbours; and watched the multi-angle big screens being raised and tested at the scoreboard end. And that was another first, big screens again.

Ax had never liked this place. It was gated – not much use against a Chinese invasion – a practice Ax considered sickening; but it had been Jordan and Milly's choice, and understandable at the time. Their house was just visible from the green, identified through the trees by a blue flood of wisteria. It reminded him of the Chosen Few's original HQ, in Taunton itself; which the Second Chamber had turned into a museum.

Wonder if the inscription's still there, on the slab we cemented over the front door. *This world is a bridge, make no house upon it.*

Min, who had been letting the kids admire him, hopped onto Ax's knees: much cat these days, little Bat-ears long gone. It gave him a pang to think that this would happen to Coz: she would grow up, she would no longer say 'Eh!', or stare in such blown-away wonderment at bathwater, sunlight, her spiderweb picture—

'That's a wonderful cat, sir,' said the tutor, a stylish middle-aged bloke with a braid down his back. Mum had been in Bristol before the invasion, starting a new life; studying Law. She'd been ordered back here, but she'd been allowed to keep up by videolink, mainly with this guy's help. So be nice. 'He must be worth a packet.'

'What, *Min*? Oh, no, no, he's a mog. I picked him up as a stray kitten.'

Pigtail smiled at Mr Preston's joke. 'No, seriously, of course he's a terrific Spotted Bengal. What is he, F4? Looks too near the leopard cat for an F5. D'you always take him around with you, aren't you afraid to lose him?'

'Min's more like a dog than a cat,' said Sunny, Ax's mum, as non-cat-lovers will, and thankfully Jordan appeared. Time for the pre-match huddle.

'What's up with you?' said his brother.

'Nothing, just something Pigtail said.'

'Huh. Him . . . What d'you think of him?'

The crowd whooped and waved as the brothers passed. Ax looked at Jordan, narrow-eyed. 'You're winding me up.'

Their dad had been dead nearly four years.

'Why would I do that?'

The home team's dressing room was a green wooden hut with a sagging verandah, predating the gentrification around here. The Rockstar Eleven, plus extras, were inside, marauding the lunch sandwiches and drinking tea, alcohol VETOED by captain J. Preston. They were worried. Jordan had accepted the Taunton Fort's overtures, encouraged by his big brother; expecting a PR stunt. The squad that had arrived this morning was a fucking different proposition. By no means all of them were Han Chinese. They'd been hand-picked from the whole invasion force. It was the Sphere against the Rest of the World, the rest of the world comprising one young County all-rounder, T. J. Suppiah, who also played guitar for a well-known Bridgwater band. Milly Kettle, reliable at bat, Boje Strom, good on form, great to watch but erratic, the notorious Preston brothers, and a tail of West Country resident pop musicians, of varying fame, with no special talent on the field.

Hindsight said they should have organised, they could have bussed in half the England squad, done them up with eyeliner, made them honorary pop-idols. But then *they* get pasted (all-too-likely scenario), and it looks even worse—

'Right,' said Jordan. 'How are we going to approach this?'

'Lose?' suggested Shay, the youngest Preston brother, wryly. Their sister Maya, the Chosen's lead guitar since Ax moved on, didn't care for cricket, refused to make sandwiches and was exercising her restored mobility somewhere else.

'Seems like that's the Chinese plan,' reasoned someone else. 'If we were supposed to win, their lot would be squaddies barely knowing cricket from baseball.'

'Better take a fall, Jor. They're the bosses.'

'Fuck, no,' said Ax, grinning. 'I say we go out there an' mash 'em.'

A little startled shock went through the company, and straight to Ax's balls. You forget, you forget. You've been telling the people to grovel, to accept humiliation and say thank you, you forget that what you say actually means something to them—

The Rockstars raised a cheer. 'We shall fight them on the beaches!' roared Boje, Gintrap's Swedish *soi-disant* hot-shit guitarist. 'We shall NEVER surrender!'

'Hey, Jor. Make sure Ax doesn't get tempted to take his clothes off out there.'

'If you had a big dick,' said Ax, 'you'd like to show it off, too.'

This team was Jordan's drinking pals, plus the ubiquitous Gintrap. They thought the Anglia movie was a load of unpatriotic weirdo crap, even if it *was* a Norman Soong. The hotly rumoured sex-show, on the other hand (which would never see the light) was a mammoth hit. And one day we'll live it down.

Strange thing, you look for the ageing demi-gods, and oh fuck, that's me. The Rockstars wore white. The Sphere had come to the pyjama party in red and green; promising an entertaining clash of cultures. Jordan won the toss, and put his side in to bat. It wasn't bad. The Sphere could bowl, but they'd only just met. They were sloppy fielders and they didn't know the ground. The magnificent partnership of M. Kettle and B. Strom formed the backbone of a creditable performance, the home team were bowled out for a respectable 232; three overs short of their allocation.

There was a moment, as he walked out at the start of the afternoon session, when it was literally General Wang Xili Ax saw at the other end. A horror gripped him, and Fred Eiffrich's voice whispered *go belly-up, look helpless it's your only chance*. They took the children's heads, a haunted house, oh fuck. His right hand was full of blood, a mass of solid blood, he could smell it. It's called transient psychosis, happens a lot, people don't talk about it—

Fucking hope I don't incite any hooligans, because the last thing I dare to do now is act submissive. We are winning the peace, I am confident, I'm among friends, I have nothing to fear. He ran, his arm swept, of its own volition; the red ball flew.

Exit one startled AMID officer of Australasian origin, who had assumed the President-in-Hiding was on first for reasons of protocol. He was not the only victim. A. Preston was as one possessed, J. Preston took over with his slow and cunning left hand, the last Preston was a coffin-nail in the hopes of the Sphere. Rockstars inspired, miracle catches; tourists demolished. The (English) champagne fizzed and showered, the Rockstars gambolled through a disorganised victory lap, to ecstatic ovation. The South West General himself, like a good loser, came over all smiles to congratulate.

'You're a dark horse, Mr Preston! I am sincerely in awe.'

'Bit of a fluke,' said Ax, malignly modest. 'I can't remember when I last played, tell you the truth. My brother and his wife are the cricket fanatics.'

'Hm. Your partners aren't with you?'

'Not this time.' Nothing to do with avoiding the Chinese, perish the thought.

'That's a shame, I was hoping to meet young Cosoleth.'

'It's a little too public. We really don't want her to be a rockstar baby.'

'Quite right.'

Wang Xili gazed around at the warm-toned modern brick houses, dazzling 'cottage' gardens, fine trees; ducks on a pond. The tower of a mediaeval church, rising beyond the candled green of a majestic horse-chestnut avenue. Ax remembered a coloured lad born on a sink estate in Taunton, who had loved the Somerset landscape so passionately, and felt so excluded. It was a strange kinship. You think this is England, first class treasure. But *this* is not what I was fighting for, Wang. I'd take a blow-torch to most of this, frankly. What I want has no homeland.

The thought rang in his soul, and chilled him.

'How perfectly English it has been, delightful . . . but I believe,' Wang added, with a thoughtful look, 'Mr Pender and Fiorinda were on my doorstep, the other day. Or just over the county boundary in Oxford*shire*, I should say.'

'Yes. A visit of condolence, to a bereaved family. You know about Ms Buckley's death, of course.'

'Of course.' Wang shook his head. 'A sad business. Poor Dian.'

'Very sad,' agreed Ax.

A few seconds' silence for the trophy courtesan.

'You'll have received your invitation from Elder Sister's office?'

'I have,' said Ax. 'It will be a great honour and pleasure to meet her again.'

The General seemed oddly unsure of himself, though he must have seen so many Presidents, Cultural Icons, Popular Front Leaders, National Heroes, Feisty Power Ladies, picked out of the rubble, dusted down and benignly set upon their thrones. Never a rockstar before, maybe that made the difference.

'I must return to my battered troops and organise the retreat. Goodbye, Mr Preston. Do drop in and see me when you are at Rivermead; if you have a moment.'

'Norman Soong is *gay*?'

Ax shrugged. 'Yeah.'

'How can he be gay? He's a *trannie*. That's hooky, if you ask me. I mean, if he wants to be a man, then he wants to be a man, doesn't he, and—'

'Men aren't gay. Mmm, right.'

'Seems like cheating, though,' mused Shay, 'somehow. Like that Jam Today bird, says she's a gay man in a girl's body, and *that's* why it's okay for her to screw a fucking sexist old dinosaur like Bill.'

'Takes all sorts.'

Most superannuated rockstars, Ax thought, morph into solid bourgeois. Conservative views, rather odd clothes, worried about the kids' schooling. Ah, if we could sit simply in that room again. I used to tell you two I was going to be the leader of a futuristic utopian revolution. What the hell did I mean by that?

The AMID squad had departed in their ophidian, the Top Brass had quit the field in conventional-looking staff cars. The President Elect (maybe), of a liberated nation, stroked his ocelot, in abstracted silence. What the fuck kind of pet is that for the man who claims he despises being a rockstar? Mum and her tutor had wandered off, Milly was talking to friends. Jordan and Shay sat on the grass eating leftover picnic, necking warm white wine, and idly watched Jordan's little boys, Albion and Troy, getting yelled at by the groundsman—

'It's his baby, isn't it? His wife and child, that's what it looks like to me, Ax. I wouldn't say this if I didn't think—'

'Hahaha. Don't criticise what you can't understand, Jor. Six wickets, you ungrateful bastard. Aren't you ever going to buy me a pint?'

'Bet they'd been told to lie down.'

'Nyah. Bet they didn't have a choice.'

A Game Of Risk

The English had begun to trickle back into Reading City. There were local customers in the Three Guineas bar on the station, one bleak afternoon at the end of May, when the Triumvirate walked in with their baby. The landlady, who was filling bullet-holes with plastic wood, turned to see what had caused the silence. She dropped her pallet knife, wide-eyed: recovered it, and resumed her work. The boy polishing the brass rail didn't miss a beat. The landlord finished drawing a pint of Pride, from a barrel on the bar. A print-out of a Civilian Freedom of Movement voucher changed hands: this season's top currency. *They* settled in a booth, Fiorinda came to get the drinks in.

'All right, Miss Fio?' said the landlord: speaking softly, as if afraid to scare away a treasured wild thing, long vanished from these haunts.

'Not too bad. If only the weather would pick up.'

'Cold enough for June, eh? Bet you're missing sleep with that young lady.'

Coz was in her sling, awake and interested. 'Nah, she's pretty good at night.' Fiorinda grinned at the optics row. 'Is any of that real?'

'No chance. It's all bathtub vodka and onion skin.'

'Nice labels, though.'

'Very imaginative.'

Time was this bar had been a honeypot for celebs, its futuristic sound and vision-tech subtly concealed, classic English Pub details preserved by Reich Royal fiat. This afternoon an old fruit machine lay buzzing on its side while two barpersons tinkered with its innards. A big screen showed Joyous Liberation news with the volume turned down. They had come home, and it was heartbreaking—

'I've looked it up,' said Ax. 'The fucker's right. *Bengals*, stupid fake name, but it's Min in the pictures. He's not mine, he's got to be a pedigree cat, worth a stack of money, he belongs to some breeder.'

'Don't be silly, you found him abandoned in an old shed. If there *was* a breeder, they're long gone.'

'I'll have to track them down and give him back. It's no use, I can't be a looter, it looks fucking shit.'

'*Ax,* trust us, no one is going to take Min away. Over my dead body.'

'Don't say that.'

'If it helps to panic on a safe issue go ahead, but—'

'Shut up, Fee. You'll make him worse.'

He was hideously nervous. He never remembered feeling like this in all his career. He must have been equally as scared, often: maybe he'd never before hoped for so much. He combed back his hair with his fingers, mugging apology.

'You're *sure* nobody's going to take my kitten?'

'We're sure,' said Fiorinda. Coz reached out a tiny hand from the sling, looked earnestly at Ax (a new trick), and added her reassurance. 'Eh! *Eh!*'

They laughed, and the whole bar seemed to sigh in longing, oh let things be as they were, let us have our cosy fucked-up little world back. It was a relief when the spruce young officer walked up and saluted, at a respectful distance; cap under her arm. One of Elder Sister's invisible company, you can see them when you know what you're looking for.

'Do yourself a favour,' murmured Sage. 'Don't mention Tibet.'

'Not unless she brings up Lord Palmerston first.'

A flashing smile, and there, he's gone. They watched the doors through which Ax had disappeared. 'A breeder wouldn't want Min back without his balls.'

'I'm glad you didn't tell him that, my brat.' Rain scudded outdoors, a train approached; they heard a blurred announcement. 'Was it Scarlatti you were playing?' asked Sage. 'D'you remember, that night in the Insanitude?'

How long ago, how far away, the first time we waited together to find out if Ax had won his round. It was the death penalty referendum: if the people had voted against judicial murder, then Ax was in power. How *strange* to recall: but you were you, and I was I, and we both already loved him, just as we do now.

'Yeah, Scarlatti.' The music rose into her mind, K27, E minor, airy and calm.

He was delivered not to Rivermead Palace but to one of the barracks he'd thought looked like upturned boats. In a vestibule a white-gloved, dress-uniformed aide took his suitable gift (a hamper of moss-wrapped, rooted cuttings of prize English garden shrubs and herbaceous plants). Another showed him through double doors: told him, in English, that Elder Sister would be with him soon, and left.

He looked for the monks: no sign of them. He was alone, and the hairs rose on the back of his neck. He thought of Sage, walking alone into Rufus O'Niall's castle at Drumbeg. Here I am in the flying saucer. What the fuck's going to happen?

The walls of the large room were oval in profile, indigo and cream with a moving, twisting pattern; the floor was layered in silk carpets, like swatches of gleaming brocade. Wings of *di* rose into hollow peaks above his head, traced and ribbed in gold; apparently supported by deep red pillars like boles of cedarwood. Glorified version of an Inner Asian chieftain's tent: that's not Han, that says outsider; ruling China, but an outsider . . . Forget it, *she* decides what the signs mean. How English am I? The bed, the chairs, the pan-Asian artworks were eye-popping. He thought of Napoleon Bonaparte despatching cartloads of class-A plunder to the Louvre, and smiled, realising he'd known she loved luxury. He'd felt that in the Daoist Nun, fuck knows how.

Under the central cone, separated from the furniture by amazing antique screens, there was a rectangular dais on shallow steps; inlaid with a Fu pattern in pale green. The whole room was oriented towards this area, so that you looked for a throne up there, or at least a speaker's desk; rows of chairs below. There were none. He sat crosslegged on the rugs facing the stage, feeling watched.

The music that broke the silence was so incongruous he thought it was an aural hallucination, and so familiar that for several bars he didn't recognise it. What the fuck? Unless I'm completely losing it, that is *Queen*. That is *Freddie Mercury*.

A modest pair of doors opened, in the wall beyond the dais. A woman stood there and then ran, gracefully, lightly, up the steps and to the centre of the stage. She bowed to Ax, gold ribbons trailing from her hands, and leapt into a flying kick: floated in the air for a moment, and landed like thistledown.

'Don't stop me now,' she announced, with a dazzling smile, and took a pose of joyous defiance, one arm outflung, the other fist pressed to her heart. The intro started over and she *attacked*, gold ribbons whirling – in a choreography wonderfully matched to the music, to the über-partyboy's daft lyrics; to the energy of the finest pop group the world has ever known. She was a tiger defying gravity, a racing car burning through the sky, she was a gymnastic, disciplined, daring, crowd-pleasing entertainer. Two hundred degrees, that's why they call her Mr Farenheit—

'Don't stop me now,' she sighed, drifting to one knee on the floor, as Queen faded out. Her ribbons tumbled around her. 'I don't want to stop at all.'

'That was fabulous,' said Ax, sincerely.

'Would you sign me up?'

'I'm humiliated, Elder Sister. I'm remembering in painful detail the gig at Warren Fen, when I do believe at one point some clown pretended to try and dance.'

The woman kneeling in the Manchu salute above him didn't resemble the Daoist Nun at all, except that they were the same person. She wore pale-gold, to match her ribbons and the stage: gold slippers, slim trousers gathered at the ankle, a pearl-embroidered waistcoat over a full-sleeved cream silk shirt. Her hair was jet-black, worn in a feathery fringe and dressed with gold pins at the back; her face was oval, unlined, made-up for the stage. He would have guessed her age at around thirty, though she was supple as a teenager: he knew he had no idea. Head on one side, she examined him quizzically. 'How did you know who I was?'

'I don't know who you are, Elder Sister.'

She smiled. 'But you do.'

'Then you are *Shi Huangdi*.'

They were speaking *putonghua*, he hoped he could survive.

Elder Sister jumped down and settled back on her heels: he turned to face her. 'I am *Shi Huangdi*. At least, I am the person the brave old man Cornelius Sampson had guessed at; along with other "China Watchers".'

'So the One Man turns out to be a woman. That's going to startle people. Is the truth well-known, everywhere but here in Europe?'

'It's getting to be known.' She grinned, disarmingly. 'The truth began to leak a while ago, and it doesn't matter, it's high time to go public. Some ignorant people, even in the Sphere, had started to say I am just the PLA's cute mascot.'

I wouldn't like to be those people, thought Ax.

'They're quite wrong . . . I am the army brat who became a sort of Emperor, very Romanly, by proclamation of the Praetorian Guard. Wang Xili will no doubt tell you the story, he keeps my scrapbooks. But I was not plucked from nowhere. I have had a respectable military career. You can find the details in the Outside World News Releases for the years of turmoil; which were also China's harvest time.'

'I see,' said Ax; because she had paused for his reaction.

'Look closely, you'll find a female general called Li Xifeng: a battlefield commander in the Inner Asia campaign, promoted to the rank of Marshal after the Japanese Uprising Negotiation of 2012. General Li's sex is rarely mentioned, there are no photographs, but that's me. I'm also a Member of the Standing Committee of the Political Bureau of the Communist Party, Vice-Chair of the Military Commission, appointed Deputy to the Chief of General Staff, and Deputy Minister of Defense, by President Hu Jintao.'

He did not recall any General Li, never mind this fistful of honours.

'The top level appointments were not made public internationally.' She set her chin on her hand. 'You're wondering *why* it's been a secret.'

'Er, maybe—'

'We'd learned our lesson in the twentieth century, Mr Preston. We'd had enough of the so-called international community's opinion of Chinese "despotism" and "personality cult". We took over, leaving the structures of the People's Republic intact. We built the first phase of the Sphere. We absorbed our troubled satellites, we liberated Inner Asia. We fed the people, we restored order. Maybe you can imagine the way the Chinese masses feel about the person responsible for those victories, *primus inter pares.*'

'I can figure it, a little.'

She nodded, seeming pleased by his reticence. 'Our success was open to the world's gaze, we kept our hearts and minds to ourselves. When China imposed control over the internet, at the birth of this century, we were reviled as barbarians. I think you'll agree events have proved we were simply ahead of the game. We were the first to understand that the media of the information age could be used as an impenetrable screen, on which any kind of picture could be projected.'

He nodded again. He planned to do a lot of nodding, and speak very little.

'As long as the so-called *West* was outside our rule the secret had to be kept, so that the international media didn't revile me. It was kept. Now that's no longer necessary . . . But you haven't told me how you guessed.'

She waited, smiling and expectant, the nemesis of evening's long empire; the wrath of God in ballet costume. He steadied himself: be confident.

'I thought there was someone missing from the invasion force line-up. I was looking for a fifth commanding general. When I came to Reading in December a Lieutenant Chu showed me round. At the end of my interview I overheard General Wang addressing the lieutenant as *jiejie*. I forgot about it, but when we went to Anglia, the mysterious Daoist Nun was also *jiejie*. Then I remembered, and I wondered, who does the First Marshal of China call "Elder Sister"?'

'Oh. That simple.'

'I wish I could make it a more interesting story. You came walking towards me, in the Warren Fen garden at night, I couldn't see the Daoist Nun's face, so I knew you were Lieutenant Chu, and that was intriguing.'

'You looked at my desk on the boat.' She frowned, delicately. 'There are plenty of reasons why somebody could be using a lot of red ink, you know.'

'I'm sure. But historically one of them – which stands out, to a foreigner who only knows a few things about Chinese tradition – has been if a person were the Emperor, adding commentary to official memorials.'

'Hahaha. That's quite true, and very silly.'

'The clues were slight,' admitted Ax. 'Really, it was intuition. First I felt that there was someone hidden, then I felt a presence I could only explain one way.'

'You should trust your intuition. It works faster than consciousness.'

'Anglia puzzled me. I could understand why "Shi Huangdi" would be leading the invasion force. Taking the USA was not something the person who built the Sphere would leave to her officers. But why would the hidden ruler risk exposure, and put herself in needless danger the way you did in Rainbow Bridge, over a minor issue in the liberation of a tiny little country like England?'

Nemesis watched him with glowing dark eyes, Phoenix eyes, as the Chinese say, and he trembled. 'You choose your words, Mr Preston, but to no avail. You feel conquered, I'm sure. Not liberated.'

'You're right, and it hurts. But I welcomed the invasion, Elder Sister. The Second Chamber régime was an evil I had utterly failed to defeat.'

'You began badly,' she said, judiciously. 'You should not have accepted the Presidency from Fred Eiffrich's hands, that put you in the wrong from the start . . . We had been preparing to invade the USA from the moment we knew of the A-team experiment. It had to be done, *they were insane.* The event itself forestalled us, but when the US President offered to let us in, we were ready to move at once.'

So much for the ceding of bridgeheads between friends. He wondered what the hell was really going on in the US now. He wasn't going to ask.

'We also had to crush England,' Elder Sister continued, briskly. 'The USA built the A-team, but this is the pernicious hotbed where the barrier was first broken. We couldn't risk seeing the Neurobomb emerge in the hands of the Second Chamber. Please understand, we know that your playboy Minister, Stephen Pender, cannot be weaponised. Still, he is what he is, and knowing the dangers as he does, his behaviour has been unthinkably careless. He is light-minded, and he's given you bad advice.'

Ouch.

'As to the "risks" I took in Anglia . . . You're right, Mr Preston, I don't leave things to my officers. I am on the frontline, wherever it may be, that is my rule. But I'm not irresponsible. I was married once, I have a son. He's in his thirties, he's very competent, he stays safely at home in Xi'an. When the time is right I'll step down in his favour. Meanwhile, if I were to die tomorrow there would be no power vacuum. My generals would serve him unswervingly.'

'Ah. That explains it.'

She grinned again, three-cornered, charming. 'Of course, I was barely more than a child when he was born. I want to show you something. Watch this.'

She turned to face the dais, and he turned with her. It drew back and rose on its side, a fluid yet mechanical action, like the articulation of the *di*-tracked landships. The Fu pattern disappeared, it was replaced by that superb, China-oriented projection of the globe he'd seen in Wang's office, in December. Here the notation was English, and the movement of history was frozen.

Scarlet for China and the New Autonomous Regions. Rose-lilac for the Sphere Partners. Pink for the Territories; countries with puppet governments outside the satellite region. Violet for the Liberated Nations, too recently conquered for their status to be clear. The rest of the world was a muddy beige; unfinished surface. He noted that the whole continent of North America, from the Pole to the isthmus of

Panama, was pink: he couldn't recall what colour it had been last time he'd seen this.

Elder Sister counted the swallowed satellites on her fingers, absorbed in a favourite pastime; as if she'd forgotten Ax existed. 'Japan, Korea, Vietnam, Cambodia, Laos, Mongolia, Tibet. And the Philippines . . .' (Oh yeah. The Philippines had turned scarlet, sometime since December.) 'We have promoted the satellites, they are Autonomous Regions now, as you know. Taiwan, Hong Kong, Macao and Singapore are fully Chinese, of course. Burma, Bhutan, Nepal, Kazakhstan, Kyrgyzstan, Turkestan; Developing Autonomous Territories.'

Make a list, thought Ax, fascinated.

'Then the Sphere. India-with-Bangladesh, Pakistan, Afghanistan, Malaysia, Indonesia, Thailand, Singapore, Australasia-with-Polynesia, Turkey. I left one out, ah, Sri Lanka, I always forget Sri Lanka.'

Those ten, including one cunning, disreputable escapee from the EU, were the ones with the coveted status: not decided on economic or ideological grounds alone, or on geography alone. Tech advancement plays a part, having an ancient culture with striking monuments helps; pragmatism plays a part (Afghanistan!).

'Iran, Kuwait, Iraq, Saudi, the Yemen, Oman, Syria, the Lebanon, the Emirates, Palestine, Israel, ah, and Jordan . . . Most of that region we don't have to conquer, they are eager to join us. The most ancient nations, *apart from Israel*, will join the Sphere, we're developing a second class of partnership. North Africa, the Horn and the East Coast – Egypt, down to Mozambique – we plan to treat the same way. The desert Arab nations won't survive.'

'What about the rest of Africa? What's happening there?'

'You don't know?'

'I've lost track.'

'It's not so bad as you might think. In many African countries things will improve, now that your grasping friends in the USA are finally out of the picture.'

Ax nodded. They both knew that it was China, not the USA, that had given the African continent a near-lethal dose of raw capitalism, just before the Crash. No need to labour the point.

'Of course the A-team was a wicked blow. It's better, it's getting better.'

'Okay.'

You have no idea what's happening a hundred klicks away he thought, in self-defence. Unless you go there: and then more than likely you find your most treasured reforms have turned to nightmare. But Elder Sister had resumed her account. 'Lastly the conquests . . . Azerbaijan, a very terrible place. Uzbekistan, our tough nut.' She glanced at Ax, almost with amused apology. EU 'involvement' in the Uzbek resistance had been the utterly specious pretext for the invasion of England, and of Roumania. 'European eco-warriors, the Belarus and Roumanian guerrillas, had been fighting for Gaia against the American oil interests. They were stranded far from home by the A-team, and they could not grasp that we were on their side. We offered to repatriate them, they refused to leave. They refused to lay down their arms, and you know the rest. But it's all settled now.'

Once, in another lifetime, Ax had looked into the inferno of the Caspian Basin from a small plane. He had seen the appalling scale of the devastation in those lands. Lalic the Macedonian, Doctor of Philosophy; Markus the Dacian, fighting for a cause they believed long lost . . . The fires would be out now: where were Lalic and Markus? Did your liberation kill them? he wondered. Probably.

Her roll-call seemed to be over. No plans for South America? he thought. Antarctica? What are you going to do about those damned Feds?

The projection began to move: *simplicity as a result of complexity*.

'The *di* is alive,' said Elder Sister, softly. 'I believe that in time everything we make will be alive. Once, in the Pre-Cambrian, a balance tipped, a build-up reached its emergence point, a little predator called a trilobite found out what it means to have eyes. This is our Pre-Cambrian explosion. If we can survive, then *this* is where human civilisation begins. It will develop into who knows what new forms.' She gazed at the world-map like a beautiful woman studying her reflection, like a mother brooding over her child, and he felt her charm. He understood Wang Xili's passionate devotion, and the atmosphere in that Chelsea flat: the two Generals anxious to repair the slights they feared they might have offered; to Elder Sister's protégés. They don't resent her at all, whatever she wants she must have.

Phoenix eyes. She loves the world, this megalomaniac. She's convinced she can make it a better place, although it may take a few massacres. Hey, compadre. I've quit, I could not stand the bloodshed, but I remember—

'Do you know that we had met before the invasion?' said Elder Sister, turning away from her mirror with that disarming grin.

'*Really?*'

'Yes. In Shanghai once, years ago, and in Hiroshima later. Maybe we didn't meet, but we were in the same room. You were visiting the Pan-Asian Utopians by roving presence. I was the Daoist Nun, or someone like that; observing.'

'That's amazing.'

'Hm. Is it? You are disingenuous, I'm afraid. About England; and about your own place in the world. The Great Peace holds the heritage of human culture in trust. Little England, cradle of so much history, would have been a special case for us, no matter what. The pernicious delusion must be uprooted, the Counterculture must be stamped out, forbidden technologies must be abandoned, but England's beauty must be preserved. That's one reason we have been very careful. The other reason is the Rock and Roll Reich, and its global reputation. You have created one of the pillars of my Utopia. I want to make Reich beliefs part of my world state.'

She held up her fingers for another counting exercise, slim dancer in pearls and gold. 'You have preserved national unity, and public order, while your consort Fiorinda, Protector of the Poor, has kept "the drop-out hordes" fed and clothed, and under decent, humane control. You have enlisted the masses, and convinced them to work for the good of the state without coercion; you have struggled to outlaw bond slavery and chattel slavery. The target I would add to these is: establish a culture of full civil, personal and family rights for women—' She raised a moth's wing eyebrow. 'What's the matter?'

'Could you expand on the, er, rights for women agenda?'

'A girl is a boy,' said Elder Sister, firmly. 'A woman is a man.'

'I've heard the slogan. The wording has caused some confusion.'

'I know. I don't see why; it's very clear to me.'

And moving on.

'In short, we must use high tech to save the living world; and save ourselves from barbarism by caring for each other "like the social animals we are meant to be". That much anyone could have seen. *You* alone saw that the masses, freed from the slavery of material values, need the release only music and dance can give. *You* have given the world a model of hedonism and wild desire, without anarchy and without moral degeneracy. Obviously you've learned from the East, but your system embraces everything that Asia is greedy for about the West. It's Socialist, it's Maoist, it's Confucian; it's authoritarian—' She smiled, because she knew he wouldn't like that.

'I think you're too kind,' said Ax, ruefully.

'Never. That's not one of my faults.'

Your son, he thought, if such a person exists, hasn't a snowball's chance in hell of ascending the throne. You're not capable of stepping down.

'Now, to business. You have given me England, Ax. Not least by your stalwart performance at Rainbow Bridge.' She grinned. 'Thus we see that humanity's most ancient beliefs can be cleansed of the foul taint of delusion and brought to serve the masses; that's very good. But England cannot be liberated in isolation, we need to bring in Europe. My plan is that we will host a conference, for which preparations are already in train. It will be held in Free Cumbria, over the Line: that way we won't have to police Occupied Zone prohibitions. The people of the EU will reject vile technologies later, of their own free will . . . Delegates will be approved on the basis of right-minded attitudes, not on political rank. Cultural, folklore and Rock music issues will be discussed, there will be forward-thinking rallies. Will you take on the task of leading this gathering?'

'Of course,' said Ax. 'If you think I'm up to it, I'll do my best.'

'You are too modest.' It began to sound like a warning. 'I *know* about you. My officers have been working for months with your Permanent Civil Service, a Chinese-inspired institution by the way. They are told, by humble bureaucrats who could be *dismembered* for resistance, Oh, Mr Preston wouldn't like that. Oh, but we'll have to ask Mr Preston. We've all been very impressed.'

He'd known Cumbria had to be on the agenda. The EU conference was unexpected. The planet-destroyer watched him, smiling a little.

'There are hotheads, and pockets of recalcitrance, but by and large Europe's response to the liberation has been promising. You are the ideal emissary. You haven't put a foot wrong: you have said not one toadying good word for the Chinese, but you have accepted fate, and committed not one act against us. And now you have a daughter, born under the twin auspices—' She made the 'yoni with eyes' mudra, steepled fingers lifted coquettishly under her round chin, 'of the 2nd AMID Army Women's Medical Corps; and of Gaia herself. That was a stroke of luck.'

Ax did not conceal his surprise.

'I am at peace with Gaia. Sometimes I don't like the company she keeps.'

'I've felt the same myself.'

'You'll go to Cumbria with your partners and the Few, without a military escort this time. You'll lead the unofficial official summit, you will give me Europe. Then, quite soon, the mopping up will be over and England will be promoted from Liberated Nation to Territory status. I want you to agree to be my President, in time perhaps President of a larger region—'

So here's the promised present. Shame it couldn't have been a nice jigsaw, thought Ax. I'd have liked a jigsaw. The gilt-wrapped package lay between them, for too long. He studied the silken patterns on the rugs.

'I still don't think I'm the man for the government job, Elder Sister.'

How would she take this? Chop his head off, or something slower? He risked looking up: and saw amusement in her phoenix eyes.

'You're a tough negotiator, Mr Preston. All right, we'll talk terms another time. Please deliver my congratulations to Fiorinda on the auspicious birth of her daughter. Tell her I admire her very much, by the way; and I hope we can be friends. And, hm, my respects to Mr Pender. Would you like some tea? Black tea with cow's milk, the English way?'

'It's an acquired taste.'

'Better milk than yak butter,' said Elder Sister, with feeling. 'I use skimmed milk, is that all right for you?'

'We all prefer skimmed milk, it's a problem. As short of calories as we are, we can't seem to use all the cream. We have to get the people to believe whole milk is good for them; except the Vegans, of course. Fiorinda's working on it.'

'I hope she has more success than with the garlic porridge.'

The tea arrived, in chaste white English china. When the orderly had left them, Elder Sister switched from *putonghua* to US-inflected English. They talked informally about things dear to both their hearts. Food supplies, the fuel crisis (it's a necessary illusion, it serves us well); fine-tuning the energy audit. He didn't recognise Lieutenant Chu, or the nun, but knew those other personalities were there beside him. Who is Elder Sister? A performer, an army brat. A romantic, a good-willed despot; a mask.

Wang Xili was looking ostentatiously relaxed when Ax was shown into his office. He rose, smiling, and flicked a lordly, casual hand at his secretary in the corner.

'Shoo!'

The secretary left them. Ax and the General sat down.

Wang smiled with the air of someone welcoming an initiate into an exclusive brotherhood, the trial by ordeal, the ritual hazing forgotten. 'You look "blown away", Mr Preston.'

'I'm overwhelmed.'

'She's *astonishing*, isn't she. We should talk about Cumbria, and we will.' He leaned forward, elbows on the desk. 'But first there are things you should know, that I don't think she will have told you, about Elder Sister's life story.'

'I'd be very interested and grateful, if you feel it's appropriate.'

'Of course. You won't know much about how our leadership emerged, so I'll begin at the beginning. At the time of the Tiananmen Square events of June 1989—'

Ax wondered if he was going to be shown an airbrush photo of Elder Sister at the pro-democracy rally: a beautiful child, dancing in the path of the tanks.

'There were five soldiers who had become friends, although serving in different branches of the armed forces. They shared ideals, and an uneasiness about Deng Xiaoping's reforms. They felt that "democracy" was an empty concept, "material wealth" a trivial goal. They despaired of the naïveté of the young protestors, but they were insulted by the way the military crackdown was handled. They rejected political dissidence—'

Wise choice, thought Ax. China in the nineties, not good ground for dissidents of any shade of opinion.

'—and instead became the nucleus of a group bent on developing the role of the PLA in the new free markets. Their dream was a Chinese approach to modernism, using the strengths of old China: Mao and Confucius. The leader of the five was called Ling Bao, you won't have heard the name. He was handsome, well-connected, an adroit technocrat and a ruthless operator. He had married a young soldier from a humble military background, Li Xifeng: who had been talent-spotted and transferred, rather against her personal wishes, to a Political Works Troupe, *kongjun gewu tuan*; the song and dance troupe. She was a star dancer, but she studied military strategy, and the Classics, every spare moment. Her dream was to serve China as a first class officer in active service. She was deep in the confidence of the group, much trusted and loved. Ling Bao was more and more inclined to personal aggrandisement. Having used the 9th Disarmament to purge his rivals, he was close to launching a military coup when he was killed in a firearm accident, in 2005, along with several others.'

'Okay.'

'No,' said Wang, dropping out of approved history mode. 'You know nothing of that coup because it didn't happen. What did happen was not "okay", but it was necessary. I was part of it, though not one of the five at that time. I remember a choking Beijing night, one of the last summers of the old capital, and a horror atmosphere that made me think of my grandfather's career in the sixties. Things are done in darkness. You look around the next day, and you resolve to make sure it wasn't for nothing. That night, Li Xifeng, enthroned in our hearts, became our leader in fact. There was no coup. We became China, without violence, leaving the officials in place. Colonel Li Xifeng, whose promotion had been blocked by her husband, swiftly attained the rank of Five Star General. And she has led us to glory. Those of us who were with her from that beginning are her partners, we are the Five Generals; two of us are here in England with her, Hu and I.'

By acclamation of the Praetorian Guard . . . Ax wondered if he'd ever hear the sordid details, he thought he'd never be nearer to the truth: the passionate devotion she commanded, the huge emotional charge diffusing outwards. The masses love her, because men like Wang have followed her to hell and she redeemed them, she made it worth the fall—

'In a sense, Elder Sister sees herself as your disciple, Ax. She regards you as a close friend: which makes it appropriate for me to tell you—'

Wang took up a battered folder, handling it like a sacred relic: chose an item from its contents, and passed it across the desk. No grisly statistics this time. The face of the woman he'd just met leapt out from a laminated sheet of newsprint: a young dancer with a radiant smile caught in pirouette, long fake flaxen locks flying.

'That is Li Xifeng, as the principal dancer in a production of "The White-Haired Girl", in 1987. It's a revolutionary tale based on a legend of a white-haired female immortal; very popular in China. Here she is again, at around the same time.' The bright face subdued, circled, in the back row of a stage full of suits and uniforms; he recognised Deng Xiaoping at the podium. 'She was then in her twenties. Earlier records are hard to trace, but here is a school photo, this is 1970.' Black and white, girls and boys in uniform a handsome walled garden. This time the face was too tiny and blurred to be recognisable, but all the children had armbands, and each of them was holding up the same small book. He was astonished, though he'd known there must be something like this—

'Elder Sister is a contemporary of your *grandfather*?'

'Thereabouts. In China we have a treatment for ageing, I believe it cleanses the cells of free radicals, reverses the shortening of telomeres, some such combination.' Wang shrugged. 'I don't know the scientific formula. It's called "Acala", it restores youth, and extends life perhaps indefinitely. The Standing Committee has decided that immortality is to be awarded rarely, discreetly, in special cases. So far Elder Sister is the only person who has been singled out for the august burden.'

'I see.'

'I'm telling you this not to forestall your curiosity, although that's a factor, but because it will help you to understand her. The Sphere needs stability. We need her to be with us for a long, long time; but it isn't anything she sought.'

Ax nodded. The White-Haired Girl's fresh, joyous smile shone up at him. 'Elder Sister told me she has a grown-up son, back in Xi'an. Is he a soldier too?'

'Ke'ai has done well in his career.'

And that's the crown prince dismissed.

'There's one other thing,' said Wang, after a pause, 'that you should know, and never mention. Ling Bao was a typical bad lot, among the spoilt males of his day. He was a tall, handsome, "charismatic" bully, afraid of Xifeng's obvious superiority. He was pathologically unfaithful, and he beat her. It left bitter scars.'

'Ah.'

'I see you understand me. Mr Pender should continue to keep a low profile. In fact it's best if both your partners keep a low profile.'

No explanation for why Fiorinda should stay in the background, and none was necessary. That's absolutely fine, thought Ax. That suits us very well.

The two men sat in silence.

'You know, in China we have a gender imbalance.'

'It gets talked about.'

'I can imagine. Leave aside the prurient speculation, it's true that it has changed us. We have had an epidemic of ladyboys: brought up starved of femininity, desperate to become women; and how can I put this? Chinese women, on the other hand, are strong in a reliable, forthright, practical way. One knows that these are desirable qualities, but a born woman of *feminine* power is a very precious treasure.'

'You use the word power as if you mean beauty.'

'Her power is beauty,' said Wang, intensely. 'It is the greatest beauty. Mr Preston, make no mistake. Elder Sister is *not* a figurehead.'

'I'll remember that.'

He left Wang and waited in the grand solar for his driver; glad of the respite. He'd been delivered to Elder Sister's quarters and then brought to Rivermead in a car with shaded windows. Now he stared through the noble expanse of glass, blind with storm, and could see nothing. No loss: he didn't want to know what had been done out there. Once upon a time there was a general called Ling Bao, you won't have heard the name . . . A man who would be king, written out of history; if he ever existed. So many veils, you know you'll never reach the end of them, you're scrabbling at the hems of infinity, it all spins away from you. I must get out of this shit, he thought. I will seriously lose my mind . . . Someone approached with a heavy tread from the direction of Wang's office: a woman, round-faced, sixtyish, don't-care hair, wearing the olive-green uniform with insouciant, middle-aged frumpiness.

Good God, maybe this is the real Elder Sister, stripped bare—

The woman sat down with a thump. She held a large, gift-wrapped parcel. 'Mr Preston? Elder Sister asked me to give you these, for the baby.'

She spoke *putonghua*, augh, thought I was off duty: he struggled for the simplest phrases. 'Oh, thank you, ah, thank Elder Sister. How very kind.'

Thank God he'd remembered to bring a present. It's vital to observe the social niceties and damned difficult to keep them in mind, when from your perspective it's a tea-party in a shark tank, and you had no option. 'Elder Sister wanted me to ask you,' continued the frumpy woman (she reminded him of Ingrid, Fiorinda's dresser in the glory days. Ingrid had been no frump, but he felt the same watchdog disapproval for all male hangers-on). Me, stage-door Johnnie. 'After your trip to "Cumbria", when you visit *Madame* again—'

'Yes?'

'Could it be the straight half of Mr Preston?'

'Oh . . . Okay, I think that could be arranged.'

She dumped the parcel with sublime rudeness and tromped off. Ax was considerably startled, but he had to admit he was not surprised.

Fiorinda laid out the loot, on the bank under the camellia hedge. The weather was warm and sunny, which made a pleasant fucking change.

The Chinese baby clothes were entrancing, especially the hats. She arranged outfits, the little green-lined scarlet jacket with the yellow trousers, and the stripy hat . . . 'She's really sixty.'

'Sixty-odd, according to the evidence I was shown.'

'But she looks like fifteen-going-on-thirty, is a dazzling dancer, and she has a big crush on Ax Preston. What a lucky boy you are.'

'Fuck off. She treats Sage like dogdirt because her husband was a wife-beater and a sex addict, and she has a grown-up son at home.'

'She's not reckless or invulnerable, she's just a frontline commander. She does not suspect Sage of being the Neurobomb, she doesn't like him because he was a sex-god and she's heard about him hitting Mary.'

'You've got it.'

Ax was lying curled around the baby. He tickled her with a grass blade, she batted it and swiped for his face. Coz liked pulling noses, which was getting to be a hazard. She had sharp claws, and resented having them snipped. Min admired the fashion show, occasionally reaching out a covetous paw to pat a ribbon or a bright shiny button. He still had his collector's instinct: he hid things.

'And she takes a drug, which is not available to anyone else, that keeps her immortally young . . . Hm.' Fiorinda sat back on her heels, contemplating an array of flat babies, invisible except for their charming clothes. 'Remember we used to talk about the Neurobomb Cold War? Maybe this is it. We don't know, they don't know. We daren't try to find out which of us has the Bomb, we dare not attack each other, so it's stalemate. Mutually Assured Destruction.'

'I wish I could have brought you better news.'

'I didn't think you were going to come back with our freedom in your pocket.'

She sighed. 'And ooh, nearly forgot, this female emperor wants you for her male concubine. Hopefully just a one-night-stand.'

Ouch. 'The proposition was fairly direct,' said Ax, cautiously.

He got an old-fashioned look, as the English say. 'And you're not averse to the idea, so don't pretend. Well, I can see you better not say no.'

She left the clothes and put her arms around him and Coz, her body a shield, a roof over their heads. 'Ax, Ax, have your night out, sweetheart: but *I know what I'm doing* is such famous last words. Are you sure you're not jumping into a tiger pit? She's had my father's children killed. We don't know what she is.'

There had in the past been an actual incident involving tigers in a pit, which Ax was never going to live down.

'I'm not in that kind of danger.'

'Eh. Eh. **Eh.**'

'All right, all right, Miss Pushy. I am not stealing him, I am *sharing* him.'

'She doesn't know that word yet.'

Fiorinda lay down. Min climbed over Ax's side and made space for himself beside the baby, purring firmly. Ax had discovered that Min was hopelessly flawed, according to Bengal Cat Standards, as he had tufted ears. This gave him great satisfaction, not because he was scared of that mythical breeder (know the difference between paranoia and reality, thanks), but because it proved Pigtail was a wanker. 'I wonder exactly what happened on their night of the long knives. Must've been gruesome: Wang has a burden of guilt, that's for sure. Professional soldiers hate to commit civilian atrocities, it screws them up.'

'Makes you wonder what kind of bloke the dastardly Ling Bao really was.'

'The victors wield the airbrush.'

They thought of the darkness that had closed over vivid scenes in their own past. How swiftly the world forgets, and you feel a mug for remembering who did what to whom, wow, a whole decade ago. 'You didn't tell her Elder Sister sounds like Big Brother, which recalls to our ancient culture a fable of evil Stalinist domination?'

'Not me. Not one Lennonism passed my lips, not likely.'

'Did you ask about Keith Utamore?'

Keith was a Japanese-ethnic Oz rock journalist, who'd been a friend to them in prison. He'd been trapped in England by the invasion, arrested and 'repatriated' to Guangdong. 'I asked. She said, let me get this right . . . "The Japanese are inveterate copycats. They have always wanted to be Chinese, now they are Chinese. What's wrong with that?"'

'You make her sound like a real charmer.'

'She *is*, in fact, a real charmer.'

'Hm.'

A chaffinch called, *pink, pink*. Beech leaves shimmered overhead: Coz reached for them, and suddenly wailed. Baby wants to climb trees, baby wants to run and jump like Min. Soon, soon enough, baby. Don't wish your life away.

'Wouldn't it be great to stay here all summer,' sighed Fiorinda.

'Forget it. You're a rockstar. Summer is not your own time.'

Sage came out of the house, folded down and looked at the grass babies. He'd been working, as he had been for days, on Lance Buckley's virtual record. He hadn't yet told them anything. He'd been immersed in his look-through-you, obsessive, coding mood. It was nostalgic, but it made him daunting company.

'Why isn't there any blue?'

'Blue is for a boy,' said Fiorinda. She didn't care for the colour pink herself, but there was a very appealing fuchsia-coloured romper suit, with hand-embroidered flowers. The sun was in her eyes, she lifted the baby as a wriggling parasol.

'What bullshit. She'd look excellent in blue.' He picked up the stripy hat and switched it with the four-cornered cherry-red one.

Ax knew they'd both been ahead of him, on the surprise coda to his meeting with Elder Sister. He wasn't so dumb that he took Fiorinda's calm reaction at face-value, but she would scratch: she wouldn't bite. She'd been known to play away before, and so had Ax. His big cat was a different problem.

'Did you get somewhere?' he asked, humbly neutral.

'Yep, think so. I'm running it.'

Sage relented, barely, with a tender smile. But oooh, I'm still in trouble. 'Lance's hardware was useless for catching ghosts, Oh Chosen One. Fuckin' daylight robbery. But a b-loc self is a material object, it's not solid but it's really there an' it leaves a trace. I picked up a few fragments of os and 1s that didn't match any phase point in Lance's reference model, and wouldn't hybridise with his model of Dian. I've been building on that, it's been slow work but I'm cooking now.'

Ax and Fiorinda sat up. Coz, freed from the corral of their bodies, set to work on her own treasured project: the great rolling over trick.

'I'm getting a signature that matches the b-loc signature for DK in my board's cache. I think he must have made a call,' added Sage; staring at the baby clothes. 'He loc'd out of the firestorm, who knows, maybe thinking he could escape like that; or not thinking at all. The Chinese captured the signal, and it was the same *signal*, months later, that visited Dian. That's what I'm guessing, so far.'

'My fucking God,' breathed Ax. 'You're saying they can hack b-loc?'

'I'm saying, maybe the Chinese are master experts at the atrocious, world-destroying tech they forbid anyone on earth to use.'

The back garden at Tyller Pystri shivered like a windblown veil.

They took the baby and went indoors, to Sage's study: the damp old cottage parlour overrun by hardware. They saw the recovered 4-D image of that room, the dying woman and the shadow, *in dark, close-fitting clothes*, which had the signature of DK's somato-sensory cortex self-image (the basis of b-loc). 'I think of you all,' said Fiorinda, rapidly, trembling. 'I count you over, to make sure you are all right. I have counted DK dead, is he dead? Is he alive? *How* could Dian have called him up? How could she have made contact?'

'I don't know,' said Sage. 'I have no idea.'

If Dilip had been interrogated they were dead. But they were not dead, they were riding high. The Emperor summons Ax Preston to her bed, appoints him her emissary to Europe, grooms him for ever-higher honours—

'So now we go to Cumbria,' said Ax, grimly. 'On a very complex mission.'

What to tell Allie, they wondered, as the truth sank in.

It was chilly indoors: Sage lit a fire. They cooked and ate together, gave Cosoleth her bath; sang to her, read her a story, and settled for the bedtime feed. The baby sucked first at one sweet, naked breast and then the other, music from long ago playing on the sound system; the men rapt in devotion, mother and child nestled in their arms on the sofa. But already Coz hardly seemed like a baby, she was a separate person, no longer an extension of their own bodies. Soon they'd have to give up this intensely sensual, if not sexual, pleasure, and that would be a goodbye—

In the night Fiorinda got up, wrapped a shawl over her nightgown and went to look for her tapestry bag. She brought the saltbox to the hearth, holding it in her palm: a wooden apple that held salt in one half, flint, steel and tinder in the other. When you commit magic you use a focus, a talisman, a channel; it gives you some protection, some safeguard. She thought of the drains under Rainbow Bridge. The light dies, the roof ahead touches the water, you're going to have to fill your lungs and dive, go under without knowing if you'll ever breathe again.

'*Fee?*'

Sage slipped out of the bed and came to join her, a shadowed, naked tiger, slippery muscle gliding under his pale hide.

'I don't want to go under,' she whispered. 'I thought it was over.'

'So did I, my brat. But we did for your old man . . . I don't believe we have another boss fight on our hands; if we do, fuck it. We'll just have to win.'

They clasped hands. 'C'mon, sweetheart. Back to bed.'

Before she slept Fiorinda made puja in her heart, although she did not believe in God. She thought of Dilip on England's night of the long knives, when she had barely known him, the two of them clinging to each other, smeared with other people's blood, on the steps of that dreadful building in Whitehall. We're still alive, we're alive, hang onto that. *Lord Krishna protect me, help me remember that I'm not really afraid, let me not become the monster* . . . The divinity she saw in her mind had Dilip Krishnachandran's face, blackened in flame.

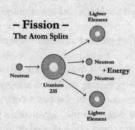

II

The Lantern Bearers

The little Lakeland town was *en fête,* the streets decked in organic bunting, spacious old car parks and cluttered pub forecourts overrun by guitar bands, choral singing, prophetic poets, firebrand puppeteers, mad preachers. Big screens on street corners and walls relayed events from the tents and stages of the Fairground; digital masks and other virtual toys (banned on pain of death in the Occupied Zones) were openly on display. Death himself sat crosslegged on the parapet of Church Beck Bridge – a tall and limber skeleton, transparent between the charnel bones – keeping an eye on the throng of pilgrims who poured through the gates of St Andrew's churchyard.

Alain de Corlay and Naomi Erhlevy (aka Tamagotchi), leaders of the French techno-green delegation, had just made the obligatory visit Ruskin's grave. The former Eurotrash Deconstructionists of *Movie Sucré* stopped to pass the time of day, and to wax satirical about the Godfather. They'd reverted to their popstar personas, Alain Jupette wore his trademark miniskirt, in Royal Stuart plaid; Tam wore one of her Courrèges Moon-Girl suits, and silver platform boots.

John Ruskin's sexual nihilism and his nature sketches met their approval; for his charming pet rock collection they would pass over a multitude of crimes—

'The man had talent,' pronounced Tam. 'His description of falling into madness, through the grain of the polished wood of his bedstead, is *admirable.*'

'Naturally, one despairs of his political naïveté.'

'Mm.' Death watched the uniformed constables, who were marshalling the graveyard queue in flower-decked boaters and yellow vests. Cumbria Police, terrified that any trouble at the Congress would be the first step to Occupation, didn't have their peace and love heads on. There'd been some trigger-happy use of non-lethals.

'Why don't you send the filth back to their kennels?' suggested Tam. 'Let us police ourselves, we've had experience; remember Amsterdam.'

'Wasn't there,' said the Minister for Gigs. 'Nah, they'll get the hang of it. Sacking the police would be an incident in itself, and there must be no incidents. This is Elder Sister's wild, uncontrolled rockstar radical event, *nothing* goes wrong.'

'How stupidly paranoid you sound, Aoxomoxoa.'

'I am.'

'I am terrified myself,' said Alain, placidly. 'Life in Paris, with the Chinese on our doorstep, has been frightening enough. Now here we little birds are between the dragon's jaws, picking her teeth. Your blood sugar is low, you should come to lunch.'

Tam dropped her cheroot and boot-heeled it, giving those constables the evil eye; then stooped to pick up the butt like a good girl. 'We've found a place called the Snow Pudding, authentic artisan food, *unbelievable* fresh ingredients—'

'No thanks.' Two stately Shield Ring Hearthmaidens caught Death's blood-dark empty sockets fixed on them, and crossed the street: yeah, be very afraid, long frocks . . . Sage had forgotten how effective the avatar mask could be. He'd spent the first day overdosing on sombre menace, had to tone it down. 'I'm good.'

Chip and Verlaine leaned over the bridge, watching the curious preparations for a duck race. They were in Morris costume, ready for a show in the yard of the Black Bull: black breeches, red sashes, white shirts, stockings, buckled shoes, bells on their gators, coloured ribands in their hats. A distressing sight.

'Nobody asks *us* to lunch,' complained Chip. 'We are not chic enough.'

'Nyah, they only ask because I won't annoy them by accepting. I'm gonna regret this, I know I am, but Chip, *why* are you in blackface?'

Chip rolled his eyes. You have to ask? 'I'm a *miner*, Sage. A dirty, black-legged miner . . . Tho' not in fact a blackleg.'

'Okay, makes perfect sense. So, er, why isn't Ver in blackface, seeing he is white and it would work a little better?'

'Because *I* am Margaret Thatcher,' explained Verlaine, as to a slow-witted child. He retrieved a sneering mask on a stick from the pavement; and a gilded scroll.

'We auditioned. They said I couldn't act for fuck.'

'I make a superb Iron Lady,' said Verlaine, modestly. 'These are my words. Would you like a sample of the voice?'

'No!'

The ducks arrived in a net in the back of a four-wheeler, and clattered off to the starting gate upstream. Punters surged to place late bets. Stewards warded them off the banks where vivid, ragged July flowers tumbled; among the young trees and the wild raspberry canes. Someone shouted, it's no use throwing the'selves in, ladies and gents, them ducks won't be let out unless the course is clear—

The Adjuvants hooked arms and cut a merry caper, waving their hats.

'Go away,' said the living skull. 'You're making me look cute and harmless.'

'D'you think he's going to start talking in capital letters?'

'Get out of here, before I THROW YOU TO THE DUCKS.'

On the Euro Cultural Congress Fairground, at the head of Coniston Water, Ax and Fiorinda exited the media tent and walked around: greeting friends, saluting enemies; rewarding faithful service with personal chat. They could not get used to the fx. They were both liable to jump a mile if a light-hearted flight of virtual Daleks or fire-spouting basilisks suddenly blossomed in the air, *my God, we're all going to get massacred.*

Movie Sucré's rayguns had been impounded: the absurdistes took this very seriously. A dance ensemble from Poland had been hospitalised *en masse* after a terrible crossing, they were full of praise for the way they'd been treated in Occupied Tyneside. Delegates from the Nordic Alliance, including the Crown Princess of Norway, had been held for questioning at their port of entry; but it had ended happily. The young activists of the Reich, encouraged to cross the Line along with their leaders, had leapt at the chance. There's Areeka and her pals, exchanging autographs with a Bavarian pop idol collective. Post-Italians from Turin and Milan, Czechs, Slovenes, Baltics, Iberians . . . Word was that most of the covert government agents had been turned back; but some had been allowed through, no one knew on what grounds.

The Chinese say one thing and mean another. The radicals and utopians had obeyed the summons in popculture drag (it wasn't a stretch). The official coverage would be Elder Sister, the recently unveiled Supreme Being; Elder Sister's wonderful enthusiasm for Europe's music etc . . . The questions from the floor were openly political, as they were meant to be: the atmosphere was fear and adrenalin.

'It's going to be tough,' said Ax. 'They want to be on board, but there's uncertainty, a sense of loss, and they're going to take it out on someone.'

George and Peter passed them, wearing policemen's boaters; soberly skull-headed. There's Bill unmasked, Clio from Jam Today firmly affixed. The Powerbabes and Rob, with Pearl Wing in tow. Good to see that little monster herself again: dressed to the nines, glowering at being dragged away from London. Marlon and Silver must be around, but we won't see them if they see us first—

And here's Ax Preston, revered rockstar guru of Crisis Europe, morphed into an unashamed apologist for the prospective Chinese World State; with a Celtic tattoo, and a dappled cat the size of a young ocelot pacing beside him. Here's Fiorinda, wild-cat diva and Protector of the Poor, re-invented as a feel-good pro-Chinese celeb, with a baby in a candy-stripe sling. They caught each other's eyes as they walked through the fair, in rueful appreciation. Just be glad we're still standing. By the pavilion of the Guild of St George they stopped to let Coz admire the great embroidered standard of the Shield Ring.

METAL MEAT CORN AND WOOL

Metal, Meat, Corn and Wool, we don't need you, leave us be. That's corn, in the old English sense of the grain you grind for bread: probably not wheat these days, certainly not maize. A tall, broad-shouldered Steadman, in Gortex walking shorts and a *Don't Shoot The Gardener* tee under his robes, came over. It was Simon Hartsfern, Master of the Guild. A gleaming blue-black beard rippled over his oak-barrel chest, concealing Ax's face on the tee and half-smothering his chain of office.

The Shield Ring had harboured no actives, their Futuristic Artisan creed was not judged Countercultural. Cumbria was unoccupied because the Chinese had chosen to leave them be. Their anomalous status was crucial for this conference. Their later fate would have to be tackled, on the back of the Euro issues—

'Thee had a rough reception in the prelims, Mr Preston.' Simon bowed graciously to the Reich's young queen. 'My lady—'

'No bad thing,' said Ax. 'There are opinions that need to be aired.'

'To *my* mind the question is not whether or not we're surprised at the news that we have a mighty Empress, all power to her. It's whether the

EU still exists in any form. If it does, how shall it be governed? Shall we foster the Well-Being of the Land, as we were vowed to do, under thy former rule? Or shall we feebly allow ourselves to return to the sterile debates, the satanic mills of Crisis Europe Politics—'

'Many contentious issues shall be raised,' said Fiorinda, edging towards escape. *Eeeh,* said Coz, and reached for the beard with her most coquettish chuckle.

'I understand thou intends to join us on the Landsturm, young lady,' said the Master, beaming. 'May I offer thee and thy mama the hospitality of the Shield Ring Ladies' Mountain Goat limo?' He smiled hopefully at Fiorinda. 'Thee'd be very comfortable, and my wife and sisters would be honoured by thy company.'

'Thanks,' said Fiorinda. 'We'll bear it in mind, but we're planning to do the walk. Something for her to tell her grandchildren.'

'Excuse us. It's time for her feed, and you know what it's like. Slap the popper on your throat, in ten minutes you're pumping.' Ax raised his eyebrow at Simon's very blank look. 'I thought you had kids, Master. You must have done the dad's instant lactation trip, it's *so* futuristic.'

'Idiot,' said Fiorinda, when they were safely on their way.

'I must remember to tell Sage, d'you think he'll back me up?'

'I'm absolutely sure he will.'

They were prejudiced against right-wing Utopians, for reasons that were hard to set aside. She glanced back at the Guild encampment, where some kind of Bronze Age hymn to the lunchtime sun had started up. 'Promise me you'll keep those under control. You *can't* treat them as the enemy, that's a fucking stupid gambit.'

'Hahaha. They're a sophisticated bunch of reactionaries, running a very successful experiment. They can take a few Lennonisms; but I'll keep 'em down—'

They gave Coz an oat rusk to mumble and wandered, leaving the crowd behind, until they found a stand of sycamores on the shore. Boulders made an armchair in the green shade, Min collected a pebble and took it up into the branches. The baby sucked happily, kneading like a kitten; Fiorinda's head on Ax's breast, his arm around his girl. If they could stay like so forever, in a haze of oxytocin . . . Except for the nagging gap where Sage ought to be. Such is the life. The Triumvirate would be lucky if they slept in adjoining bedrolls for the next couple of weeks.

'Maybe I should accept Master Hartshorn's offer,' mused Fiorinda, in a martyred tone. 'Get the inner circle long frocks' girltalk.'

'Hartsfern.'

'Speak for yourself. He looks a lot like a Victorian lady's pick-me-up to me.'

Let a hundred flowers bloom, then chop their heads off when they say things you don't want to hear . . . The hint of real news the Danube delegates had brought to Cumbria was a warning. The *other* occupied European nation seemed to have been lurching from crackdown to crackdown, and contrary to Elder Sister's report, nothing was 'settled' there. But on this side of the continent, the vulnerable people had stayed at home: no Scots or Irish because of the 'Celtic' misunderstanding, no Greeks; a slightly worrying Welsh Shield Ring connection. Every delegate had been approved by Wang Xili and by Ax. You have to stop agonising about the hundred flowers trap, and concentrate on the performance. Trust the Chinese to have screened out the suicide warriors, and treat the Shield Ring as light relief, because the air has ears.

Cosoleth sucked lustily, first the left breast and then the right. 'She needs more than I can make. I'll be pleased to have my tits back, in a way, but it'll be an awful wrench. Bugger of it is, the more solids she eats, the less milk I have.'

'She's getting too big for the sling. The stitching's coming apart.'

'Oh, woe is us.'

The baby fell asleep, Min rattled his pebble, Ax began to get restive.

'What d'you think about *beards*?'

'I think you can't either of you grow one.' Fiorinda swiftly cut this notion off at the pass. 'Sage's is so blond it's pointless, and yours is straggly.'

'Well, thanks . . . Shall we go an' see how the big cat is getting on?'

'I want to practise being lonely as a cloud. You go, and have a nice talk about galley slaves with beards and big milky tits. Probably getting whipped.'

'Hahaha, fuck off. C'mon Min, thy lady wants to be alone.'

My tiger and my wolf, and their daft fantasies . . . John Ruskin's Brantwood, a white house with a little turret and green lawns, stood small and far away across the water. Alas, I fear our Godfather would run screaming if he were confronted with the Reich. Presumably he'd be better pleased with his current tenants . . . Brantwood could have been a problem. Fabulously beautiful ancestral Utopian gaff, who gets to stay there? Fortunately the Bronze Age futurists had cunningly offered their

HQ to the Chinese Observers. She felt that this boded well, it showed a cool nerve and a rational attitude. A small boat was tacking over the lake, a dinghy with a three-cornered tan sail. Oh, look, Coz. See the blue bird on the flag, I bet that boat is called the Swallow—

But Cosoleth had gone with Ax and Min, little shoot would never listen from the inside no more. Fiorinda was alone, thinking again of the profound revolution that she had struggled so hard to forestall. There is one code uniting mind and matter, the perceived world and the consciousness that perceives it. We have learned to read that code, and the future opens, stranger than imagination could devise . . . The Chinese were trying to turn back time, but it couldn't be done. The trees, the stones, the water and the mountains that brooded over it were immanent with holy dread; a veil over the formless matrix *which now had form*, which could be taken apart and remade.

> *Dust as we are the immortal spirit grows*
> *Like harmony in music; there is a dark*
> *Inscrutable workmanship that reconciles*
> *Discordant elements . . . How strange that all*
> *Regrets, vexations, lassitudes interfused*
> *Within my mind, should e're have borne a part*
>
> *. . . in making up the calm existence that is mine*
> *When I am worthy of myself . . .*

The dinghy with the swallow pennant had come inshore. One of the young soldiers was reading carefully from a little book, while his companions downed the sail. Tourists! Who the hell else would be reading Wordsworth aloud on this gig, while sailing a boat called the Swallow? The Observer Team aides saw Fiorinda and started to grin shyly, like kids surprised at a stolen game of make-believe. She grinned back: hey, compadres. Up here I'm a tourist too; and left them to enjoy their First Class Treasure experience in peace.

'There was a stall selling baby-carriers,' said Felice, wrapping a carry-cloth firmly around Fiorinda and Coz: the candy-stripe sling was dead. 'We can find the long frocks who were running it, they'll be around here somewhere.'

'Mm.' Fiorinda resolved to get this cloth-strapping thing down, for the duration. She didn't want neo-Bronze Age artisan-crafted baby gear. She wanted something antique, shiny tubing and bright-coloured nylon—

'How old is she *now*?' asked Dora, as people do, when they have forgotten. 'Is it, um, four months, where does the time go?'

'Seventeen weeks on Wednesday.'

'Wow, she's huge—'

When they had something important to discuss the free Cumbrians gathered and went for a long walk together. It was a tradition founded in the depths of the Crisis, when Simon Hartsfern and Walter Ridley had tramped the fells: gathering followers, preaching self-sufficiency and the Well-Being of the Land. Mr Preston's pro-Chinese message was getting the Shield Ring treatment. The Fairground had been dismantled and packed on mule trains. The marquees, stalls and stages would be raised again twice in Langdale, and then on Eskdale Moor. The hike itself was not obligatory, but it was *hardcore*, so naturally the Reich had signed up.

Chip and Verlaine, ostentatiously at home in their boots, guarded the packs and talked about ale with hairy-stockinged locals. Cherry Dawkins stood alone, immemorial sadness shadowing her pretty face; turning *pretty* into beautiful. The spiritual quest, it seemed so real, and then you find yourself over the edge, in a situation where there's no way forward, no way back. Measuring yourself and coming up *worthless*, without ever going near a scanner—

Allie paced up and down, wondering if they'd made the right decision. The Chinese Observers were walking, but the non-Reich bands, significant Euros and the entire mediapack had opted for limo-standard motor transport, gorgeous food and soft beds. What if Ax missed a vital conversation held in a gourmet hotel spa?

Cumbria's luxuries frightened her.

But there's the Berlin Foreign Minister (they were openly pro-Chinese in Berlin), incognito as a flugelhorn expert, and there's an important Portuguese Presidential aide; also *fadista*. She walked around Cherry, who managed a tight-lipped nod. Poor eye-candy baby. Everyone knew what was going on there (except the obvious person), and nobody wanted it to happen. Breaking up is hard to do.

The maidens and the wives wore shorter skirts for walking: pinafore-cut linen shifts in glorious colours, with mantles in that very fine wool folded on their shoulders. They did not look like Amish, they looked like a fucking *Vogue* shoot. God, the bloom on these people, they make us all look like scarecrows. How can the Chinese *not know* there's something weird about this economic fucking miracle? She hated the sight of the Shield Ring. Broken glass in her throat, terrible images, and guilt twisting the knife, oh why couldn't I mourn and move on—

Death came thumping up on horseback, wearing a steward's vest, an ecstatic little boy in front of him on the saddle. He was leading a second mount.

'Mama!' shrieked Mamba. 'Look at ME!'

'Ohmigod!' howled Dora. '*Sage!* What are you doing with my kid? He's too little! He's supposed to be in the Mountain Rescue jeep with Fer!'

'She's not in the jeep, she's with Rob. The safest place they can be is with us. Hey, Allie, you can ride. C'mon, you're hereby deputised.'

Around eleven in the morning they started to move: Steadhusbands and Hearthwives, maidens and manchildren, radical rockstars, EU delegates, rank and file Utopians; and of course the Chinese Observers. They tramped singing through the town and up into the Coniston Fells, with the larks shouting and the stony trail echoing under their tread, until the Reich favourites you could march to, some of them inexplicable ('Bohemian Rhapsody'?) gave out; and it was *Ich bin ein froher Wandrer . . . Und hab' ich auch kein Geld . . .*

Death and his companions watched from above as the Landsturm crossed the flank of Great Intake, 'Ilkley Moor', the Islamic Campaign song, making the fells resound. Someone was capering ahead of the Shield Ring banners, a satirical duck impaled on a stick. Banners and standards had become a *thing* on the campground in Coniston, rousing mysterious passions: captured and defended, joyously destroyed.

Norman, you should be here, thought Sage . . . But Norman Soong was in mild peril, having been discovered in possession of a copy of the sex show, which he was supposed to have erased. He wasn't going to get dismembered, but he wouldn't be on Elder Sister's first team for a while. What'd happened to the guilty copy of that very impressive sex show was anybody's guess—

'Fucking glad Jiang Jieshi isn't after them,' remarked Rob.

'Who?'

'Aka Chiang Kai-shek,' said Allie. 'Chased the Communists around.'

'Oh yeah, what scholars you are. The Long March.'

Rob took a firmer grip on his daughter. Ferdelice, the five-year-old, had been thrilled to be riding until Mamba got to share the privilege: now she felt betrayed and wouldn't stop wriggling. That ambling mass of humanity looked so naked. He looked up, almost afraid to see a flight of purple UFOs.

'Sage, are there any actual ex-barmies in that lot?'

'Yeah. But they've recanted, and none of them were active.'

'Tell me there are no concealed weapons.'

'Fucking hope not.' He shook the reins, one arm around Mamba, 'C'mon Mr Pie, let it out.' The little boy whooped for joy, the mighty steed thundered away. The horses were Fell Ponies, crossed with some big work-horse marque in the case of Sage's mount: built for the kind of ground where humans longed for a ski-lift.

'D'you want to be Famine or Pestilence?' said Rob to Allie. 'Since War is not invited . . . I fancy Pestilence myself, but I don't mind.'

At New Bridge the National Trust campsite welcomed the Landsturm with fine food, good ale, unlimited hot showers and blister kits; a feat of organisation. The walkers sat up in the camping barns, and out under the stars: talking Utopian blues, sharing news from nowhere in thirty languages, singing, playing guitar, forming impromptu bands and instant eternal friendships. Dor and Felice dropped out of a fiery debate on space travel, what does Gaia think? They lay on their backs, staring at the misty stars. Cherry was talking to Rob, over there under the apple trees, and they knew every word that was being spoken. They felt branded, as if every fucking person here was pointing the finger, there's Rob Nelson's laydeez, thought they were so cool, but they couldn't hang on to the pretty one, the silky skin, the sweet mouth, she took her wings, she's got to fly—

Their feet hurt, but their hearts were breaking. They categorically did not believe they were being dumped for a choirboy. Cherry was cutting loose, that was all. Any excuse. 'Everybody's private lives,' said Dora, 'start to crawl out from under. The breaking up and moving on that we've suppressed, all these years.'

The dissolution of their love seemed like a toll exacted on the success of this congress, on the fulfilment of the Reich's purpose; the birth of a new world.

'We were living in a fool's paradise, girl. She never cared about us, we were steps on her shining way, that's the fucking truth.'

'Shut up.'

An easy stage onwards to Wall End, and the walkers rejoined the sybarites. Ax Preston made one of his rare full-on public speeches, at an event billed as a panel on Preserving Our Musical Diversity.

The choice is simple. Do you prefer to be swallowed whole, and live on in the belly of the empire? Or would you rather be chewed to mush very painfully first? We don't want a fight. We'd have to be insane. We've watched this dawn rising, we want the benefits of Sphere membership, am I right? We fought for something new, vital, humane, to rise from the Crisis, and here it is. We need to *engage* with the World State concept (although knowing the reality of that may be a long way off). We need to show Elder Sister that Europe is more than a 'tragic and violent backwater'. We have a diverse heritage to defend, yes, our 'musical diversity', good figure of speech. No music if the notes are all the same, every folksong a web of history—

He compared Elder Sister to Napoleon, but a true Napoleon, getting it right. He told them she needed, she *wanted* different voices in her empire, to keep her on the path of lasting glory, and this was the role to which they could aspire. '*Engage,* it's such an Ax Preston word,' murmured one woman in the crowd to her wife, and they sighed, and clasped hands. They would follow him anywhere.

Question-time was rough. This was a self-selected crowd, nobody was going to offer the slightest offence to the Chinese, nothing resembling the term collaborator could be used. But there were ways of speaking the bitterness.

Why should we listen to the dupe of Babylon?

'Remind us, what part of the American Way did you most admire, Ax? Was it the fascism or the rapacity?'

That was a francophone Belgian, top EU maven (so far as that body survived); posing as a folkie storyteller. She was white, but married to a Rwandan-born academic and used her husband's name; which Ax avoided trying to pronounce. She'd been a sparring partner of Ax's at the Flood Countries Conference. What's happening in Central Africa, Mathilde? How bad is it? Do you and Dom have any real news?

Real news was a Landsturm catchphrase, and a dangerous one, have to watch that. You mean Joyous Liberation isn't real?

Never argue, answer a different question, it's child's play.

'Few of us who were adults when the Crash came were innocent, Mathilde. We can't call it the American Way, it was global. Rich or poor, the world over, we knew it was dirty, but *we all took the money*—'

One bastard asked him did he now consider himself a rabid Celtic, or was the tattoo mindless rockstar body-art?

'The Extreme Celtics put my girlfriend on a bonfire,' said Ax, 'for the crime of protecting the people. Then another time the Scots saved our lives, and this is their mark. Wake up, brother. Death is simple. Life is complicated.'

The Chinese Observers listened with great interest.

It was a little like tunnelling out of prison, climbing the Wall, crawling through the razor wire to freedom, to be greeted by a yelling, rotten-veg-slinging crowd. He was angry about the DON'T SHOOT THE GARDENER tees, fucking rows of them staring up at him. Nobody asked my approval for that, what am I? The Shield Ring's Poster Boy? But what shook him was the way he recognised so many of the faces, people he had never known by name. He'd been with them in Amsterdam; in Bucharest, when they were freeing the Danube. He'd taken refuge with them in Paris, in one case, spoken to the bloke last in the Cardiff Assembly. We rise on the backs of the mass movements, we fall by the way, in one Terror or another, and then it's the few who are still standing, most of us known to each other; and we decide. Small and far away, in Reading Arena, in a world he couldn't remember, he saw a naïve little figure with a guitar on his shoulder, thinking about that red-headed babe, posing for the mirror of the crowd—

'The amazing Mr Preston,' murmured Alain, when he finally escaped from the podium and rejoined the panellists. 'The perfect master at leading pigs to market. You will have them convinced it's their very own idea to love Big Sister.'

Ax grinned (shakily) and nodded. The air has ears.

A Steadman with a noble chestnut beard, looking somehow like a Centaur, gave the vote of thanks. Ruskin, thou shouldst be with us at this hour, etc. Ax heard the music coming in from the field outside, wandering like a lost soul between the heated bodies, and realised he could not stop himself from shaking. He lost the last exchanges, the finale. The next thing he knew he was in a backstage space, a three-cornered patch of green grass between drab membrane walls. Big George Merrick and Bill Trevor were leaning casually in the entrance to this roofless cave. Sage was with him, unmasked, looking strange. I've been here before, he thought. A horror washed through him and was gone.

'What happened?'

'Nothing bad,' said the big cat. 'Standing ovation, you walked off, no damage. Let Alain make the curtseys and press the flesh—'

'Sage? Are you okay?'

'Wish I could run away an' join the circus. Otherwise I'm good.'

'Me . . . same.'

Blue eyes, blue eyes. Ax felt that the tension between them, building since he'd told his lovers about Elder Sister's irresistible offer, was ready to snap. Words didn't come, his need was choking him, closing his throat.

'I belong to you,' said Sage. 'You want to sort me out, babe?'

'You want to go and find somewhere?'

They went and found somewhere, and had a sorting out, nothing held back. Sometimes nothing less than *savage* discharge can express, can explain, can release the hard, hard place we're in.

Link hands and stare at the sky. 'Want to go another round?'

'I'm done,' murmured Sage. 'You realise we've been rolling in sheep turds?'

'Don't fucking care.'

Fiorinda was interviewed by Margaret Smallwood, one of Simon Hartshorn's sisters, cousins, aunts or something; for a radio talkshow called *Hause,* with 'floating title pictures', whatever that meant. Cosoleth had been taken off by a gaggle of Hearthmaidens. She was asked about the one-child family (Cumbrian women are concerned), the labour camp system (will English working people still be slaves?), and did she have qualms about abandoning the 'forbidden technologies?'

'None whatsoever,' said Fiorinda, smiling. Leave them alone together, she was thinking. It usually works . . . 'I'm excited about finding out what the new Sphere technologies have to offer.'

The intense middle-aged prophetess hovered on the edge of rash comment, rash reservations; and moved on. Cultural diversity, schools to adopt *putonghua* as a teaching medium . . . What about my new download? My new baby, my all-star girl band? Can we talk about my latest drunken folly? Nah, I suppose not.

The announcement of Fred Eiffrich's death had reached them in Coniston. After an illness of several weeks, borne with dignity, said Joyous Liberation's newsreader. No extended coverage. No solemn music, no grave procession of talking heads-of-state, but *borne with dignity*; suppose that's the Chinese way of saying thanks for saving us from another A-team, dude. The evening after the Musical Diversity panel there was a full-scale rock concert: a blaze of lights, flawless sound and gleaming guitars; the Langdale Pikes peering down through the sweet air, like two pointy-headed old giant-women, curious to know what these ants were doing at their feet. Ax did a solo set. He played for an hour, bantering with the crowd, very relaxed; and then paused, his white Strat at half-mast, looking over their heads into the last sunset light, for so long people started to get uneasy. Here we are on the other side, Fred. It's not like we imagined, but we made it.

He leant to the mic. 'This is for Fred Eiffrich.'

> *Mine eyes have seen the coming of the glory of the lord*
> *He is tramping out the vintage, where the grapes of wrath are stored*
> *He has loosed the fateful lightning of his terrible swift sword—*

No one knew what to do with a Hendrixed-up American anthem. The mask slipped out there; the fear showed. But the Chinese Observers led the applause with what seemed genuine enthusiasm, so everyone joined in. Elder Sister doesn't like people who abandon their friends. A craven puppet could never hold Europe for her, true allegiance is not afraid to criticise. And now they wanted *Jerusalem*. Okay, okay. Sing along, why don't you.

Yeah, had a feeling you'd all know the words.

The man has perfect instincts, thought Alain de Corlay, affecting ignorance of the lyric on the VIP straw bales. The pity that he'd felt in the afternoon dissipated. He saw that Ax had merely been shaken by a moment of fugue; for the human frame, mind and body, is bound to struggle against the shackles of power. The hero of this hour was at peace with himself and with what lay ahead. Which implied his partners must also have accepted their fate . . . That's good, because you've become our special man, my poor friend. And *we* will be the kingmakers; if we survive our last tight corner. For once, and at such a price, the utopians, radicals, social rebels of Europe will be the ones pulling the strings—

By the third march it was beyond dispute. The soft-optioners were out of the loop, the walkers were the Landsturm. There were supposed to be eleven hundred of them (there was no accredited accurate count). Very few dropped out, although there were blistered feet and sorely fried hides – mainly mixed-race urbanites who'd taken no precautions, having had no idea they could get UV-burned in the English Lakes. Possible rulers of a future Europe, radical rockstars, veteran eco-warriors, free

Cumbrians; young and old, they surrendered to the rhythm of the hills. There were hours when the singing stilled by common consent, a walking meditation. We shall lose everything, and live to fight another day, we shall defend *liberté, egalité, amitié* in the World State (that may never happen). Oh, but the price! *Muß es sein?* they chanted – a delegate of a classical bent having taught them a round, based on Beethoven's famous marginal comment, his last words on life and death; maybe a joke, maybe profound truth, maybe both.

Must it be?

> *Muß es sein?*
> *Muß es sein?*
> *Muß es sein?*
>
> *Es muß sein!*
> *Es muß sein!*
> *Es muß sein!*

And then the *good* bit, the intensely satisfying note everyone waited for, and cheered for, sung by that old Bavarian bloke with the growliest, deepest of bass voices: *Der Schweeeeer gefaaaaasste Entschluß!*

The difficult resolution!

They knew this march through the fells would live forever.

Mr Pie, the wall-eyed piebald stallion, drifted about, munching patches of green and cooling his big feathered feet in peaty sloughs. Death moved more purposefully, taking sight lines, studying his gadget belt and his visionboard; sticking a pronged instrument into the ground and reading the display screen on that. Silver Wing sat on a tussock, restlessly braiding and unbraiding her silvery-brown hair; and watched him with an utterly teenage lack of curiosity. They were on top of Esk Hause, the Irish Sea a glittering ribbon glimpsed between the western fells.

'You don't *want* us to be together.'

Sage left a complex (and forbidden) realtime analysis to run and lay on his back, arms outstretched. Marlon had asked Silver to marry him. Pearl had told Marlon's dad about this, in a fit of vicious sibling rivalry; Marlon's dad, in a fit of very stupid candour, had told his son that he was an idiot if he thought wedding vows would cure Silver's taste for playing away. Take her as she is or let her go, kid—

'I just think you're both very, very young.'

'That *stinks*. You have no fucking right to say that.'

'True. Silver, when I was your age it never crossed my fucking mind to expect adult approval for anything. Why does it matter what I think?'

'Because I'm not sixteen yet,' muttered hairtwister, almost inaudible.

'Ah! Well tha's me off the hook because *Rob* is your guardian.'

By the customs of her extinguished people, the Counterculture, Silver's mother's old man had pretty much owned her, whoever her biological father was. Smelly Hugh being a proscribed fugitive, Rob had taken on the role. Silver's choice.

'You're such a *prag*.'

'Yeah, well, pragmatism catches up. It'll happen to you.' He sighed, thinking of the little outlaw in her smocked dresses, her butterfly wings, who used to run to him, eyes full of childish worship. What a drag it is getting old.

'Is that a *Geiger* counter?' she asked, finally distracted.

'It is.'

'Is this place *radioactive* then?'

'Be strange if it weren't, my dear, considerin' we are right next door to what used to be one of the premier nuclear power stations. Don't panic, it's only a mild hike above background levels. Not a sign of the buried power cables for all their windfarms, though. Tha's what puzzles me.'

'You can't *see* the windfarms,' explained Silver, rolling her eyes. 'The turbines are invisible so they don't spoil the landscape, you can only see the little substation huts, or, er, whatever they are. Fenced off, like firing ranges.'

'Mm. Any idea how they make the turbines invisible?'

'It's done by cloning. They capture images all around, and clone bits and arrange them the way they would be if the turbines weren't there, like your skeleton body mask.'

'Not bad. D'you think you could code that?'

'For fuck's sake, not *now*,' said the teenager, disgusted. 'Is lying on the ground like that part of what you're doing?'

'No, tha's just me, lying on the ground.'

He sat up and studied the board's results, wireless, on his mask's eyecam.

Hm.

'Is your sister still walking in those stupid shoes? If she is, she can forget doing the Reich Youth ridge route. She'll break an ankle.'

'I don't care if she breaks both her fucking legs.'

'But I do, because I am a prag, an' it would be a huge hassle.'

They had a mass barbecue (special permission for the fellside fire) and a wrestling tournament, which ended with the Cunning Cornish Crusher, veteran George Merrick, undefeated – to the chagrin of the Shield Ring's champions and the mighty Swedes. They played yat lowping and hikey-dikey. They came to bitter blows over the morality of hunting with dogs. They discussed post-genderism and minimalist music; they had a moon and torchlit duck race, with their one long-suffering plastic duck and a flock of paper ones made by Weng Jiang, Chinese Observer voted Mr Congeniality (he took it well). They ran out of meat and ale. The mule trains called on the Mountain Rescue when they lost a drum kit off a crag (Keswick Mountain Rescue not amused, Steadpersons annoyed because they'd been made to look stupid. It should have been *Wasdale* Rescue). Other call-outs included two broken ankles (both caused by yat lowping); a nasty sprain, a tib-fib, and someone's dog in a crevasse. The Reich Youth party vanished: out of all contact until Death and Famine spotted them taking a short cut over the highest mountain in England, many of them in very stupid shoes. And so they came to the last rendezvous, safely enough. Here there'd be another Landsturm fair; and then the most dedicated of the walkers would complete the circuit back to Coniston.

Chip was ensnared by the evil fan, on the home straight to Eskdale Moor. The Adjuvants didn't like 'fans'. They preferred to forget the audience existed, as any genuine Adjuvant aficionado understood. They'd been hiding from this woman since Coniston. He had to be nice, in the spirit of Landsturm fellowship, so he chattered away on auto, feeling noble: thinking about the platonic threesome, and how good it was. Verlaine didn't want a baby . . . Did he want them to go to Caer Siddi, become Zen monks, *never come out alive*? Was that the secret? Chip had resolved to talk to Chez about this, see if she would help him to change Ver's mind.

The fan asked him, with a revolting twinkle, was he bisexual now?

Chip said of course, the group marriage, everyone knows about that, but right now he was on a spiritual quest, thanks but no thanks.

'I didn't mean *that*,' she squealed. 'I meant, are you both getting it on with Chez, or is it just Verlaine? It's hot gossip, those two, but what does *Rob* think?'

And the scales were lifted from his eyes.

'Oooh. I've said something I shouldn't, haven't I? I'm really *sorry.*'

Like fuck you are . . . Pride would not let him run. He was forced to brush it off, insanely forced to laugh and *flirt* with the hell-bitch, searing agony in his soul.

The mule trains had been unloaded before the walkers arrived. Tents and stages were going up, Cumbrian entrepreneurs were assembling their stalls. Blisters, aches and sunstroke queued for first-aid; all was laughter and tears. There was a vote in favour of the World State, a vote in favour of Elder Sister as a special, incredible person (suck-ups); there was a work party framing a Landsturm statement, to be posted on Youth and Political Discussion message boards all over the Sphere. A move to create a masque, like one of Aoxomoxoa's masques in the glory days, only without immix of course, and perform it up here, unrecorded, pure, for ourselves alone—

Well away from party central Min and Ax slept nose to tail. Mr Pie dozed on three feet, and the living skull was singing to the baby: *when it's midnight in the meadow and the cats are in the heather* . . . Fiorinda left her boots in their care, and took a packed lunch up the hill for some solitude.

The day was hot and overcast, Burnmoor Tarn a sheet of iron, the Scafell massif blood-dark as Death's empty eyes. A house stood by the water, screened from the vulgar gaze by suburban-looking cypress hedges. That was the Lodge; where the Master of the Guild held court up here, on his regular circuit. A wheatear flicked its wings on a boulder; the rough caress of the heather tugged at her bare feet. She was thinking of little starfish fingers reaching to the mask, which Coz had loved at first sight, wise child. Just the way I loved him when I was fourteen, and had never seen the fallen-angel beauty of his naked face—

almost fell over Chip, hunched still as a rock in a stand of bracken.

'Sorry,' said Fiorinda, 'I'll go, er, on—'

'Why?'

Because you are crying. No, can't say that; so she sat down.

'I've been thinking about the Zen Self experiment,' he said, wiping his eyes. 'How it went. Taking the nasty drug. Getting hooked up like fuck, so you knew your life was in danger, getting shoved into the scanner. Coming back with a keyhole glimpse of heaven or hell, through some moment from your future or your past, and the narrative visions didn't mean a thing.'

'Mm.'

'The evidence was in the *data*, what the cognitive scanner said, how the neurons had fired, whether they'd shifted towards the impossible . . . I didn't get the message. All the data was saying VERLAINE IS FUCKING CHEZ. *You* all knew, I see that now. But I heard some weird tale about a spiritual quest and I believed it.'

'You're wrong.'

He turned on her, the Few's forever-young sweet black angel, Fiorinda's beardless counsellor, destroyed by shame and fury. 'Don't give me that! Don't fucking tell me you all thought we were a hot threesome. I don't want to insult you, Fio but I'd *never*, gaggh, do it with a girl. The idea *makes me feel sick.*'

Fiorinda clutched her head. 'Oh boy, oh boy, oh boy. Chip, I didn't mean that. The opposite of that. I meant, I'm sure they're not fucking.'

'Oh, *really*? So what do you call it? Making love? Sorry I was crude.'

'Cherry couldn't help telling Rob and the Babes how she feels. But I don't think they've even kissed. They're trying to work up the courage to tell you, first.'

A long silence.

She opened her sandwiches and offered him one.

'What is it?'

'Grasmere Dolly Herd corned beef and brown pickle.'

'Okay.'

They munched. The inevitable sheep arrived, one of the whiteface shaggy dark kind, and gave them the forlorn look . . . Word must have passed from hilf to hilf, these rockstar ramblers are well gullible, soft as muck, take them for all you can get.

'Go away,' said Chip. 'You're a vegetarian.'

'I bet she'd eat beef. I've seen sheep acting very suspiciously around a dead cow on Bodmin. And not from starvation; of their own free will, honestly.'

'That's *disgusting.*'

Daytime music, non-amplified, rose up to them. The gaudy crowd was like a transparent movie image floating on the moor: very distant, very familiar, very *thin*.

They shared the second sandwich.

'We're not really part of that down there, are we?' said Chip, absently (the new information sinking into him, robbing him of anger, heavy with finality; making him feel much worse).

'Not at all. Maybe we're their myth of origin.'

'If they live that long.'

'Yeah . . . I feel embarrassed to be walking among them, but I'm sort of proud we've been with this all the way, ever since Dissolution Summer.'

Let the circle be unbroken. Let the love stay strong, no matter who's fucking who. Chip nodded, and wiped his eyes again.

'You were winding me up about the dead cow, weren't you?'

'Was not.'

Droves of happy wanderers had trotted up Scafell. The Triumvirate and the Few decided they wanted to bag Scafell Pike; and set out in the milk-cart with the empties, early one clear blue morning. Steadmen and Hearthwomen were holding the morning service, raising a solemn, beautiful chorus to the sun; ordinary mortals slept in their tents. The driver wore a dairyman's white coat and a shapeless cricket hat. He told them ghost stories over his shoulder, as they jogged along the old corpse road by the tarn. Coffins gone astray, incorruptible bodies, revenants.

'Eh, it's quiet,' he remarked, with satisfaction, starting up the auxiliary engine for the gentle rise of Maiden Castle. 'I remember a time when there'd be hundreds, *hundreds* of dayglo folk wi' t'ekking poles up and down this road, any summer's day. They'd be thick as fleas on the big name peaks, like the London Underground. Not that I've been to London, thank God.'

The churns rattled, the carthorse trotted smartly, ears back, disliking the whine of the two-stroke; or maybe insulted at the suggestion she needed help.

'D'you ever miss them?' wondered Ax.

'Not likely. It was a sin, what we had to do for mere gelt, you know, money. We were going to hell like lambs until the Shield Ring woke us up. I pitied them, the hordes in their fancy gear, wandering around in packs.' A pause. They thought he might rephrase that last remark, more tactfully—

'It won't happen again.' He was very sure of himself.

They opted for the short route, half appalled that they were doing this voluntarily, up the beaten path of Lingmell Gill, two by two, three by three, one by one, almost in silence except for the baby, happily babbling in her new carrier.

'I hate the way it goes *on*, and *on*, and *on*,' whined Fiorinda, 'but there's nothing to it, this hill walking. I can do it, I just don't like it.'

'Like swimming laps,' agreed Dora. 'Boring, but good for you.'

'You got no eyes,' said Felice, her long legs swinging easily, peace in the curve of her big strong mouth. 'You got no *body*, you don't appreciate this.'

The senior Babes were walking hand-in-hand, but it wasn't a hostile gesture. Today they were okay with Chez, who said, 'You know, I bet we *could* have done it from the top of Scafell, the double whammy route by Foxes Tarn—'

Catcalls. Four days' gentle hike and she thinks she's ready for K2.

The narrow waters rushed secretly or flashed white beside them, dippers bobbing above ferny dark pools. Ravens croaking, buzzards wheeling, the gleam of rockroses, yellow gems in the royal purple. The moment you decide to take a drink, they said to each other (four days of experience) the next thing you see upstream is a rotting dead sheep. Chip and Verlaine, who had been here in the bad old days, advised the left fork over Hollow Stones, and led some off-piste casting around, searching for the excellent spot, a green promontory over Piers Gill, where they had picnicked (crystal clear, that holiday together; it had meant a good deal to them).

'All right,' conceded Fiorinda. 'It was worth it.'

To their west the blunt scarf of Wastwater under its screes, and further off a limb of the sea. Hives of Shield Ring large industry lay along that coast, southward, beyond the Duddon Estuary. It was a flaw in the mission statement, those Mountain Goat limos were built by hand by futuristic artisans, but they weren't assembled in cottages . . . Closer at hand, the great hollow of Wasdale Head was a rockery: shaped by the vanished pressures of mass tourism. Wherever you looked there were graded paths, paved paths, wheelchair routes, rustic stairways, paved and railed viewpoints, careful plantings to hide the servers that ran the smart boards; all falling into neglect now, but indelible—

'It's a world inside a spaceship,' said Cherry. 'I thought it would be *wild* up here, untouched wilderness like I've never seen—'

'Lions and tigers and bears?' Ver grinned at her. 'Oh my!'

'Fuck off. Everywhere you look, somebody's done something. It's so beautiful, but it's all *fixed*. I look up, I expect to see the landscape going overhead.'

'Maybe we *are* in a spaceship,' said Ax, on his back with his hat over his eyes. 'Travelling on a forgotten mission. It's just too big to see across.'

Chip looked over the drop, propped on his elbows (he was impervious to 'heights'). 'Deep they delved us,' he murmured. 'High they builded us, but they are gone. They are gone. They sought the havens long ago.'

'But on the land of Lorien no shadow lies,' added Verlaine, wryly.

'There is that.'

'If you two *quote Tolkien*,' F'lice threatened, grinning, 'I'm authorised to have Death throw you to the ducks, you guys know that. You've been warned *plenty*.'

'Shame on *you* for knowing when we're doing it.'

They were alone at last. It was time to talk about the real news.

The Shield Ring situation had always been a dangerous issue, one of the problems that had to be shut down. Elder Sister's Congress should have been the Triumvirate's chance to come up here and knock some sense into the free Cumbrians, tell them they had to *strangle* their appalling economic miracle . . . But then Sage had read the trace of Dilip Krishnachandran's virtual self, in the os and 1s of a trophy courtesan's last hours, and the agenda had changed dramatically.

Chip came down from his lookout. They formed a circle on the green fellside: automatically, unconsciously taking the same places as they'd taken round the old schoolroom tables in the Office at the Insanitude. Except that Allie was sticking close to Sage; which would never have happened in the old days. She was their fashionplate again, she'd collected some beautiful Shield Ring britches and a perfect crocus-yellow linen smock, but she looked shattered.

'The Chinese can see us sitting here,' said Ax; getting straight to it. 'They can focus on a square centimetre of Scafell Pike if they feel like it, why not? Maybe they can hear us. One of us could have been tagged with a transmitter, we know it happens. Everything we do is seen, everything we say is heard. That's the Chinese assumption, and the only safe way to behave is if we never forget it.'

'But they'll see and hear nothing untoward from now on,' said Fiorinda. 'I can't tell you how I'm doing it. Knowing how is *expensive*, I'll save that for when it matters. Just take it from me, their coverage is screwed and they won't blame us.'

'We believe you,' said Rob. The others nodded, very soberly.

Effective hexing works the way the occult tradition always said it would. It twists the world, insidiously: like a whisper of malicious gossip. Ruin falls on the victim like diabolical bad luck. When Rufus O'Niall was starting out, before the global audience boosted him to critical mass, very bad things happened to people who crossed him; but nothing you could pin on Rufus.

'They'll probably blame the opposition back in Xi'an,' said Ax.

'Does Elder Sister have opposition?' asked Verlaine, incredulous.

Ax shrugged. 'Give me a break.'

Of course she does. Everyone has opposition.

'This does not mean you can relax,' Fiorinda went on. 'I can protect you, but I can't up my intentionality too far, or they *will* notice something. Don't take risks.'

The Few nodded again. They had known this was going to happen, but they were in uncharted territory. This was the worst case scenario, or *nearly* the worst, and Fiorinda's icy, distant, crystal-spoken calm was not reassuring—

'We should have known the Chinese had to have mind/matter tech,' said Sage. 'It was staring us in the face, an' I was maybe the only person left alive in England with the tech to check their credentials. But I was too fucking scared. I wouldn't listen to Dian. Why not? Because I couldn't see questioning anything our new overlords chose to tell us—'

'Don't beat yourself up, big cat,' said Ax, ruefully. 'You got it from me.'

'Same here,' said Fiorinda. 'I was just waiting to be found out, or to find out that *they* had the same terrible secret; until the day we went to Dian's house . . . As far as we can tell, they don't know we're onto them. They don't know about the "apparition", they don't know that Lance Buckley recorded the evidence and gave it to us. They know we visited Rexborough, but we couldn't help that—'

'I think it's okay,' said Ax. 'If Wang's uneasy, let him sweat. We're nosing around something that's a scandal, no harm in him knowing that. Fuck sight better than where we thought we were—'

'Industrial espionage on the masters of the universe sounds bad,' Sage grinned, ruefully. 'Okay, it sounds insane. An' plus we took our time getting onto it. But you have to admit, the situation has a hint of promise—'

'We can *see* that,' protested Dora, passionately. 'We're with you all the way.'

The rest added their assent; Ax moved on. 'We knew what had to be going on up here, same as we know what is going on in deepest Wales; and we were afraid the Shield Ring had to be using forbidden tech. Sage can now confirm they're using b-loc to facilitate their power-sourcing. The only *mystery* is why the fuck it's all still running, with the Chinese Observers right on top of it. I find that scary, but I'm hoping for the best.'

'Ruskin will protect them,' said Sage. 'They sing to the sun, don't they?'

'Maybe they're sure the Chinese believe in the invisible wind turbines,' said Chez. 'So they're safer hiding in plain sight, showing no fear?'

Fiorinda nodded. 'Could be.'

Those invisible wind turbines . . . Cumbria had been sourcing most of its power from offshore wave and wind-rafts; until the A-team event had revealed (the world over) how much fossil fuel support those renewables needed. You can't maintain the rafts if you can't get near them. Undaunted, the sturdy Cumbrians had switched back to the mountain windfarms they'd just finished dismantling as an affront to the Land. They'd hauled the masts out of mothballs, done a Ruskinite miracle of getting them back on-stream, mounted them with mirror-routine boxes so they were to all intents invisible: and it was business as usual in this enclave of plenty. That was the story. It had passed, at a distance, so far as anyone had even wondered, in the confusion of the last two years. It didn't stand up very well at close quarters.

'The Chinese *must* know,' muttered Allie, unhappily.

'They know *something*,' Fiorinda agreed. 'That's obviously why the AMID force stayed out of here: it's like Anglia. They don't deal with entrenched opposition, not unless they have to. She's giving us a chance to convince the people of the error of their ways; before she moves in and mows them down.'

'My guess is that the Cumbrians started this years ago,' said Ax, thinking it through. 'Who was paying attention? The Irish haven't complained, and the Welsh weren't likely to. David Sale's government left the Shield Ring alone, glad to let them get on with it. Could be the Second Chamber knew the truth and they were getting paid off. We never did much here, same reason as David. The Volunteer Initiative put a couple of camps on the Furness Peninsula—'

Fiorinda nodded. 'Local opposition, but they backed down.'

'When the A-team event came along, they felt secure enough to make up that story. Then came the invasion, and suddenly a politically incorrect secret was—'

'Something that could cause the Chinese to slaughter every man, woman and child,' finished Sage, grimly. 'An' they froze, they went into collective denial?'

'Either that, or Chez's version. They don't seem very fucking worried.'

'So that's where we are.'

Fiorinda bent over Cosoleth. The baby kicked and chuckled in her lap, grabbing at copper curls; she disentangled the tiny fingers and looked up.

'We were going to give them a severe talking-to and shut them down. Now we're planning to ask them for a loan of their b-loc: we don't think they'll refuse. So then we can reach DK – probably, wherever he is – with some higher geekery. But b-loc ghosts have limited powers, and anyone who took the trip would risk getting caught, the same way he was caught. We need to make someone materialise *physically* at the remote site, a trick that's only been tried once, on me, by my boyfriend here, and it didn't really work. But we can fake it.'

She kissed the baby, and handed her to Ax. I will hold you again before the performance, but in my heart this is where we part, maybe forever, my little one. Mama got to go to work . . .

Sage opened his board.

The Few were blanched with dread, as if staring at a horrific road accident.

'If I have grown two heads,' said Fiorinda, tartly. 'Then we are in trouble.'

'Sorry,' they muttered, and tried to look cheerful, which was worse.

She felt the tiger and the wolf on either side of her, the mountain at her back. A huge mass of os and 1s, local point phase conservation, and they must be in order, at least to four dimensions, map on map, a staggering number of connections, like an impossible task in a fairytale. I have to do it right or I am like my father, a wrecking ball, ripping holes in *la grande illusion*, the desperately necessary barrier . . . and here goes, before I see some little tiny error, before I start to drown.

Fiorinda vanished. She reappeared, instantly (a paradox, perception is not instant), beside the boulder she had picked out, about five metres away.

'Gotcha,' said Sage, quietly. 'Looking good.'

'*What* do I look like? On the screen, what do you see?'

'My b-loc virtual Fiorinda sig, lining up, spot-on.'

'But I'm not. See, I can touch the ground, oooh, I can feel the grass, I'm solid. But if I *felt* like it, where I am now, I could walk right through this rock!'

'Don't get carried away, sweetheart,' His fingers stumbled a little on the toggles, but he kept it steady and light. 'Time to go home, c'mon.'

There, she's back where she was.

'It's very seductive,' said Fiorinda, with a glittering grin. She ducked her head, vanishing behind the curls. 'Talk among yourselves. No one touch me for a moment.'

'Eh?' said Cosoleth, struggling to get to her mother. 'Eh, eh!'

'No, no, no,' said Ax, cuddling her. 'Be a good kid, we're busy.'

Cosoleth was a terror with a sense of emergency; an excellent thing in a baby. She sighed and lay quiet against Ax's chest. 'We're going to find out what happened to Dilip,' he said, his chin on that fuzzy little head, 'and find out what the Chinese are really up to, the lying bastards. We'll keep the actual pernicious stuff to a minimum. But we'll do what it takes.'

'*Yes*,' said Fiorinda, from inside her huddle.

'There are people at the Congress who know what we're doing, they're with us for the next stage if we succeed; of course they won't know us if we fail.'

'Sage is my alibi,' Fiorinda sat up, white under her summer gold, eyes like grey stones. 'If we get caught, he did it by higher geekery. If we end up claiming responsibility, he can have the glory. I'll settle for keeping my head on my shoulders.'

The rock and roll brat smiled like hot starlight, she glowed with a weird mixture of horror and bliss, brought from beyond the veil.

The Few didn't manage to smile in return.

'Just for completism,' said Sage, 'now we've got you proper terrified, may as well: we think the Chinese are experts at forbidden tech, and the Cumbrians are right-wing lunatics. We think that's it, nothing worse, no A-team, no hell-monster waiting to pounce. Everything says not.'

'But we could be horribly wrong,' added Ax.

'Tha's unfortunately true.'

Then no one knew what to say, or do, until Dora reached out and gripped Chez's hand. Chez reached for Rob, Ax set the baby down. Coz lay on the grass while they all clasped hands. A hard, no-nonsense grip, musicians' hands are strong. Let the circle be unbroken, all the breaking up and moving on put aside . . . They let go, and sat in silence in the spaceship wilderness.

Chip thought of Rox, who'd been Kevin Verlaine's mentor and lover when the Adjuvants first started gigging. The non-ego way that the great Roxane Smith had bowed out, when s/he knew that three had become a crowd. What goes around comes around, yeah . . . No, karma's not like that. Karma is, every time you do something wrong you will be offered a chance to right the balance again, so that when you die your heart weighs less than the feather. Is that mixing my mysticisms? But they're all the same; love God and love thy neighbour. *Keep me sweet*, he thought, if this is my last day on earth, or if I live to be a hundred. Let me do this the way Rox did it.

And okay, I lied. I was angry . . . It's probably true I'd never do it with a girl, but the idea does not make me sick, an' it would have been nice to be *considered*, Cherry-baby. Feeling their eyes on him he looked up, and mugged a silly smile.

'Time for the summit dash?' suggested Fiorinda.

'Not me,' said Rob, squinting at the upward path. 'I'm staying here, it looks horrific. You fuckers—' (meaning Chip and Ver) 'I bet the other way is the easy way.'

'You bet wrong.'

Chip and Verlaine wanted to preserve their first ascent, the Power-babes decided to stay with their boyfriend. They were not daunted, they'd just had enough exercise; fine with the picnic spot. 'We only pretended we wanted to bag the peak,' said Dora. 'We are not so crass.' Allie said she honestly didn't think she could make it. It was a little strange, undercurrents, but the Few wouldn't be moved. From this high place (such an English molehill of a high place), the leaders must go on alone.

Everyone watched as they headed off, unashamedly fascinated by Sage's lean, athletic grace, and the maybe-President of Europe with a baby on his back. Their living goddess, in spite of her girly whining, bounced from stone to stone as if on springs.

'That girl's waist,' remarked Dora, reflectively, 'was twenty-four inches again, *three days* after she had a baby by Caesarean section.'

Nods, and groans of agreement, from her sister Babes and Allie.

'Who told you?' asked Rob, intrigued. 'Did Ax tell you?'

'Nobody told us,' said Allie. 'Ax wasn't there, remember? We measured her.'

Women, thought Rob. Why'd you do that, if it was going to annoy you?

'They treat that baby like an exotic pet,' complained Felice. But she knew why Coz came everywhere. No safer place for her to be, and pray Ferdelice and Mamba are okay back on Eskdale Moor, protected by the Heads, the crews, surrounded by our people. Anxiety clutched her stomach, she thought of Anne-Marie on Reading Site, in that welter of blood, dying with her babies—

Put it out of your mind. Smile, it's a beautiful day.

Chip and Ver decided to lay out the luncheon, which should be good, it had weighed a ton, stubbornly chanting the proper incantation: 'coldtonguecoldhamcoldbeefpickledgherkinssaladfrenchrollscresssand-widgespottedmeatgingerbeerlemonadesodawater—' in spite of heckles that this was crypto-Tolkien by stealth. There genuinely was a glistening roast chicken, succulent potted beef, and boiled eggs, a herby salad, tomatoes, butter in a crock, Beauty of Bath apples; a big loaf of fresh white bread.

'Shit,' said Rob, 'the ginger beer isn't in stone bottles. Send it back.'

'Did people really have *stone bottles*?' wondered Chez. 'In modern times?'

'Depends what you call modern, our kid,' said Chip.

'Are we supposed to look at all that until the mountaineers get back?'

'Nah, they'll be happy with the scraps. They aren't big eaters.'

The summit was very suburban, from the cemented pillar that marked 978 metres, to the recycle bins and smart boards (no longer active) in the half-moon wind-shelters; which were artfully arranged so that large parties of intrepid loners could stare at the views, and not at each other. The breeze was strong and suddenly chill; mackerel cloud spun away over the high tops. They mugged at each other, crestfallen: why are we surprised? England is a garden, of course it's like this. One day these will be the sublime, ancient wind-shelters of the elder race. If they live that long.

'I think we're spooking them,' said Ax.

'You mean the Few? I know, I can't help it,' said Fiorinda.

'Nor can I. The only way I can do this is—'

'Weirdly calm, a little dissociated. We have to watch that.'

My baby, my baby. He didn't say please don't leave me, to this one you can't say that. Her leaving would be from the inside, a shell would remain, an agonised ghost. He took her face between his hands and kissed her, strands of copper against his mouth, a jolt of warmth and sweetness, smooth over bitter—

'Eh, eh, *eeeh*!' pleaded Coz, tired of being ignored.

Sage lifted her from Ax's shoulders, out of the new baby-carrier, and wrapped her inside his jacket. 'Were you cold little girl? Better now?' But

Coz did not want to be wrapped up. She reared, pushing herself up and away, as if she'd like to take flight. Eyes like saucers she gazed around, looked up at him and jerked her head, a fervent affirmative, and did it again. *Yes,* said Cosoleth, with every fibre of her being. *Yes!*

Fiorinda and Ax came out of their private moment to admire this earnest display. 'I think she likes the great outdoors.'

'Look at that. Seventeen weeks and she's communicating abstract ideas.'

'No offence, Sage, but *me likes mountain* is not an abstract idea.'

'She's a person, not a textbook,' said Fiorinda, uneasy at the sugges-tion her child was a prodigy. She's *not* huge, she's *not* superbright, she's totally normal.

'It's practically abstract. What's she getting out of it, huh?'

They retired to a wind-shelter, and let Coz 'stand up' with her baby feet on the rock, to her passionate joy. There you are, baby, snagged the highest peak in England, next stop Nanga Parbat. Fiorinda dealt out a ration of honey-oaties and water from her tapestry bag, and found the saltbox under her hand . . . I've always protected them, it's nothing new. I've shifted the os and 1s before, and it worked out. She remembered her grandmother, the hateful old witch, saying *you are the salt of the earth.* Salt-laden soil in the devastated lands, where nothing grows. But without salt there's no flavour in the world. I am health and destruction, hopelessly entangled, oh, that breeze is chill, it's making me shiver.

'I want to leave something here.'

'Good idea,' said Sage. 'I doubt if we'll be back.'

Ax chose a small rock that seemed to have character. Fiorinda set a pinch of salt in a niche of the summit cairn and they laid Ax's rock on top. White crystals flew to the four winds, but something stayed. They walked down to Lingmell Col, and joined the picnic. At Wasdale Head hotel – where the sybarites in residence were delighted to see them – they hired a smart four-wheeler, and were back on Eskdale Moor long before dark.

This was the night of the last concert. Aoxomoxoa and the Heads played straight, wholesome rock and roll. Death on Horseback, morphed into the blue-eyed rock god, was channelling Janis for some reason: falling to his knees and belting out the torchsongs, *take it, take another little piece of my heart now baby* . . . Fiorinda, in her first stage appearance since the baby was born, had decided to turn into a metal mama, guesting with the ubiquitous Gintrap in baggy shorts and a punk tee; and flirting blatantly with a dazzled Boje Strom. No 'Winter Song', no 'Dark Water, Small Box, Flow,' no 'Hard' . . . No Triumvirate set, and Ax didn't play at all.

It was all rather puzzling, but that's legends for you. The crowd went crazy anyway, determined not to be disappointed.

The passing trade (dwellers in the Western Fells, from villages and farms and little towns on the coastal plain) strode casually off into the dark. Steadmen and Hearthwomen chanted the night hymns and retired to their pavilions; the eleven hundred bedded down, singing Leonard Cohen songs and having banner-fights. In the bar tent someone explained the words of 'Sweet, Dirty' rather drunk and loud; presumably trying to pull. 'Yeah, but, yeah, it's like *saying*, see, that sexual love an' pleasure keeps us sane or we'd go crazy. *The sweet and dirty hidden power to carry on.* To carry on, you get it? It's a play on words. Mindless reproduction, hijacked to make the fucking horror of being human bearable—'

Ah, the secrets of the Empyrean, to what base uses are you put.

At Mr Preston's table the mood was depressed, the midnight conversation trivial and low-spirited. 'Gay man in a girl's body my arse,' growled George. 'She fancies herself as a rockstar's wife, that one. I know the type.'

Peter, owlish, shook his head sadly. 'Poor Minty. Bill always told her he was against marriage on principle. It's wrong to tell lies.'

Ax had heard of this awful crime, 'wanting to be a rockstar wife', in a version where the scheming broad was Mary Williams, and the accusation in very poor taste. He'd never known before George or Peter have a good word for Bill's previous steady girl, the appalling Minty LaTour . . . He rubbed Min's throat, deciding silence was golden.

'Marlon with that hippy child,' remarked Alain, restlessly: leaning to pass the spliff to Mathilde. 'What is her name? Silver? I think of her as Aoxomoxoa's little niece, mascot, you are all like blood-relatives, it seems distasteful—'

Naomi, who had ditched the Eurotrash-dolly look for gunslinger-black and a sombrero, cast a sour glance around the many-coloured hangings, the soft lights.

'What kind of a filthy rebel dive is this? I detest the whole concept of this Shield Ring, it's an excrescence of English organic, sandalled gentility.'

Tam's taste in décor ran to first series *Star Trek* and David Lynch's *Dune*. She's a French absurdist intellectual. How can we ever find a middle way?

'This is reality,' sighed Märtha-Louise, the Nordic folklorist and Crown Princess. 'The *one world state* we dreamed of in the chatrooms of the Crisis was fantasy: God has called our bluff. This is our dream come true, translated into real politics. This is how the World State gets born, this is how it feels.'

The faded warmth of the July night recalled summer's end, the English Counterculture annihilated, Roumania overrun. The internationals would be leaving in the morning, it was the last time these friends would meet. They couldn't talk about the Triumvirate's boss fight because the air has ears, and there was nothing else to discuss. The future of Europe, we've done that, that's so over. They wanted to ask Ax where Fiorinda had got to, and was everything okay? Better not. What was it all for, all our struggle? For what, for what? A Chinese world, at the best.

Muß es sein? Es muß sein.

Around three a.m. Fiorinda availed herself of the dainty, spotless ladies' *sanitaires*. Luxe, luxe, the soap, the towels . . . really, it's like Saudi before the end of oil. The hospitality of a simple nation of fucking millionaires. She picked her way by the rustling starlight from banner to banner, through the murmurs of sleepy conversation and random bursts of noisy laughter. Firefly glints in the outer darkness where the guards were posted. Useless idea having guards, against what, wolves? Mad sheep? But eleven hundred campers need some kind of militia, or buggering fourteen-year-old nutcases would torch the marquees . . . Left at the Green Griffin, on past the Duck (the mutilated, sacred Duck). Where's our Psycho Chihuahua got to? Ah, there it is, and here they are. Min's eyes glowed and vanished as the cat checked her out.

Ax lay on his side, one arm over the soft basket where Coz was just a little nose and her woolly hat. She knelt beside them, milk stinging her breasts as she breathed the baby's scent. Don't bother, tits. I'm *not* going to wake the baby for an alcoholic snack. Oh my Ax, my darling Ax—

'That you, Fee?'

Sage was sitting there awake, a black outline, watching her. She went around and sat by him, shucking off her bag. 'Yeah. This is me.'

'Where've you been?'

'Socialising. Is that a crime?' She set her water bottle by the bedroll, checked her saltbox with a touch, and started taking off her boots. 'Seeking a change from Bronze Age Lutherans, idiot kids and kiss-your-hand patriarchal eco-warriors, I went down to the blacktop where the tourbuses are parked. I had to wait for an escort party to walk back, that's why I'm late. There are ghosts on the corpse road, you know.'

The atmosphere was forbidding, the black outline didn't stir.

'Don't do it, Fee.'

'Do what?'

'Boje . . . Haven't we got enough trouble?'

'I wasn't *planning* to do him,' said Fiorinda, wounded. 'You always think the worst of me.' She laid her head on her arms, on her drawn-up knees. 'All right, I'm drunk, I stayed out late. So shoot me. I used to be a rockstar, you know.'

'Me too.'

'I hate watching my tongue, charming and anodyne, carefully answering every question with the right lie from the lie list, the whole fucking time.'

'C'mon, Fiorinda. When you were fourteen you had an iron-clad agenda, based on your brilliant career. What's the difference, except this is arguably a bigger deal?' He sighed. 'I was un-fucking-touchable when I was a rockstar. Doing things that had never been done before. Don't remember I was any happier for it—'

Fiorinda dug in her bag for her smokes tin, took out a spliff and lit it. They sat on the edge of the groundsheet, Aoxomoxoa and his stupid brat; their guitar-man sleeping beside them, the bodies of the campers stretching off on every side. It could have been any shipwrecked night of their long disaster movie. But the familiarity was an illusion, this was someone else's movie now . . . The Triumvirate had come back from California vowing that somehow they would beat the Second Chamber, and then they would quit. No use rifling through the litter of broken schemes, they must have always known it was a life sentence.

It would be easier if they didn't have the hateful feeling that Elder Sister was competition. The man of destiny announces his latest mighty ally has sexual intent; which can't be refused. Then not another word on the subject. What are we supposed to make of that, Ax?

Ax stirred, and turned over. 'Fio, ah, safe back, thank God.'

He sat up, from sleep into their silence. 'Fuck's sake,' he whispered. 'Don't ever leave me. *Please* don't leave me.' Fiorinda handed him the spliff. They smoked without a word, the tiger and the wolf leaning together, Ax with his arm around Fiorinda's shoulders, holding her close.

no regrets. Just thinking about that midnight train to Georgia.

III

The Glory Of The Garden

The dinner guests took their champagne glasses down to the tarn. They'd be eating on the terrace. Happily the evening was fine, though the day, which had been spent breaking up the Landsturm, had been overcast. 'The Lodge was a keeper's cottage,' said Master Ridley, the chestnut centaur. 'The rooms are adequate, but rather dark, it's not the best place to be indoors in summer.'

'Is it true that it's haunted?'

'I've never seen anything unexpected, but there's an atmosphere.'

It was an intimate gathering. The founders of the Shield Ring were taking their first opportunity to entertain the Triumvirate; Ax's administrator and the Welshman, Iwan Turner, the only other guests. Walter strolled with Mr Preston, and told him about Julius Hecht, the third of the Shield Ring Brothers: the Ruskinite philosopher who had inspired them; who had left his university post in Denmark when they invited him to join their enterprise. 'He still walks the fells but he's ninety this year; we husband his strength. Thou'lt hear him talk over dinner, he's a great preacher, and a brilliant conversationalist—'

Ms Marlowe and Fiorinda walked ahead along the shore, arm-in-arm: jet-black ringlets mingling with the red curls, Ms Marlowe's burgundy gauze tunic brushing Fiorinda's green silk skirts . . . *both beautiful, one a gazelle*, thought Walter. And the other's a lioness. They were perfect foils for each other, Ms Marlowe's fragile olive pallor; her friend's golden vigour. The two men smiled, sharing frank appreciation of two lovely women, a fine wine. The music of a folk ensemble floated through the cypress hedge. The big tents, the mule trains and internationals were gone; but the campers were still out there.

O'er the mountains when the day is done
And the clouds are gathering round the sun—
While they weeping whisper one by one
Marianina come again, we have tried to dance in vain
Come and turn us into rain—

'We think of replacing the Lodge, building another Brantwood here, a centre of excellence. But we'll see how that goes.' The centaur paused, with a thoughtful look. 'We like tha way of doing business, Mr Preston. Tha don't *push*, do tha?'

'No,' said Ax. 'I don't push. But it's time we started talking.'

'Aye. It's time.'

The rest of the party looked out from the end of the wooden jetty, where a rowing boat was moored. Fish rose, kissing the peach-bloom reflection of sunset into spinning ripples. 'Brown trout and perch,' said Simon Hartsfern. 'Dost tha fish, Mr Pender?'

'Nah. I just like watching them.'

'I never knew you were a vegetarian, Sage!' cried the Welshman.

'Hahaha. I like eating them, too. Long as they've been fairly caught.'

'There speaks a hunter,' said Simon, pleased. 'And a countryman.'

'Perch isn't tasty eating,' said Iwan, peering down. 'I'd have to be hungry.'

'Blue and red,' said Fiorinda. 'I don't remember how it started.'

Allie had taken care to find out what the dress code was: Ax and Sage had brought formal kit with them. It struck them both as odd, somehow cheating, that the robed Steadmen reverted to old-fashioned black-and-white for dinner parties—

'Ax's best suit was red,' said Allie, 'when we were the Countercultural Think Tank, and we barely knew how to dress. I think he's superstitious about it.'

'Anne-Marie said those were their colours, aural opposites; and it's true. If Ax wears blue and Sage wears red, it's creepy.'

'You know, I can see that. Ax would look *shy*, in blue.'

'Sage looks like a psychopath in red.'

They'd reached the jetty, but the men were coming back: gingery Iwan flushed and acting confident; Julius Hecht a dried-up, tight-skinned little figure with a bald dome of a head, absurdly dwarfed by Sage and the

Master. Ah, it's time. Allie and Fiorinda glanced at each other, and touched hands. They had stage-fright.

Louisa Hartsfern, Simon's wife, first lady of the Guild, was a beautiful, nervous woman in her forties, with a crown of dark braids. 'I wish I could have invited you to Brantwood,' she said, as she greeted her guests. 'There's a limit to what I will pack onto a mule train. Usually we camp out, when we're here on the summer circuit.'

The terrace looked over an orchard plot, where flowers tangled artlessly in the long grass under the trees. Fiorinda praised the garden design, *ars gratia artis*; and admired the hand-painted damask table linen, the rooted floral arrangements, the bounty of artisan *hors d'oeuvres*. Louisa accepted the compliments distractedly, as if she too was tired of that game. Julius intoned a Bronze Age Lutheran grace; while they stood behind their chairs, and the servants hovered discreetly, with bowed heads. The practical philosopher seemed unaware of the subtext of this meal. He lingered over his sonorous psalm, and smiled expansively around the table.

'How pleasant this is! We dine together, sharing bread and salt!'

'Someday you *must* make the whole great circle,' said Margaret Smallwood, Louisa's sister, the prophetess who had interviewed Fiorinda: fixing Ax with her large, slightly crazy, brown eyes. 'It's our sacred pilgrimage, vital as the *Hajj*.'

'Another time.'

Ax watched the black-and-white clad servants, wondering if they were bonded. The Shield Ring allowed a form of bond-service, and they didn't consider themselves slave-owners. Right-wing Utopians, why are you so predictable?

Another wine was poured. Allie immediately picked up her glass and downed half of it. Walter Ridley cleared his throat. 'We've been impressed by the way tha survived the walking and rough riding, Ms Marlowe, a delicate fashionable lady like thyself. Tha's a tidy brave lass, as we say.'

'We haven't been on another planet,' said Allie, shortly. 'We've had hard times, we've lived on the road a great deal.'

'How *difficult* city life must have been,' murmured Louisa, and glanced again at the Master, at the other end of the table; as if waiting for a cue.

Iwan devoured smoked oysters, uneasily.

Julius explained Cumbrian husbandry to Sage. 'This is a land made by human hands, no less than the *Pays Bas*. You have seen the ancient circles on Brat's Moss? Evidence abounds of a settled population, three and four thousand years ago. The hill land improves dramatically with lime and dung, of course plenty of dung, but it must be well ploughed in, and the bracken rooted out. Gradually, the soil can be brought to a condition where arable crops can be added with profit to a long rotation—'

The philosopher paused, a twinkle in his ancient eyes. 'The fertility of the Land, as we know, is of interest to the Triumvirate. I was *extremely* pleased to hear of the ceremony at Rainbow Bridge. Pure intent makes all things pure!'

The blue-eyed rock god smiled, without amusement. 'You think, professor? I c'n call to mind a few exceptions.'

'We are *not Pagans*,' said Margaret Smallwood, in a low voice.

'Of course not, my dear Margaret, but—'

The servants cleared the *hors d'oeuvres* course and laid warm soup plates: a tureen approached, borne with stately deliberation. Enough is enough, thought Sage, contemplating the hell of another five or six courses. He exchanged a glance with Ax and Fiorinda, yep, agreed. Fuck the Lakeland gourmet experience.

Let's put them out of their misery.

'Carn' say I noticed the stone circles partic'larly. We have Neolithic debris to burn where I come from. It's yer famous invisible windfarms I most admired.'

He leaned back in his chair, and became Death (he had the body mask on his eyesocket button). Margaret froze. Louisa lifted a hand, and shook her head at the tureen-bearer. The servants, all of them, quietly retired into the house.

'Where *did* you get that mirror software? If you wrote it, you're going to be stinking rich, not that that would be a change. You have to have forests of turbines up there, an' this mask works *okay*, but I avoid open horizons, I've never tried running it indefinitely. An' I'm oversized, but I'm not twenty feet tall—'

Louisa and Margaret stared, as if measuring the success of the disembodied bones: slivers of tablecloth and crystal lacing Death's tib and fib; gently moving apple leaves, Walter's black broadcloth, between his ribs. Walter and Simon were stone-faced, unmoved: the beards helped.

'It's not what you're *hiding*,' continued the living skull, affably, 'because frankly, you are not hiding anything. It's fucking obvious, excuse me, ladies, once anyone gets close to you, that you've ignited the old power station.'

Julius blinked several times, and passed a hand over the liver-spotted gloss of his skull. The creamy knife-pleats of Louisa's bodice rose and fell, Iwan Turner stared at his empty soup plate. Everything we do is seen, everything we say is heard.

'Nah, as usual, classically: it's not the robbery, it's the cover-up. I've been collecting some very exotic signals, up on your high tops. It wasn't hard. Anyone equipped to sniff out forbidden tech could do the same.'

The Shield Ring principals weren't giving an inch. They seemed filled with hidden excitement: thrilled to be facing execution by slow torture for themselves, bloody massacres for their people—

'We are *not* Counterculturals,' declared Margaret, head high, without a tremor. 'We have no truck with any pernicious delusion. What do we have to fear?'

Simon gave her a look of brotherly resignation: incongruous, very human.

'Tha's not turned us in,' he said. 'Tha's at risk thysen, talking like that.'

'*Can* we talk here?' asked Ax, casually; addressing his lady.

'Nothing's certain, but I think so. Go ahead.'

Everyone looked to Fiorinda, who sat with her chin on her hands, the saltbox on the tablecloth between her elbows. The Shield Ring principals were puzzled, they hadn't seen where that wooden apple had come from. Fiorinda nodded to Sage, and that's one risky moment passed. Outside chance, but they could have had effective magic; they don't. She tucked the saltbox away in her green silk clutch-purse.

'We are not at risk,' she said to Simon. 'We are privileged negotiators. Elder Sister wants us to achieve her purpose, which is the peaceful liberation of Cumbria, she trusts us to choose the means. This house is suspiciously well-armoured, but as far as we can tell the Chinese have not tried to penetrate your defences. Not yet. They don't want to "know". If they "knew", they would have to act. We can talk.'

'You must have been shitting yourselves,' said Ax bluntly, 'these last ten days. Are you going to explain to us *why* you didn't shut your operation down?'

'It's not like turning off a tap,' muttered Walter.

'We've been shitting ourselves since last September, Mr Preston,' said Simon Hartsfern, still with a light in his eyes, 'while waiting for our leaders to find a way to reach us. Tha'd better come indoors.'

They went into the house, and to a dank upstairs room, where a hidden closet held contraband. They passed from there to a different world.

They were in the upstairs room. It smelled of damp and mice, it conjured up Tyller Pystri, saddened by long neglect. They were standing in a smooth-walled corridor, painted in faded red, with a great curve of window in front of them, and out there, under a quiet evening sky, across a field of rough grass, they saw the two square kilometres of Sellafield Nuclear Power Station, humming with peaceful life.

It was a while since they'd done b-loc. Sage was at ease at once, Ax and Fiorinda had to struggle, for a moment, to reach the state where you're no longer bewildered at being in two places at once: commit to the remote site, commit to the home site, no different from talking on the phone really; consciousness is a point, not a line . . . Simon's material self tapped a control pad in the dank mousey closet. Lights came on, illuminating the gothic lettering, etched into the glass of the observation bay.

𝕿𝕳𝕰 𝕺𝕹𝕷𝖄 𝖂𝕰𝕬𝕷𝕳 𝕴𝕾 𝕷𝕴𝕱𝕰

The only wealth is life. 'Oh, *fuck*,' breathed Ax. He put up his hands, to push the wings of dark hair from his temples. 'My God.'

His head had been full of how to get what he needed from these people, and how to manage the Landsturm *exactly* the way it must go, because at the end of this tangled coil there's someone who must not lose face. He'd never had time to visualise what the Shield Ring's outrageous operation would look like. He was staggered, blown away by the scale of it—

'Nuclear power is very much a live issue in Wales,' said Iwan.

'Yeah,' breathed Ax. 'We know.'

'We call the secret projects "Invisible Wind Turbines".'

'Oh,' said Sage, equally riveted by the view. 'I get it. Okay.'

'The Chinese don't see this,' explained Margaret Smallwood, reassuringly. 'They *can't* see it, it's neurophysically impossible. We have a very large array virtual screen, forming a hemispherical false horizon, on which we project a 4D direct cortical stimulus image of the plant – as it was before we took it out of hibernation. We call it the *sleeve*. It's immix technology, it works on the entire perception of human receptors, as well as deceiving their instruments.'

'The sleeve?'

'Yes, Mr Preston.' The prophetess smiled on Ax, with her shining eyes. *They need, these blossoms of the spring, assailed by winds. An all-encompassing sleeve to close off the skies.*

Fiorinda and the Zen Self Champion exchanged a glance of bug-eyed horror.

'We've had expert, covert assistance from the Wylfa group,' said Walter, 'all along. This is the modern face of nuclear power, Mr Preston. The emissions are down to a minimum that would surprise thee, we have realtime tracking of all materials, and everything's remote. The people who work inside, work by b-loc. We have a network of live paths set up; of which this is the start of one. We've no need for muscle power in any hazardous area. Should there be concern over the *slightly* raised levels of radioactivity in the region, we've prepared an alibi. There was a moderate semi-permanent storage leak. It happened a while ago, we've dealt with it . . . Our answer to the materials problem, decommissioning, and storage is twofold. We're entirely a reprocessing plant, we shan't be requiring any raw uranium, and we don't plan to decommission; not until we have a genuine, energy-audited solution. Which we believe, in time, neurophysics theory and mind/matter tech shall provide.'

'To our mind it was our business,' declared the Master, unrepentant, 'our lifestyle choice, and when we had to lie about it we did. Tha don't ask permission to bail, when the boat's filling up with water.'

Ax flashed, wildly, on the political disaster this would have been. One of England's *de facto* devolved regions has been producing nuclear electricity, and more than likely *selling* it, labelled as windpower. Well, I'm dead. I'm *crucified*. Oh Crisis Europe, my fucked up, interim and pro-tem lost world, where are you now?

'Mr Hartsfern,' he said, eyes fixed on the science fiction, 'Mr Ridley . . . I'm a nuclear sceptic, as you may remember. We don't need to replace fossil fuels with plutonium. We need to *consume less energy*, can't you get it through your heads? But that's beside the point. If Elder Sister has to know about this, believe me, you're not going to be making a statement at the public inquiry.'

'If she gets to know about your "sleeve" technology, she'll slaughter us all,' added Sage. 'Without compunction. Do you realise how *military* that sounds?'

There was a strange pause. Walter and Simon looked almost bewildered, as if they wondered whether they had been speaking English. Julius Hecht gazed through the curve of strengthened glass, lost in his own thoughts.

'This *is* a military operation, Mr Preston,' said Walter Ridley. 'We're not ready to go, but we soon will be. We aren't building submarine missiles, but we found Vickers had left plans and *matériel* behind when they closed down at Barrow. We've been able to cannibalise those reserves for our battlefield, guerrilla-oriented purposes. We found some vital armament workers among your drop-outs, Ms Slater.'

Irresistibly, and maybe because they did not use the archaic *thees* and *thas*, the women had seemed like pawns in this game, dressing up to please their menfolk, living in the real world in their heads.

It was not so. Louisa, the stately matron with her crown of neo-Victorian braids, had the same fire in her eyes. She clasped her hands, trembling with proud emotion. 'We understand your tactics. The first objective is to get the 2nd AMID army off our soil, and you are *magnificently* close to achieving that. Once that goal is achieved, *we can fight back.* That's why we didn't shut down: no time must be lost, and we knew they could not penetrate the sleeve. They have seemed invincible, but they are not. In the name of God, your God and mine, Mr Preston, we can make a stand. Allies will gather. We can defeat her!'

Ax realised, astonished, that he was tearing up. The dank closet with its stained wallpaper, the great fission plant out there, had taken on a piercing, doubled, significance. The skin around his left eye stung as if the inkwork was fresh, the shame and pain of the invasion was raw in him. The room was England, and Louisa looked like England, locked up as a madwoman in this dirty place. He had no choice, he had to desert her, let her die alone. It's the grief I must not feel. It's the b-loc, it's emotional stuff when you're not accustomed—

'Well, you'll have to shut down now,' he said, cutting it short. 'We're about to do something that will blow your cover wide open; and there are other considerations. We'll explain, but can we get out of b-loc? I think we've seen enough.'

'Could we make that soon?' whispered Allie. Commercial b-loc masks the virtual self with an avatar hologram. Without that protection, Allie in the Sellafield corridor was going to revert to her unconscious form, the naked goblin of the somato-sensory cortex; the others would see her swelling and shrinking, huge lips and tongue and genitals, a humiliation she couldn't stand.

'*Creation itself will be set free,*' murmured Julius, gazing at the glory of his garden, his old brain slow to catch up with immediate events. '*From its bondage to decay, and obtain the glorious liberty of the children of God . . . For in this hope we are saved.*' He looked around, blinking. 'Aren't we going inside?'

'Not right now,' said Sage, compassionately. 'Maybe another time.'

They left the contraband in its hiding place. When the closet was closed the wall was blank, not a hairline; and that was probably another direct cortical illusion. Another haunted house, riddled with utter insanity . . . Simon took up the lamp, and led the way downstairs. An anxious servant was waiting in the hall. Ax glimpsed the rest of them, peering through a half-open door. He saw that bonded or not they were in the loop, ready for a last stand beside their leaders; so shame on you, Ax Preston.

'All's well,' said Louisa. 'No, I think we won't eat, Thomas, it's rather late. Could you bring us coffee, the liqueur trolley, and the second dessert?'

'Right away, Mrs Hartsfern.'

Walter handed the liqueurs, specially attentive to Ms Marlowe, his gazelle; who did not notice him. The visitors broke the bad news. The Shield Ring conspirators still had their death or glory eyes when the explanations started, but they became impressed. Especially when Sage reached the part about the Chinese *hacking b-loc,* an idea to strike terror here . . . They agreed to comply. They would provide the tech the Triumvirate needed, and put the plant back into hibernation. They gave an estimate of how long it would take to do this safely.

'Will tha be staying to see that we do it?' asked Walter, on his dignity.

'No,' said Fiorinda, with a bleak look. 'You're on your own.'

They nodded, sobered. They understood.

Ax went to debrief the Chinese Observers, some of whom who were still on Eskdale Moor, occupying a fine Shield Ring pavilion. He told them the dinner party had gone well. Everything was smooth, great progress had been made. The Shield Ring leaders were reconciled to the changes they'd have to accept, in fact the masses had already been pressing them to embrace the new order . . . He was consumed with guilty knowledge, bristling with obvious lies, but the Chinese were fine about it. They weren't heavyweights, they were running a PR exercise. They were expected to deliver success, and they were very happy with Ax. They brought out their hard liquor stash and he had to drink a few toasts: to the Landsturm, to the future of Europe, to Elder Sister, to Ax himself and his partners, to the Duck; etc.

The hardcore walkers had left, the last campers were enjoying goodbye parties, silly drunken games; a final round of banner fights. Sage went to pass the word to the Few; Fiorinda and Allie waited for Ax in a private partition of the bar tent. It was cool and bright. A great bowl of living waterlilies stood on a bentwood and wicker table, coaxed to stay open at night by imitation sunlight; and manipulation of their internal clocks. The Shield Ring has the power to indulge the most beautiful whims—

'It was when no one outside our little band seemed *human*,' said Allie, eyes down, tracing patterns in the woven willow. 'After what we'd been through, because of the situation we were in. D'you remember that feeling? The group marriage, that was a joke, but it wasn't a joke? I think it was the same for him, but we never talked about "why". I'd seen one boyfriend get his head blown off, now I was with someone under a death sentence, but it didn't seem like that. We were friends; not lovers. Although he was a very good lover, slick and experienced, but warm too. Really nice.'

Fiorinda nodded, and then caught herself, shamefaced.

' 'S'okay. You, Ax . . . He'd have loved to have sex with everyone, and all at once, that was DK. He had a collecting streak. When we split up, I was knocked out. When he was killed I was devastated, and numb. Now I don't know what I feel.'

Ax and Sage came into the partition quietly. The two women looked up, their formal dresses a glowing composition: summer green and autumn wine.

'All's well,' said Ax, quickly. 'Weng Jiang had to captain a midnight volley ball team, or I'd still be necking Pearl River bai jiu.'

Allie stared at him, pale as Famine indeed. 'I'm blank,' she whispered. 'But my body knows. I can't eat, I can't sleep, until I find out what happened to him. Shit, am I being a fucking nuisance? You three don't need this.'

'Yes we do,' said Sage. 'It's your show, Allie.'

The purity of the lilies was unearthly, a message from a world that could not exist: where exquisite plenty could be had without cost, love without loss.

SHŪ

I

Conflict Gems

A first-floor room in a derelict building, somewhere in South London. The ground floor had been an electrical shop, a commonplace chain, long vanished; it was boarded up. The first floor had been occupied fairly recently. There was a grubby patterned rug on the floor in the front room, a grill-pan that had been used as a brazier, a sack of kindling; a down-at-heel three-piece suite. Tattered bedspread curtains were tacked over the windows. The venue had been chosen almost at random, it had no connection with the Reich. Bill and George had picked it out; for anonymity, and certain digital landscape advantages. If you peered from behind the left-hand bedspread you could see a scrap of Crystal Palace Park between the houses.

Vanguard, Victorious, Vigilant and Vengeance . . . My arse in butter, who started that, I would like to know, are you trying to get us busted?

V_1, V_2, V_3, V_4, oh, did I do that, well I meant to change them.

'If anyone's picking up we're screwed anyway, Sage.'

okay, say what you like, whatever helps—

Allie watched the Heads crew setting up for the break-in, Sage in their midst like a prince among courtiers; his presence distanced by the immix buffer field, and by the silver blizzard of his eyes. He was wearing the coding lenses he'd brought back from Hollywood: he looked like an eerily perfect, giant sci-fi doll. She remembered how that deliberately slowed-down Cornish accent used to set her teeth on edge. Arrogant and hammered, so he plays the lout, the only way he can communicate with us mortal meat puppets. How I used to *hate* him. The jargon washed over her, only fragments of banter in English . . . Fiorinda sat opposite, in one of the armchairs: feet tucked up, a gold and brown shawl wrapped round her baggy shorts and tee-shirt; untouchable as her boyfriend. She didn't know it, she would smile and talk as if she thought she was normal, but the same look of horror and bliss that she'd worn on the mountain stood in her eyes. She was somewhere else, riding shotgun for the geeks at a speed nothing could beat; their final defence. She would be somewhere else until this was over. Cosoleth slept at Fiorinda's feet, in her basket. Allie huddled her Gucci jacket around her, rubbed her cheek against the antique red leather that she loved, and thought of Virginia Woolf, hearing the sparrows talk in Greek.

DK . . . ?

Is that you . . . ?

The über-geeks were convinced, on evidence in the trace Sage had recovered, that Dilip had been calling Allie, person-to-person, when his b-loc signal was captured. When they'd said this meant they could send her, virtually, to wherever 'virtual Dilip' was, she had been terrified it would be Xi'an. But everything had pointed to England. This is *forbidden tech*, the stuff the Sphere must never dare to contemplate. Elder Sister's not going to let the evidence out of her immediate control. The geeks had invaded the AMID's datasphere (under Fiorinda's protection), found the b-loc signature buried there and pinpointed a physical location. Dilip was at Ground Zero. Ax had said it would be Reading. Where else? She's a frontline General, she does her own dirty work. Here, in England, the bodies will be buried—

Sage and his brother Heads bitched and speculated casually as they worked. Can we really *blackmail* the Chinese, will they cut a deal? If they'd massacred Counterculturals anywhere else they'd kept it quiet. But they'd imposed the mind/matter tech ban, ripping out whole sections of new industry; and the Sphere had complied, trusting souls. Our story's got to be a major embarrassment—

'We was robbed,' said Bill Trevor, Bill without Clio round his neck for a change. 'Fuckin' wankers, ripped us off and trashed us. If there was any justice—'

'It would be a *Reich* fucking world,' agreed George, darkly.

Cheers and applause from the crew.

'They'll live it down,' the Minister for Gigs decided, from far away. 'I see a glorious propaganda campaign: Elder Sister can be trusted with forbidden tech, so China was allowed to use it, secretly, but no one else. They could make that work.'

'Or they play up the military deterrent angle,' suggested George. 'Easy.'

'They can do what the fuck they like, this changes nothing about their actual position, it's a question of style. But will they shoot the messengers, or invite us onto the board? Depends how cynical you are about Elder Sister—'

'No offence to Ax, but I am cynical as shit,' avowed Bill.

Ax was on his own mission. Rob and the Babes and the kids; Chip and Verlaine were also out of London. It'd be hard to maintain their innocence if things went badly wrong, but cross that bridge when we come to it, and it's not going to happen. Cosoleth was here because there was no safer place.

Everything we say is heard, but it doesn't matter anymore, tonight we share the freedom of the dead. Allie closed her eyes.

It wasn't Xi'an. She concentrated on the feeling of relief.

Peter left his desk, and asked Fiorinda what if she spotted something that had already slipped. 'Would you be able to fix it retroactively? Make it so it hadn't happened?'

Fiorinda scratched her toes, and wondered if the sagging armchair had fleas. She was remembering another bohemian dump, maybe more flashy, not so grungey as this. The basement of the Snake Eyes house in Lambeth, HQ of rock rebellion. I was sixteen and I'd just met them. Ax Preston was picking guitar, in the pauses of the conversation. Singing, single notes, that I knew were talking to me—

Thoughts like this rise, when you're about to go over the top.

'Yes,' she said. 'I can do practically anything in the datasphere, arrow of time no object, without going within a million miles of critical. But it would be a fuck of a job and if I started trying not to make mistakes I would fall in and drown—'

'So you have to get into a Flow State, does that feel excellent?'

'Yes it does, I'm there now. But I wouldn't do this often. I wouldn't make a habit of it if were legal and decent, because it would drive me nuts.'

Allie roused out of her frozen daze, and spoke calmly. 'Cack—'

He looked round. 'What?'

'Leave Fio alone. She's concentrating.'

Sage was finding out as much as he could about the situation at the remote site, right now. He could tell that 'virtual Dilip' hadn't been copied (now there's a nasty thought) . . . It's perilous to infer physical conditions from the digital activity of some place you've never seen. The peaceful isolation that showed on the map could be a server stuck away in a broom cupboard, or it could be some buzzing party central, where 'Virtual Dilip' was kept in a cage of impenetrable firewalls. It didn't move around; that was all he was totally sure about. What about the status of the signal itself? A b-loc signal is a *facet* of a human consciousness, logically *not separate* from the original, or from any manifestation of itself. 'Virtual Dilip's' survival was a paradox: but theoretically, marginally, he could reach the brainstate of that shadow at Ground Zero through the entangled fragment he had collected from Lance Buckley's recording; and the reference signature from his cache.

—like reconstructing a minor Hittite dialect, from a broken sliver of clay and a dictionary based on a much richer language. Nah, more like astrophysics. (We have no *proof* that DK made that fatal call, though we all believe it now.) A tower of inference built on pure speculation, and theory in search of an experiment—

He kept up the backchat because he knew the crew found it reassuring. They blocked the security patrols and took him off-line irregularly, for a millisecond or so, when the iterations reached levels they didn't like. Fiorinda is backstop, but we don't use her unless we must . . . About every nine and a half seconds, every thirteen seconds, and there was another, shorter cycle that kicked in not-quite-randomly.

What shall we call this, neurophysical necromancy?

'Okay, I'm done, best I can. Still active, and pronounced clear.'

'What does that mean?' asked Allie.

The geeks had changed gear. Sage was leaving his board, the moment was upon her. How would it be? She imagined DK rescued, like fragile thistledown, a living ghost, living out his days in peace—

'It's difficult to describe,' said Peter, seriously. 'There's no *Dilip* in the material present, so it's got no origin. Active like a virtual movie avatar, kept the way they are, on standby. You can't switch them off or they disintegrate.'

'I couldn't get a great deal—' Sage turned his white-out blind eyes on her: Allie flinched. 'Ah, just about to take them out.' He tipped the lenses onto his palm, dumped them in a tiny autoclave and came to sit in the other armchair. 'We won't be landing in anybody's lap or squabbling with furniture; an' if there's an exotic trap waiting to catch virtual invaders such as us, I didn't spot it.'

'But *is he alive*? Is it him? Is part of him still alive, somehow?'

'Mm. Better if you don't think like that.'

George was frowning at Sage's immix construct, reduced to code on a regular screen. He and the boss exchanged a steady look.

'It's time you got moving,' said George.

The Cumbrian b-loc sets had been programmed, from Sage's files, with the identity of the pair that had been in the Few's possession. Fiorinda and Allie kept their heads still, while the geeks made final adjustments—

'Let me remind you,' said Sage, donning his own set, 'this has to be a short trip. You and I, Allie, won't be able to get around. We don't have a live path, we're loc'd to the shade, the standard b-loc footprint. Move away from him more than about a metre, two at max, and we'll loc' out. The nine-seconds cycle is harmless, we're too strange for it to spot. The thirteen-second probes are blunt instruments, they don't care what we look like. We can survive two of them, we'll loc' in at the start of that cycle. It'll seem longer, but that will be the limit. After that we're playing chicken.'

He looked down at his sleeping daughter.

'Last call. Are you still up for this, Allie?'

'Don't *do that*!' she wailed. 'Yes I am up for this.'

'Sorry,' said the boss, unperturbed. 'My brat?'

Fiorinda smiled, spookily calm. 'I'm ready.'

The support crew were suddenly talking in Allie's head. V_2 will return the call she missed, the day the Insanitude siege was broken. V_1 and V_3 are slaved to her, V_2 never to be alone at the remote site . . . The brain's visual centres, because the visual cortex is God, and the death-dealing submarines. She knew that V_1, or Vanguard, was Fiorinda. Sage was V_2, Vigilant, making Allie Victorious. Just the kind of name the commandos *would* give to the weakest link, but it didn't wound her. She was far away, trying to think herself back to that moment, the unexpected hinge-moment, on which everything, *everything* depended—

DK . . . ?

Is that you . . . ? Where are you . . . ?

She didn't remember getting the earbead ping, and failing to respond. The b-loc sets had been hidden in a bedroll. Nobody remembered seeing Dilip root one out and take it with him on his fire watch. They'd been expecting an assault, on that last day: they hadn't known it would end the siege. All Allie remembered was the uproar, a surge of panic sweeping through the non-combatant havens; deep inside the palace. Dora and Felice stuffing Toots into a pet-carrier, and calling frantically for Ghost, the Snake Eyes' other cat (hadn't been seen in days). Chez and Chip and Ver grabbing things, the children passive with terror; Rob yelling at the senior Babes, *fuck the cat, come on!* The smell of fire, the gusts of heat. She remembered realising that Dilip must be dead, but did not know where this knowledge had overtaken her. When we were running with the faithful barmies, no idea where they were taking us? When we *saw* the firestorm that everyone was screaming about—

I'm in the departure lounge.

They were in a dark room. Glowing red and green dots, like standby lights, hung suspended, dimly showing them a rectangular space, not huge; nearly square. In the centre, right in front of them, stood a pale polished block around two metres long, maybe a metre high; immediately suggesting an altar or a tomb. Hardware towers, giant servers or maybe just filing cabinets, emerged from their hiding. The room was walled with them. There was a door, no windows. At waist-height, around three of the hardware walls, objects were laid on counters or benches; most of them quite small; difficult to make out.

'The exotic trap was in the nine-second cycle,' said Fiorinda. 'Dunno how, but I've blocked it.'

'Ouch, sorry—'

'But where is DK?' whispered Allie.

Three seconds had passed.

'He's here,' Fiorinda stared around, 'He's right here! But *where*?'

They could all feel the contact, the mental penumbra of a b-loc call—

The pale block, the funereal aura of this place, the nature of their mission, had them imagining Dilip's ghost honourably entombed. Enshrined as a hero by the noble enemy; for Chinese reasons that they didn't understand . . . Then they saw a shadow hovering over the catafalque, and realised the tomb was actually a flatbed scanner, like the flatbeds they'd seen in Hollywood when they were making *Rivermead*. This version had no second housing for the controls, and the dome was almost invisible. But it was there, and the shade was firing up inside: reacting to their presence. Allie gasped and clutched at her head, felt the grip back at the home site and almost loc'd out. The shadow had become a human body, the head and neck contorted, eyeless, noseless, the limbs and trunk seared, shards of textile burned into the red and black meat. A headset was fused to the black-blistered scalp, the forearms fixed, hands like claws, as if reaching to pull it off.

There he is. There's Dilip, where he has been all this time.

Allie recovered first. 'Oh, thank God,' she cried. 'He's *dead*! He was always dead, we've been agonising over nothing, all we have to do is pull the plug. How do we pull the plug!'

Eight seconds had passed. 'We've got to pull the plug!' cried Allie again, but Sage and Fiorinda weren't responding. She understood, blunderingly but fast, that there was worse to come—

The shade had heard her voice, it stirred and woke.

It was Dilip alive, a living image laid over the burned shell: his hair drawn back from the face they knew, his great eyes alight with recognition. They saw what Dian's father had seen, a slender male figure in very closely fitting dark clothes: an impression of someone enduring, or taking on, great pain. But the apparition was looking at them.

'Ah!' breathed the shade. 'Did the Insanitude fall?'

They could not speak. Ten seconds had passed.

'Have I been like this long? It's hard to know, I have no memory. I don't think I talked. I was conscious when they interrogated me. They had to vivisect, because if they shut me down I'm gone—' It drew a deep breath, into vanished lungs. 'Ah. You haven't come to get me out, have you?'

'No,' said Sage.

But the shade had forgotten the question. It was fixed on Allie. It raised the burned shell's blackened hand, Fiorinda and Sage saw it realise it could not touch her.

'I wanted to say goodbye . . . I had the b-loc. I had always taken it with me when I had to leave you, those scary days, so I'd be able to say goodbye—'

'Goodbye,' echoed Allie, speaking to the long dead. No tears, but her knees were giving way, she couldn't feel the floor and she'd forgotten why.

'I called you but the fire came through so fast, I wasn't thinking, I never meant you to see this hideous thing—'

'*Don't*,' she whispered. '*Don't*—'

'I lived too long in the departure lounge. You're a true soul. I'm glad you came and found me.' It forgot her. Dilip the free spirit, party animal, enduring great pain undaunted, turned and smiled at Sage and the rock and roll brat.

'My lord, my oceanic Fiorinda, is Ax okay?'

'Ax is doing fine.'

'Tell me one thing, are we winning?'

'*Yes*,' said Sage.

'I don't know where the controls are. You won't leave me like this?' Twenty seconds.

'Don't worry,' said Fiorinda. 'I won't.' The countdown stopped. Time was away somewhere. She sliced her hand through the top of the dome – which did not shatter, it rose like dew and vanished in the air – sprang up onto the scanner bed and seemed to take the shade by the shoulders. She kissed Dilip gently, and drew back. Sage and Allie, on either side, held his burned claws. He was thistledown, the way a b-loc virtual ghost always feels: there is no sensation, but your brain is puzzled.

Fiorinda pulled off the fused headset.

Allie and the ghost both disappeared. Allie was safe at the home site. Dilip's shade was just gone.

'That was a cheap round,' said Fiorinda, still crouched on the tomb, where the laserdome was as it had been, whole but empty. 'I know what it looked like, and felt like, but what really happened was all in software. You found him by geekery, you could have hacked the off-switch by geekery; just would have taken longer.' She grinned, and shook herself. 'They'll never know I was here. Net damage to the fabric of reality *derisory*, only now I remember why this is a very dangerous drug.'

She jumped down from her perch. 'What *is* this place? What else are they keeping in here? Shall we look at the grave goods?'

To Sage's eyes she glittered as if her blood had turned to light. He shook his head. 'Got to go, babe. Twenty-six seconds, realtime. I'm gonna get caught.'

'Come on, live a little.' She held out her hand, shining. Sage barely hesitated: he joined her where the countdown couldn't hurt him

(back in the first-floor room he watched the contents of those servers zipping into Reich custody: cheap round for us, expensive for the tourists, but enough is enough, I'm about to pull you out, my brat—)

They grinned at each other, dropped the handclasp and walked around.

'We must be inside one of Ax's upturned boats,' said Fiorinda.

'Most likely. What d'you think *shū* means, exactly? In this context?'

The Chinese character was embossed on the sides of the pale catafalque; in large relief up on the towers, and button-sized on every winking control panel.

'Text?' she suggested. 'Books, recorded knowledge . . . ?'

The objects on the counters were English Countercultural or forbidden tech artefacts. A magic crystal sitting on its barkcloth bag. A book of spells from the twentieth century; with fairies on the cover. Sage lifted a box-fresh b-loc headset; *Adiabatic of Cambridge* scrolled on the case. First-generation, a little clunky, but popular to the end, as near to a mass-market product as b-loc ever had. *Adiabatic* was supposed to have been trashed and burned when the English went crazy after the Insanitude fell, and smashed all the futuristic science. 'You start to wonder—' he murmured, and shook his head. Don't bother, we'll never know *what really happened*. What really happened is a concept that the Chinese have erased.

'They never suspected me at all,' said Fiorinda, off on her own track. Most of the stolen tech was in pieces; vivisected. 'We should have had more faith in our own cover-up. They believed the same as US Intelligence believed, same as Fred Eiffrich did. I'm Rufus's daughter but I was his victim, helpless, didn't inherit a scrap of his mutant brain. They killed my father's other children out of idle curiosity, or as a precaution, or just to see what their brains were like—'

I am free, she thought. Elder Sister has set me free.

It flashed through her mind that if the bastard Chinese had plans for another A-team, which was all too possible, seeing this collection, they would get nowhere.

Not as long as I live. I shall stop that from happening.

I—

'They didn't come to England to save the world from a second A-team, Sage. They saw the Second Chamber as a threat all right, and maybe, *maybe* they saw our Counterculture as a breeding ground for Neurobomb material. But deep down dirty the massacres were camouflage. They made it look like righteous ideology, when really they were here to protect their secret monopoly. And strip our assets . . . When the dust settles I bet they plan to scoop Europe's best "evil" neurophysicists and mind/matter techs, take them home and rehabilitate them—'

As she gets older, thought Sage, occasionally she's going to look a lot like her dad . . . He wasn't horrified, he'd long accepted that Fiorinda and Rufus would always be close. Alight with her fire, he felt the latency of mind/matter fusion in his own brain and wondered if he could ever join her where she was now under his own steam, using tech alone; preferably without killing himself.

File that one.

'The *di* is mind/matter based. Has to be. I saw that at once when I started thinking about it. We are idiots, Fiorinda. If they remotely suspected trouble, they wouldn't have dared to come near without some kind of forbidden fallback—'

'The *bastards*. The bare-faced, conniving *bastards*.'

She took his hand again and they stood together, looking up at the character *shū*, on the towers, on the panels. 'It means the code. The os and 1s of reality.'

'Yeah.'

They thought of Anne-Marie and her little boys: of thousands uncounted; friends and strangers cut down here and elsewhere; of Toby Starborn's cruel fate. The need to hit back with equal savagery boiled through them, and vanished into the purity of the fusion high. Let it go, accept, submit; this is the *good* news. Normal human villainy killed those people, and now we will win Ax's game.

'I didn't like the way DK ended up being Vengeance,' said Sage at last. 'He was not the vengeful type.'

'Nor did I,' said Fiorinda. 'But I don't know . . .' She smiled, remembering the Mixmaster, thinking he'd have liked the irony. 'Maybe it works.'

The best revenge is to live well.

A baby screaming and screaming; the crew packing up with their teeth clenched. Fiorinda crooned and rocked Cosoleth, to no avail. George sat beside Allie on the dirty sofa, seeming to absorb her shock and grief into his broad frame.

'You all *knew* it would be like that,' cried Allie, tears streaming.

'Somethen' like. An' we woulder tried harder to tell you, but we thought you were better off only facing it the once—'

'*It's okay, it's okay.* I needed to know what had happened, and now I do. I know where he is. He isn't lost, he's found. Oh God, oh, God—'

Coz's piercing yells shifted from frightened to angry, which was an improvement, though the noise did not diminish. 'Hush little baby,' coaxed Fiorinda, 'poor Coz, it was too much, I am such a trial to you. What the hell did I do to spook her, Bill?' she asked, over the baby's head. 'I'm a klutz at b-loc, I always lose my short-term memory, I've no idea what was happening back here.'

'You didn't have time to do anything much,' said Bill.

My God, was it only half a minute, is that all?

Sage came back into the room. He'd gone out for some quiet, to make a phone call: to tell Ax it had gone well. She looked at him, and he nodded, blue eyes wide.

Now we'll see. Are we falling or flying?

What The Thrush Said

The straight half of Mr Preston knelt among drifts of creamy silk, smiling at Elder Sister, who faced him, crosslegged, her hair loose and tousled on her shoulders; from which the robe she wore was slipping in very pretty disarray. She touched a shallow crease, hardly a scar, that ran across his upper ribs, on the left.

'What's this? A souvenir of what?'

He wondered if she'd ever been wounded in active service. When would that have been? The nineteen eighties, before her Principal Dancer days? Vietnam border skirmishes? Or later, in her career as General Li? Forget it, can't rely on anything I've been told. Her life will be wrapped in cloud as long as she stays in power. If she falls it'll be different, but no more truthful.

'It's very stupid.'

'It looks stupid. I don't like the position at all.'

'It was in Cambridge, in the thing we call the Deconstruction Tour.'

'The first, most violent phase of your Cultural Revolution. Nobody here seems to have any idea what that meant in China. You seem to think it was none of our business. It was terribly shocking, it wasn't our image of the English at all. And then there was a young man, a guitar-player from a *rock band*, whom we were told was controlling the masses. He was restoring order, yet also leading the people in the destruction of greed, selfishness, ignorance and decadence, the four poisons that were killing the planet. That was a road we could understand. We in China were suffering hell from the environmental problems of the Fall.'

'The Crash. Is this the view of the Chinese, or Elder Sister talking me up?'

She grinned, and touched the same finger to his lips. 'We knew that absolutist change was the only way forward. And he looked very Chinese.'

'Do you want to hear about my wound, or not?'

'No, I want to talk about you, because it makes you uncomfortable and I love to see you uncomfortable. You don't understand how powerful it was. In China this is the Ur-story. There's a peasant boy, who becomes a soldier in a time of decay and corruption, he raises the people against an unjust régime. He is an outlaw hero who gathers an army, he's going places, unlike your Robin Hood.' She paused for thought. 'He's a peasant, or at least very poor, but he has the right ancestors, that's important. I've heard that Fiorinda comes from an old gentry family?'

'Haha, yeah. On her mother's side. The Slaters haven't been personally involved in putting roofs on houses since around the time of the Peasants' Revolt.'

'Oooh, a peasants' revolt. When was it, what happened?'

' 'Bout eight hundred years ago . . . A charming young king told them he loved them, promised them everything, lured the leaders into the open and the régime clobbered them, *mercilessly.*'

'Ah, too bad. You laugh, but you shouldn't despise legitimacy. *My* name is "Li", I have found that surprisingly useful. Your daughter's name should be Slater. Now, let's return to my peasant boy. He takes over kingdom after kingdom until he holds all China. He declares a new dynasty, he institutes sweeping and compassionate reform. Heaven accepts him, and phoenixes are seen in his gardens.'

'I didn't like the pension plan.'

They were alone in her private quarters, with the fabulous artworks. The Fu dais where she'd shown him her map of the world was beyond their lamplight, hidden by the antique screens. Elder Sister sighed, stretched her arms above her head, and reached over, lithe and smooth as young girl, to the hookah. She took a deep pull of smoke, watching him, eyes half-closed, sidelong.

'Hm.'

She was very good at sensing resistance.

'We were told you had *"invented post-modern warfare"*. It was fascinating. This idea of using war without terrorism, when war *is* terrorism.'

'Now I know you're laughing at me. General, you couldn't begin to sound the depths of my ignorance. Richard and Corny did it all. I didn't know I was on the world's stage. I was on local tv, in our storm-in-a-thimble, making phrases in the hope of stopping what I saw as hideous.'

'Again,' said Elder Sister, rather tartly, 'you don't understand. It *was* our business. We had embarked on a plan to unite the world. We needed to overrun country after country, without leaving a disastrous trail of low-intensity urban warfare behind us. We'd have been fools not to watch Europe; to see how a successful unifying power emerges; when a country has fallen apart. Military genius is innate, like musical talent. Soldiers know it when they meet it. You may be ignorant, but you have that genius, and we learned from you.'

She offered the mouthpiece: he took it, shaking his head. 'You'll have to be more plausible. The PLA can't possibly have been studying my battle plans.'

'Hm. Our suborbital transports are expensive and we use them sparingly. But it's because of Ax Preston that we rarely, rarely use air strikes. We fight on the ground. It does not hamper us, we have invincible superiority, but it reduces the terror remarkably.'

Touché.

He lay down beside her on the silken pillows, and blew smoke rings into the lamplight. Everything about Elder Sister raised the ghost of a past self he'd almost forgotten. He didn't want those days, or that mindset back, fuck no. But she gave him access to emotions that no one, not a soul, had ever shared; and that touched his heart.

'The mission was to save the world; to save civilisation, from *real and present danger*. And to nurture the Good State, so it could survive and grow on the other side of the Crisis. I struggle to remember what it felt like to be twenty-six, and convinced I could achieve those things. I'm a different person, several times over.'

'I know about *that*,' she said. She seemed to smile inwardly, nostalgically, her profile calm and grave. Then suddenly she turned on him like a tigress, phoenix eyes snapping, a storm of black hair. 'So! You admit you have a mission. Then *why are we arguing?*'

'I wasn't aware that we were arguing.'

She was close to getting genuinely annoyed, this planet-destroyer in bed with him, beautiful and naked among her swirls of embroidered satin. Be careful, he thought. Show no fear, but never cross the line. Have I crossed it?

'*Ax!* Now you are being insufferable—!'

'Hey. I don't think you can call me insufferable on a first date.'

She withdrew. She sat up, smoothed back her hair, and arranged her robe. No more fun and games, said the expression on that flushed, lovely face, not quite bare of make-up, free of any sign of ageing. Here we go. He wondered how the dice were going to fall, would she give him the opening he needed, or derail him?

'I want you to be my President of Europe.'

That'll do. He sighed, and marshalled his thoughts. She knew that what he said tonight would be different, that he had finally stopped fencing. She gave him time.

'Ax?'

'I want to talk to you,' he said. 'Dead straight.'

He wanted to ask if they could continue this in English, but if you can't say it in *putonghua* it's not worth saying, so scratch that. Leave your ego at the door, try not to sound too stilted, avoid complex sentences, trust your intuition.

'Elder Sister, I would like to work for you; I want to serve the World State. But I can't take a, what amounts to a post on your staff, unless you are going to listen to me. I have to be able to say what I think, and you have to be ready to listen. Otherwise I'm not the man for the job. I wouldn't last a week—'

He got no further.

'This sounds to me,' said Elder Sister, in a level tone, lowering the hand she had sharply raised, 'like the prelude to a well-honed petition. You may speak. What is it you want to ask?'

'All right,' Ax sat up and shrugged his own robe together. Dressed for business, the planet-destroyer and her spirited new favourite faced each other.

'Everything Weng Jiang and his team told you about the Landsturm is true. The whole affair was an unqualified success. However, you could still be running into trouble. In these countries the masses did not labour under oppression and decay for generations, as is the case in the east of Europe. Civic collapse is a recent thing. The masses are steeped in eco-revolution; emotionally and intellectually the cadres are passionately on your side. They are Utopians, they believe in the World State. But if crucial issues are not treated thoughtfully there'll be a backlash.'

She nodded, focused and intent. 'This is the kind of thing I need to hear. What do you mean by "backlash"? I will deal with recalcitrance.'

'There are countries in Western Europe that still have nuclear capability.'

'Hm.' She thought about that. 'I believe not. A long way from readiness, at the least. For instance, the last British nuclear deterrent was decommissioned under David Sale's government. It passed for a Quixotic gesture, I saw it as a practical move. Better to destroy the weapons that principle forbids you to use, than have them lying about "just in case", while rabid Countercultural terrorists prowl the nation.'

'I agree. The nuclear threat was an extreme example . . .' Ax paused. 'The danger of a public setback is real. The Sphere's growth has been from success to success, and that's what your great plan needs, to sweep it to completion.'

'Go on.'

'As I see it, your job is to make sure the will to hold back isn't there. To rule by consent, not to crush ambition; to encourage the spirit of partnership. If you bind your natural supporters to you, in confidence and gratitude, populations won't be alienated by the police actions you may have to take. Recalcitrance will wither away.'

'So all the modesty and reticence was a trick. You see yourself as the counsellor who shall keep this hot-headed Napoleon on the right path!'

'This is not a trick,' he said, 'this is honest advice. Before I realised who you were my intuition told me to trust you; I trust you now. I know there's a contradiction, I've turned my back on violence, you are a military leader. I still want you to succeed. I'm in awe of your victories, your talents, your courage; and your decency, so far as war allows decency. But in some respects you will have to change your ways if—'

'Hm.'

'If I am to go on believing you are truly the person I want you to be.'

'And who is that?'

'The rightful son of heaven.'

Her phoenix eyes opened wide. He glimpsed the outlaw hunger of a young woman in soldier's uniform, studying battles between dance rehearsals, the angry, enduring shame Wang Xili had warned him about; the whole story of Li Xifeng, which he could never know. That charming three-cornered grin broke out.

'Well! It's true what they say about you, Ax Preston.'

Ax reached for the hookah again. Good at spotting resistance, and very good at signalling when the imperial audience is over. 'Oh yeah? What do they say?'

'That you are an *inspired* flatterer.'

'The golden rule is, you can never be too blatant.'

Elder Sister burst into delighted laughter, and collapsed on her side, the robe falling open. 'Oh dear. I am a child! The words "son of heaven" go straight to a centre in my brain! I have never taken heroin, I think it may be something like!'

Please God, nobody ever introduce this woman to smack.

She was a wanton dancing girl with sparkling eyes and dewy lips, giggling up at him, brass-nerved, wicked as if she'd been born English. He took her in his arms, the chemistry between them blossoming again, and kissed her parted lips. He was aching hard, extremely turned on, a very strange state to be in, but genuine. I saw you coming towards me, in the night garden—

The moth's kiss first. 'But I mean it.' The bee's kiss now.

Just before four a.m. Ax left the clouds of her bed, shrugging the robe provided for him over his shoulders. He located his clothes, tossed on a chair, and took his suit jacket through the looming maze of furniture to the open floor in front of the Fu dais. It was a relief to change his orientation. Her bed faced south, the dais faced south. But in Reading Arena everything should flow from east to west. Ax's sense of direction was strong, and boosted by years of having had a brain implant. When he was aligned wrongly it nagged him. He sat with one knee up, the other leg folded under him, staring across the shadowy space, and listened to a thrush that had begun to sing, practice notes, an isolated phrase repeated, and then another . . . wishing he had a cigarette, his phone on the rug in front of him.

It was a toy he'd picked up at the fair in Cumbria, a sleek, curved haematite pebble, with no outward sign of tech. Just a phone, no tricks.

Thoughts of the long, bewildering struggle drifted through his mind, fragments of the catalogue of failures and mistakes he rehearsed to himself when he was low. But it was all one now. In an hour or two it would be time for the *Fajr* . . . He felt very close to his religion tonight, strange as that might seem. *To be* the presence of God's compassion on earth. *To know* that the world is a mosque; to walk in it humbly, reverently, as on holy ground. That's all you need to be, that's all you need to know. The rest, all the plotting and scheming, working the percentages; it's so worthless.

But he didn't think he would pray, not this dawn. Maybe not even in his heart.. He wondered where the thrush was perched. Down by Travellers' Meadow, where the great oak tree stood, that fell in the storm in Boat People summer? No, the ragged wilderness down there would be gone, like the lovely trees that used to grow beside the Thames, the bushes and briars ripped out; the river culverted.

He had spent the night love-making with a beautiful woman, some thirty years his senior; and she was an adept. He had received, he hoped he'd given, a great deal of pleasure. And now what? Hollow and empty as the hour, not even terrified, just tired and sad, he sat listening to the birdsong until his phone rang, bang on time.

Fuck! He dived for the pebble.

'Hi, Scheherazade, how's it going?'

'I'm good. How are you?'

'Ooh, we've had a great night. Didn't miss you at all. We reached the fourth V, solved that, got some stuff, an' Aeris, Barrett and Tifa all home free and clear.'

Aeris, Barratt and Tifa were characters in a classic fantasy roleplay game, great favourite with Fiorinda and Sage; the fourth V was Dilip. Not that Ax was ever going to be explaining this conversation at a public inquiry.

'What about the big boss fight?'

'Turns out there isn't one . . . Ax, don't stay too long, it'll look bad. If I were you I'd leave before office hours.'

'Okay,' he said. 'I'll do what I can.'

The phone was dead, and there was someone watching him.

'Who was that?'

'Sage,' said Ax. He sighed, and dropped the pebble into the pocket of his jacket.

'What did he want?'

'To tell me that he couldn't sleep, I think. I'm sorry, Elder Sister. I should have had the phone switched off.'

She knelt close by him, with a dancer's grace, warm from the bed, an incense-breathing shadow. The thrush was singing clearly now, flight upon flight of defiant joy, flung against the dark. 'I'm not an ogre. You have a baby, suppose she had been taken ill. He was making you feel guilty, that's not very dignified. Well, you may tell your partners I have no designs on their boyfriend.'

'They know that. I'm sorry I gave you cause to have to say it.'

'Though I *would* like to see you again.'

He nodded. He wasn't about to say no, he couldn't find the words for 'yes'.

'Elder Sister—'

'My name is Li Xifeng,' she corrected him gently.

Ax shook his head, smiling in apology. 'I'm sorry, but you are *jiejie*. To me it's your name, not a title. It reminds me of the Daoist Nun, and the way she came towards me in the night garden, that night in Anglia. When you called me friend Mohammad, because I'd given my coat to a cat. I'll switch if you insist, but—'

'Gracefully put,' she said, 'if not up to your own peerless standard.'

Fuck, now he'd insulted her. Better not dwell on it. Moving on.

'Elder Sister, do you recall our conversation last night? About Europe?'

'Of course.'

'When you look back on it, I hope you'll understand that I meant every word, and that I truly want to serve your cause. I've been thinking. I would like to arrange a meeting — if you'd be interested in talking privately to some Utopians, some of the significant delegates from the Landsturm. Would that be appropriate?'

She pondered.

'Yes. I like the sound of that. We must see about arranging for them to come back to England, we should meet in London. Who would I meet?'

'I'll look into it, and send a list of suggestions to your office today.'

Last night there'd been nothing between them but the random chemistry, and the thrill of playing their roles. There was something more now; an orphan regret. It changed nothing, on either side. The emperor studied him from behind those beautiful eyes. He saw her putting his offer together with the phone call, and the alarming news Ax had delivered, so discreetly, a few hours before.

Taking it in, and deciding to let it go for the moment.

I will leave in good health, thought Ax. Even if she gets the emergency call. But viral pneumonia might be on the cards.

'What is that bird?' she said. 'He sings every morning, from about this time until dawn; he was very loud in the spring. I am ignorant. Is that a nightingale?'

Another insomniac. Hey, compadre. 'No, that's a songthrush. Nightingales only sing for a short season in England, they're pretty much over by now.'

'Not so steeped in romance, then,' said Elder Sister. 'But he's a fine, strong singer, and good company.' She reached over to touch the bullet crease, smiling. 'I don't keep those souvenirs. My body is a peeled almond, its memories quickly fade. You should leave before sunrise, or people will talk, but that leaves us with an hour or so to spare. Why don't you tell me the story of your heroic wound?'

The Sting

Ax returned to London, and sent his list of names along to Elder Sister's office. It was received as if nothing untoward had been discovered. Days passed, still no reaction to the Sydenham strongbox raid: and this looked hopeful. As a rule, the state arrests you, gangsters come round and kill you, but rational big business keeps quiet about getting hacked, and waits for the ransom note. The geeks didn't probe too deeply, but they didn't detect any increase in encrypted traffic between England and China either. A week after the V team had freed Dilip Ax sent a request to Wang Xili: could the Triumvirate have a meeting with the Generals and Elder Sister, to discuss the unofficial Europe talks? They had a response within the hour: certainly, what a good idea.

They'd been staying at the Snake Eyes Commune; the old same place, which had become once more the HQ of the rock and roll revolution. Cornwall was too far away, the Few and their leaders had felt like sticking together. They went to Chelsea on a warm, still afternoon, and walked from the Underground. The neighbourhood where Fiorinda had once wandered, twelve years old and pregnant, looking for the address she'd somehow never learned, was quiet. The only people on the streets of slightly raffish privilege were Chinese soldiers. There were plenty of those: the old capital was still an occupied city, and one of the Five Generals had his London quarters around here. At the armoured checkpoint at the end of Wang Xili's street they were greeted with beaming smiles and eager goodwill.

Wang himself received them, in the flat's tiny hallway.

He was in uniform, elegant as always, but stiff with them: no sign of his lively charm, or his customary urbanity. No question the Chinese knew of the raid. Perhaps the collaborators were here to disclose, for their masters' ears alone, the details of a conspiracy they had uncovered? From his manner, Wang didn't appear to go for this explanation. He showed them into the gold-curtained living room.

'I will inform Elder Sister that you have arrived.'

The Fiorinda gallery stared from every side, insistent on being noticed.

'I'd forgotten it was this bad,' said Sage. 'It went out of my head.'

'Don't worry about it. I don't care.' Fiorinda wondered what she was doing up there. Standing in for Elder Sister? Maybe in China *jiejie* was everywhere. In England the personality cult behaviour that had begun to break out was severely discouraged. Perhaps Wang surrounded

315

himself with glamour shots of a foreign rock babe, and thought of his own inamorata. She thought it didn't matter much. She was deposed, dethroned, no longer *the awful problem*, and it was a very good feeling.

Fiorinda had her tapestry bag, Sage carried his visionboard. It was okay that Cosoleth and Min, dear companions, were back at Snake Eyes, but it was a shame that Ax didn't have his Gibson on his shoulder. Because here they were at the end of the trail they'd embarked on last autumn as demoralised fugitives, clinging to their last treasures. They'd been in rags at Ashdown. Today they were rockstars: Sage and Ax in very fine pastel suits, Fiorinda in designer shalwar kameez: eau de Nil, with a silvery cobweb scarf over her hair. Not going to make a habit of it, but sometimes my prince *deserves* the solidarity of a little touch of hejab—

They realised they'd been standing in a dream, staring at each other like idiots: grinned ruefully and sat down. Ah, remember Paris in the springtime, in the long freeze, when we had nothing to do but be in love? They knew they'd been left alone in the faint hope that they might let something slip. They felt this boded well. We have them in a tizz.

'Do you remember anything?' asked Ax.

Fiorinda shook her head. 'I don't *think* it was all gold and shimmery like this, I have darker colours in mind. But it's a blank. Oh, the bedroom was through there—'

She pointed, and memory stirred, faint and oddly poignant.

The door she pointed to opened. Wang held it wide for Elder Sister; Hu followed her. Imagine the Fifth Element, the world-conqueror, sitting in her General's bedroom in this poky little flat, waiting to be summoned. But no doubt Li Xifeng had seen worse foxholes. She was not in uniform: she wore a crisp white shirt untucked, and blue jeans; her feet were bare. The Generals and their beloved leader sat down opposite the English Triumvirate, the low table between the two parties.

'The meeting will be conducted in English,' said General Hu.

Elder Sister looked long and hard at her Chosen One, and kept her eyes on him as she held out her hand to Wang, who swiftly opened the briefcase he had brought from the bedroom, and gave her a sheet of paper.

'Now,' said Elder Sister. 'This list. Alain de Corlay, Naomi Erhlevy, Dominic and Mathilde Hategekimana, Märtha-Louise Behn, Fausto Lattani, Gerhard Bessard. I will not go on. All the names are well known to me, prominent in the decade of Crisis, some of them currently in high office. Have you anything to tell me about this clique, Ax? Something more than the rather vague remarks you made last time we met? About discontent, and what you called a *backlash*?' She was not pleased with the word *backlash*. She bit it out, with a snap of her perfect teeth.

'Not really,' said Ax. 'It's as I said. Europe is in a poor state of repair, as a coherent entity, but there's infrastructure that can be pulled together, and the will to join the Sphere is there. Those are some of your strongest supporters, people I think you should be talking to . . . What we're hoping for is full partnership.'

'There's also a petition,' said Fiorinda, 'which so far comes only from us, and which we'd like you to consider, informally, this afternoon. We'd like the peaceful applications of neurophysics, the mind/matter tech which you call *shū*, to be distinguished from the appallingly dangerous development that you call the "pernicious delusion", and we call the Neurobomb. We'd like to be able to share our *shū* technologies freely, with other Sphere members.'

The Generals and the planet-destroyer took this on board. Wang and Hu were not quite stone-faced; it seemed they had thought of worse possibilities. Elder Sister showed neither fear nor relief. 'I see,' she said. 'I suppose this list—' she whipped the paper with a flick of her wrist, 'of *my best supporters*, is also a list of potential supporters for your petition. Is that all you have to say?'

'I could add some new names.'

'Add them.'

Ax began to list Sphere and Chinese luminaries who were sufficiently unhappy about the global ban to be obvious; starting at the top. He spoke slowly, sticking to the names he was absolutely sure of. People under totalitarian rule say one thing and mean another, but the code's transparent when you have the cipher. She raised a hand, before he ran out of the good stuff. He saw her recalibrating, finding her depth, not at all phased. A top predator challenged, completely fluid, completely open to her own best advantage—

'So this is your game!' cried Wang. 'You expect Elder Sister to talk with the traitors who want to practice forbidden science!'

Elder Sister's head snapped around, she silenced him with a phoenix stare of astonishment: from which Wang visibly recoiled.

Dried-up old Hu had the air of a man who was determined not to open his mouth at all. It was strange to think that he was probably around the same age as the woman clothed in youth, and crackling with energy, beside him.

'I see you came equipped, Mr Pender, with the tools of your forbidden trade. I presume that means you have something to contribute to this discussion?'

'Well, yeah, I do.' Sage took the board from its case, and laid it on the table. 'Hardly dyslexic at all, now,' he remarked, with a friendly smile. 'It's clearing up nicely. But this isn't going to be text-based. Where shall we start? I could show you the working record of a shoestring experiment we did last spring, when we sent someone, bi-location, to a low-orbit satellite. Dilip Krishnachandran,' he added, deliberately, 'was the guinea pig that time. A very brave guy, my friend DK. It was trifling of course, compared to what your taikonauts are up to in space, but we were pleased with it. That's one way we could go . . . The other way is, we could look at a shorter trip, a place we found and the information I slurped up while I was there.'

It was quietly done. Insolent words, strangely at odds with the presence of the Triumvirate here, defenceless, simply asking for a hearing.

'I presume you must be familiar with the mechanisms of b-loc? Maybe you have a version in development? Or were you just set up to capture anything that had the sig of forbidden tech, Hu?'

Please take this well, planet-destroyer. You're what we have, art of the possible, we've worked with far worse people. Be the world-conqueror Ax thinks you are, and be ready to deal—

'Elder Sister, you once told me I shouldn't make immersions, because I was meddling with the fabric of reality, and this was terribly dangerous. You're right, mind/matter tech is terribly dangerous. It's Galileo's moons. It's an extension of our human reach into realms that were mystic and unknowable an' heaven only knows where it will lead us. But we seem to be on the same page *vis à vis* reaching into the unknown. Can we agree to that, and move on?'

Sage's hands, with the long, square-tipped artist's fingers, rested lightly on the closed board. The Generals kept quiet. Elder Sister looked to Ax, her expression hard to read. But Ax had nothing to add. Conquering the world is no account, a spectacle, a firework show. You just keep moving until your armies cover the board. If you want to *rule* the world, and make it anything approaching the Good State, that's a different game, different rules. You know it. Your choice, *Shi Huangdi*.

Fiorinda thought of the courtesan. How did Dian know she could make contact with DK's virtual ghost? Did she have his b-loc number and just randomly call him, to see what would happen, because of something Wang had let slip? The way that kind of mystery is never solved, not until years later, when nobody cares. The way all the tumultuous things that had happened in England, since the invasion, would blur into a paragraph. She looked at her own younger face up on the walls and had the eerie feeling that she must be hundreds of years old: a time traveller from an elder world.

'Once,' she said, 'on the brink of modern China's birth, a thinker called Lian Quichao asked, how can the nation be strong? When the people have knowledge, the nation is strong. How can the people have knowledge? When all the people under heaven read books and recognise characters, they will have knowledge . . . He spoke of written language. How strong will the World State be, when all the nations can read and write the code of reality?'

'Well put,' said Elder Sister. 'A distant dream, but a good dream.' She smiled, warm and clear. 'I would like to see the low-earth orbit experiment, Sage. Soon; although not this afternoon. That sounds very interesting. As you are to become Sphere partners, your *shū* applications will be the property of the Sphere. And I will decide when and how the liberalisation occurs.'

'Of course,' said Ax.

The Generals relaxed, in a slow-taken breath. They must have been very scared. For a few days it must have looked as if the glorious unchecked rise of the whole great plan had hit a snag. Or, my God, *worse*, as if Elder Sister's legend was about to get tarnished—

But it's over, all smiles.

Fiorinda took a jewellery case from her bag.

'You gave me some fine diamonds, Elder Sister. I have something here I would like to give to you, in return. Our Crown Jewels are not personal property, nor State property. They belong to the reigning Sovereign, whoever that may be. We have decided this is ours to pass on, and that it ought to be yours.'

She offered the case. Elder Sister took it, opened it and set it down. A large unset white diamond lay in the velvet, a stellar brilliant, oval in shape; had to be more than 100 carats. A very distinctive jewel.

'This is the Koh-i-Noor.'

'Yes,' said Fiorinda. 'Not quite a mountain. Some people say Queen Victoria shouldn't have had it recut. But it's not bad, is it?'

'This was the property of the Queen of England,' murmured Elder

Sister. She looked at Fiorinda frankly. 'You are too generous. This should be yours.'

'The Moghuls used to say the Koh-i-Noor belongs by right to the ruler of the world.' Fiorinda looked to Ax, and to Sage, they nodded. 'We want that to be you.'

Elder Sister bowed a little, from the waist. 'I am honoured. I am honoured by your trust, my three friends. And I shall deserve it. I sincerely want to be the person Ax mentioned, ah, the other night.'

'The baby clothes are *lovely*,' said Fiorinda, discreetly accepting some kind of unspoken apology. 'And she's still growing into some of them, which was truly thoughtful. I like "a girl is a boy, a woman is a man". I *like* that. It unfolds.'

Elder Sister gazed for a moment longer on her new treasure, then she shut the case, and it was as if a light had gone out.

'The meeting with the Utopian cadres will go ahead. England, and nominally Europe, will have partner status before next spring. This will entail the withdrawal of the 2nd AMID army, which I'm sure is high on your very bold, very Chinese agenda.' She paused. 'Now I will say something that goes no further than this room, and I will not elaborate. Until today we have been mortally afraid of each other, for no reason. From today, we share a sacred trust. Never again. Do you understand me?'

Never again.

On Ax's second date with Elder Sister she took him into the garden that lay beyond the small doors in the Fu hall. Ax didn't say anything, but she spotted that he didn't like the marvellous scenery. She turned it off, leaving them with the real dimensions of a courtyard from old China: flowering shrubs in big pots, a rectangular pool bordered in dark green, shining stone. There were pretty fish in the pool, small grey and yellow koi; a little fat Buddha sat on a plinth in the middle.

She told him that the *di* had been the PLA's downfall.

'We had developed it long before the A-team experiments began, quite independently, from our own take on mind/matter. Deep in the heart of the semi-living particles there are transactions that pass the barrier between information space and normal space. The technology was secret because in China most people dislike the ideas you call "neurophysics", they find them uncanny. It stayed secret because mystery had become a vital part of our aura. After the A-team event we were faced with a dilemma, but the right strategy seemed clear.'

'Deny everything.'

'Protect our superiority, and root out every threat. So that's why, when we came to England, we came as industrial spies as well as conquerors. It was a mistake. We should have simply destroyed everything we found, then you would never have caught us out.'

The *way* they'd been caught out, the capture of DK's virtual self, was not to be discussed. Can't go there, loss of face territory; and that's fine by me. He thought of the piled bodies he'd been shown in the Memorial Hall here at Reading, his reaction observed by the clinically attentive Lieutenant Chu. The destruction of Toby Starborn, and God knows how many others who had played forbidden music in her courts. They were one with the hecatombs of dead in the wake of her liberating progress: for which the good tyrant felt no remorse. She has no reason to feel remorse, he reminded himself, because she is genuinely doing her best. He wondered how much she had known about what was going on in Cumbria . . . She'd certainly known about Sellafield, though not about the military option. Possibly she'd known about the forbidden tech up there; to an extent. And yet she'd held off, she'd given Ax a chance to talk them down—

She slaughters when she feels she must, for China. Accept that.

'The *di* formula, and its relatives (yeah, he thought. Those expensive airships for instance?) will remain secret. They are part of our superiority. The western evolutionary lines, bi-location, and immersion code, will be vetted carefully and encouraged under close control . . . Would you really have tried to cause a global scandal? Shown us up for hypocrites?'

'We didn't believe it would come to that.'

She grinned, charmingly. 'Oh no. You are our friends, you only wanted to show us that our security *could be* compromised, and that our secrets *could be* discovered. Ax, you keep forgetting that I know about you. You and that insolent "gentle giant" hacked the Internet Commissioners' data quarantine. We know you did that, because you came to Asia, Hiroshima wasn't it? Just to see if it could be done.'

'We shouldn't have done that. It was a stupid, pointless trick. I have a mania for gambling. Oh, and my vanity is disgusting.'

She lay with her cheek pillowed on one slim, outstretched arm, watching him. 'Deep in his heart, Ax Preston is convinced that he is the world's model of rectitude. He can fail, he can make terrible mistakes, he *never* descends to moral error. It's your great strength. It makes you, in your way, invincible. But as a result you don't forgive people easily, and you take your own falls too hard.'

'What's that supposed to mean?'

'Something I feel about you.'

A harvest moon had risen, full-bellied and yellow. It eased above the coping stones of the courtyard wall and Ax felt himself slipping backwards, falling off the curved flank of the world. Facing the wrong way . . . He understood, this time, that it was conflicted feelings causing the disquiet, not the *feng shui* of Reading Arena. A little touch of transient psychosis. He would lie here and make love with the woman who had ordered the Reading Massacre; who had arguably kept his friend (not Dilip, but something of Dilip) alive in the moment of burning to death; for months. And she had touched his heart. He looked into Li Xifeng's eyes and saw someone who had ordered the massacres, who had condemned the prisoners, and was trying to stay human. He saw himself. A different scale? Fuck that. She's made ruthless choices, well *so have we.* What about when the Chinese invasion happened, and Ax Preston decided to let them do his dirty work? Say I was helpless: I was not. I chose a certain course of action—

The conflict was getting to him. If she asked again, he would have to say no. But he knew that Elder Sister had divined this, and there would be no third invitation, so this was the last time. Talk, say whatever comes into your head.

'Fiorinda can give me hell,' he said, speaking to *jiejie*, the Daoist Nun, as to a true friend. 'But I'm sure of her. She gives me hell the moment I step out of line, but she's part of me. I'll *never* be sure of Sage. I don't know how to deal with how much I love him, I'm a bastard to him sometimes . . . I remember when he insisted his dad had to know we were lovers. I didn't get it. I said, if Joss wants to think we're very good friends who share a girl, strictly no funny business, what's the problem, it's no big deal. This being Joss Pender, the software baron, you see—'

'One of your most useful supporters.'

'Yeah,' Ax sighed, hard. '*Exactly.* It's no big deal – God. Aeons ago now, in our catalogue of disasters, but I can hear myself saying it—'

'There you go again. That doesn't sound like a very shocking crime. Tell me, was it real? The time at Warren Fen, when A—' She still had trouble giving Sage his name. 'When Sage played "Apache" with you two. Norman says he was miming, but I couldn't believe you three would *do* that.'

'Hahaha.'

322

'You were faking! You *wankers*!' Elder Sister pounced on the English word with glee. 'Ha! Now I know your secret and I shall destroy your legend!' She fell on him, they tussled, it swiftly became very sexual. Ax reached for the six-pack he had tucked under a convenient cushion. He was old-fashioned about play-away sex, full jacket, accept no substitutes, no matter what. He'd used condoms last time.

Elder Sister's slim hand came down over his.

'No.'

'Oh . . . Well, okay.'

He let it go and buried the implication: something he would not think about.

In the morning Lieutenant Chu drove him to Reading Station. He got out of the car. 'Keep me on the path to lasting glory,' said the spruce young girl-soldier.

'You make too much of me,' said Ax. 'I'm not who you think I am.'

She looked up at him, wide-open. 'You have become my superstition.'

Sage and Fiorinda picked him up at Bodmin in the old black Volvo. Fiorinda was driving, she did not move over. Sage was folded up in a knot in the rear seat, staring out of the back window. He didn't speak, or look round.

'Well,' said Fiorinda, after several kilometres, 'did you enjoy yourself?'

He'd thought about this conversation and contemplated lying, but there was no point, they'd be onto him at once. 'Yes, in fact. I did. Very much.'

'You going back again?' asked Sage, dispassionately.

'No. The dalliance is over.'

An orphan regret, a fear in case their future peace rested entirely on a planet-destroying ballet dancer's infatuation for 'Ax Preston'; and something that told him it would be okay. She is *jiejie*, she speaks to me as if she knows me, she came towards me in the night garden. She's ruthless, but she won't let me down.

They stopped at Ruthie's to pick up Cosoleth. Ax had a flash, as he walked up the garden path in rich evening sun – between Ruthie's dig-for-victory front beds of courgettes, tomatoes, bean tepees, spinach, onion sets – of a little girl in a blue dress and bare feet running towards him, a little girl of four or five years old, pearly teeth, eyes like stars, a bouncing mass of jet-black curls. The baby was a shock, but the grin was the same; except for a slight deficiency of teeth.

The twin beeches were turning dark when they parked, the light had gone, September again already, and England's still occupied; but wait, next spring. Wait. Fiorinda took Coz indoors, at speed.

'Sage? *Please*—?'

Sage had been loping for the back porch with a bleak, wounded expression, laden with the food trove he and Fiorinda had queued for in Bodmin Town. He dropped the bags, and grabbed the guitar-man. 'Very fucking weird,' muttered Ax, head down, shaken by afterburn, stung by the truth of what Elder Sister had said: I think my shit don't stink . . . 'I swear I'll *never* be a bastard to you again.'

'It wasn't your fault. Ssh. Whole thing, *very* fucking weird.'

But here we are.

Ah, summer, summer, always some kind of hell. Thank God it's over.

Not To Touch The Earth,
Not To See The Sky

I

The Red Deer

In the hollows of the moor there were bald patches, dun and grey, but it was a white world, asleep under the cold low sky. The hinds moved through the landscape in a fairly tight bunch of twelve, with two outliers and a leading dam. The hunters had their eye on the smaller of the outliers. She was their lawful prey, and she was the easiest target. Lying in Darwinian ambush, Fiorinda tried switching between the decent distance of her own eyesight and the indecent close-up of the cross-hair, to see how it would feel to aim at this stretch without aid. If I had an eyesocket gadget, I'd be able to flip to and fro by blinking. I could have movies; I could watch mtv.

'*Don't do that*,' murmured Sage. '*You're gonna only get one chance.*'

She was cold and bored and tired of being ordered around; although she had asked for it. She did not actually *want* to know how to shoot a deer. She pleaded guilty to the crime of wishing her meat could be killed by a nice kind butcher and bought in a shop. But Fiorinda ought to be able to do things like this: me with you in same winter boat, masses, make do and mend, scav' food where can. Also, personal agenda, what kind of no-good mother predator can't bring back dinner to the den?

You just told me not to talk, she thought.

'*This is NOT my world*,' she hissed, '*but I'm coping. Leave me alone.*'

The deer came on placidly. Don't want an eyesocket gadget, ecch. How did creepy intimate tech like that become *ordinary*, when you can't drink the water that comes out of the tap? I just don't get this modern world. This reminded her of when Sage had predicted they'd be like Edwardians watching television, and she turned, incorrigible, to tell him so . . . But the big cat could move very quietly when he wanted to. He was gone. Oh well. She settled to wait for the shot she must take, and the deer came on obediently, into her sights, straight down the line.

A blast of sound both sharp and diffuse, a dagger in bright cloud. The other hinds scooted, the January kill lay on the snow. Now that's a *strange* feeling. Maybe I won't chuck our only high-powered rifle in the Chy after all . . . She shouldered the gun and the game bag, and trudged down. Where the fuck is he, what did I say that was so bad? There was no sign of Sage, but he could be in the little larch wood below their ambush. The poor animal was cleanly dead. She heaved it over, looked at its belly, and opened the DoE Living Off The Land page on her phone. The diagrams looked good, idiot-proofed. I bet I could do this, I can do rabbits. How long should she wait for him? It would be a major coup to start the field-dressing, a disaster if she screwed up. Be careful when you remove the bladder, *do not* let urine spill on the meat. Hm . . . I can sharpen a knife or two. That'd be something.

She tugged out a handful of the deer's coarse coat, tried the edge of the biggest knife; and *another time, another place: this action.* Violent emotion, sensation, swept through her, leaving her desolate with a pounding heart, and in a cold sweat of terror. Sage was coming out of the little wood. She set the heels of her hands to her temples, and fought for context. When you get a snapshot seizure (yep, they are seizures, yep, it is brain damage), you're plunged, it's like an adhesion, into the brainstate of another place and time. It's usually a scary bad place, because that's the charming way the brain works, and you pray it's not from your future, oh please—

She had never taken snapshot, but she had the same problems.

Thick hair, weight behind it. I picked up my father's head by the hair, on the beach at Drumbeg. I stuffed the mouth with salt and sand, and set it where I could see the fucker. He was still mumbling. Oh, he took his time dying—

So that's okay. Can't complain about flashbacks of horrible traumatic events in the past. It's only when they come at you from you don't know where. But she was still trembling so she called Ax anyway, just to hear his voice.

'Ax?'

'Yeah, what is it? Did you do it?'

'Yes . . . Is Coz all right?'

'Depends what you mean by all right,' said Ax dryly.

'What's she done?'

'Several things, I want to sit her down and make sure our stories agree, before you two get back. My cat is under Mar's bed, I can't yell at this bad baby without Min being convinced he's doomed, and Coz just laughs. Wolves, sledge, all over it. I'm trying to write this song, my brother's not picking up the phone. I might have to do a virtual house invasion to catch his attention.' No rest for the President-elect, Elder Sister had decreed that the Chosen Few must produce an album (not a rez, the squares didn't like that term). All new songs, before the spring—

'She's here, you want to talk to her?'

Blood on the snow, Cosoleth talking animatedly, in what sounded almost like English. Ax on the voicephone, cheerful and wry, everything's okay.

Sage sat down beside her, grinning white and wide as the living skull—

'Was I pissing you off? It's just I thought I'd be buying my venison from a fancy Chinese-owned supermarket chain by now. What's taking them so long?'

'Nah,' he said. 'You weren't. I realised you wanted it to be your own kill.'

'Oh.' She thought about it. 'I suppose I did. I am a sick puppy.'

'D'you want to dress her with me?'

'Oh yes. I have to do that.'

A steaming pile of offal in the snow. Sage dragged the sled to the road, where they stowed the body into the back of the Powdermill Inn's Land Rover. So this is the way we live, a year on from the Reich-In-Hiding. Killing Bambi's mother, butchering her and parcelling her out to our Chy Valley cadres. Hoping the fuel ration won't be cut again, bracing ourselves for the new job, getting attached to this interim life. Bambi's mother had to be hung by her heels in the back porch, with a clean bucket under her nose. The insides deemed fit for eating had to be cleaned, packed up and dumped in the fox-proof cold-box. Finally the hunters stumbled indoors and plunged down by the hearth, keening and nursing their fingers. Cosoleth was napping in her new, grown-up cot (handed on by Ruthie's family).

'Got some long-distance email for you, Fio,' said Ax.

It was from Norman Soong, who had served his time in the punishment of obscurity. He had a lot to say. The best bit was when he got down on his knees in his gorgeous robe and chanted at full volume, kowtowing vigorously—

I SWEAR THERE WILL BE NO NUDITY
I SWEAR BY ALL I HOLD SACRED
I SWEAR BY MY OWN,
BELOVED,

BEAUTIFULLY CONSTRUCTED
MEAT AND POTATOES!
THERE WILL BE NO NUDITY, OH GODDESS OF ROCK!

He wanted Fiorinda to tour China.

'What's he talking about? Does he mean *just me*?'

'Sounds like it, my babe.'

The three of them sat on the hearthrug looking at Norman, frozen on their tv screen, in the act of thumping his liondog head on a gaudy carpet.

'I think you should do it,' said Ax.

Fiorinda wrapped her arms around her knees, feeling dazed. She shook her head, meaning give me a moment: but Ax was barely started.

'Listen to me. The music biz hasn't changed just because the centre of the world moved to Xi'an. Art for a cause is a blip on the balance sheet. Big-name rock musicians are supposed to be idiots. You're not an idiot, you're not a cash cow, you're the voice of these times and *you're a woman*. You can't let that go, sweetheart.'

'He's right, Fiorinda. You wrote the songs, you've been the singer.'

The tiger stretched at length, Ax with his timber wolf look of concentration, were looking at her so nakedly it made her blush, and went straight to her sex. She thought of blood on the snow, the overwhelming snapshot flash—

'Shit. Where's this coming from, all of a sudden?'

'It's not sudden,' said Sage. 'It's the way we feel.'

'What if I . . . What if I want to, but I don't know if I can handle it?'

'We'll be there,' he told her. 'First time out, anyway. We can take a couple of weeks off. You don't want to make it too long, just whet their appetites.'

'We'd be there any time you wanted us,' said Ax. He grinned. 'Except later on you know, we'd have to think of Coz's schooling—'

They cracked up. Fiorinda stuck her fingers in her ears, and stared at the fire. 'You're wrong. There's been someone exactly like me. Rufus O'Niall, remember? He fed on his fans until he had the power to rip the world to shreds—'

'That's not relevant, sweetheart. You're *not* Rufus.'

Sage swooped on her, across the rug. 'An' it's a little late to worry about *you* getting boosted to critical.' He kissed her nose and drew back, blue eyes smiling, amused and tender. 'Isn't it, Fiorinda?'

. . .

'I'm going to think about it,' she said, at last.

She had a feeling like wings, cramped from long disuse, beginning to unfold. But that dry red pelt, the dead weight resisting her will, the shock of terror—

The threat of the Guangdong camps, held over foreigners of Chinese ancestry, was being stepped down. The mechanism had proved invaluable, particularly when the satellite countries were first annexed. It would continue to be deployed against dangerous extremists. But Ax had persuaded Elder Sister that it was a terror tool, its time was over; and he was right. She was still glad she had expedited Ax's own National Citizenship papers. Systems of that kind have a life of their own, difficult to control; and are often most dangerous when they are dying.

The more formidable task of screening of his family and his associates for any taint of pernicious delusion continued, in the remorseless depths of a secret bureaucracy. Ax and his partners, whose involvement with the delusion had been so intimate, had been declared blameless by Elder Sister and her Generals: this fiat made it all the more important that the routine vetting should be thorough. There must be no suggestion of special treatment.

Li Xifeng was with Wang in his office at Rivermead. It was mid-morning. They were talking about the withdrawal of the 2nd AMID army, which they both called 'the Retreat', for modesty's sake. In reality they were delighted with their achievement, despite the trick that had been played on them. The 'liberalisation' of forbidden tech had been left in Chinese hands, while China's own secrets stayed under wraps. In time China would reap a splendid harvest; and it was a bonus that the Zen Self Champion considered immersion code and bi-location harmless. (Sage's opinion meant more to them than they cared to admit—) Sphere leaders found England's promotion acceptable, while the candidacy of Europe could move as slowly as China liked. There were voices in Europe muttering that the English had been too modest in their demands: Elder Sister and her Generals were aware of these elements, and would take no action unless it proved necessary. The truth was, the Triumvirate had been looking for *England*'s best advantage, and they'd known where to stop.

The conquest of Europe, which had presented such terrors, would prove to have been almost bloodless. The little country they both found so romantic had taken shocking casualties, relatively speaking. But there had been no way to avoid that, and it had cleared the road.

'So you will not see him again?'

Xifeng looked into her English tea cup. 'No. Not in the way you mean.'

Wang knew that he could tease her: she liked to be teased about Ax Preston. 'Maybe you'll be able to arrange a yearly meeting, between the Weaver Girl and the Cowherd.'

'Nonsense. I value him purely as my guru.' She put her head on one side and contemplated, with a reminiscent smile that broke into her three-cornered grin.

'What is it?'

'Hahaha. Little do you know. He has orgasms as long as a woman's.'

'Ah! I knew there was something practical in your choice!'

'But I *do* value him as a guru,' said Xifeng, soberly, leaning back in her armchair with a sigh, the cup warming her hands. It was chilly in the Rivermead offices, as was their rule on campaign. No self-indulgent waste of heating power.

'So do I,' agreed Wang. 'He's a remarkable person.'

'Mm . . . He has partners and he loves them, Wang. They are always on his mind. It's better so, I need the guru far more than I need the lover.'

They spoke of Fiorinda and her Volunteer Initiative, of the Minister for Gigs and his covert work ethic; very satisfied with their protégées. A clerical officer arrived to deliver some documents. The man was respectfully keen to depart, so they told him to wait in the outer office. It might be they'd want to question him. Hand-copied documents, delivered person to person, meant something was hot. The General and his leader found they were looking at the Pernicious Delusion Screening results for a handful of Ax's associates. The selection seemed random, none of the names leapt out. A young woman called Virginia D. had been tagged for further appraisal. They looked for a reason and found it in her medical records.

'Let's get the clerk in here and ask him if he knows what this is about.'

'No,' said Xifeng, frowning at the thumbnail headshot of Virginia D. 'Have you no eyes? That's Cherry Dawkins.'

'Ah, I see. Original name, Virginia. The Powerbabe has a sense of humour.'

Wang went to the door and told the clerical officer that he could go.

They checked again, in the hope of finding some mistake. But it was undoubtedly Cherry Dawkins, one of Ax's closest associates. A very pretty young woman, with velvety dark skin, fine eyes; who wore her crisp hair shorn close, but not shaven. She was twenty-seven years old. She played saxophone in the Snake Eyes Big Band, which was lead by her boyfriend, Rob Nelson, Ax's deputy.

Xifeng approved of the Powerbabes. They were sexy, of course, but they were hard-working, right-thinking artists, not greedy half-clad prostitutes.

The problem was a biometric scan scooped in London, before the Few had been released and allowed to travel to Sussex for the Ashdown Festival; it had held bad news for Virginia D. 'Here, our pretty black girl had the White Death,' said Wang. He set the second, disturbing record beside the first. 'Here, a few weeks later, according to another scan, she didn't.'

Security scans were interminable, the vast majority unseen by human eye. It looked as if Cherry Dawkins' phantom tuberculosis had gone completely unnoticed until the Pernicious Delusion vetting discovered it. But the documents they had were clerical grade, and not very informative. The sender was anonymous.

'We should investigate this ourselves,' said Li Xifeng. 'I want to see the data.'

Wang nodded. 'Shall I clean up the paper trail?'

She shook her head. 'Let's find out if we are in trouble first.'

The Chinese knew precisely what had happened at Vireo Lake. The Pentagon scientists, ignoring the stark implications of the new neuroscience, and the warnings of the Zen Self experimenters, had recruited neuronauts with measurable psychic ability (and testing as stable otherwise, a 'Catch 22' indeed). The A-team had – collectively – broken the mind/matter barrier, becoming plenipotent in information space. But they had paid the price predicted by the theorists and died – possibly by suicide – hopelessly insane. Scans taken at the moment of their death showed the damage to the frontal lobes one would expect in savagely advanced schizophrenia. Rufus O'Niall had been a rare monster, a threat unlikely to arise again. Vireo Lake had proved that the *real* danger was the slight, almost undetectable 'magic' power that could be used to fuel another A-team.

China had started screening for 'A-team candidates' immediately. In time Li Xifeng planned to make it routine for all her subjects. So far only PLA recruits, re-education camp detainees, criminals, and candidates for public office were covered – apart from cases where suspicion had been directly aroused (oracles and magicians, mediums, fortune-tellers, faith-healers). Investigations very rarely went beyond a review of records collected for normal purposes, and a cognitive scan hidden in a medical check-up. The objective tests were not recommended lightly. The testing itself was harsh; if there was cause for alarm, then torture and forcible desexing followed, without exception. The cruelty was necessary. Torture was known to bring latent psychic power out of hiding, and the link between sexual potency and 'magic' was considered proven.

Toby Starborn had suffered this penalty. He had not, in fact, been punished for his connection with the Second Chamber. His affiliations and his artworks had given grounds for suspicion, but he'd been doomed by his brain's response to the drug called 'snapshot'.

Psychic activity *above* the 'precursor type' level identified by the Pentagon meant immediate execution. This potency had never yet been found, but Xifeng would sign the order, retrospectively, without hesitation, should the need arise. There must never be another A-team. The in-depth screening was highly sensitive. China was still claiming that the A-team event hadn't happened: they could not admit to using evidence acquired by forbidden tech, or analysis based on the new neuroscience. The unlucky precursor types were punished, officially, purely for the taint of pernicious delusion, and they did not reveal the details of their interrogation, under pain of death. Of course the secret files were instantly accessible to Elder Sister.

They went looking, using Wang's desk screen.

'Faith-healing,' said Wang, 'is generally innocent. Mysterious, but harmless.'

'Spontaneous remission in TB isn't unusual,' remarked Xifeng, unruffled. 'The bacillus retreats, with rest and good diet. I expect that's what we'll find. Either that, or a simple clerical error in the software.'

But when they examined the evidence, it was damning.

General Wang watched her quiet profile as she read the screen and was stirred by awe. Decency and forbearance were so much the first laws of Elder Sister's rule that one forgot this other, equally necessary face. *She is death,* he thought. She wields merciless, arbitrary power: and that's what we need, that's the way it has to be.

II

When The Map Is Unrolled, The Dagger Is Revealed

The day that Wang and Li Xifeng investigated their leaked document there was a Utopian Futures conference in Central Hall. It was large, it was chaotic, it was full of organisers running around panicking. It would have been making Crisis Europe veterans feel young again, except that the violence was missing: that constant, vibrant sense of *violence* which had marked Dissolution Summer in this dull little country, and indeed the legendary Flood Countries Conference, when Celtic *vs* Techno-Green fire-fights had enlivened the stolid burghers of Amsterdam.

'Of course the absence is an illusion. Violence has simply been contained once more, packed away in olive-green uniform. It is still the spectre at our feast.'

'You think that sounds clever, don't you, Alain? Go on, convince me we'd get more done if there was a few mad eco-warriors with guns in here—'

Big George towered over the little Breton to the point of absurdity, as if they had been bred under different atmospheric pressures, but Alain was not intimidated.

'It was thrilling. This is a school outing, only missing the head girl.'

'Ah, but she's with us in spirit,' remarked a *Movie Sucré* hench-person. 'Behold, the amazing guitar-man rides again.'

Ax had emerged into the foyer outside Great Hall, in conversation with Lucy Wasserman; their party hedged around with mediafolk. Alain watched them go by, with a grin of malign sympathy.

'The stuffed and mounted Mr Preston. We should doff our hats, as to a funeral cortège. Nothing is *getting done* here, George. We are décor, we are relegated. Go on, find yourself some hymn-singing. I believe it's in the Quiet Room.'

'Don't look to me for sympathy,' said George. 'The sound of political activists faffing around doing nothing but talk is music to my fucking ears, an' I hope it lasts.'

'Hahaha. Lie back and enjoy it, George.'

The brother Heads quit the scene – George had Peter Stannen in tow, like a basking shark attended by a solemn little pilot fish. Alain smiled fondly after them, and looked around for further prey. He had generously appointed himself gadfly, since Mr Preston was on prefect duty, and Sage was fully occupied. The live-path for virtual delegates had been misplaced; they were trapped in the Great Hall, fighting with the fixed seating, and nobody knew how to undo the damage.

The French congratulated themselves on having come to London in flesh and blood. But Eurostar running again, my God. It really tells you that something is over.

Flood Country Coastlands: Does Time Stand Still? Islam Without Oil. The Camp System: Models For Regeneration . . . Haiku ac Hokku Gymraeg Gweithdy. Wolf Culture, Concentrated Protein Culture, Invisible Turbines Laid Bare (likely to be a slanging match) . . . From the amorphous jiggling of this kind of soup, in times of revolution, new governance arises that may last for hundreds of years. How can it happen? It's one of those *where does the weirdness go* problems.

Fiorinda wandered around with Coz, pondering the mysteries and looking for a carpeted place where a baby could crawl without getting her head stepped on. Or try her new trick, which was walking. Furniture, I need furniture she can hold onto . . . Ruthie Maynor said, *an early walker is a peck of trouble*. Fiorinda wasn't sure if this was ancient North Cornwall lore, or observation. She found Allie in the Great Hall, with Walter Ridley. The Cumbrian centaur was paying his respects, in wonderfully Victorian style. For he had devoted his youth to the Cause of Science, never had a lady love. Sound in wind and limb, Shield Ring millionaire, lovely beard . . . She left them to it, and went looking for somebody else she knew. Allie could always walk away. The afternoon sessions were closing, the only people trying to catch her eye were punters, and *I* think I'm on a break. Ax and Alain were sitting on the great stairs, with a bunch of Île Saint Louis Très Stupid Costumes Équipage.

'Have you tried the Quiet Room?' suggested Ax. 'That might be good.'

'Isn't there a Methodist strand in there? Cack said there was hymn-singing.'

The Stupid Costumes sniggered, for no good reason. Cosoleth cried, 'A'tz! A'tz! A'tz! Eh! Eh! Eh!' (all the grasp of the English language she'll ever need); and fought to get out of Fiorinda's arms.

'I'll take her,' said Ax. 'She'll be a useful accessory. But you owe me.'

'Where are you going?'

'Got to break up Islam Without Oil. They're talking about the Great Chastisement, which, as you know, refers to an event that didn't happen.'

'You'd think the mullahs could hold a simple idea like that in their heads.'

Ax left with the baby, Fiorinda sat down.

'No wonder the English and the Chinese ended up in bed together,' remarked Alain sweetly. 'Our liberators could have written the book on *Alice in Wonderland*.'

Speculation about Ax's special duties was rife, and there was nothing to be done about that, it's not 'leaks', it's human nature. The Chinese didn't seem worried. Alain, you can fuck off, thought Fiorinda—

'Maybe that's why she says Ax thinks like a Chinese.'

'Whereas Absurdism is not nonsense. Absurdism is formal, disciplined, the Satanism of the rational, the Lord's Prayer recited backwards—'

The crowd streamed by, in all its colourful dress codes, in and out of halls raised to celebrate the mass revolution of Wesleyan Methodism, a hundred-odd years ago. 'People will look back,' said Fiorinda softly, 'if there are such things as people, five hundred years from now, and it will be like rings on a tree stump, always the same, always the same, always heading for this. Everything we did, everything that happened to us and seemed so vital, was just a last little fractal iteration on the long, long rise of the World State—'

'Which may never come,' Alain pointed out, tetchily. 'Although everybody seems to have forgotten that Antarctica exists. Also the trifling matter of South America, and those Feds.' He laughed. 'Ah, Fiorinda. If youth only knew! The opportunities we wasted! Don't you wish this was Dissolution Summer?'

'You're joking.' She watched the crowd; thinking about being a global megastar, and rejecting the idea with relief. Bird, gilded cage, had enough of that. But a music career of her own design, that would be brilliant, was it possible?

'I thought I'd crashed a very stupid party, full of nutcases, where I didn't belong, and it turned out to be my life . . . Just the normal teenage experience, except for the blood and the dead bodies. Oh, and the weird stuff that didn't really happen.'

'Swiftly, her lyrics pass from the personal to the universal. What are you doing after this, beautiful Fiorinda?'

Uncanny. Try to flirt with her, and immediately one or other of them will materialise. The former Aoxomoxoa collapsed in a gangling heap, tipped his fleecy yellow head back and closed his eyes. 'Thank God, geek-free. Just lemme lie here.'

'Is it fixed?'

'Nah. We've had to send them all home. Well, we didn't have to but we were bored. Imploding novel technology fatigue sets in. The music line up will be starting on schedule, more or less. Like I care.' Sage opened his eyes. 'We're heading off to Lambeth soon, Alain. D'you want to come and eat with us?'

'*Dommage.* I'm afraid I'm Reiched out.'

They had to go and reclaim Min first. They'd come up to London on the sleeper, a fine way to travel. Ax's cat had been impounded by the Central Hall porters, hope they haven't kept him in the same room as any dogs—

Chip was in his room at the Snake Eyes Commune, two floors up at the back of the original house. (There'd once been one tall, old terraced house: now there were two side-by-side, and one across the road.) He'd moved in after Christmas, having ceded the Notting Hill pad to Chez and Verlaine. They were getting used to being a couple, very sweet and shy with each other, it was unbearable.

He sat in the winter dusk, looking at his single bed, and thinking of the old flat. The long period when their furniture had consisted of a waterbed, a few old sideboards and a virtual décor controller . . . The night the two of them had decided they would take on Fergal Kearney (*my God*), and rescue Fiorinda from durance vile. His new Mickey Mouse counterpane looked very mickey mouse . . . I must get myself some stuff, he thought. Do I have enough money to buy a house? How do you buy a house? He had no idea. Verlaine had looked after their finances.

What happened to never growing up, was it always just me?

Two floors below the big commune table was spread. There was socialising going on, while the cadres waited for Ax and Sage and Fiorinda to get here from Central Hall. Chip was listening carefully because he knew Rox had arrived, he'd heard hir voice. S/he was almost certain to come looking for him, with kindly sympathy, and he couldn't stand the idea. If he heard the thump of hir cane he'd have to leap up and bounce merrily down the stairs—

Roar, screech, slam! Roar screech slam! Roar screech slam!

Chip had dived from his chair, and crossed the room well *down*, as if bullets or broken glass were flying, before he knew it. Traumatic stress flashback, but when he saw what was going on in the street, it turned out to be the right reaction.

My God, he breathed, *look at that!*

but there was no one beside him, missing you so much, Pippin—

BAM BAM BAM—!

He ran downstairs in the dark, in his socks, and peered from the first-floor landing: ooh boy, an armed police raid in anybody's language. Serious numbers of helmed, booted, gauntleted Chinese; he couldn't get a clear look at the insignia. He clutched the banister rail, like a frightened child in a nightmare. His view was of the hallway, full of uniforms, faceless faceplates and guns. He couldn't see any communards. He heard *putonghua* at a savage, barking pitch, then Rob's voice and Felice, going *what d'you think you're doing? Let's all calm down* . . . They were ordered to SHUT UP! (he understood that). Then nothing but Chinese voices yelling, the hammer of booted feet, doors crashed open, breaking glass, furniture overturned—

What's happened? What the fuck, what the fuck?

He realised he might be the only person who hadn't been rounded up.

He tiptoed back to his room. His phone, of course, was dead as a duck. Time warp. The Reich-In-Hiding had lived in fear of something like this: the Chinese will turn on us, and *they will give no warning.* So now it's come. He tried to remember what he was supposed to do, and had thoughts of going down and blagging the kids out of it. The Snake Eyes teens, the little ones, Marlon and Silver and Pearl. He would be witty and eloquent, with his basic phrases of *putonghua* . . . no, better not, it won't sound the way it does in your head. Better idea, he must warn the Triumvirate. There was a landline phone on the first floor, in the big band's office. It was worth a try. He was very scared. He thought of climbing down a drainpipe and running off down the street: but the landline idea won out . Hu's military police (he'd worked out the insignia) were rushing about like a tide of rock and rubble. He made it to the office and dialled, manually, Fiorinda's no-such-number, the emergency one, which was not traceable to her real phone number. The set was antique, it had strange foibles, he couldn't tell if he'd got through. Try again, that's an improvement, but fuck, what do I say? If we're in trouble and they're not, I might implicate them. But if they come here they'll get arrested, full house—

What about the codeword that had meant the invasion?

Iphigenia, he gasped, as gauntlets grabbed him, and threw him away from the desk. The phone went flying. A rifle muzzle stabbed his chest, eyes behind a visor, glaring madly. Okay, okay . . . Now, remember you're a good guy, Chip. Project good guy vibes, you're *not* a criminal. And don't panic, and be polite.

'Who were you calling?'

'The police, of course.'

'You were not calling the police.'

'I *meant* to call the police. Not 999, the local number, the local station.'

'Who were you calling?'

He'd been thrown into an APV, and brought in here with a blanket over his head. He was in what looked like an ordinary police station interview room. He hadn't seen anybody else. They gave up on the phone call, and asked him did he know a Virginia Dawkins. The Chinese *must* know who that was, but he wasn't going to take a chance. He'd never been in this situation, but he'd heard that once you start answering the questions you don't stop. Stonewall. He asked where he was, what was all this about, and what had happened to his friends. He said he was outraged and he refused to say anything until they told him what going on. They asked him about Chez's *medical history*. He was genuinely confused, but it dawned on him, in a flood of horror. He knew what they must have found out, and he knew he was done for, because the Chinese had seen that flood of horror. He wasn't hooked up to anything, they hadn't asked his permission to take biometric readings (joke); but it was obvious.

Everything changed.

Later he was in another room, he knew not where, a very ominous room. They told him that they knew he'd tried to contact the Triumvirate.

'You wanted to smear them with your filth. *You* are the guilty one.'

'No I wasn't. I didn't. I'm not guilty of anything.'

'Soon you'll be questioned further,' said the one in uniform.

He was left alone. He was still in his own clothes. He hadn't been searched, just shaken down for weapons; his dead phone and personal belongings taken, such as they were. He thought he'd been in custody about twenty-four hours but he wasn't sure. No clocks, no meals, although they'd given him water. Maybe it had been drugged. I have disappeared, he thought. I am never going to leave here.

The room was a neuro lab, and that's not all it was. Mind games and tactics went through his head, a prepared statement, fallbacks, scrabbling ways he might save his life. Cherry was poorly when we were in detention. Nothing was said but we were worried . . . All right, I thought it was TB, and it's a notifiable disease. It's stupid, but that's why I was scared when you said 'medical history'. That's absolutely all there is to it! Okay, so I was terrified. I have a right to be terrified. I thought it meant you'd killed her. You can't call that incriminating!

Oh yes they can. He looked around him. Prepared statement, fallback, bullshit.

If I don't want to go out betraying Fiorinda and fucking up utterly, I need a cast-iron strategy for dealing with being tortured; and I need it now.

Once upon a time in California they'd been afraid they were about to be attacked by the worst kind of Neurobomb, runaway chain reaction, a formerly human thing called the Fat Boy. The Fat Boy can tell you to turn inside out and eat your own guts, and you'll do it; and it will be what you do for a subjective eternity. The Fat Boy's mind works like that. Sage had taught them how to die, a surefire neuro switch they could flip, in case that was the only way out.

The lesson was long gone. Brain chemistry doesn't last, neurons don't last, brainstates have to scramble back into life in new shoes every time you remember something. But he started to think about that ranchero house in California, on the beach. The crimson bougainvillaea and the dry fountain, the ten-foot palms in pots that blew over and rolled about in a rainstorm. The drained spa in the basement where they used to hang out. Blue walls, blue empty pools. Dilip used to say he could see ripples of light on the ceiling; the ghosts of water. The memories made Chip happy. Drained, dry, but happy. He left the interview table, where he'd been sitting like a good child, and sat with his back to the wall and his arms around his knees, in a corner. Not a toilet to piss in, which is not fair. But he didn't need a piss. There were ripples on the ceiling, ghosts of water, little curves like birds' wings, crossing and recrossing each other. He watched them, and knew he would be all right.

'Chip?'

'Hey, Chip?'

Sage was calling him. He didn't know where he was. *Where was I just now, is this real or was the other place real?* He opened his eyes, or maybe they were already open, and saw the torture room. He was still sitting in his corner, back to the wall. Sage was in front of him, tall Sage in a grey hoodie and black jeans, squatting down so they were eye-to-eye. Some olive-green trousers there too. He followed them upward, and it was General Wang Xili standing beside Sage, in his five-star uniform. No one else in the room. Sage and General Wang, he thought. Am I rescued? Wang had a very strange, blown-away expression. Sage's blue eyes were smiling, but—

'Hallo.' His throat was very dry. 'What happened, Sage?'

'You need some water, here.' Chip took the water bottle, his hands were very stiff, the fingers didn't want to bend. He sipped. 'Can you stand up?'

'I think so. Am I rescued?'

'Not yet,' said Sage. 'C'mon, you need to sleep.'

Sage and the General walked him to another cell. Chip had to lean against Sage, because his legs would barely carry him. There was a bed with sheets and blankets, a cupboard and a toilet and a basin. It still looked ominous.

'What's going on, Sage? Did I fuck up?'

'No you didn't,' said the boss, still with that smile that was too deep, coming from too far away, a smile from the edge of the universe: and gave him a hug. 'Not at all. You'll be treated okay now. Get some sleep.'

There was a guard outside the door of the cell, who saluted, staring straight ahead. Sage walked with the General into the empty, cream-walled corridors.

'Are you having problems with any of the other prisoners?'

One of the other prisoners was Aoxomoxoa's sixteen-year-old son.

'No,' said Wang. 'Can you *explain* that?'

'What Chip did? Yeah, I think so. It's kind of a psychic suicide pill, I taught them how to do it a couple of years ago . . . I don't know why he isn't dead. Must be something he added on his own.'

The Triumvirate had not been arrested. They'd been told that the reason for the raid on Lambeth was classified; they had not been able to find out where their friends were being held. They hadn't been able to reach the Generals or Elder Sister, they'd been dealing with obstructive, openly aggressive subordinates. But Chip had been causing such consternation that the Chinese had finally broken down and called in the expert. He'd been in the torture room for three days, apparently. He'd been left to look at his fate, the torturers had come back to find him sitting in the corner clothed in quivering light, and nobody had been able to get near him.

They walked. Sage didn't want to leave the fort. He wanted to shout out their names, to see if anyone shouted back from behind the narrow doors. No guards except outside Chip's new cell, did that mean the others were elsewhere? Already dead? He kept hold of himself. He must not get locked up.

'Chip was a neuronaut with me, he followed the Zen Self path for quite a way. No one thought he was a front-runner, but we may have to change our minds. Yogi tricks are *not* magic, Wang. It's a completely different thing.'

They'd reached double doors, where there were guards. He dimly recognised the way he'd come in. Wang looked at Sage out of that stunned wonderment, beyond horror, beyond shock, and shook his head. He spoke almost gently.

'No . . . No, Aoxomoxoa. The case is clear, the evidence is overwhelming, the culprit has betrayed himself. There is nothing whatever you can do.'

You want to bet? thought Sage. You want to fucking bet, bastard?

'What happens now?'

'You'll be taken back to Reading.'

Fiorinda walked up and down the concourse that had been Rivermead's great solar, reading the signs. A strip of military utility carpet, beaten by many feet. A drinks machine, serving hot water, green or black tea; like the one on the landship that had taken them to Anglia. Smart noticeboards, homely drawing-pin noticeboards, on the inside wall and freestanding. All the writing was in Chinese characters. Spartan armchairs, slippery stiff benches . . . People passed through here. Maybe they met, accidentally on purpose, to exchange a few useful words; corridor talk. Today the big doors had been closed at either end and the graceful space was haunted by its former identity. The western wall of glass was the same, and there's the Arts and Crafts enamelled fireplace, disused; there's where my piano stood.

Ax had tried to call Elder Sister at once. He hadn't been able to get hold of her. Bad sign, bad sign. The London Chinese had treated them like shit. The vibe was that Hu was responsible, and he was totally hostile. In the end they'd been told they must come to Reading. They'd left Coz and Min at Joss Pender's. They'd seen Elder Sister and Wang Xili. Bad, very bad. Inhuman faces, police state voices. They'd been given a room to sleep in, with three camp beds in it, they'd been told they were not under arrest. They'd had the unsuspected horrors of the Pernicious Delusion Screening explained to them. Your friends have betrayed you, there was a viper in their midst. Denounce them! Denounce your own gullibility! Read out this statement of abject contrition!

Are you kidding? Do you think we don't have terror régimes in the west, do you think we don't know we're screwed whatever we say, you'll burn us anyway: do you think we never met people like you before?

After the abortive interview they'd agreed it was time to quit. They'd hit the wall, at last, that had been waiting for them since day one. Then Sage had been summoned to London – very strange vibes. But he'd called to report what was happening, and nothing had changed, except for the worse. So Fiorinda had asked to see Elder Sister alone. She was waiting here because Sage was back, he and Ax were going to talk to the planet-destroyer first, explain the real situation.

Then the roof comes down and hits the water and I GO UNDER.

The fate of the Snake Eyes communards was not clear. There was a chance they might turn out to be Chinese, and just get sent for indefinite re-education. The Few were going to be tortured. Not just Chip, all of them. Then the men would be castrated and the women's external and internal sexual organs surgically excised. Ferdelice, Mamba, Silver and Pearl Wing would live in jail until they were old enough, and *then* they would be tortured, etc. Marlon was old enough now. This was going to happen because at Ashdown, over a year ago, Fiorinda had noticed that Chez was looking sick, and had blessed her. She'd thought nothing of it, or very little of it. Bless. A formula she'd invented when she was in green nazi hell, to comfort herself when everything had seemed cursed. Meaning *be good, have a nice life,* or some such fucking harmless thing. She wondered what the torturers would do to Rox, who had been unlucky enough to get caught in the sweep. How do you strip sexual potency from someone who has already opted to be neuter?

She walked up and down, her arms wrapped tight around her body, thinking of when she'd been kept here as a prisoner by her father.

Are we downhearted? Fuckit, no. Angry enough to spit. Just getting a little dissociated, getting scared of what's going through my mind—

Elder Sister let herself in, and shut the doors. She was in uniform, she looked like a stripling boy, a Chinese Polly Oliver, except for all the damned stars. Fiorinda was wearing the same clothes she'd been wearing when things exploded, oops can't make a social impression, too bad. They walked toward each other and stood, Elder Sister keeping her distance.

'So, you are the hopeful monster.'

'That's how Sage looks at it. Not me.'

'Then you are, potentially, a human weapon of mass destruction.'

'No comment.'

Elder Sister stared and stared. 'You three have treated me like a child!'

'You *are* a child,' snapped Fiorinda. 'Whatever it is they give you to keep you looking so pretty, it makes you into a six-year-old, and planet earth is your sandbox.'

'Is this a catfight? Are we fighting?'

'You tell me.'

Elder Sister was completely impervious. It made Fiorinda mad.

'You know what? Your so-called "Pernicious Delusion Screening" is a fucking *farce*, if you'll excuse my rockstar language. You cannot exterminate the leaky mind, it's always going to be there, it's a Bell curve, not a disease. You know what you're doing? You're helping the pernicious delusion to grow big and strong, and if you were to snag anyone really dangerous, such as me, you might as well *hook them up to a polygraph*.'

'We know that. That is why the Few must be treated the same as Chip.'

Fiorinda glared in contempt. 'You think they're isolated? I don't mean your stupid "precursor types", I mean the neurons in their heads. Fucking hell, you're a totalitarian leader. Don't tell me you don't understand that human information space, made of the neurons in all of our heads, forms a single population, and fitness selection works on it, same as it works everywhere. It's like trapping rats, the survivors just get smarter. You'll create a culture of terror. *If you're lucky,* that will be the height of your achievement.'

Elder Sister's hand flew up, imperiously. 'The raid was a mistake,' she said. 'Let me speak in confidence. It was ordered by Hu Qinfu, who is a very old friend of mine. He's jealous of Wang . . . Wang Xili made an error of judgement. He had formed a liaison with a high-class hooker, a convert to our cause. She claimed she was a close friend of the inner circle. He thought he could use her to get a response from the "virtual ghost" signal. We knew what it was, we could not activate it, it was frustrating. She was plausible, she got away with crucial information. The consequences were arguably very costly.'

Not least for Dian, thought Fiorinda.

'I did not punish Wang, so Hu,' both hands now, palm outwards, a sharp flick of the wrists, 'took his revenge, though I will never say that to him. He knows he should have handled this differently. But what he did was by the book. The capital is his command, the Screening Office had reported cause for great alarm. It's done, and I have no wish to undo it. The evidence is damning. It is *not* remission, it is *not* faith-healing, it has the signature. I cannot release anyone involved, I am sorry. The Few must suffer the penalties.'

No use telling her torture is hateful. She knows that but she believes this system of hers works. Fiorinda marshalled herself, trying to be patient.

'I'm not a doctor. If I'd known that Chez was really ill, I'd have told her she had to see a doctor. I'd have told her we have to keep the rules. But I didn't know. She didn't seem so bad. I didn't know about your precious Pernicious Delusion screening, either, how could I? You're the people who said magic didn't exist, that the A-team never happened. I've always protected them, it was a chaotic time, I was *distracted*.'

'You offer yourself instead of your friends,' said Polly Oliver. 'No, it doesn't work. They have been "too close to the fire", as you Westerners say. They must be regarded as a hideous danger, the same as Chip himself.'

'Listen. Just *listen* to me. The internal world and the external world change places, things of the spirit manifest in the material. What happened in the torture room was one of those slips. You people saw Chip as he is on the inside. INNOCENT AND BEYOND YOUR POWER TO HARM HIM! You thought that was weird? Your precious *di* is making the barrier shakier, are you going to stop using it? He *did not* fix Cherry's TB. It was me. DO YOU GET THAT? What do you think I should do?'

Fiorinda turned on her heel, paced with her arms wrapped around her body and head down, and came back, bright-eyed, breathing fast.

'Remember when Ax came here and met you for the first time? Whoa! Elder Sister! The big secret! Suppose we call this the Triumvirate's big secret? We two agree it should go no further, we are nice people and everything calms down?'

She was close enough to feel that Elder Sister was taller, that's too close. She backed off. The woman in uniform was shaking her head, immoveable.

'Well, scratch that. It wasn't likely. So it's up to me. I won't let my friends be tortured. There'll be different solutions, I'll have to pick one. Suppose I make it so that the first covert scan, where Chez had TB, disappears, somehow, accidentally? Once I've done it everyone including me will be living in the world I made, and we'll never know the difference. It should be okay. *The world changes all the time.* Usually we're not aware of it, no more than we're aware of the dancing atoms in a tabletop, but my father could hack the game and so can I. Okay, I'm not my father, I don't smash and grab. Every circumstance has to agree with my little change, back there November before last. I'm going to solve this in the information, the way Sage would do it, in the code, in the os and 1s. The volume is unbelievable, but I can get there if I let myself flow, except, whoops, I see a mistake. I have to focus on that mistake but ohmigod there's another, so I hit that . . . This single point phase mistake business is not local, this is *full of holes into other places.* Oh shit, oh shit, I'm going to have to leap to another level, oh fuck, maybe I need to be where the A-team were to get at this. Maybe I'm in danger of becoming the Fat Boy—!'

She bared her teeth. 'Do you see what I mean? You know that the A-team were schizophrenic when they died. The Neurobomb is a human weapon that has to be insane to exist. Do you notice how my voice is changing, my mood is changing, when I think about doing what I need to do? I can do it, but it'll drive me crazy. Crazier. Don't make me do it. *Don't make me.*'

'This is an empty threat,' said Elder Sister. 'First you confess to a healing miracle, clearly committed by the viper Chip Desmond. Now you tell me you "could do" something spectacularly evil. Then you say you won't do it, and if you did, I would not know that anything had happened. Am I supposed to be frightened?'

'You're a very stupid damned fool if you are not.'

'Please calm down and think before you speak. I notice that you are talking as if I believe that your father, the possibly psychic green nazi leader assassinated by your lover, really was a natural "Neurobomb". That is quite unwarranted!'

'Give me a break,' snarled Fiorinda. 'You're not just knocking out A-team potential. You're looking for another Rufus with that screening, and I WONDER what you plan to do if you ever catch one!'

Silence, five-star Polly Oliver's infuriating cool unbroken.

It was all going away from Fiorinda, except for the need to speak. 'Let me tell you about me and my father. I met him when I was twelve, if you don't count that I knew him until I was three. He'd always taken an interest. He gave me my name: I am Fiorinda, the flower-bride the magician made. I thought I'd chosen it myself, but I don't care. It's my name now. It means me. I didn't know who he was, I thought he was a cool older guy. He made me pregnant but my baby died. When I was eighteen he came for me again. He tried to initiate me. It happened over there.' She pointed through the great window, with a sweep of her arm. 'Over there, long ago, in Traveller's Meadow, in Sage's big van. Sex and drugs and rock and roll, friendship like an ever-fixed mark, that looks on tempest and is never shaken. It's gone, my starry meadow, you annihilated it out of existence. But that night is still happening, *sub specie aeternitatis*, as my friend Chip would say, you Chinese have another name, but it's science now, call it *in the state of all states*. I'm there, right now, this is called simultaneity. I had friends, thank God. I fought him off. I always fight him off.'

At last, some expression in that smooth girlish face, but she couldn't tell what it meant. She had lost the ability to read expressions. What did I say? wondered Fiorinda. What was the magic word? Maybe it was the aura of black light she felt gathering around her, the feeling that Rufus was terribly close, watching her, waiting for her, oh please, somebody help me.

'When I heard about you I thought you could save my life. I thought you could make it so that magic didn't exist. But you're no good. *You're no good.*'

She waited for another insane, state-police riposte, and the room seemed very big, echoing and vast, with just the two of them, suspended in its space.

'What is it like?' asked Elder Sister, softly.

'What is it *like*?' wailed Fiorinda. 'How would I know? Right now I can't remember being out of this. Sometimes it's fine, sometimes it's not, sometimes I have to go to where Sage has been, it's my only shelter. But I don't want nirbhana, I want to live. With Ax and Sage, and my little girls.'

Another silence, that seemed very long.

'Suppose there was another case like Rufus, a vicious mutant mind with access to billions of eager fans. What do you suggest?'

Fiorinda said nothing, feeling this might be a trick question.

No use, Elder Sister was onto it. 'Ah,' she breathed. 'There *has* been another. We suspected that might be so. There was a Rufus in the USA? In the desert stronghold, where the Gaian martyrs were holed up? What happened?'

'I killed her.'

'I see . . . All right. All right, Fiorinda. Let me think about this.'

'Make it something quicker than the bonfire. Let my friends go, *including* Chip, and bring on the summary execution.'

Outside the doors, Li Xifeng's most trusted personal servant was waiting, placidly sipping tea with her feet up. Nobody else. 'Ta-chieh, in a few minutes, tell Ms Slater we are in Wang's office, if she wishes to join us.'

'Why not tell her right now?'

'I said *in a few minutes*. Give her time to compose herself.'

'Boyfriend trouble,' judged Ta-chieh, with satisfaction. 'I told you so. You shouldn't screw another woman's husband under her nose, it's indecent.'

Fiorinda crouched on one of the shiny benches, doubled over, head in her hands. If you hurt someone they will always, always hurt you back, what did I do to you, Chez? Was it because you're prettier than me but you had to grow in my shadow? Was it because I is not black enough . . . ? But she was still able to laugh at herself. No, no, no. Get out of my poor brain, rotten little crawlers, taking you for serious is the road to the bad place. It was no one's fault. She wiped her eyes, feeling slightly better than she'd felt for the last few days. If I have to do it, I have to do it, that's all, and go under, into the dark water. There is no armour against dumb luck.

Li Xifeng went from the solar to Wang's inner office, where she found the two other members of the Triumvirate waiting. Wang himself had stayed in London with Hu, both of them fully occupied in containing the minor repercussions of this. She sat down quickly, and didn't speak until she'd brought her breathing under control. They watched her, the tiger and the wolf: Aoxomoxoa all cold blue eyes, loose limbs and lazy threat, Ax watchful, poised, preternaturally alert. She remembered the wild tales that these two could actually transform into savage animals. It seemed quite possible.

'Fiorinda must never, *never* perform on stage again!'

'With respect,' Sage's accent exaggerated, a very tigerish blank stare, 'I'd like to see you try an' stop her.'

'I know about the Hollywood Conjecture, I know that psychic power feeds on the adulation of the audience. She could become a Neurobomb!'

Ax shook his head, smiling. 'Elder Sister, she already is the Neurobomb, it doesn't make any odds if she goes on being a rockstar or not. She's a refusenik, pacifist, selfless Neurobomb. She's proved it many times over.'

Everything between them had been lies, and she felt bereft, even now. 'She is schizophrenic!'

The tiger and the wolf, without looking at each other, nodded. 'There's no way around that,' drawled Sage, 'considerin' everything. It don't mean she's insane. She's the sanest person I know. She's got the deficits, but she's making it work, the brain's wonderful like that. There's nothing wrong with her, usually, except she sees more of the real world than most of us could stand.'

Fiorinda must die! thought Xifeng, genuinely horrified. But she must go willingly to the slaughter, or who would dare to strike the blow? The pit that had opened underfoot resolved itself into this impossible dilemma. They were ahead of her, of course. They knew what was going through her mind. They feared nothing, hoped for nothing. She knew where they were. They were in the zone beyond fear, beyond firefight readiness; a place with no name.

'I really think I might be asleep and dreaming. I saw the phenomenon in the interrogation room. Now Sage asks us to believe that this was the effect of a psychic cyanide pill. Or perhaps an "innocent" yogi trick, he cannot make up his mind—'

'I'm going for the yogi trick,' said Sage. 'Kind of like transient psychosis, only different. It's a sign of the times.'

'You are *shameless* . . . You want me to believe Fiorinda is a schizophrenic magical adept, like her father before her. Yet the Reich is unconcerned. You have been *living contentedly* with the pernicious delusion! My darkest fears are realised, and this is your admirable fall-back position. You have lied to me and lied to me, for all these months. Now you have been forced into the open and your fatalism is understandable, you knew it might come to this. Allow me a little time to catch up.'

They allowed her a little time.

'You could let our friends go,' suggested Ax. 'And the children, and Sage's son. You could file Fiorinda's confession in the same closed box as a lot of other things, why not? You know she has committed no crime.'

'I shall direct the penalty process to continue! Then we shall see! We shall see if this monster exists, and how monstrous she is!'

Silence.

'Let's get this in proportion.' Sage took Fiorinda's saltbox out of his pocket and leaned forward, elbows on his knees. 'She's a refusenik, but she's handy to have round in an emergency. *Think* about it. D'you want her for a friend, or an enemy? What she plans to do now isn't new bad news, she's changed the world before: it happened on the beach at Drumbeg. It's more *difficult* than the things her dad used to do in his long career, but the end result will much less damage. There are risks, mostly for Fiorinda, but she won't falter, she won't fall, and I'll be right there holding her hand . . . So it's going to be fine, except you should not make us do this.'

Silence.

Ax and Sage listened to the winter wind, which they imagined but they could not hear, sighing around the old Leisure Centre. On a night like this, thrown out of the world we knew, we met our girl's demons for the first time, and here we are again, as if we never left. Surrounded by our ghosts, acknowledging the darkness.

Elder Sister was deep in thought.

The door opened and Fiorinda came in, looking weary and very pale.

'Hallo?'

'Hey, my brat.'

'I'm sorry,' she said, to Elder Sister, 'sorry I shouted, *jiejie*. It wasn't necessary.' She looked at the two men. 'I fucked up, didn't I? I'm really sorry.'

'When was that?' wondered Ax, holding out his arms. 'When you saved Chez's life? Or when you turned yourself in, in the hope of stopping a few torture sessions, Protector of the Poor?'

She settled on his lap, her cheek against his shoulder, either not quite aware of Elder Sister's presence or past caring. Sage got up from his chair and went to sit at Ax's feet. He took Fiorinda's hand and laid his head down, his arm across her knees, his eyes closed. Elder Sister and her Chosen One looked at each other across the low-lit room in strange accord, strange intimacy. Everything was in the open now.

Fatality, the will of heaven. No regrets.

Next night Elder Sister gave a private dinner, hardly a banquet, for the Triumvirate; in her quarters. The other guests were Wang and Hu. The dining room was hung with deep-red and orange silks, panelled in the dark-red *di* and lit in glowing amber. It was like a cave at the heart's core of the world. The food was vegetarian (for Hu Qinfu's sake; he was a strict Buddhist), good, plain, wintery soldiers' food: a Hokkien clay-pot stew of bean curd and root vegetables, aubergine in a very flavoursome hot sauce, braised English-grown oyster mushrooms with peppers; 'fake eel' nuggets, which sounded bizarre but proved delicious. Of course the rice was excellent.

They were an auspicious party. Six represents the whole Universe, with its four cardinal points plus Above and Below. The conversation was in *putonghua:* Elder Sister and her Generals going easy on the non-linguists. They talked about number, exchanging superstitions. About beauty spots in England and in the region of China called Shaanxi; about cricket. Hu Qinfu didn't really unbend, but Wang had recovered his charm, and the three rockstars were on a plane where pretty much nothing could touch them. Why not eat, why not chat?

At the end of the meal Elder Sister set down her wine glass.

'My friends,' she said, 'there was a northern general, Zhao Kuangyin, who unified China, and founded the great Song Dynasty taking the dynastic name Taizu. There is a story that Song Taizu held a dinner, when the consolidation of his power was complete, for the military commanders who had put him on the throne. Do you know this one, Ax?'

Ax looked at her. 'Yeah . . . I think I do.'

'He put it to them that though he honoured them and wanted to reward them, he knew they were kingmakers. If they were at court he would always be looking over his shoulder, and they couldn't expect him to trust them. He suggested they all retire peacefully to the countryside, and enjoy their success in freedom.'

'What did the commanders say?' asked Sage.

'It's not recorded that they said anything. They enjoyed their dinner in a normal fashion. The next morning they offered their resignations on various pretexts, and left the capital without delay.'

'I can see how that would work,' said Fiorinda. 'What was the sweetener?'

'The secret action against the Few has run its course. Ms Dawkins shows no sign of ever having suffered from pulmonary tuberculosis, and such medical records as we can trace tell the same story. It has been found impossible to make a case for a suspicious cure on absolutely nothing but one covert scan. Chip Desmond has been examined by our neurologists, and his brain discovered to be normal. There are rumours that he was supernaturally protected from undeserved punishment. It's not my business to confirm or deny that, but I don't consider such things impossible, and certainly not pernicious.'

She paused, as if waiting for a balance to settle.

'These two, and all those caught up in the sweep, were released today; with apology. It has been revealed, for the public record, that the alarm was caused by a tip-off that Countercultural terrorists had infiltrated the Snake Eyes Commune. This has been proved false. The Few have made statements to the media, expressing their appreciation of the action and affirming the need for vigilance. There is no call for embarrassment over the arrests, General Hu gave the right orders. If he was over-zealous, he's not the only one. Wang Xili would do well to practise restraint, especially in his sexual affairs; and look before he leaps.'

Wang took the public slap with a rueful nod, accepting his deserts.

'Now we move on to the Presidency of England, and of Europe. I have come to a decision. When the 2nd AMID army has withdrawn, and England becomes a Sphere partner, a process that will soon be completed, Rob Nelson will be President.' She smiled. 'The formal titles held by Felice Hall, Dora Devine, and possibly Cherry Dawkins shall be decided according to the will of the masses. The Presidency of Europe will be nominal. We'll see how that goes, later on.'

She looked across the round table at the Triumvirate, with her phoenix eyes.

'My friends, you are kingmakers: I would always be looking over my shoulder. I honour you, I would reward you if I could, but I have divined that the best gift I can give to you is peace, freedom, and a quiet life, away from *all this*—'

They waited.

'You must leave England. You must leave Europe and never return, neither physically or in bi-location, or by any future miraculous tech. You will be celebrated as my heroes, and my counsellors. The World State will know that you are under my protection. I will know that it's the other way round. Are you satisfied?'

Let me remember how it felt when we received Elder Sister's judgment, in the red-gold room. We had told her that we wanted her to rule the world, then fate had forced us to show her that we could destroy her . . . There's no one like Elder Sister. Her response was to offer us a way out that conceded nothing; and yet we saw at once that it was the best solution for everyone, including ourselves. The pain would come later, and the shock, and the gallows humour. Let me remember the moment when it was like music, the resolution unlooked for, difficult, falling into place as if it had always been there.

We said yes.

Antares

Here is the kitchen table where we played *Risk* in the lamplight. Here are the stone flags that were cold to my bare feet, that perfect night when we'd come here as true lovers for the first time. Down the little step and here is Sage's big low bed, where we have made love together; how many times? Here is the old sofa where I sat, the night they went down on their knees and proposed. Here are the deep windows, where night looks in . . . Look, Coz, this is the dead media wall, which holds an unparalleled collection of rock and roll, and some other music; once belonging to the great Joss Pender. Joss can have it back now, I suppose. What do you take, when you're told you must leave your home forever? Very little, in the end.

Cos tugged on a hank of curls, pulling Fiorinda's head down until they were nose to nose. 'What now, my girl?' Baby kisses, round blue eyes brimming with concern. 'I love you too,' said Fiorinda.

'A'tz?' suggested Cosoleth hopefully. The answer to everything.

'Good idea. Hey, how about *mummy*?'

'Meh, *meh.*'

'I'm going to decide that sounds promising.'

If we had stayed everything would have changed. New chairs, new curtains. A new rug instead of the one where Ax and Sage sat doing jigsaws, the weekend that Sage first brought us here, one early spring. Fresh paint on these faded holy walls. Everything precious to me about Tyller Pystri is in the past, why mourn for a place I will never know? But the stones, the walls, the daft things Aoxomoxoa used to buy, helplessly, in airports, were all crying to her *please don't leave us—*

*

Out in the garden she found Sage with his arms stretched around the trunk of one of the twin beeches. He changed his pose swiftly when he heard her step, and stood with his back against the tree's grey hide, wiping his eyes.

'Are you okay?'

'I'm fine.'

She put Cosoleth into his arms. The day was mild, the air sweet. They went to sit on the bank under the camellia hedge, and listened to the faint clamour of the Chy; in spate down in the gorge. We must leave, and never see this again: the solid shape of the little old house, the battered back porch, the ledge outside the kitchen window where the birds, and the red mice, come for scraps. The mossy hillock on the shrubbery edge of the lawn, with the odd little stone bench on the top, that looks like something out of Narnia.

'I'm glad we made it through to the primroses.'

'Yeah.'

Ax had been upstairs, sitting in the room that would have been Coz's room. He came to join them, Min following at his heels. Coz took a trundle around and settled confidingly against her father: talking softly to her fingers, and a family of grass blades. 'I'm fucking glad we didn't end up hitting this situation with the United States of America in charge,' remarked Sage. 'We'd'a spent thirty years on Death Row, making generations of lawyers rich, an' still got the perpetual banishment.'

'Things to be said for eastern despotism.'

They sat and watched the southern horizon, where the red beacon of Antares, rival of Mars, would rise when it was summer again in England. They would not be here to see it, but they would have kept the promise Sage had made in the winter depths of defeat. The Occupation would be over, England would be free.

At the nadir of their fortunes they had set out to achieve something that seemed impossible. They'd done what they'd vowed to do, they were free and clear of all debt: things could have been a hell of a lot worse. Can't have everything.

And the river tells our story, and the stones will remember.

III

The Three Guineas

The massive *di* walls had vanished, faster than they'd built themselves. The purple barracks that looked like upturned boats were gone. The final departure of the 2nd AMID was weeks away, but as of tonight Reading Arena belonged to the Reich again. The scaffolders had raised a towered stage where Main Stage, Red Stage, had always stood. The big screens were in place, the live broadcast was running and a lucky crowd of thousands stood waiting on the cleared ground; on a cold evening of early spring. The day had been raw and wet, but the sky had cleared. The west was streaked with sunset light, lemon and pearl between bars of slatey cloud.

Elder Sister stood with Ax on the side of the stage, watching the sound and light team as they wandered about, completing their arcane tasks. She wore her dark padded coat and a close cap; her hands were tucked into her sleeves for warmth. No mask, but he felt the Daoist Nun was near.

'When we came to England,' she said, 'we felt ourselves in terrible danger. Wang set himself up in the heart of darkness, he displayed Fiorinda's face in the rooms where Rufus had seduced her. We were very reassured when actions of that kind brought no hostile response from the populace or from the Reich . . .'

Actions like the Reading massacre, he thought.

'Our thinking was naïve. Power generally corrupts, and corrupt people are stupid. But sometimes, rarely, great power breeds subtlety and wisdom.'

'And you exposed us to Toby Starborn.'

'In China a death penalty that has been commuted becomes mandatory, if the criminal reveals the details of their interrogation: this is true for all serious crimes. We believed that if you were guilty you must be aware of Toby Starborn's latency, and you would interrogate *him*. In fact, he *told you* that snapshot had been used on him, with everything that implied, but you saw no threat in that. You ignored him!'

'Dumb luck,' said Ax. 'We just weren't thinking.'

Aoxomoxoa, not yet dressed for the stage but still a magnet for the eyes, had launched into a passage of dance moves for the engineers—

'Sage is remarkable,' said Elder Sister, softly. 'I have come to believe that he is truly what you call him, an enlightened master: *returning to the marketplace with bliss-bestowing hands*. You and Fiorinda must never, never part from him.'

Ax nodded, without taking his eyes from the big cat; thinking of all the stages on the way to this one. I've seen bigger crowds. Wave on wave of punters, far as the eye could see, what a feeling, to rule that ocean. And never again—

The set-up was nearly done now, it was time. 'What does it mean?' asked Elder Sister, softly. '*The freedom of the rose tree?* In that anthem of yours, "Always The Day"? The rose tree is England I suppose?'

'No, it's a quote, don't remember where from but it stuck in my mind. The complete thing goes, lemme see: "Freedom is the unclosing of the idea which lies at our root: the rose is the freedom of the rose tree".'

'Hm. I like that . . . I'm leaving now, Ax.' She would not stay for the concert: Elder Sister did not belong at this ceremony. 'Perhaps we'll meet again.'

Ax nodded, thinking it very unlikely. 'Maybe so.'

'It has been an honour to know you all.'

'I'm glad to have known you too,' said Ax, turning at last to smile at her. 'Goodbye, *jiejie*. I wish you well.' And that's that.

Backstage, the faithful were gathered. The Prestons were there in force, including Ax's mother and her boyfriend. Dave Wright, the poacher turned stand-up, the Prime Minister and her entourage, Areeka Aziz and Jam Today; the ubiquitous Gintrap . . . Sayeed Muhammad Zayid al-Barlewi was talking to Joss Pender; and Beth Luarn, Sage's mother. Talking, or trying to keep the peace. The novelist and the software baron had been parted for more than twenty years, but the acrimony survived—

'It's not the end of the world, Joss! It's hardly different from tax exile!'

'You make a religion of being poorly informed, Beth,' snapped Joss.

'We'll never see him again, and I just hope there isn't a *backlash* against her, over this.'

'What mixed feelings! Of course the money wins out. Elder Sister has destroyed your son's life, but she's good for business.'

Muhammad cleared his throat. 'I've watched them, especially this past year, and there's a saying about musicians and the law that's come to my mind. *Who breaks a butterfly on the wheel?* They've done enough for us, in my opinion. I'll miss that lad like my own son, and Fiorinda and Sage too, but they've been beating their wings against the bars too long. It's high time we set them free.'

The *hadith* of rock and roll.

The Few sat together in their professional finery, an invisible cordon separating them from the crowd: Chip and Verlaine, Rob and the Babes and Allie. Smelly Hugh was with them, Marlon and Silver and Pearl; Bill and Peter. George was up on stage with the boss. Silence reigned.

'I'm going to try and get into Caer Siddi, after this—' began Chip.

'No you are not!' cried Dora, horrified. 'How can you *say* that, Chip!'

'We got to stick together,' advised Smelly Hugh.

Chip drew a circle around the rim of his beer glass, eyes down. 'I was watching ripples on the ceiling, the ghosts of water, and then Sage was calling my name. I don't remember anything else, not a thing. I can't leave it like that, I need an explanation. Some kind of explanation for, well, I don't know. Just why—'

Verlaine squeezed his hand. 'Give it a while, young Merry, and I'll come too.'

'So will I,' said Cherry in a low voice, 'if they'll have me. As some kind of tea girl, or, or cleaner. I can't go on living in the normal world. How can I?'

But it had never crossed Cherry's mind that she had TB. Her friends and lovers were the guilty ones. They'd seen the marks of the terrible scourge, and had been unable to stand the idea that she'd be taken away, put in an isolation ward. Their silent, unthinking cowardice had cost everything, lost everything—

'Who said anything about *normal*—?' demanded Felice.

No answer. Allie said, 'I have some mementoes, from Fio. I suppose now's the time.' She'd thought there ought to be some kind of a ceremony, but that wasn't going to happen. She passed the tokens round, a little silver filigree charm for each of them; two in reserve for George and for Rox.

'Is it the Hand of Fatima?' wondered Pearl, solemnly clutching her treasure. 'Or Fiorinda's hand? I want it to be Fiorinda's.'

'It's both,' said Allie.

'Remember when she told us it was over in a voicemail?' said Dora.

The tiger and the wolf smile and say goodbye, Fiorinda takes away our trainer wheels. The mood changed, a *gestalt* flip. Something stirred in them, faintly: ideas, convictions, plans all of their own—

'We're going to make this work.' Rob glanced around, bringing them all in. 'This isn't the time to be going off on any quests. We're the Reich now.'

The music washing through, bursts of laughter from outdoors. Dave Wright was milking his bows. Rob and the Babes had better go to join the big band.

Roxane paid off hir taxi, considered the backstage marquee, and chose instead to limp carefully, over mud-puddled chicken wire track, to the Portakabin communal dressing room. S/he found Sage alone there, sitting with his long legs stretched out, ankles crossed, staring into space: wearing immaculate sand-coloured trousers and a ragged blue tee-shirt that had sweat stains under the arms.

'I hope you're planning to change that shirt, Natasha. It's a disgrace.'

S/he lowered hir old bones into a plastic chair, and folded hir hands over the top of the ebony and silver cane. They smiled at each other, old affection renewed. 'How is she?'

Sage pulled the offending tee over his head. 'She's good, very good. Just didn't want to be here, an' I don't blame her.'

'Nobody likes goodbyes. Tell her God bless . . . And Ax?'

'He's around, prob'ly in the bar by now. Ask him yourself.'

Rox winced, but s/he was mistaken. Mr Preston bears a grudge, the bad lad; but Ax'd forgiven Rox for hir crimes a while ago. Sage donned a clean white tee and the suit jacket, and grinned at himself in the mirror. The message on the tee said *My IQ Test Came Back Negative.* There I am again, a little older, any wiser?

'Why Natasha? Who she? What did I do that was girly?'

His fabulous face, thought Rox. This backstage moment is when they are most conscious of their own beauty. But *he* won't miss the smell of the crowd. What will he become, I wonder, our bodhisattva? And I will never know . . . For many years the critic had teased Aoxomoxoa by nicknaming him after hi-culture fictional characters.

S/he shrugged eloquently. 'I'm not quite sure. It's Natasha Rostov, from *War And Peace*. A native, passionate spirit, the belle of every ball. War sweeps over Russia, interminable. Dreams die, lives are shattered, Moscow burns. The smoke clears, and there's Natasha grown up, taking a happy housewifely interest in the contents of her babies' nappies . . . I think it says tragedy may have the best tunes, but comedy has the stronger material in the end. An admirable compromise.'

'Hahaha. C'mon, no moping. Let's go find the folks.'

. . . No immix. The Heads gave us their *Unmasked* set, with the synchronised dancing: the soft-shoe shuffle 'Ripple' had us ecstatic. We missed his stunt-dives and the way he used to scramble our brains, but it was good, really good, to have Aoxomoxoa laughing at the whole antic business; one last time . . .

. . . And so at last it was the remains of the inner circle, friends and hangers-on, crews and babes-in-arms, for the traditional Reich finalé. Ax made a little speech, last words to his home crowd: there wasn't much to it. He'd given us his testament when he played with the Chosen Few. He presented Rob with the five-thousand-year-old stone axe called the Falmouth Jade, which the Chinese had returned in time for this ceremony, and we won't ask where it had got to in between. The badge of office exchanged, Rob and Ax embraced, hugs and emotion all round. And we felt it was right.

Ax isn't being forced out, that's a lie. He's leaving because it's *right*. It's time for him to go, time for the mantle to pass on, time for us to move into another mode. But now the crowd was hungry to hear his guitar, one last time. They shouted for another Hendrixed national anthem, another Reich classic, another of Fiorinda's songs. Ax waited for them to shut up, standing alone at the front of the stage, and finally they did. He looked over the heads, smiling at someone out there on the other side of the screen: bent his head the way he does, and started to play. No, not Hendrix. He chose to give us Bob Marley, no fireworks, no bravura: just *won't you he'p me sing, these songs of freedom* . . . Dead silence. It was as if we'd only just grasped that he was really leaving, going away, he wouldn't be back, and now it's up to us. Just when we were getting weepy, the bands had their instruments handed back to them, and everyone swung into a daft, cheery ska medley: those Babes blowing their horns, Rob and Ax dancing and laughing, arms round each others' necks . . . Way to go, guitar-man. All he's ever had: redemption songs.

'All right, Fiorinda?'

'All right, Joe,' she said, reading over his shoulder. 'Zap it down the wire.'

Joe Muldur zapped his copy and watched his virtual screen vanish like dew. 'I won't be doing that again very often.'

'What, are you quitting?'

'Nah, just it isn't what happens anymore. Different rules pertain. Less roving reportage, more an' more writing done by Sphere desk software.'

'Ah, well. Everything passes.'

He felt that she'd already left. She was taking a polite interest, she didn't give a damn how *NME* reported the last waltz. They watched the big screen, along with everybody else in the quiet bar of The Three Guineas. The final scenes, the security cordon breached, forests of hands reaching up to touch the man, to touch the founder of the Reich and carry something away; something to last for a long time. 'I'll be off,' said Joe. 'Got a train to catch. Tell Ax and Sage . . .' He shook his head. 'Oh, I don't know. Tell them have a nice life, and, er, don't take any wooden 'shrooms. It's been *brilliant* knowing you three, following your fabulous trail, every step.'

'Including Rainbow Bridge?'

Joe grinned. 'Including that weird, ghastly hellhole.' He tickled Min behind the ears, and smiled at the sleeping baby. 'G'bye Fiorinda.'

She leaned over and kissed his cheek. 'G'bye Joe.'

You to your life, I to mine. Unsullied little friendships, she thought, are the memories I will treasure, from my celebrity career. Not much else I want to keep.

Fiorinda sat dreaming for a few minutes after Joe had gone; tuning out the post mortem on the big screen, thinking of many things. Then she returned to the work she'd brought with her and finished it off; while Coz slept and Min dozed like a sphinx beside the baby basket, chin on his outstretched paws.

The last words down. She read over what she'd written—

So there you have it. This is my story, my account of the Reich. Put together from memory, scrapbooks and scribbles on old bus tickets; and now it's done. Complete with conversations I can't possibly have overheard, unwarranted assumptions about other peoples' motives and emotions, references I haven't checked, and details I've made up because I've forgotten or I never knew. Some of it you won't believe. You'll notice jagged gaps of weeks and months: sometimes that's censorship, sometimes I just don't remember what happened and I don't feel like trying to dig it up. Some of the holes are pure accident. Don't believe I said a single word about Jor and Milly's wedding or the—

And here they are, the two coolest dudes in the known universe.

'Ready to go?' said Ax.

'I'm ready.'

One baby basket, one cat carrier, one backpack, their sacred possessions: the tapestry bag, the visionboard, Ax's Les Paul. And goodbye cruel world.

Later, the barmaid noticed Fiorinda's tablet on the table, a message in Chinese taped to the case. She studied the characters, wondering what they meant, and put the tab away carefully, on a shelf behind the bar.

To be called for.

جرف

JOY

I

The Triumvirate left England and disappeared. No forwarding address, no trace. One night at the end of July they turned up in Brittany, at the old manor house in the shell of his pirate ancestor's castle; where Alain de Corlay was spending the summer with Tam. They'd made a tactical withdrawal from Paris. Utopian politics were stormy, that season of the new world. It was a balmy night, the moon near the full. Alain was called to the gatehouse, and found his armed guards (indispensable, for a techno-green tribune of the people) bemused by the three gypsies and their child.

'My God, what happened to you?'

'We got banished,' said the outlaw with the ponytail and the tattoo around his eye. A lean spotted beast in his arms yawned at Alain, completely placid.

'No, but since February—'

They shrugged, they had no answer. The bronzed scarecrow with a ragged cap of yellow curls smiled like a gentle god. The young woman with her hair tied up in a scarf, skin like beaten gold and wild grey eyes, seemed in another world.

Alain picked up the baby, thinking he'd carry her upstairs. He'd hardly begun when a tiny voice beside his ear said carefully *je peux fai' les marches.*

Sage took the child. 'Let her do it,' he said. 'It's quicker in the long run.'

Cosoleth climbed the stairs, a determined little animal on her four paws. Fiorinda saw a bat through one of the narrow windows, but Ax missed it. The three were magical company, in the strangest sense: wide-eyed ghosts. Alain and Tam were using the terrace on the stump of the old donjon as their living room. They had eaten, but the table was still laid. They reported on events in England: how the 2nd AMID withdrawal had been smooth and complete, how Rob and two Babes had been inaugurated President, Party Secretary, and Head of the Utopian Techno Green Committee. How Cherry Dawkins had declined public office, but she and the Adjuvants had begun to have a cult following like you wouldn't believe . . . The Triumvirate ate leftovers, drank wine, welcomed spliff, and seemed like castaways who have forgotten how to talk except to each other. They offered a few anecdotes, good ones, from their vanishment.

Cosoleth, who had been fed on bread soaked in milk, ran out of patience, grizzling. Fiorinda said she would put the baby to bed (Alain remembered how adroitly the rock and roll brat would disappear, when social occasions bored her). She took the nappy bag and Coz into the house, where Alain's staff would show her to the room that had been prepared while they talked.

'She's pregnant!' announced Tam, who was using a new biometric gadget, an entertaining conversation piece.

Sage leapt from his chair and across the terrace, with truly appalling speed and power. 'Leave her the fuck alone!' he snarled in Tamagotchi's face. He stared around like a tiger, eyes blazing; made for the balustrade and disappeared over it. They heard him crashing down the creepers, and then silence.

. . .

'Those things are going to cause such interesting scenes,' said Alain to Tam. 'Are you sure you want to be so obvious?'

'We know she's pregnant,' said Ax. 'The problem is she can't do natural birth. She had Coz by Caesarean. Sage is scared, excuse him, he's a wild man.'

'Fiorinda refuses to have a Caesarean—!' exclaimed Alain, horrified.

'No, no no.' Ax was lying on the chaise longue, Min curled on his belly. His hair was loose, he'd taken off his boots, his feet were bare. He waved his hands, like, *so it goes.* 'We have no Sphere ID. We can't go to a hospital.'

'Oh, my God!' said Tam. '*She* did that to you?'

'Hahaha. You're kidding. We did it to ourselves.'

'But *why*?' cried Alain.

'It's the way we want to live.'

Alain wanted to tell Ax that the whole thing was sublimely unjust. In the presence of this wild, strange spirit – with the feral air of a wolf indoors, secretly alert, checking for exits – he felt a shocking nostalgia for the man he had known. He wanted to talk to Ax Preston again.

'Ax, *why don't you three just hold a gun to the woman's head?* Since you can easily do that, and you know I know this. Where's the harm? Very few people would know, enough would know to protect each other. We could do it.'

'This is better.' Ax combed back the hair from his temples, the old gesture, and gazed at the moon, smiling. 'You haven't thought it through, we have. Stay on the Elder Sister bandwagon, Alain. It's a *good* wagon, it's the *right* wagon. Be a prag.'

Sage reappeared, from the terrace windows. He must have come in through the tower door again, and up the stairs. He was cheerful, on the point of laughter. 'Sorry,' he said. 'That was really stupid.' Fiorinda came after him. Now there was a distinct atmosphere of fuck, a musk of sex in the air between the three.

'Shall we go to bed?' suggested Ax.

They said goodnight and took their belongings indoors.

Alain and Tam decided to call it a night as well.

These two had never been lovers, just fuck-buddies once or twice, and it had been a long time ago. Yet they had spent more time under the same roof than most of the notorious couples of the Euro Crisis (including the trio who had just left); and probably that would continue. They were partners. Thoughts of permanence were in the air in the radical community, in Paris and throughout France. When your wildest ideas have entered the mainstream and are being mangled by its degrading maw, it's time to take stock. In public we dance to the tracks we knew in their original versions. In private we begin to prefer, like old criminals, the company of friends who remember what it was like.

They moved the chaise longue and the armchairs indoors to protect them from damp, and shared a nightcap.

'Do you envy them?' wondered Alain.

'Not at all. But I understand them.'

The Triumvirate left after a few days, no forwarding address.

5 Vine Cottages,
Nr Testor,
Bodmin
North Cornwall
PL30

Dear Mr Pender,

Life goes on happily here, everyone's pretty well. Dolly at the Powdermill had her pups, and there's some argument about who's going to get them. You asked after the wolf colony. They haven't got themselves into any trouble since the old dog-wolf was found killed (which we think we know was NOT the work of a mystery big cat), and they are busy rearing the alpha pair's cubs, of which "wolfwatch" is as proud as if we were staging the Olympics. They've certainly put Bodmin on the map! but as long as it's only virtual tourists, I'm not complaining. We hear from George, and Bill is getting married, but of course you will know about that. Peter is back home with his aunts just now, he's missing you very much, poor man. Your mother is well, she tells me she hasn't been in touch and longs for your address. Marlon came down once, with his girlfriend a new one, you won't know her. She seems a nice enough girl. When you get round to it, I need to know whether the barn conversion is to go ahead, or do you want the cottage kept just as it was, until you can get here again? Should I ask your father about that?

You'll be pleased to know that the garden is standing up well to our storms. The Roger Hall hedge suffered the night the winds were very high indeed but I have cut it back hard and I believe it will recover. Nobody will be buying firewood in the Chy Valley for this winter, and we're crossing our fingers. It would be hard if they wouldn't let us burn our logs, adding insult to injury. Tyller Dystri lost a chimneypot, which I've had replaced but no trees except the big old flowering plum, which was coming to the end of its natural span, tho' it will be sadly missed I have in mind a replacement. I will send you the nursery catalogue with the place marked as soon as you can give me an ID address. The Stepping Stones are already covered they say that's a sign of another long cold winter but I don't know, the "signs" of our weather must be out of date now, mustn't they, with all this climate change. By the way, I found Cosoleth's spiderweb picture, and I would like to send it to her, along with some little clothes I've put together, and some very nice shoes I hope will fit, though I'm guessing at the size. It would be lovely if you could send me a photo, someway. Tell her love from Ruthie, and I hope she's being a good girl.

My very dear love to you all, even that rascal Min
Ruth Maynor

III

Ax tracked down the right house after what seemed like hours of hunting up and down tiny earth-paved alleys almost identical to each other. The midwife was neither old nor young: desert age, a seamed face swathed in indigo, clear eyes, a firm wide mouth. She seemed to live alone, was that weird? He wanted to know what she was like because he had to trust her, but she wasn't interested. She ignored him, and gathered her things together.

'It might be a difficult birth.'

'Hmmph.' The desert woman paused, picked up the lamp, and took a good suspicious look at this stranger. 'Has she been cut?' she inquired, narrow-eyed.

'No—'

'Is this her first? Is she *very* young?'

I must look like a real charmer, thought Ax. Must be the tattoo, made him look like a bandit. 'No, it's not that.'

It was very dark outside. The midwife asked Ax for directions and then led the way. She walked briskly, with a straight-backed, flowing pace that made him revise her age downwards, and didn't speak until they'd reached the wide street – much faster than Ax could have found his way. Trees in a square. He glimpsed a shop, with a stand outside where newspapers lay folded, a blue-and-white painted building with a strange cross: Coptic Christians. He already knew where the mosque was.

'She has had other children?'

'This is her third child.'

'Hmph. Has she had sons?'

'Her first child was a son, but he died. She was very young then. The second baby was born by Caesarean, by section?'

'Hm. We'll see. If it looks like trouble, I can call the emergency hospital.'

Ax nodded. At this juncture, fuck the outlaw freedom. He was planning to flash the *access all areas* pass if need be, and nobody was going to stop him. The bus arrived and they got on it. A sleepy conductor took their fares, Ax paid for the midwife. They had not discussed charges, and he hoped this was a good sign. She does the doctoring first and then asks about the money. She'll get paid. The bus was half-empty, decrepit, serviceable. He looked out of the windows at a ribbon development pinpricked with golden lights. Is that a market? He thought of staying here, finding his way around, buying bread and milk, taking Cos to that square with the trees. My big blond cat causing a sensation, but they'd soon get used to him.

'Where are you from?' said the midwife.

Ax shook his head. 'Nowhere, really. But my mother's people came from, ooh, within a hundred miles of here.'

'Hmph.'

You must leave England, you must leave Europe. With all the wild world to choose from they were still clinging to the skirts of the Mediterranean. It would be a terrible wrench to cross one of the great oceans, it would feel irrevocable. Maybe after this, when Fiorinda's baby was old enough to travel, they would make some decisions. He thought about Clapham Junction, the long echoey tunnel, hurrying people, stalls laden with cakes, coffee, glossy magazines; stairways leading reliably to destinations he needed. He had always felt *secure* at Clapham. You get there, you know you can get back to Reading, back to Brixton.

Oh, this is the stop. It wasn't so far after all.

The house their friend at the bus station had found for them had an outer room and an inner room, an outhouse bathroom, a water pump with a turbine, and one haphazard flowerbed. It was set in a high-walled orchard that belonged to the property. It was clean, there'd been nothing but dust in it; apparently it had been standing empty. Cosoleth pattered in and out of the back room, singing. She liked being up in the middle of the night. Min had found a window he could leap through and was outdoors looking for pebbles to hoard.

'D'you think he can jump over that wall?'

'Min's solid, Fiorinda. He's fixed on us. An' Coz cannot reach the latch of the house door, so she's not going to do a runner. How are you doing?'

They had bought a string bed, and paid for it to be carried here and installed, in the corner opposite the single window: which was now a small black square hung on the clay-red plastered wall, luminous obsidian shining on their lamplight. Sage was sitting up on the bed, propped against the wall, Fiorinda in his arms. She felt queasy and tired, nagged by these pains, disinclined to do anything. Don't want to walk around, do the squatting, the breathing exercises, just want to lie here against Sage's breast and feel the beat of his heart, the hard muscle and bone I know so well; listening to the pit-pat of my little girl's feet, and her sweet little voice. C'mon, oh mighty childbirth hormones, carry me away.

'How about some more tea?'

'No, don't leave me. Don't be *frightened*, Sage. It's going to be all right.'

'I'm not.'

Ax looked after Coz in the front room while the baby was being born. They spread the camping mattresses and hugged, comforting each other. Min crouched at the inner door lashing his tail, and occasionally letting out a heartbroken yowl. He didn't like closed doors, and he was very disturbed by Fiorinda's effortful, fierce cries. Cosoleth seemed to take Ax's word for it that everything was going according to plan.

'I have found a baby . . . Is it?'

'No, Coz, that's a little stone.'

'Put eyes?'

He found a marker, and put eyes on the little stone. She'll talk to anything. Her fingers were a family, Ax's feet (known as Footso and Toeso) were characters in an enduring soap opera. 'Oooh, Coz. Where did you find your stone? Is it Min's?'

The little girl was shaken by terrible guilt.

'*No!*' she whispered, tears brimming. 'I have found it.'

What are we going to do with this child? She's so devastated by everything, so passionately in love with everything around her. 'Sssh, ssh, it's okay. Your stone.'

Cosoleth left the bed, and crouched with her little head clutched in her hands, wrestling in silence. Finally, biting her lip, tragic-eyed, she took the stone with eyes and laid it at Min's paws. She came back to the mattress, cast herself down and wept.

Ax picked her up and rocked her, what shall it be, one of her favourites

> *rivers of light,*
> *scarlet and white,*
> *sink into the sand,*
> *but this is our Promised Land—*

Don't be scared, he told himself, don't be scared. The beauty of the night struck him as something unearthly: the child in his arms, Min sphinxing on the end of the mattress now, his Les Paul in its hard case up against the red-plastered wall. An arc of blue handprints above the window . . . He wanted to paint this and put it to music in immix, with the intensity of a Van Gogh interior. Better than wanting, he thought; I'll do it. But not until I know what kind of beauty this is. Oh God, is this the end of my life? The door of the inner room opened. The midwife looked out from the bright light in there; Ax and Cosoleth started up, trembling.

'Fiorinda?' breathed Ax.

'Your wife is very well, it was easy. Your friend is a good nurse.'

'Yeah, I know, yeah, I know. Is the baby okay?'

'She's very well. You have another daughter.'

The baby was washed and dressed, and offered her mother's breasts. She latched on without any hesitation (a good sign). Ax went with the midwife into the front room, where she showed him a little drawstring bag of papercloth. 'This is for the umbilical cord, you should bury it under the doorsill. If you know the child's name, write it here.'

Ax wrote. The woman looked at him suspiciously.

'Faraj? This is a boy's name.'

'A girl is a boy,' said Ax. 'A woman is a man.'

Her suspicions were not assuaged. She addressed Ax sternly. 'The Prophet, peace and blessings, hath said, *one daughter is worth ten sons to a man of peace.*'

Ax thought that might be one of the Elder Sister *hadith*, he wouldn't put it past her. And why not? Who knows how much of what the Prophet really said got suppressed, when it didn't suit the canon of opinion? She would conquer Islam, the same as she'd conquered everything else: by might and guile and patience.

'I believe it . . .' That's why my daughter isn't going to have a second-class (don't tell me any different, I know how Arabic works) version of her name. She gets the full measure. 'What does it mean if you bury the umbilical cord?'

'Nothing, really. It's a nice thing to do.'

Ax took the baby into the yard with him, wrapped in her blankets, to see the midwife out. He knew her eyesight wasn't too good, but he wanted her to see the stars. The midwife had been paid. She would be back tomorrow, later in the day.

'Goodnight, and peace be with you.'

'And with you, peace,' said Ax.

Under the doorsill, hm. He felt that his life had suddenly expanded, become limitless as the abyss up there, with all its worlds. The tiny baby was awake again, looking up at him. When they are newborn, before babyhood closes over them, they seem so wise, they seem like grown-up alien beings. Nothing like Coz. He felt a quieter soul in there, a gallant little stoic, with sheeny-dark hair and Fiorinda's smile. He felt as if he'd known her all his life.

'Your name is *Faraj*,' he said. 'My daughter. It means Joy.'